A COMPENDIUM OF EVER-INCREASING MAYHEM

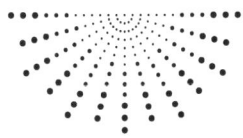

COURTNEY MILAN

UNLOCKED

A perpetual wallflower destined for spinsterhood, Lady Elaine Warren is resigned to her position in society. So when Evan Carlton, the powerful, popular Earl of Westfeld, singles her out upon his return to England, she knows what it means. Her former tormenter is up to his old tricks, and she's his intended victim. This time, though, the earl is going to discover that wall-flowers can fight back.

Evan has come to regret his cruel, callow past. At first, he only wants to make up for past wrongs. But when Elaine throws his initial apology in his face, he finds himself wanting more. And this time, what torments him might be love...

CHAPTER ONE

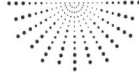

Hampshire, July, 1840.

I T HAD BEEN TEN YEARS SINCE EVAN CARLTON, Earl of Westfeld, last entered a ballroom. This one was just a moderately sized hall on the Arlestons' country estate—a dance at a house party, not a great London crush. Still, standing at the top of the stairs he felt a touch of vertigo—as if the wide steps leading down to the dance floor were instead a steep slope, and the swirling pastels of evening gowns the rocks that waited below. One wrong step and he would fall.

This time, he had no safety rope.

He blinked, and the illusion passed. The figures at the foot of the stair coalesced into whirling pairs of dancers, not sharp crags. Everything was normal.

Everything, that was, except him. When last he'd been in polite society, he'd been its most ardent participant. Today...

His hand tightened deliberately about his cousin's arm. She turned and gave him a quizzical look.

"Don't look so hunted." Diana, Lady Cosgrove, was resplendent in peacock-blue shimmering silk.

Evan had returned to England nearly fourteen months ago when his father had passed away. Since then, he'd been burdened with the details of the funeral and the estate he'd inherited. And, to be truthful, he'd dreaded the thought of reentering society. Foolish, that; enough time had elapsed that everything must have changed.

"You'll see," Diana was saying. "Nothing's changed—nothing that matters, that is."

"How enticing," he said flatly.

She chattered on, oblivious to his unease. "Isn't it, though? Don't pull that face. You've been in mourning so long you've forgotten how to have fun. I must put my foot down: the great explorer *will* enjoy himself."

He'd been a *mountaineer*, not an explorer, but there was no use correcting a trivial point of vocabulary.

Diana patted his arm, no doubt intending her touch to be bracing. "You were the most popular fellow in all of London. When last you were here, you dominated society. I wish you would *act* like it."

Not comforting, the unquiet memories that brought to the surface. Evan looked out over the group. A large house party; but even with the addition of a few souls from the neighborhood, it was still a small ball. Of the nine or ten couples, only a handful were dancing. The rest were clustered in a loose knot on the edge of the room, punch glasses in hand.

The evening was young; only Evan felt aged.

When last he'd been here, he would have been the center of that crowd. His jokes had been the funniest—or at least, they had made everyone laugh the loudest. He'd been the golden boy—handsome and popular and liked by everyone.

Almost everyone. Evan shook his head. He had utterly hated himself.

"If it must be done, it's best done bravely." He drew himself up. "Let's go join the throng."

He took one step toward the massed group.

Diana pulled his arm. "Goodness," she said. "Have a little care. Don't you see who is present?"

He frowned. He could only make out a few faces. They blurred into one another at this distance, the bright silks of the ladies' skirts contrasting with the dark, sober colors of the gentlemen's coats. "Is that Miss Winston? I thought you were friends."

"Next to her." Diana would never have been so uncouth as to point, but she gave a little jerk with her chin. "It's Lady Equine."

Ah. *Damn.* He'd not let himself even *think* that dreadful appellation in years. But Lady Elaine Warren…she was the reason he had left England. His breath caught on a mix of hope and furious shame, and just as he had all those years ago, he found himself scanning the women for her, searching faces.

No wonder he hadn't seen her at first. She made herself easy to overlook. Her arms were drawn tightly about her waist, as if she could squeeze herself into insignificance. Her gown, a pink so anemic it might have been white, left her muted in the crowd of bright colors. Even the pale color of her hair, twisted into an indifferent chignon, seemed to declare her inconsequential. It was only his own memory that made her stand out.

He kept his voice calm. "I suppose she isn't Lady Elaine any longer. Who did she end up marrying?"

"Really. Who would wed a girl who laughs like a horse?"

He looked at his cousin. "Do be serious. We're not youths any longer." Even from this distance, Evan could see the ripe swell of her bosom. When she had come out at seventeen, she had attracted attention, her body mature beyond her age. He had noticed. Often.

She'd been entirely unlike all the other debutantes: not just in body, but with that laugh, that long, loud, vital laugh. It had made him think that she held nothing back, that life was ahead of her and she planned to enjoy it. Her laugh had always put him in mind of activities that were decidedly improper.

"I *am* serious," Diana said. "Lady Equine never married."

"You're not still calling her *that* a decade later." He wasn't sure if he intended his words as a command or a question.

But he felt the truth with a cold, sick certainty. He could see it in the set of Lady Elaine's shoulders, in the way she ducked her head as if she could avoid all notice. He could see it in her wary glance, darting to either side.

"Come, Evan. You wouldn't want me to give up my fun." Diana was grinning, but her bright expression faded as she saw that look on his face. "Don't you recall? You said once, 'I can't tell if she laughs like a horse or a pig, but—'"

"I remember." His voice was quiet. "I remember very well what I said, thank you."

He only tried not to.

She'd never stopped laughing, no matter how he teased her. But when she had looked in his direction, her eyes had begun to slide over him altogether, as if he were nothing but an irrelevant *objet d'art*, and one that was of no further interest. Over the course of a Season's worth of mockery, he had watched her draw in on herself until the vital stuff he'd lusted after had simply faded away.

"Don't worry about her," Diana was saying. "She's nothing. There isn't a man out there who would consider marrying a woman who laughs like the unholy marriage between a horse and a pig."

"*I* said that." His hands clenched.

"Evan, *everyone* said that."

He'd run from England, ashamed of what he'd done. But whatever maturity he'd found in his travels abroad, he could feel it slipping now. It would be so easy to be the selfish swine who thought nothing of ruining a girl's prospects simply because it would make him popular and make others laugh.

Diana watched him expectantly. One smile, one comment about Elaine's whinny, and he would seal his cousin's approval—and his fate.

He'd been right. There *were* rocky shoals below, and gravity was doing its level best to dash everything good he'd made of himself against the waiting crags.

Gently, he removed his cousin's hand from his arm.

"What are you doing?" she asked.

"What do you suppose?" He bit off the words. "I'm going to dance with Lady Elaine."

But she misunderstood the martial set to his jaw, because instead of looking worried, a sly, pleased smile spread across her lips. "Oh, Evan," she said, touching his cuff lightly. "You really are too awful, baiting her like that. This *is* going to be just like old times."

⁓

L ADY ELAINE WARREN SCANNED THE WALLS OF THE BALLROOM. Choosing the place where she would spend the evening was always an exercise in delicacy and balance. It had grown easier over the years, as the leaders of fashion had found new, more interesting pastimes than making fun of her. She had a few friends, now—real ones. She might go entire evenings at a time without having to school her face to a pleasant, stupid blankness. All she had to do was choose her company wisely.

This house party was mostly safe—she'd interrogated her mother closely as to the guest list. None of her closest friends had come, but her remaining tormenters were absent. Her mother had wanted to attend to pass the time while her father was off overseeing his estates.

"It's a beautiful room," she said to her mother. "Why, just *look* at the carving on the paneling. The details are utterly exquisite."

Her mother, Lady Stockhurst, looked puzzled and then peered at the wall. Like Elaine, Lady Stockhurst was tall and blond. Like Elaine, her mother was well-endowed, corsets barely containing her ample curves. Like Elaine, her mother was not respected at all.

If they pretended they were more interested in the walls than the dancing, there could be no disappointment.

"Why, Mrs. Arleston," she heard behind her, "what a lovely gathering."

Elaine stilled, not turning. She didn't need to turn; she wasn't being addressed. But she knew that voice. It was Lady Cosgrove—one of the women who still took delight in needling Elaine.

She leaned in to her mother. "You didn't say Lady Cosgrove would be here."

"Didn't I, then?" her mother responded. "How remiss of me. I must have forgotten. Or maybe I never knew?"

Unlike Elaine, her mother somehow failed to notice how little she was liked.

"Let me introduce you to an old acquaintance," Lady Cosgrove was saying.

The murmured introduction was too indistinct to reach Elaine's ears. Instead, she smiled and nodded. "Never mind, Mother. It's nothing." And maybe it *was* nothing. So few of Lady Cosgrove's compatriots were here. She wouldn't continue to pursue her game without an appreciative audience, would she?

"Yes," Lady Cosgrove was saying, "but do look—here's another old friend. Why, Lady Elaine. How do you do?"

Elaine could not ignore so direct a query. She fixed her smile in place so firmly that her cheeks ached.

"Lady Cosgrove," she started pleasantly. And then her gaze shifted behind the woman. Her hands grew cold. She stopped, mid-greeting, feeling as if she had just been struck. For just one second, her amiable expression slipped, and Lady Cosgrove's grin widened to sharklike proportions.

But Elaine couldn't force herself to beam in placid unconcern. Not through *this*.

She had fallen into a nightmare: the kind where she entered a ballroom wearing nothing but her drawers. She'd had that dream before. Soon, everyone would start laughing at her. And when they turned to her en masse, the people who pointed and mocked all wore the same face: a thousand incarnations of Evan Carlton—now the Earl of Westfeld.

She always awoke from those dreams in a cold sweat. She would succeed in coaxing herself back to sleep only by repeating to herself that he was gone, he was gone, he was *gone*, and she wouldn't ever see him again.

But *this* horrid dream was real. He was back.

He was older. He was bigger, too, shoulders wider, his jacket unable to hide the ripple of muscles fit for a laborer. Back when he'd tormented her, he'd been almost scrawny. Faint lines gathered at the corner of his eyes, and he was dressed in sober browns. His hair was no longer tamed in the fashionable, sleek look that she remembered. Instead, he'd let the dark gold of his hair fall into tousled curls.

He stood too close to her—three full steps away, true, but even that seemed unconscionably near. Cold gathered in her hands and a knot formed in the pit of her stomach. She wanted to turn on her heel and run.

But she'd realized long ago that running was the *worst* thing she could do. Deer and rabbits ran, and the sight of their hindquarters usually only spurred the dogs to the hunt.

"Lady Elaine," he said, giving her a stiff bow.

She had been Lady Equine for as long as she could remember. But now he was calling her by her real name and looking into her eyes, and it was almost as if he *respected* her.

He had always had deceptively compelling eyes—dark and fathomless. She felt as if she might glimpse hidden secrets if only she peered into those depths. He looked as if he were about to reveal some extraordinary truth, one that would explain everything.

An illusion, that. He was nothing more than a snake who could hold her spellbound in his gaze. As for the fluttering in her belly...*that* was nothing so mundane as attraction. Instead, Westfeld made her feel the vital, vicious pull of a might-have-been. Even after all these years, some foolish part of her believed that she might one day be respected. One day, she would not have to watch over her shoulder, constantly wary. One day, she could enjoy herself without fear that she would become the object of ridicule. If the Earl of Westfeld would treat her with respect—well, then she'd know she was safe.

She hated that he made her think that the impossible might be attainable.

Right on cue, Lady Cosgrove asked, "Indeed, Lady Elaine. How *are* your horses?"

Long years of training kept Elaine's face unruffled. It was a triumph over both of them to curl her lips into a smile, to reach out one hand in polite greeting.

"Very well, and *thank you* for the gracious inquiry," she said, ignoring Lady Cosgrove's delicate smirk. "And do tell—how are *yours?*"

"Leave off the talk of horses," Westfeld said shortly. He wasn't smiling, not even a little.

"True. Westfeld has been all round the world," Lady Cosgrove put in. "He could talk about more exotic creatures than *pigs* or *ponies.*"

Westfeld didn't glance at his cousin. Still, his lips thinned further. "Don't." His voice was steel. "Besides, I spent most of my time in Switzerland. I don't consider the alpine ground squirrel to be particularly exotic."

"Don't tell me you saw *nothing* exotic." Elaine let a hint of breathiness invade her tone. "Didn't Hannibal lead all his elephants into the Alps?"

At Lady Cosgrove's befuddled look, Elaine felt her smile broaden, and she gave herself a mental point in this match.

"You see," Elaine said, "I know all about foreign animals. I haven't any need to hear from Westfeld on that score." And with that, she laughed.

Laughter was an act of defiance, although these two would never understand it. Elaine knew her laugh was *awful*: high-pitched and so loud that people turned to stare at her. When she laughed, she snorted in the most indelicate manner. Her laugh had been the cause of their torment all those years ago. And so when Elaine laughed without holding back, she sent them a message.

You cannot break me. You cannot hurt me. You cannot even make me notice you.

"Yes," Lady Cosgrove said after a telling pause, "I can see you're quite the expert."

"Indeed." Elaine beamed at the pair of them. "I attended a lecture given by a naturalist just the other week. He had traveled *all the way* to the Great Karoo."

"The Great Karoo?" Lady Cosgrove asked. "Where—never mind. The animals there must be different indeed. Do they snort? Or squeal?"

Elaine waved a dismissive hand. "It's a desert. There aren't many creatures that make their homes there."

Still, she had pored over his sketches of giant, flightless birds. He had said that the creatures put their heads in the sand when threatened. Apparently they believed that if *they* couldn't see *you*, you could not see them.

She hadn't seen why anyone would need to spend nine months traveling to Africa to find specimens that hid from the truth. No; one had only to travel half a mile to the nearest ballroom.

She had been the butt of jokes for so long now that denial had become second nature to her. It didn't matter what people said; if you pretended not to hear it, they couldn't embarrass you. She need show no reaction, need have no shame. If you didn't acknowledge what they said, you need shed no tears. And so she'd hid her head in the sand and locked away everything about herself but a pale-haired marionette of a lady. Marionettes felt nothing, not even when they were presented with their biggest tormenter of all time.

She smiled, this time at both of them—Lady Cosgrove and her petty jabs, and Lord Westfeld, who had not so much as cracked a smile the entire time since he'd returned.

"No," Elaine said brightly, "there's nothing in all the African continent that could be considered the least bit foreign."

Westfeld was watching her intently. That abstracted look on his face had always heralded a particularly cruel remark.

Beside her, her mother tapped gloved fingers against her skirts. "Lady Cosgrove, Lord Westfeld—I do thank you for giving your regards. It has been so long since we've seen you." Her mother paused, and Elaine could see her drawing in breath and doing her best to make polite small talk. "The stars. They'll be bright tonight. Did you know the moon is almost new?"

"Indeed," Lady Cosgrove said silkily. "Tell us more of the *moon*, Lady Stockhurst. You know a great deal about it."

A muscle twitched in Westfeld's jaw. "No," he said. He looked surprised to have spoken. "No. I didn't come here to... That is, Lady Elaine, I came here to ask you to dance." He turned his gloved hand out—not reaching toward her, just offering it up. Incongruously, she noticed that his gloves were kidskin brown—not a fashionable color.

How odd. Westfeld had always dressed at the height of fashion.

Despite that lapse, she would almost have thought him handsome, if she let herself forget who he was. Since she'd last seen him, the lines of his face had grown harsher, more angular. She could almost pretend he was a different person.

But the passage of years had not dimmed her memory of how this form of recreation would proceed. It was the game of "let's be kind to Elaine," and it had been played on her before. *Let's invite Elaine to our exclusive party. Let's invite Elaine to dance. Let's make Elaine believe that we've forgotten how to be cruel to her.*

The next step was always, *Now that we've lured her into exposing herself, let's humiliate her in front of everyone.* She would have given up on society altogether, except that doing so would have left her mother alone and unprotected.

"You needn't accept," Westfeld said, so softly that only she could hear. "I would understand completely."

And that was the hell of their jests. If she refused, he would know he had the capacity to hurt her. He would know that she feared him. He would *win*. And that was the *last* thing she wanted him to do.

And so Elaine smiled into the eyes of the man who had ruined her life. "But *of course*, Lord Westfeld," she said. "I would love it above all things."

CHAPTER TWO

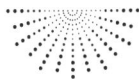

ALAS. LADY ELAINE DID *NOT* love dancing with him, Evan thought ruefully. She hated it.

Her hands were warm in his, even through gloves. She danced beautifully. She smiled the entire time. She also did not look at his face, not once. Instead, she concentrated her attention on the second button of his coat, even though she had to look down to do it.

What Evan needed to say to her was too important to be delivered cavalierly. But with talk so momentous on his mind, his skill for small conversation seemed to slip away.

Finally, he managed, "Your gown is lovely." It was, he supposed, although he was hardly the judge of such things. Pink silk, large sleeves, a skirt so wide he might have tripped over it. Might *still* do so, if he didn't watch his step.

Her gaze flicked up, and then back to his button, its touch on his face as temporary as a hawk moth flitting by a window.

"I've lost all sense of fashion myself," he told her.

Her perusal of his coat became more marked, and too late, he realized what he'd said—he'd praised her gown, and then implied that he had no taste. It came out as the worst sort of backhanded compliment.

Lady Elaine raised her eyes to him. He felt a sort of shock travel

13

through him as she did so. Her eyes were gray and luminous. She was smiling at him, but there was a knife-edge to her expression. "Indeed," she said, her tone solemn. "I can't recall the last time I saw a gentleman wearing *brown* gloves."

A little bit of an insult in return. Good for her; he deserved it.

"All my gloves are brown," he confessed. "It's a habit remaining from my mountaineering days. If your clothing is too dark, it absorbs too much sun and you become overheated. If it's too light, the dirt shows. I long ago abandoned fashion in favor of function."

She raised an eyebrow in disbelief.

"It's the truth," he said. "Would you believe I still have my waistcoat pockets lined with mackintosh?"

"I hardly know what to think," she said. "I cannot envision you as anything except an outright *leader* of fashion. You were always quite the dandy." She spoke lightly, but he could almost hear the accusation underlying her words. He *had* been a useless fribble.

His hand tightened about her waist. "People change." *He* had changed. "I wish I didn't have to do this."

Her hands tensed against him, and her face went as still as a deer sighted in the forest. But she didn't flee. Instead, that smile of hers broadened.

"How ungallant," she replied. "You *did* ask me to dance. And here you represent yourself as a gentleman."

"You misunderstand," he said. "I do not wish you out of my presence. I wish I had not made it necessary to say what I must. I am sorry."

She had never flinched at any of his insults. But at his apology, she jumped.

"I am sorry," he repeated. "You cannot know how dreadfully sorry I am."

"Whatever for?" Her face was so guileless that for one instant he believed she might forgive him. But then her eyes widened slightly. "Oh, there's no need to worry about *that*," she said. "It's quite easy to misstep in the waltz. You must keep time carefully—*one* two three, *one* two three—"

She was addressing his button once again. He hadn't misstepped, the little baggage. Somehow, over the years, she'd developed the talent of delivering the most splendid snubs in that breathy tone of voice. She hid her claws behind that innocent demeanor. But, by God, she was insulting him.

And, by God, he *liked* it. He liked that the fire and zest he'd seen in her that first Season had not completely faded. He glanced down and his gaze fixed on the creamy skin of her throat. For just one second, he contemplated leaning down and setting his lips right *there*, on her shoulder. He wondered, not so idly, what she would taste like.

She was probably counting the minutes until the waltz ended.

He shook his head. "You know what I'm referring to. My conduct all those years ago was inexcusable. I cannot ask for your forgiveness, because I don't see how I could merit it. But I must let you know I regret it."

She fixed her eyes on him. "You know, Westfeld," she said, in that same breezy tone that she always employed, "I have no notion what you could *possibly* be apologizing for." Her eyes cut away. "In point of fact, I scarcely recall you at all."

Ouch.

A hint of color touched her cheeks. "If you are perhaps referring to the last time we danced—"

Oh, hell. He didn't want to think of that.

"—I assure you, I thought nothing of your inebriation. My father, Lord Stockhurst, says only a very weak fellow drinks to excess, and I am not so unkind as to hold your incapacity against you."

He hadn't been *drunk*, damn it. He'd been rude and boorish. And the venom in her words—coupled with that sweet, placid smile— answered his question. No, she wouldn't forgive him. He could have guessed that from the start. As languorous as the waltz could be, she did not relax against him. The muscles of her back were tense and stiff against his hand. She was wary, as if she expected that at any moment he might savage her.

She had every reason to think ill of him. Yet, for all that, some errant corner of his mind paid avid attention to the pale pink ribbon threaded through the neckline of her gown. He couldn't help but wonder what would happen if he were to pull on it. Would the gown stay up, or…

God. Ten minutes in her company and he was fantasizing about her breasts again.

He was a beast: there were no two ways about it. He had apologized to her. And if she hadn't accepted it…he might well be a beast, but he wasn't the sort of man who would make a lady feel uncomfortable just so he could have the satisfaction of obtaining false forgiveness. If she wanted to pretend that she'd never been hurt, it was not his place to gainsay her.

She was light on her feet, and her gloved hand in his made him feel a whole range of uncomfortable things, from the unquiet stirrings of his lust to a pained, wistful sadness.

Damn, but remorse could run deep. There was nothing to do about this one, though, and so he folded it up and left it inside him. If he lived his life with only this one major regret, he'd count himself lucky. The waltz came to an end. And if his hand covered hers a little too firmly as he escorted her back to her mother, well, there were worse ways to apologize.

"Lady Elaine," he started to say, and then could not find a way to finish the sentence. He gave her a little bow, and slowly relinquished her hand.

"Lord Westfeld." She turned to leave, and then stopped, her gaze darting to the figures before them.

Diana had seated herself in a chair near Lady Stockhurst. The two appeared to be engaged in earnest conversation. As Evan watched, Diana leaned forward and set her hand on Lady Stockhurst's shoulder.

Next to him, Elaine's breath sucked in.

Lady Stockhurst looked up. Her eyes brightened as she saw her daughter, and she made a beckoning motion. Elaine slunk forward, each step slower than the last. Above her shoulder, Diana caught Evan's eyes, and she gave him a slow, dangerous smile.

No. Not this again.

"Elaine," Lady Stockhurst was saying, "I have just been talking with Lady Cosgrove."

No, no.

Lady Stockhurst brushed at her hair, and a smooth, pale wisp came tumbling free. "And guess what she said? She told me that everyone here was interested in my work—so very interested! She suggested I might deliver a lecture on the final evening of the house party. She'll present the notion to Mrs. Arleston. What do you think?"

It did not take a particularly intelligent man to tell what Lady Elaine thought. She stared straight at her mother. At her side, her gloved fingers compressed into a fist.

Because if there was a bigger laughingstock in all the *ton* than Elaine, it was her mother—her mother, who seemed dreamy and insubstantial half the time, never quite aware of her surroundings, entirely unable to follow a normal conversation. Ten years ago, she'd been prone to lapse into the most incomprehensible discussions at the drop of a hat, on retrogrades and periodicity of orbits. It appeared that hadn't changed, either.

"I was thinking of discoursing on my comet," Lady Stockhurst was saying. "They *did* tell me I might be made an honorary member of the Royal Astronomical Society, if ever my findings were verified. Although they haven't quite come round to that yet."

Poking fun at Lady Stockhurst would give Evan about as much amusement as jabbing a puppy with a sharp stick.

But what was her daughter to do? She couldn't very well say, "No, don't give a lecture—they all just want the excuse to laugh at you."

"That's lovely," Lady Elaine said. As she spoke, her eyes cut toward Evan, her glance sharp and unforgiving.

It didn't matter what he wanted. How could he have thought to paper matters over with a mere apology? He'd left this behind, unfinished, all those years ago.

And now his old sins were returning to haunt him. This time, he wasn't going to let them win.

~

"WASN'T THAT A LOVELY EVENING?" Lady Stockhurst, Elaine's mother, hummed to herself as she moved about the tiny sitting room that had been allotted to them. She flitted like a butterfly, light and graceful. Like a butterfly, her interest landed on a silver-backed brush that lay on a chest of drawers. When she picked it up and turned it about, the light from the oil-lamp reflected off its surface into Elaine's eyes.

Elaine winced and looked away.

"And you danced *three* times."

"Yes," Elaine said uncomfortably. "I did." She sighed. "At least that's three times better than the last ball."

Her mother set the brush down with a click. "No, it is *infinity* times better, the ratio of naught to three being boundless. If you continue to attract dance partners at an infinite rate, at the next ball you attend, every man in all of England will ask you to dance."

Elaine smiled. "You're being ridiculous, Mama."

Her mother frowned. "Yes," she finally admitted. "It is rather optimistic to extrapolate a geometrical trend from two data points."

Elaine sighed. Her mother was…well, she definitely wasn't *stupid*. Lady Stockhurst probably understood more than half the Fellows of the Royal Society. On the subjects of astronomy and mathematics, she was the most discerning person that Elaine knew.

For just about everything else…while her mother was not stupid, she could be remarkably oblivious. A more attentive mother might have looked at Elaine and seen a daughter who had failed to find a husband after eleven Seasons. Any other parent would have realized that Elaine was a social failure. But Elaine's mother looked at her daughter and saw perfection.

Elaine tried not to overturn her mother's illusions too dreadfully.

"It is *so nice* that Westfeld is back." Her mother traced a dark imperfection on the mirror and then inscribed an elliptical orbit around it.

"Mmmm."

As she spoke, Lady Stockhurst marked the perihelion on her orbit and measured it with her fingers. "You know, I always thought he was rather sweet upon you."

Elaine stared straight ahead. Out of the corner of her vision, she could catch a glimpse of the maid they had brought with them. Mary paused in the act of brushing her dress, her eyes bobbing up toward Elaine's in an unspoken question.

Elaine looked away and chose her next words carefully. "Perhaps you overestimate. You thought Viscount Saxtony was interested, too."

An annoyed wave of her hand. "And he was—if only he had not been so fickle as to marry elsewhere."

"You said Sir Mark Turner was in love with me."

"As well he should be, if he's any notion what is good for him. You should make a fine couple—both blond and tall. He needs a wife. And you are both so popular."

Elaine bit her lip. Sir Mark Turner was wanted everywhere because he'd been knighted by the queen. If Elaine was wanted *anywhere*, it was to serve as the butt of their jokes.

Lady Stockhurst smiled faintly, and smudged out the orbit she'd drawn on the mirror. "Did I mention I'm to give a lecture?"

"Yes." Elaine shivered. Her mother *would* give a lecture, and everyone would snicker at her. Elaine had sat through those before— the snide whispers about how amusing it was to see a woman aping a man. It was hard for Elaine to ignore insults when they were directed at her personally. But it was excruciating to bite her tongue when those voices mocked her mother.

Still, her mother never seemed to notice. She would take their sarcastic jeers at the end as honest applause. Elaine alone would seethe on her mother's behalf, furious and humiliated and unwilling to steal the brightness from her mother's eyes by telling the truth.

"I'm glad we came," her mother said with a decisive nod.

Elaine stood and walked to her mother, and set her arm around her shoulders. "I am, too," she said. And she truly was. Her mother would enjoy it, and if she didn't know, could it hurt her?

But her mother's shoulders seemed thin and fragile. Lady Stockhurst was brilliant and confused and...and utterly dear.

"Tell me," Elaine said, "surely you were not thinking of Westfeld in the ballroom. What *did* you have on your mind?"

It was the right thing to say. Her mother smiled immediately. "Yes, well. I was thinking that it is a matter of simple mathematics to determine the gravitational forces between any two bodies. Add in a third, however, and the equations turn to a mess. There were so many bodies in the ballroom—so many forces. One could not simply apply perturbations to project the future." She shook her head briskly. "This is why people are so hard to understand. I cannot even estimate their gravitational pull."

In spite of herself, Elaine smiled. Her mother would never figure out that her daughter was practically a pariah. She would never be able to fit the censure and laughter and insults that her daughter suffered into equations.

Perhaps that was why, after all these years, her love for her daughter had never altered. She was impervious to social reality. She saw only what she wished to see, and for that, Elaine loved her fiercely.

Her mother turned and walked to the door of her bedchamber. "I can't wait to see what tomorrow brings," she said in parting.

Elaine held her smile until her mother disappeared.

Lord above. The party would last another two days. Forty-eight hours with Lord Westfeld and Lady Cosgrove? It was going to be hell.

CHAPTER THREE

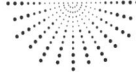

I F DANTE HAD CHOSEN TO MAKE AN EXAMPLE OF EVAN, he could not have crafted a more particularized version of hell.

Evan had tried to warn Diana off Elaine—at first subtly, then more pointedly. The afternoon after the ball, Diana had spent a good ten minutes encouraging Lady Stockhurst while the other ladies subtly tittered into their gloves. And so Evan had taken her aside.

"Leave her alone."

She pretended confusion at first. "Why, whatever do you mean? Lady Stockhurst *loves* to share her ideas." A dimple peeked out on her cheek, and her eyelashes dipped down, as if she expected him to share in the joke.

Once, he would have. "That's not what I mean. You're doing this to humiliate Lady Elaine, and I've had enough of that."

His cousin continued to smile, but her dimple faded. "I'm doing this for you."

"I don't want it. Cease. Immediately."

Her face fell. He shouldn't have felt like a cad for remonstrating with her, but he did.

He scrubbed his hand through his hair and tried again. "We started the game when we were children."

They'd been cousins, growing up on neighboring estates, ignored by all but their nursemaids and tutors. And even though Evan had gone away to school, when he'd stayed there summers she had been his only companion. After their quiet, somewhat solitary childhood, they'd entered society together. The heady whirl of constant company had been overwhelming—frightening and fun and impossible, all at once.

He protected her. She protected him. Together, they'd been unstoppable.

Truly, someone should have stopped them.

He shook his head. "We're not children any longer. There's no need for this."

She set her hand on his wrist. "You've been gone, Evan. You don't remember what London society is like. They're wolves out here, and it's devour or be devoured in turn. If you don't grasp your place in society, you'll have it torn from you. Just like your Lady Elaine."

"I remember perfectly well what London society is like."

Diana's eyes sparked, and she looked up at him defiantly. "Perhaps you think very little of me now, as I'm only a stupid, foolish girl who married an older man and stayed home while you were out exploring the world. But my husband is forever on the continent. It was a godsend for me when you returned. You are the closest thing I have to a brother, and I will *not* let you throw away your reputation or your good position in society, simply because you've got some antiquated notion of chivalry in your head."

"There's nothing antiquated about basic human decency," Evan snapped.

"Listen to yourself! This is not who you are—this stodgy fellow, dressed in brown. I *know* you. You haven't had a bit of fun since your father passed away. I did *not* drag you all the way to Hampshire so you could wallow in boredom."

"I don't mind a bit of amusement," he said quietly. "But I no longer think that ruining a lady's life is a reasonable way to pass the time."

She shrugged one shoulder. But she didn't understand, and she didn't believe him. He could tell, because throughout dinner she needled Elaine with a constant stream of sly innuendo, and no amount of repressive throat-clearing on his part would cut her off.

Dessert was soured by the tiny barbs his cousin delivered. And when Evan and the other gentlemen joined the ladies once more after port and cigars, he could see immediately that she'd not let off her sport. Lady Elaine sat on a long divan, bracketed between Diana and her mother. Even if he hadn't known Diana, there was a particularly hunted look in the lines around Lady Elaine's eyes that told him everything he needed to know.

Someone suggested cards; another person a game of charades. The discussion continued, as servants handed out delicate flutes of dark-red wine punch, chilled until condensation collected on the glass.

It was Diana who stopped the argument, gesturing with her glass of punch.

"Please," she said, "my cousin has not been in company at all. And I have been *dying* to have him tell of his adventures." Diana smiled at him prettily.

"Do tell," Mr. Arleston said. And like that, everyone turned to regard Evan.

"Lady Cosgrove makes it sound so interesting." Evan settled into the cushions of the chair. "But I only did the usual, I suppose. I wandered a season in Italy, a summer in Greece. I spent most of my time in France and Switzerland, though."

"Oh, Paris. I love Paris." That, from Mrs. Arleston.

Evan had forgotten what it was like to be the center of attention, everyone watching him, waiting for his next words. *People* had a pull for him, and even though he'd vowed he wouldn't do it, he felt some of that old energy return. "I passed through Paris on a weekend, but I didn't stay. I spent most of my time in Chamonix."

The knowing looks turned to puzzlement, and all around people leaned forward in their chairs.

"Chamonix is a town in the French Alps, near Mont Blanc."

"Is it beautiful, then?" Mrs. Arleston was frowning. "I can't quite imagine spending all my time in a small town."

"It is beautiful," Evan said quietly. "But it huddles at the feet of the highest mountain in the entire alpine region. I climbed Mont Blanc three times."

"Three times?" Mr. Patton set one hand over his rounded belly and shook his head. "Once, I can understand. It gives you a dubious set of bragging rights, I suppose. But thrice seems to be the product of an excess of ambition."

"First time anyone has ever accused me of that," Evan replied.

The ladies in the crowd smiled and shifted.

"I thought of attempting the Matterhorn, but I prefer to remain among the living. But my accomplishments are not so many. In that time, my cousin has married and produced four children. Surely that is the greater achievement."

Diana was watching him now with a curious stare, and she took a sip of her wine. "Good heavens. How long does it take to climb Mont Blanc?"

"Depending upon the conditions? Not much more than a few days of grueling work, across desperate traverses covered in snow." He paused to let the desolation of the landscape sink in.

Across from Diana, Mr. Patton frowned. "Well, you've accounted for a week out of ten years. What were you doing with the rest of your time?"

Evan raised an eyebrow. "Preparing to climb Mont Blanc."

"Preparing? For ten years? Does it take so long to buy rope and the like?"

Evan shook his head and bit back a smile.

But Diana burst in hotly, almost shoving her elbow into Lady Elaine at her side in her haste to speak on his behalf. "Mountaineering," she lectured, "is quite dangerous, as anyone would know. There are...well, mountaineering *moves* that must be learned. Special ones. I'm sure we can't understand the time that must be involved."

His cousin had always had a hot temper—and while she might seem fickle to many, Evan knew that she was loyal at heart. She *would* defend him at all costs.

"And then," Diana was continuing, "one must be quite particular about one's gear. For there is not only rope to consider, but the boots, and the, uh, the special packs, and also the tampons."

"Crampons," Evan supplied.

"Crampons," she repeated, without missing a beat.

"But in my experience," Evan interrupted, "those who spend all their time making purchases and arguing about whether to use wrought iron or forged iron for boot-nails spend no time on the mountains at all. The most important part of climbing a mountain is not choosing rope, but learning to function as part of a team. You can't go out by yourself. What would you do in a rockslide? What if you misstep on the edge of a cliff? If you cannot trust your compatriots, you risk death."

"Nonsense," Mr. Patton put in. "You only hear about those puny Frenchmen expiring in such gruesome fashion. A strapping English lord? The mountains wouldn't dare kill him."

"What an amusing thing to say." Evan didn't feel like smiling. "I would not be here, had not a puny Frenchman saved me."

"Nonsense," Patton repeated, but with less certainty.

"We were on a glacier." Evan fixed his gaze on the man's eyes. "I don't know what you've heard of them, but they're quite dangerous— every step is slick, and you can't trust the surface beneath your boots. There are crevasses that are miles deep, covered by only the slightest crust of ice. One step, and you could fall to your doom."

The ladies gasped. All of them, except Lady Elaine. Her gray eyes met his, as if she too knew what it felt like to plummet to her death.

"You try to be as careful as you can, but you never know if you're walking on a shelf of ice. The ground beneath your feet could swallow you up at any instant. Entire parties have vanished. Like that." Evan snapped his fingers.

Diana looked faintly horrified. "How do you guard against such a thing?"

"Pray," he said shortly. "And you rope together, so that if one man missteps, his mates can pull him out."

There were wise nods all around.

"But—" That was Lady Elaine, speaking for the first time. "But if you are roped together, would that not mean one man could drag you *into* a crevasse as easily as he could be pulled out?"

"Don't be ridiculous," Diana snapped. "If any one man falls, the others can surely pull him out. It's a sound plan, and safe."

Elaine pulled back.

"It is *not* safe," Evan heard himself contradict. "It is d—that is to say, it is entirely dangerous. You see, if a man falls fast enough, he could jerk a companion off his feet before the other man has a chance to brace himself. If a shelf of ice collapses, it could take two men at once —and that sort of dead weight could pull a whole party into the abyss."

Diana's eyes widened. "What do you do if more than one man is pulled in, and you cannot retrieve them?"

"What do you suppose? There's no choice in the matter. You cut the rope."

Diana gulped more of her punch. "What? And send the ones who are dangling to their death?"

Evan gave a curt nod. "Yes. And you plan for it in advance. You practice on safe ground before you ever go onto a glacier, so you know exactly what your capabilities are as a team. You know when it is a choice between having one man fall and sacrificing the entire group."

"How horrid!"

"The Bible got it wrong when it intimated that the valley contained the shadow of death. Death dwells in the high places."

Everyone was listening to him now.

"So," Diana whispered. "You nearly died. How?"

"It was just as I said. The ground vanished beneath my feet. I fell six feet in the blink of an eye and had the wind knocked out of me."

"B-but your friends pulled you up, did they not?"

"My fall jerked Meissner off his feet, too. He was luckier—he caught the ledge, and was left dangling at the top, barely able to hang on. We had only one other man roped in—Dutoi."

"Good Lord. It was a good thing you had practiced for such situations."

"There had been no practice that could help," Evan said. "We knew what we could manage. One man down, one man barely holding on… we couldn't survive that. My weight was going to pull Meissner off the ledge, and when it did, all three of us would perish. We had tested it, you see."

Diana sipped at her punch once more, and seemed surprised to find the glass empty. She gestured to a servant to refill it as she spoke. "What did you do?"

"What do you suppose I did?" Evan said. "I told them to cut the damned rope." Nobody even flinched at that blasphemy in this mixed company, so rapt was their attention. "If I could have reached my knife, I would have done it myself. But it was in my boot, and I was at such an awkward angle… Those idiots nearly killed themselves, saving my life."

Afterward, the three of them had never talked of it. But as soon as he'd been able, he had bought them a drink.

"I suppose there are worse things than owing a favor to a French aristocrat."

Dutoi had not been an aristocrat. His father had been a bourgeois, a wealthy merchant. Meissner had been a commoner, too—the young nephew of some natural philosopher who lived in the Kingdom of Hanover. But he didn't see any reason to try to explain that to these people. They wouldn't understand how much he'd transformed.

"What a peculiarly intimate friendship," Lady Elaine said. "To know that someone has the power of life and death over you."

Or maybe…maybe one person *would* understand. Evan's throat went dry. Her gray eyes met his, and he felt almost naked before her, as if she could see the extent of his transformation. As if she alone, of all women, had been given the power to comprehend who he had become.

"Outside of marriage," Evan said, "it is the most intimate relationship a man can have."

Diana giggled, breaking the mood. "Well," she whispered, none too softly, "no wonder Lady Elaine shows such curiosity. She'll not be finding intimacy any other way."

Lady Elaine closed up, shuttering like a seaside cottage in the face of a storm. All sense of intimacy disappeared, as if she had recalled that he was her enemy.

But I'm not. I've changed.

"Diana," Evan said in warning.

His cousin's eyes met his in outrage, and a little spark of defiance ignited. She lifted her glass of wine punch to her lips one last time… and then, before Evan could intervene, held it to one side and quite deliberately tipped the contents onto Elaine's lap.

The liquid spilled over her gown.

"Goodness," Diana was saying. "How clumsy of me. I must have been quite overset at hearing that story. Westfeld is one of my dearest friends and—oh—" Diana burst into tears. Immediately, the crowd gathered about his cousin, soothing her, telling her to lie back and breathe deeply. Servants rushed to find the *sal volatile.*

Elaine was shoved unceremoniously out of the way. She stood and took two steps back. The pale blue of her gown was ruined by angry red. One gloved finger touched the stain, and her chin went up.

She was like a queen, Evan thought, utterly elegant even in her distress. She didn't look at him.

Instead, Lady Elaine found her mother. And while Diana gradually let her false case of the vapors subside, Lady Elaine and her mother slipped out the door.

"There," Diana was saying through a watery smile, "I believe I've got control of my nerves now."

She caught Evan's eye, and tried to give him a smile.

He didn't return the expression.

"Westfeld, we can't provide the same danger you faced abroad," she said. "But still—is there not intimacy in fun and laughter?"

There was only one thing to do. Evan crossed to his cousin—once his dearest friend—and took her hand in his. He bowed over her.

For the entire party to hear, he said, "I've upset my cousin with my tale. I suppose that is my cue to bid you all a good evening. I'd hate to disturb your *fun* any longer."

"But, Westfeld—"

Diana made him remember who he had been all too clearly. Hurting her would feel like cutting himself. But that was what he needed—to excise that person he had been. Perhaps that was why he leaned in closer and made no effort to moderate his words.

"If you'd been there that day," he whispered, "I do believe you would have cut the rope."

It was a cruel thing to say. She flinched, and he dropped her hand.

Still, he left the room without looking back.

CHAPTER FOUR

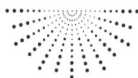

"**W**HAT A SHAME," ELAINE'S MOTHER SAID, peering at the marred fabric. "It is such a lovely gown. Do you suppose it will stain?"

The pale blue had been one of Elaine's favorites—the color of a winter sky. With that delicate lace edging the sleeves, it had made her feel like an icicle—cold and unmelting, no matter how hot the fires of gossip burned.

"A good thing this didn't happen tomorrow," her mother was saying. "It would have been so disruptive to my lecture."

Behind her, Elaine felt her maid, Mary, pause, her hands on the laces of the dress. Mary had heard the whole story. And without Elaine having to say so, Mary had undoubtedly understood what it meant.

"Yes," Elaine said. She'd meant to speak soothingly, but her bitterness came through anyway. "Because *surely* your lecture is more important than having a glass of wine punch spilled on your daughter."

But her mother was as impervious to sarcasm as she was to sly innuendo.

"It is!" she said brightening. "I'm so glad you agree."

Elaine had been holding all her emotion inside her so long that she was unprepared for the flare of anger that hit her—fierce and hot and unstoppable. "No," she heard herself shouting. "No, it isn't." She whirled and Mary hissed, reaching for the laces that trailed loose behind her. "I have taken their insults and the innuendo and the glasses of wine punch for *years*. You never take me to task for my failings, but just *once* I wish you would notice that it hurts."

Lady Stockhurst stared at her. "Elaine, you're not getting put out over an accident, are you?"

"An accident?" Elaine turned from her maid once more. "Of course you would think it was an accident. Mama, they hate me. They laugh at you. Nobody likes us. *Nobody.*"

"But Lady Cosgrove is always so friendly."

"She takes pride in humiliating you."

"But how could I be humiliated? My lectures are quite erudite, and—"

"You humiliate me every day." The words were out of Elaine's mouth before she had even properly thought them. And there was no taking them back. Her mother turned utterly pale.

But the dam had burst, and there was no stopping the outpouring of anger.

"Do you know what I hate most about the lot of them downstairs?"

A confused shake of the head in response.

Elaine's eyes stung and her vision blurred. "They make me hate you," she said. "Sometimes. I hate them for it. I hate them. I *hate* them. But when they mock you, and you play into their hands so easily… sometimes it makes me hate you, too."

"Elaine."

She couldn't say any more. She couldn't let a decade of anger spill out of her lips. But she couldn't stop herself either. Instead, Elaine turned blindly and flung open the door to the hall, striding furiously away.

She would *not* break down, she would *not* break down. But her dress was half undone, and the tears began to track down her face before she'd taken more than half a dozen steps. She stopped at the end of the hall, collapsing against the wall, and took great gulping breaths of air.

She'd held all her furious rage back for so long; why should it be so hard to contain now, merely because she'd realized she would live with it for the rest of her life? What difference would another half-century make?

The squeak of the floor nearby cut her tears off entirely. She looked up…and her heart dropped.

Of course. It wasn't enough that they douse her in punch. Lady Cosgrove must have sent her cousin up to complete her humiliation.

For there stood Lord Westfeld himself.

～

THE LAST THING THAT EVAN HAD EXPECTED TO SEE at the end of the hall was Lady Elaine, with her gown falling off her shoulders, revealing the linen of her shift. She sat on the floor, curled almost in a ball, her fists clenched.

She was crying silently, choking back great sobs. Elaine *never* cried —at least she didn't do so publicly. It made him feel that he was intruding on a painfully intimate moment, one that revealed more of her than the ivory of her chemise.

She glanced up, saw him—and gasped as if he'd shoved his elbow into her stomach.

But that moment of scalded shock passed. Her eyes narrowed, and she drew herself up in scorching fury.

"Lord Westfeld," she said, "*whatever* are you doing here? Why, the evening is quite young."

She tilted her head toward the stairs. The low rumble of voices rose up even now, faintly mocking to Evan's ears.

"I found the company below not to my taste."

He'd meant to reassure her, but instead she rolled her eyes and pushed to her feet.

"What *will* you tell the rest of them?" she asked almost conversationally. "Will you tell them that you found me in disarray? Will you and your cousin gloat that you finally broke me?"

She took one step toward him. If she'd had a knife in her hand, he suspected he'd have been bleeding already. But instead, the sleeve of her gown shifted and spilled down her shoulder.

"I told you I was sorry. I would never do anything to hurt you further."

Her eyes widened. "Never?" She took another step forward and pushed the heel of her hand into his shoulder—not hard, but not gentle either. "You must think I'm *stupid*. And why wouldn't you? I've acted the buffoon long enough."

Her left hand rose and she gave him another little shove.

"All this time I've let everyone think that I'm easy game—that all you have to do is abuse me a little and you'll have your fun. But I am done with that. The next time you push me, I *will* push back. What can I lose? It is not as if you could respect me *less*."

"I never thought you easy game," Evan protested. "In fact, you always seemed remarkably elusive."

"Don't lie to me. I let you hurt me every time. Every time I looked away. Every time I pretended not to hear your vicious remarks. There was never any cost to you when you hurt me." Her face was beginning to turn bright pink in blotches. It should have been unbecoming, especially as her eyes were red with irritation—but by God, she positively smoldered.

"Not easy to insult," he explained. "I thought you impossible to pin down, to unmask. To…to catch."

"To catch? Whatever do you mean?"

She stood close to him, so close that he could have reached out and run his hand around the impressive curve of her bosom, sliding her sleeves from her shoulders as he did so. And at that uncertain twinge in her voice, all his reason shut down—all reason but the clean smell of her hair, the brilliant shine in her eyes.

And so he leaned in and kissed her.

She tensed in shock as his arms snaked around her. She was so hot against his lips—blazing hot—and soft all over. He had just an instant to savor the taste of her.

She wriggled away from him, glowering. "I see how this is. The poor little spinster—I'm so needy and desperate that you think I'll surrender my virtue at the first opportunity."

"No," he breathed. He was the needy one, the desperate one. He needed to think, but his thoughts were slipping from his grasp. It didn't help when her breasts lifted with every inhalation.

She put one finger on the edge of her wayward sleeve. "Well." Her words were sharp, but her hand trembled. "Maybe I am." And then she slid the fabric down her arm, exposing creamy skin.

His lungs were in agony. He couldn't breathe, couldn't think anything except—*oh God, please keep going.*

"Maybe I *am* desperate." Her voice was low. "I have nothing to look forward to but decades of loneliness. Maybe all I ask for is one night of passion." She glanced up at him through thick eyelashes. "Is that what I am supposed to say? I'm supposed to beg you for a night?"

"Yes." The word came out before he could think better.

The corner of her mouth curled in distaste, but she didn't draw back.

"I mean, no. I mean—" He wasn't sure what he meant, but his erection was growing. He would mean anything, if he could just kiss her again.

"Maybe I am supposed to beg you to make a woman of me."

"Hell." Lust had always made him stupid. "You don't have to beg." His voice grew hoarse. "I've—look, I've always wanted you."

Stupid he might be, but even he could tell that something was wrong. Her nose scrunched in an adorably pugnacious fashion and she glared up at him.

"Always," she whispered, her voice silky. "Of course. How *obvious.* There is one little problem, isn't there, Westfeld? I don't trust you."

"You don't."

"You see," she continued, "I am very vulnerable—and you are not. Not at all."

That brought another heated image to mind—this time, of how

vulnerable he would be if he placed himself in her hands. Literally. He groaned, and tried to suppress the vision, but it was replaced by another—his kneeling before her, lifting her skirts—and another, in which she ran her hands all over him.

Not good. He needed to think with his brain, not his hardening prick. But she reached up and hooked her finger underneath her other sleeve, and all he could think of was her gown unfastened to her waist, her corset undone, and her breasts spilling out.

"Christ," he swore aloud.

Remember: you hurt her. She doesn't want you. She just wants to hurt you back.

"Here's the way it is," he said hoarsely, fumbling in his pocket for the key to his room. He turned the lock, opened the door. "I'm not going to ask you to come inside."

The high flush of anger was beginning to fade from her face.

"At least not yet," he amended.

He held his breath and strode into the room. He rummaged about in the dim light until he found the *rücksack* he'd brought with him. When he found it on the chest of drawers, he looked up. She stood in the hall, a foot from his door, watching him warily.

"You want me vulnerable?" He sat on the edge of the bed, pack in hand. "That's easy enough to manage."

He tossed the bag across the room. It landed on the floor in front of her and skidded to her feet. His evening shoes came off with little effort; the coat required a little more work, the fit being tight. But he undid his waistcoat buttons easily. He looked up from his task to see her watching in horrified fascination.

"What are you doing?"

"Making myself vulnerable," he bit off. "Now open the *rücksack*."

Her brows drew down at the unfamiliar word, but she bent and picked it up. She turned it around a few times before loosening the drawstring cord.

"What you're looking for is on top," he said. Was it too much to take off his shirt? He decided it was. Instead, he sat on the bed, watching as she gingerly reached in and removed a thick coil.

It was old habit that made him travel with rope—that, or some misguided desire for safety. That rope had saved his life more than once. She frowned at the heavy fibers and touched the ends, carefully waxed to prevent unraveling.

"There," he said. "Want me vulnerable? Then tie me up."

"Why?"

He shrugged. "You said you were curious. You said you wouldn't trust me. Tie me up, and you can do with me as you please."

And oh, how he wanted her to be *pleased* by him. Still, Evan had his own less pleasant suspicions about what she *wanted* to do to him.

She bit her lip, turned to glance down the hall. Moments passed while she seemed lost in contemplation. And then slowly she came forward. She pulled the door almost shut behind her and then paused, her fingers resting on the handle, as if waiting for him to spring forward. There was a strange quality to her movements, purposeful and yet uncertain. She didn't speak as she advanced, did not say a word as she wound the rope in a loop round his left hand.

"That," Evan said as she completed the knot, "is an excellent version of a middleman's noose."

She looped the rope to the left post of the bed, and then pulled the rope taut.

He felt a hint of nerves, and continued. "So-called because when three men are roped together, it's the knot you'd tie to secure the man in the middle."

She wound the rope around the post to his right, her mouth set in a grim line.

"Don't worry." He flashed her a smile. "We shall be just fine with only the two of us. No need for a third."

Her head bowed, and her loose hair spilled over her face, hiding her expression. But the knot she tied round this wrist was tighter, her hands jerking the ends of the rope into place.

He really couldn't move much at all, just wiggle his arms a little and twist his hand about. He hadn't thought she would tie him quite so tightly. But when he shifted, the friction of the rope burned against his skin.

He wanted her to trust him. And for one brief second, she leaned over him, her hair brushing his throat. She could touch him anywhere, and he'd not be able to do anything about it. Her throat contracted in a hard swallow.

But she lifted her head and looked him in the eyes.

"And what," she asked quietly, "do you think I am going to do *now?*"

He was scarcely capable of thinking at all.

"Well," he said, "I can tell you what I *want* you to do. I want you to kiss me."

Her pupils dilated.

"I want you to run your hands under my shirt. I want you over me. I want to taste you, and I definitely want to be inside of you."

"Do you?" Her voice shook.

"If I'm to list the things I want, I want to own your quiet possession," he continued, "and drive the wariness from your eyes."

She swayed just a little at those words.

"But you didn't ask me what *I* wanted. You asked what I thought you would do."

"And what do you think I will do? Do you think I will kiss you? Touch you?"

He smiled at her. "No. I didn't really think you had planned to lose your virginity to me over a wine spill. I think you are planning to walk out that door, leaving me tied to my own bed."

Her eyes widened and she took a step back. "If you knew, then why did you agree?"

He couldn't even shrug properly. "You wanted me vulnerable. I suppose I owed you that much."

"No." She shook her head violently. "No. You can't trick me into this. I know how you are. You'll pretend to be kind. All the while, you'll coax me into exposing myself, and once I do—"

"And what if I don't?"

She didn't hear him, though. She paced away, and then turned back to him, her cheeks flushed once more. "It is not going to be easy for you, not any longer. I am done being the butt of your jokes." She glared at him.

"That much," he said quietly, "I can safely promise you."

"I don't know why I ever feared you." She gave him a wintry smile. "You always were a bit slow around me. And…you always did watch my bosom. If I had realized you were so easily led years ago…" She shook her head. "But never mind that." She took the last steps to the door and then opened it. "Good night," she said.

The door shut behind her.

Evan inhaled night air and pulled at his arms. There was barely any give in the rope. He was burning from head to toe. But it was not just the fire of want that he felt inside him.

He turned his hands in his bonds, feeling the fibers rub against the naked skin of his wrists. He didn't bother to try to break free. The rope he used could hold more than two thousand pounds; he'd always insisted on good gear. For all that he wanted to swear in sheer frustrated lust, he felt a grudging smile play over his lips.

Damn, but she was good. He hadn't actually supposed she could tie a knot—but she'd surprised him. She had always surprised him.

Ten years ago, during that awful first Season of hers…

But remembering what he'd done was enough to rob him of all enjoyment of the evening. That thought was less comfortable than the ropes that bound him. Still, he twisted his left hand about and got to work.

CHAPTER FIVE

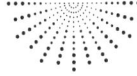

E LAINE EASED OPEN THE DOOR to their small upstairs sitting
room once more.

The lights had been doused and nothing but navy-blue
shadows awaited her. Her mother must have gone to bed and sent
Mary away. Elaine sighed and fumbled with her gown in the darkness.
Mary had already loosened it; she needed only to push it over her
petticoats before it slid to the floor in an ignominious heap. And what
did it matter if the silk crumpled, stained as it was?

She attacked the more delicate matter of her corset, twisting so as
to undo complicated laces in the dark. And then a figure near the
window straightened.

"Elaine?"

"Mama." Elaine paused, uncertain of her reception.

"Oh, Elaine." Her mother moved closer, reaching out. Their fingertips met in the darkness, and then her mother pulled her close. She
could feel her mother's heartbeat, the desperate tide of her breathing.

Any other parent would have demanded to know where she had
been. Her mother was just glad to have her back—with no uncomfortable questions about what she'd been doing in that state of dishabille.

And thank God that she didn't have to answer queries as to her whereabouts. With her mother's arms around her, she could remember what she'd let herself forget these last hours: that even though her mother would never comprehend the complexities of society, it brought her grief to know her daughter was unhappy. Her mother stroked her back, and in return, Elaine held her tightly. She wasn't sure who was comforting whom. She didn't know whose pain it was anymore.

"I never knew," her mother murmured into her ear. "I'm sorry. I don't understand when people laugh. I always thought they laughed because they were happy." She spoke in rueful bafflement.

"There, there," Elaine heard herself say.

"I know there are some things I don't understand. Maybe, if it hadn't been for me, you *would* have been the belle of the Season. Although—" Elaine could almost *hear* her frown "—I still do not understand why you are not. Are you sure you are not?"

"If it hadn't been for you, I would have given up years ago."

"I won't give my lecture tomorrow."

Elaine swallowed and thought of what might await her on the morning. Not so far away, Lord Westfeld was tied to his bed. She'd left him there. She still didn't understand what had happened between them. She'd thought him so arrogant, so sure of himself and his own golden attraction. She had thought him so confident that he could despoil her, if only she gave him a little trust.

She had meant to teach him a little lesson.

But he'd made even her revenge feel flat. It wasn't just that he was handsome. It wasn't just that once he'd shed his jacket, the muscles of his arms were visible through his shirt. She could easily imagine him as a mountaineer, holding onto a bit of rock and pulling himself up with one hand. But as strong as he looked, when he had been tied up before her, she'd felt full-blown want. She could have touched him anywhere, done anything to him—and he couldn't hurt her back. A dangerous thought.

An illusion, too. He'd never made her fear any physical danger— not even tonight. No, the danger in him was precisely the opposite: that he made her want to trust him, want to believe in him. But he was her enemy. And when tomorrow came, he would be angry and more implacable than ever.

On the morrow, her mother was supposed to deliver a lecture on comets. What would he do about that?

"We can leave," her mother said. "It would just be a day early."

She could flee.

But no. Elaine took a deep breath and set her hands on her mother's shoulders. "We'll stay. You will face them all, and you will tell them about your comet. I shall applaud you in all sincerity." If nobody else clapped, she would cheer loud enough for everyone. What was the worst that could happen?

Westfeld could ruin her if he told anyone she'd been in his chambers alone. But at this moment, the thought of being cast out of polite society seemed more blessing than curse.

Her mother's arm tightened about her. "If you want me to do it," she said, "then I shan't care about anything else." And so for the second time that evening, Elaine was kissed—this time, just the dry touch of her mother's lips against her forehead, sweet and without complication.

~

I T WAS AMAZING HOW DIFFERENT THE WORLD LOOKED to Elaine when she stopped dreading the future. She didn't have to pretend to join the ladies at breakfast—although the conversation she overheard was sadly devoid of gossip about a certain earl being found tied to his bedposts. She went walking with her mother in the morning; in the afternoon she helped her prepare for her lecture. When evening came around, she sat in the front row.

The chairs had been set up in the ballroom, but tonight Elaine had no desire to contemplate the walls. Instead, she took pleasure in hearing the brilliant Lady Stockhurst speak. Everyone else might giggle at the light that came into her mother's eyes, or the excited way she jumped from topic to topic. But Elaine drank in the sight.

Still, she was all too aware of Westfeld, sitting a few chairs behind her. He was close enough that she could imagine the heat wafting from his body, could almost feel the echo of his kiss on her mouth. She'd given herself leave not to care if he insulted her. But aside from sketching her a tiny bow from across the room, he'd not made the slightest attempt to seek his revenge. That seeming benevolence made her nervous. After last night, his vengeance would come. It *had* to.

And sure enough, when her mother had come to a breathless halt, and she asked if there were any questions, he was the one who stood.

He could not hurt Elaine. But if he hurt her mother, she would claw his eyes out in front of the entire crowd.

"Lady Stockhurst," he said, and Elaine cringed—the respect in his voice must have been false. "In your calculations of the periodicity of the orbit, you assumed it was purely elliptical. What effect does the gravitational pull of the larger planets have on your calculation?"

Was that an insult? Did it hurt? Elaine held her breath and frowned.

But a sunny smile burst over her mother's face. "What an excellent question! I have been calculating second-order perturbations since February, and…"

And she was off, bubbling over with excitement and mathematics that Elaine scarcely comprehended.

Westfeld simply watched. He was still standing; instead of exchanging looks with his cousin, he nodded as she spoke. His civility made Elaine feel uncomfortable. What was he planning?

Her mother's explanation had devolved into one of those uncomfortable moments where she simply listed the formulae in her head—she could perform derivations aloud almost as easily as on paper. This was often the point when people started laughing into their hands. And when Lady Stockhurst started in on a string of *x-noughts*, Westfeld finally did look away: he glanced at Elaine. She saw no mischief brimming in his eyes.

The worst possibility of all occurred to her.

What if he wasn't planning anything? What if he had meant it when he'd apologized to her? What if…what if he'd kissed her because he wanted to do so?

Those thoughts started a nervous flutter in her belly.

And then Lady Cosgrove yawned audibly and stretched. "Goodness," she said, "How we *do* indulge our elders in their foibles."

Lady Stockhurst stopped mid-phrase and glanced uncertainly at Elaine.

"Don't be rude, Diana," Westfeld said mildly. The expression on his face hadn't changed, not one bit, but Elaine felt her stomach knot. "I was hoping that Lady Stockhurst would be so kind as to forward me a copy of her remarks. I have a friend who might have some interest."

In response to this, her mother gave a gracious nod.

What if he didn't hate her? If he didn't, then last night…

But she was not the only one thinking along those lines. "Don't tell me you're *interested*," Lady Cosgrove spat. "Everyone *knows* what you think of Lady Elaine and her mother. We've all heard it before."

Westfeld's eyes darkened. He turned to face his cousin. "No. *Nobody* knows. But as you're bored with mathematics, perhaps I should tell you that story instead."

The entire room went silent. Elaine didn't dare breathe, for fear that her dress would shift and the sound would interrupt him. Her heart had seemed to stop in her chest.

"You see," Westfeld said, "ten years ago, I met a lady. She was very pretty and quite fearless. She spoke her mind, and she laughed with abandon. I fell in love with her over the course of about an evening."

It *had* to turn into a joke.

But he didn't look like he was joking. "I was nineteen at the time, and therefore foolish. And so, to my mind, there were two important things I had to do. First, I had to make her notice me in the way I noticed her. I wanted her to look for me every time she walked into a room. I wanted her to miss me when I wasn't there. I wanted her to be aware at every second of where I stood." He paused. "Also," he said, "being a young man, and thus having no thoughts to speak of, it seemed of utmost importance that nobody know I had fallen in love. If they knew, I would be embarrassed. And that would have heralded the end of the world."

It wasn't a joke. Elaine felt the palms of her hands grow cold.

"Somehow," he continued, raising his head and looking directly into her eyes, "what started with those simple requirements—make her notice me, but guarantee that nobody understood how I felt—turned into the cruelest thing I have ever done to another human. I started to poke fun at her laugh. At first, it was one of those things I said to explain why I was staring at her—'Good heavens, have you all noticed how Lady Elaine laughs?' And then, as everyone eagerly took part, I found myself helpless to stop it."

It wasn't an excuse. It wasn't an apology. It just *was*, and she didn't know how to take this much truth.

He stopped and shook his head. His lips thinned. "No. I wasn't *helpless*. I could have stopped at any time. I was merely too weak to do so. I wish I could say I just kept my mouth shut, but I didn't. I was the worst of the lot. I made up half the cruel names. I would go up to her, speak to her face, just for the thrill of talking with her—and as soon as someone looked my way, I'd slip in an insult, so nobody would think I cared."

Elaine's entire world had been upended. Right had become wrong, and had turned back to right again.

"She never did look at me. But I could tell that she knew when I was present, because over the course of that year—over the course of that horrible year, when I hurt her time and time again, she gradually lost her fearlessness. It was near the end of the Season when I realized how completely I had succeeded in my aims. She came into a room. She looked around—just as I had wanted, when I'd first fallen in love with her. Her eyes passed over me. And yet she knew I was there because she turned and left. She *was* aware of me, every second of every day. I was the man who tormented her, and for her, knowing my whereabouts had become a matter of self-preservation."

Did it make it better or worse that he'd understood what he had done to her? She couldn't decide.

"So I did what any young, senseless idiot would do. I ran away. A retreat to the country wasn't enough; I couldn't bear to stay in England. I had to outrun the person you all believed me to be. I spent a summer in Greece, but every woman I saw brought me back to Lady

Elaine. Finally, while passing through Switzerland, I talked to a man who had attempted the ascent on Mont Blanc. He told me that he'd nearly died in the process. To my mind, that seemed like the best thing I could do with myself."

Westfeld gave the entire room a tight smile. "And so that was why I started mountaineering: because I was too cowardly to come home, apologize, and try to make things right."

Right. She didn't know where right lay any longer. But what he'd said was irrevocable. This gossip would race through polite society. She'd wanted him vulnerable, unable to hurt her...and here he was.

"And so here I am," he echoed, as if he'd heard her thoughts. "Older, wiser, and I hope a good deal braver. Lady Elaine, you have my sincerest apologies for what I did to you. I don't hope for your forgiveness, but I am in your debt. Deeply. Should you ever need anything—anything—you have only to ask, and it is yours."

"You see," her mother said into the resounding silence that followed. "I *told* you Westfeld was sweet on you. And I was right!"

Elaine could almost see the rising speculation in the eyes of those around her. After a declaration like that, she could guess what would come next. She could feel the future pressing against her, like a crushing weight of humid air overpowering her lungs.

He was looking at her. His eyes had always fascinated her, and this time she could see nothing of the snake in them. No lies. No jokes. Just a painful, awkward, humiliating truth. He was going to ask in front of all these people, and...and they would all expect her to say yes.

She stood so swiftly her chair was knocked over behind her. And without saying a word, she turned and left the room.

She knew even as she did so that he would follow.

CHAPTER SIX

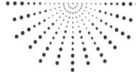

VAN FOUND HER IN THE GARDEN, sitting on a bench amidst a quiet symphony of cricket calls. She looked at him as if she were holding court—regal and unattainable. There was almost no moon to speak of, but the stars were bright, and her eyes were, too.

Finally, she spoke. "How did you escape last night?"

He hoisted his sleeve and turned back his cuff. In the darkness, it was almost impossible to see where the rope had rubbed his skin into agitated redness. "A middleman's noose can be converted into a slip-knot. With a good bit of effort, it turns out. I'd never done it one-handed before."

She looked at his wrist and then glanced away.

He sat next to her on the bench.

"I feel as if I should apologize for that," she said, "but...but I can't quite bring myself to do so. What was I supposed to think? You were talking about seducing me. That wasn't a sign of respect."

"I've wanted you for years." He scrubbed his hand through his hair. "Respect doesn't enter into it. Had anything happened, I surely would have married you."

She hid her face. "Oh, Westfeld. Don't."

"But I must. Will you marry me?"

The silence stretched into awkwardness.

"I know you'll have a hard time believing that I am serious. But please—I beg you to see that what happened all those years ago is in the past. I'm not the same man today."

She raised her face to his. The starlight reflected in her eyes, gray and silver together.

"Do you really think I would want to marry *you*?"

No. Still, it was a blow to hear it out loud.

"I had hoped—I had so hoped I might convince you. Let me court you, then. You don't know who I am now, and perhaps once you come to know me…"

He reached over to take her hand. The contact was inadequate—after last night's intimacy, the mere feel of glove-on-glove seemed confining. She didn't respond to his caress. But at least she didn't push him away.

"I don't think it matters what I know of you," she said simply. "Do you know what you did to me?"

He could feel the tips of his ears flush. "I remember."

"No." She pulled her hand from his now. "You only saw the public moments. You cannot know." Her voice dropped. "You are handsome and wealthy and titled. Perhaps I might someday believe that you are kind, too. But let me tell you what I *feel* when I look at you. In my first year out, two months into the Season, I tasked my maid to tell me a series of jokes. We filled a bath. And every time I laughed *my* laugh, I told her to duck my head under the water. I hoped I might cure myself."

He didn't know what to say to that.

"The first few times, it was just funny. And that made me laugh all the harder. So I asked her to hold my head under longer and longer."

"No," he breathed.

"Yes." Her voice was sharp. "But it never worked. After the eighteenth time, I couldn't stop laughing. Not for anything. I inhaled water into my lungs and was bedridden for days on end."

"Oh. God."

"What did you *think* you were doing to me when you called me those names? When you egged on your friends to poke fun at me?"

"But you were so serene. I wasn't even sure you heard me half the time. You never—" He swallowed his protests. She shouldn't have to break down in public for him to have a conscience.

"I'll be the first to admit, Westfeld, that you're an attractive man. When you're not being cruel, you can be quite charming. You're handsome." Her voice dropped. "And I'm very curious about what we spoke of the other night."

Such a bare recitation. Any other lady would have gladly accepted him for half as much reason, and he'd be kissing her already. Too bad he didn't want any other lady. He wanted this one. He was only beginning to realize how much.

"But none of that matters. When I see you, I remember that you made me want to drown rather than be myself."

He'd known he had been cruel. But this was the first time he'd really *felt* it, a deep ache that went straight to his bones. He didn't want to believe that *that* could be chalked up to his account. How could he ever make up for that?

You can't, you ass.

He'd never understood what regret meant until now. It wasn't the pallid sort of wish he'd entertained before. He wished he could reach inside himself and take back what he had done. He didn't want to be himself any longer.

No words could make it up to her. And perhaps that was precisely what struck him at that moment. He was always going to be the man who had done *that* to her. No matter how hard he wanted, his past followed him around as faithfully as his shadow. He would always cast darkness on her.

"Well," he said eventually. "That's it, then."

She met his eyes. She didn't pretend to misunderstand him. "That is it."

When a man was nineteen, he felt invulnerable—as if nothing could touch him. That stupid belief had been the basis of a great many idiotic things that Evan had done in his life. But this notion that all the hurt he'd caused could simply disappear because he *wanted* it to—that had been the last childish dream he'd held on to. He let go of it now. What you did when you were young could kill you. It just might take years to do it.

"We can still be friends," she was saying calmly. "Just...not anything else."

"Friends."

"Even...even back then, there were times I almost thought I could like you."

"You are too generous." The words came out sounding bitter, but he didn't intend them that way. He wasn't bitter. He *wasn't*. Friendship and kindness from her—it was more than he deserved. Less than he wanted, true, but...

"I haven't got it in me to give you any more trust than friendship. I'm still not sure I can trust you past three minutes."

He swallowed. If he'd been his young self, he'd have stalked away in a fit of pique, furious that she'd thwarted him. He would have had his revenge upon her for rejecting him. But he was a great deal older now. And he'd cast enough shadows.

"Good." He leaned closer to her. "Then in three minutes, we can be friends."

"Three minutes? Why wait three—"

"Because friends don't do this," he replied, and leaned toward her. This time, he didn't put his arm immediately about her. His lips touched hers. She was still—too still—and for a moment he thought he'd read her wrongly. But then she kissed him back.

She tasted like mint and wild honey. She was soft against him. And, oh, how easy it would be to let his control snap. To see precisely what he could do in the three minutes he'd given himself.

She *liked* kissing him. He could tell by the tenor of her breathing, by the sound she made in her throat as his tongue traced the seam of her lips.

He could tell because she hadn't slapped him.

He set his arm around her and pulled her close. When she opened up to him, it felt even better than any of his fantasies. His mind could only envision one part of her body at a time—lips or breasts or buttocks, but never all three together. But here in the flesh she was a solid armful, an overload of good things. He could not break her down into constituent parts. It was just Elaine leaning against him, Elaine that made that sound in her throat, and then, by God, she moved *closer*, until her chest brushed his. He was on fire for her.

Still, in the back of his head, he could almost hear the inexorable tick of clockwork, as if this tryst were timed by the watch in this pocket. Three, and his other hand crept down her waist, cupping her close. Two, and his tongue sought hers out. One...

One kiss, and he'd come to the end of her trust.

He pulled back. Her fingers had slipped under his elbows, and they bit into his arms, ten little needle points of pressure. He wasn't sure if she was holding him close or keeping him at arm's length.

"Westfeld." Her voice was just a little rough. "I...I...Please don't do that again."

He wanted to ask if she'd liked it. He already knew the answer. She'd liked it, but he'd reminded her, once again, of drowning. He wanted to curse.

"No," he said softly. "We're simply friends now, and friends don't do that to each other. Not ever again."

CHAPTER SEVEN

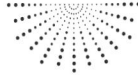

London, nine months later.

WHEN WESTFELD HAD FIRST OFFERED HER FRIENDSHIP, Elaine hadn't believed it. *Friendship* was a concept men bandied about to save face when they were rejected.

But he had nonetheless become her friend. He didn't dance continual attendance on her, but he talked to her on regular occasion and he made her laugh. He introduced her to his friends—all his friends, that was, save Lady Cosgrove—and he talked with hers. As word spread of what he had said, she simply stopped being an object of fun. For the first time in a decade, she could go to a ball and *breathe*.

She couldn't forgive him—how could she?—but was it so awful to enjoy his company?

"I think," he said to her on this evening, his voice barely audible over the roar of the crowd at the soirée, "that your seamstress needs a new palette."

A year ago she'd have bristled, hearing an implied insult. Today she smiled at him indulgently. "Why ever is that? Just because *I* happen to like pink doesn't mean *you* must wear it."

"That wasn't why." He grinned. "Although I'll have you know that I turn out very nicely in pink. And purple. Any man can don white and black. It takes a truly masculine fellow to manage lavender."

She laughed. And that was the best part of it: she could laugh without flinching. It was still too loud and still too long, but she no longer drew whispers from around the room.

"Then why?" she asked.

"Because one day, I want to see you walk into a room not in any of these watered-down colors." He reached out and flicked the pale rose of her gown. "I want to see you in vibrant red or dark blue. I want to watch you walk into the middle of the room." He dropped his voice. "And I want to see you take ownership of it."

"I—oh—I couldn't." But what an enticing vision. Still, she would have to be as unaware as her mother to do that. Everyone would look at her. Everyone would talk, and *laugh*. "I'm not a middle-of-the-room sort of person," she said apologetically.

"Yes, you are. You've hidden it deep inside you, but you are." He was watching her, and she felt something all too familiar stir inside of her.

At times like this, she wished he had never kissed her. She could almost call to mind the feel of his lips against hers. It was a disconcerting thought to have about a friend, and he *was* a friend.

Just a friend, and friends didn't think about kissing friends. He certainly had put all thoughts of kissing *her* out of his mind. He was affable. He was amusing. He was even reliable, something she never would have predicted. It was just that he wasn't going to kiss her, and she wasn't going to kiss him back.

"I prefer to enter the room like a mouse," Elaine said, joking to dispel her uncertainty. "I creep very quietly along the wainscoting. Have you ever tried to creep wearing bright red? It can't be done." She glanced across the room and caught sight of her mother.

"If something is worth doing," he said, "it's worth doing bravely."

"I'm brave," she protested. "As brave as a mouse. It takes quite a bit of courage to enter a room populated by people a hundred times your size."

He gave her a look. He didn't quite roll his eyes, but he glanced heavenward, as if in silent supplication.

"Very well, then," she said. "If that won't wash, I'll be brave as an ostrich. The instant I see something frightening, I'll stick my head in the sand."

This brought her only a sorry shake of his head. "My dear," he said, "ostriches don't put their heads in the sand. That's a myth."

"Oh?" On the other side of the room, her mother was talking to a group of ladies. Lady Stockhurst seemed to be quite excited, Elaine guessed by her exaggerated gesticulations.

Westfeld lectured on. "An ostrich weighs upward of fifteen stone. It can outrun a horse. What need has it for cowardice?"

The ladies who spoke with her mother waved fans. She could not make out their faces, but Elaine could imagine them biting back cruel smiles.

"Very well," Elaine said. "I promise you, when I weigh fifteen stone I shall relinquish all fear."

The crowd shifted, and in that moment Elaine saw that the woman standing closest to her mother was Lady Cosgrove. Over all these months, Elaine had begun to relax. But her mother was still her vulnerable heart. She had no protection of her own, and Westfeld couldn't save her. Without waiting for another word, she started across the room.

"Elaine," Westfeld hissed, following along beside her. But he'd seen it, too.

They'd talked of a great many things since they had become friends—Parliament and fashion, agriculture and the latest serial from Dickens.

They had not mentioned Westfeld's friendship with Lady Cosgrove. The woman had kept her distance since the Season started, but Elaine had seen her all too often. It was impossible to escape her; she lived just across the street, after all. Elaine had often wished that it was Lady Cosgrove who was absent, instead of her never-seen husband.

"You know what she'll do," Elaine said.

"I know what I won't let her do." They were his last words before they joined the group.

"Why, Lady Elaine." Lady Cosgrove smiled at Elaine while somehow avoiding her cousin's gaze altogether. "Your mother has just agreed to speak for us a few weeks from now."

"A lecture?" Elaine tapped her fingers against her skirts. A lecture wouldn't be so awful. Not many would come, and her mother would enjoy it.

"Better!" her mother exclaimed. "In three weeks' time, Lady Cosgrove is holding a gala at Hanover Square. There will be music, and *hundreds* of people, all interested in—"

"Mama," Elaine interrupted blandly, "they've thrown tomatoes at some of the larger entertainments." *Remember. Remember. Lady Cosgrove doesn't wish us well.*

Behind Lady Stockhurst, Lady Cosgrove bit back a smile.

And, it seemed, this wouldn't be one of the days when her mother recalled such things. "Why would they do that?" her mother mused. "I can't account for it. Even the lower orders have better things to do with a perfectly good tomato. And genteel society…"

"They throw *rotten* vegetables to express displeasure."

"Or boredom," Lady Cosgrove put in. "But, then, Lady Elaine, you don't believe your own mother is boring, do you?"

"This is all nonsense," Lady Stockhurst proclaimed. "I don't know what you're speaking of, Elaine. The tomato is a *fruit*, not a vegetable."

By Elaine's side, Westfeld took her arm. "It will be well," he said quietly. "It will be well."

Lady Cosgrove's lips pinched together.

"How can it be?" Elaine whispered. "I've seen how these things go. To expose her to more people, more indignity… How can it be well? I know *you* will be kind, but you cannot control how two dozen people will respond—and there could be as many as a thousand present."

Westfeld simply shrugged. "What did Archimedes say? If you want to move the world, all you need is a long enough lever. It *will* be well."

She huffed. "You also need a fulcrum on which to rest your lever, I believe."

He smiled at that—an expression as arrogant and certain as any she could remember seeing on him.

"Well." His deep drawl seemed to resonate with some deep part of her. "If ever you need to...rest your lever, here I am."

She glanced up at him. He was watching her, and she felt as if she might burst into flame. She snatched her arm from his before he could notice. "Do be serious, Westfeld."

He gave a resigned shake of his head. "And here I thought I was."

⁓

OVER THE NEXT WEEKS, EVAN TRIED TO MAKE JOKES to lift Elaine's distress. None of them worked, and finally he stopped jesting altogether. But despite every attempt he made to make her smile, he still held back the truth of what he was doing.

The truth was deadly earnest. By the time he'd found a seat in the hall at Hanover Square before Lady Stockhurst's lecture, he was feeling the cost of the last two weeks of frantic work. He'd written letters, found couriers, and gone in person to speak to more than half a dozen men.

He'd had to. He understood too well how Diana operated. His cousin had planned for her evening of entertainment to be a stunning success. It started with a scene from the *Pickwick Papers*, performed by the Adelphi Theater. The acting was crisp and believable, the characters expertly portrayed. There followed a concerto by Mendelssohn for piano and violin, and a short intermission for light refreshment. It would end with a performance by the famed soprano, Giulia Grisi.

Lady Stockhurst, sandwiched between these shining lights, seemed to serve all too clear a purpose: she was to be the comic interlude. As she started, she did seem to fit that role. She'd had great star-charts made, showing the course of the planets and the placement of her comet in the night sky. She spoke with great animation; her exuberance overcame all ladylike boundaries. She ended her talk with an impassioned speech on the course of the stars, predicting a return of the heavenly visitation in twelve years' time.

One either had to laugh or applaud...and when she finished, no applause was forthcoming. Instead, when she asked for questions, the audience sat in near-silence as if not sure how to react. The next few seconds would be crucial.

"Lady Stockhurst," a woman said in the front. "I could not help but notice that your presentation included calculations that are tradition-ally left to gentlemen. As a *lady*, have you ever considered that perhaps you are unsuited to such work?"

It could have been worse. Still, across the hall from him, Evan could see Elaine tense. Her chin lifted, as if she were daring the world to speak ill of her mother. He felt his own heart contract, as if he were flinching from the pain she might receive.

Lady Stockhurst, however, simply frowned at the woman in confusion. "No," she said tersely. "Next?"

A low titter swept the room. Evan had himself prepared a few queries. But he'd hoped that he wouldn't have to intervene. After all, if the rest of his plans did not come to fruition, his solitary efforts could hardly sway a crowd this large.

He couldn't pinpoint when he had started feeling this way, but now that it had been going on for these many months, he would personally take on every man and woman in the room just to win a smile from Elaine. It was stupid and pointless...and utterly inevitable. It had nothing to do with making amends any longer. He didn't want her hurt; it was that simple. At his side, his hand curled into an invol-untary fist.

"Lady Stockhurst?" A man stood in the back of the room. Evan had never seen him before—at least, not in person. But he'd seen a portrait of the fellow. Slowly, his hand unclenched.

The man was older, perhaps of an age with Lady Stockhurst herself. His face was thin and framed by short, unkempt hair that was beginning to go gray.

Lady Stockhurst beamed.

He fumbled with some papers in his hand, unfolding them, and then looked about the room. "I've not yet had the pleasure of reading your work myself, Lady Stockhurst, but my aunt saw an early copy of your monograph, and asked me to convey to you her appreciation for your meticulous work."

"Oh." Lady Stockhurst rubbed her nose in puzzlement. "But I've not given copies of my work to anyone, not except…" Her eyes darted to the left and fell on Evan. Evan tried not to smile.

He failed.

Two rows away, Diana stirred. Over the last months, they'd continued to talk—but their relationship had become strained. She wouldn't talk with Lady Elaine, she wouldn't apologize—and he half suspected that she'd designed Lady Stockhurst's part in this evening's entertainment as a way to prove to Evan that she wouldn't change her mind.

"Nonetheless," the older gentleman was saying. "I have some correspondence from her."

Diana folded her arms in disapproval. "Well, there's no need to listen to the old crones exchange their regards," she said. Not too loud; but then, not too quietly either.

It was her typical style—a cutting insult delivered with a smooth smile. But it was not met with the usual response. A murmur swept through the room. Those nearest her repeated her words, until the hall practically rumbled with displeasure.

"Crones?" The gentleman turned to Diana, his expression perplexed. "Ma'am, my aunt's recommendation brought fifteen members of the Royal Astronomical Society to this event. The instant Lord Westfeld sent word of Lady Stockhurst's presentation, I knew I would have to attend."

Across the room, Elaine shot Evan a glance. He smiled at her. *There. I said it would all be well.*

"The…the Astronomical Society?" Diana blinked at the fellow, no doubt trying to place him. "Who are you? Who is your aunt?"

"I am Sir John Herschel," the man replied. "And my aunt is Caroline Herschel—the only woman to have been presented with the Gold Medal of the Royal Astronomical Society. She was unable to come from Hanover, where she currently resides, but she asked me to read a statement on her behalf."

Across the room, Elaine was looking at him. Her eyes had gone wide and luminous. And in that instant, Evan knew precisely why he'd gone to so much trouble. Not only to make her smile. Not merely out of friendship. Not just because of his poorly-contained, ill-conceived lust. He'd done it because he was in love with her.

"When Lord Westfeld forwarded me Lady Stockhurst's manuscript," Sir John began, "I feared the worst. But it became clear to me after moments that I was reading the work of one of the finest minds in all of Europe."

Elaine shook her head at him—not in reproof, but in uncontainable delight. The letter was half over Evan's head—replete with mathematical references. In a way, it felt as if he'd come home—as if he'd righted a wrong that had long troubled him. It was worth all the trouble he'd endured to see Elaine smile without fear.

"I can safely say," Sir John was concluding, "that Lady Stockhurst's name should be linked with that of mine and Mrs. Mary Somerville for her keenness of understanding."

Evan would have ridden through hell and back for the look on Elaine's face—that brilliant, incandescent happiness, one that could not be smothered.

He felt the joy so keenly it almost hurt.

CHAPTER EIGHT

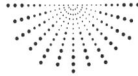

FTER THE CROWD BEGAN TO DISPERSE, Elaine sought him out. How could she not? He was on the far side of the room, and yet as soon as her eyes landed on him, he turned to her. She could feel herself light up as their gazes met, like an oil lamp screwed to full brightness. So why, as she drifted across the room to meet him, did her innards seem to tangle in knots? What *was* this excitement that collected on her skin?

He was just a friend. *Just* a friend. A good friend, yes, and one who had done her an extraordinary favor. He stood on the edge of the hall as the crowd flowed past him, standing with a group of her friends. There were the Duke and Duchess of Parford, a smattering of ladies… and the duke's younger brother, Sir Mark Turner, which rather explained the ladies.

"Duchess," Elaine said, and her friend turned, smiling, and extended her hand. The Duchess of Parford was one of Elaine's dearest friends. She had known of Elaine's worry, and had come to lend her support. "Your Grace. Sir Mark." Elaine nodded to the other members of the party, and then swallowed before addressing the last man. "Westfeld. How very, very good to see you all."

Westfeld met her eyes. "We were speaking on the nature of friendship, Lady Elaine."

"*I* was saying," the duchess interjected, "that Westfeld has been a very good friend to you."

"Yes." Elaine found herself unable to break away from his gaze. "I'm very grateful to him."

But *grateful* was altogether the wrong word. She knew it looking into the dark brown of his eyes. She might have looked into them all evening and not noticed the passing of time. No; it wasn't *gratitude* she felt. It was something rather more electric.

"Grateful," he said, the syllables of the word clipped. And then he shook his head and smiled ruefully. "Of course you are. But there's no need to be."

"There is. Every need."

"That is what friendship means." His voice dropped and so did her stomach.

She felt almost weightless, ready to blow away.

"In fact, tonight happened because of another one of my friends—Fritz Meissner, an old partner from Chamonix who hails from Hanover. I sent him a courier, and he badgered his uncle to show the work to Miss Herschel. From there, I had only to make certain that Miss Herschel's response was widely known. It was nothing."

"I assure you," Sir Mark put in, "few friends would think the same."

"Oh?"

"Most friendships," Sir Mark continued, "are nothing more than a similarity of temperament, or a smattering of common interests. Friendship is about jokes told and laughter shared."

While Sir Mark spoke, Westfeld shook his head. "I used to think the same—that so long as we were laughing together, it was enough. That was before I took an interest in mountaineering." Westfeld was talking to the entire group, but his gaze kept returning to Elaine. "My entire notion of friendship altered when I depended on someone for more than just the pleasant passing of time. Once you've trusted a person with your life, it changes everything. It's no longer enough to call someone 'friend' simply because you visit the same haberdashery. Once someone has risked his life for yours, and you've risked yours for his—once you've yoked yourselves together, knowing that one misstep could kill the both of you—well." He shook his head. "Everything after that seems very pallid in comparison."

"Ah." Sir Mark smiled. "We're boring."

"Not at all. Maybe that's what I have been looking for. When storms and rockslides threaten, I am looking for someone who will hold on to me and not let go."

He was talking about friendship, but the way he looked at her... She would crackle like fire if he touched her.

"Is that what you were doing?" she asked softly. "Not letting go?"

"We're friends." His smile twisted ruefully. "And what that means is this: I won't let anyone hurt you. Not if I can stop it."

She couldn't stop the stupid grin, too large and too painful, from creeping out on her face. She could feel herself lighting up under his perusal. And his smile—that awkward quirking smile, just a twitch too bitter. He had said they were friends. But...

She'd managed to put all thought of his long-ago proposal out of her mind. He joked with her so often that she'd assumed that it had been offered out of a sense of duty and obligation—and perhaps a hint of the desire he'd felt a decade before. He'd wanted to make up for past wrongs. And he knew—he *knew* she couldn't marry him. She'd thought he had accepted it, because until this moment, until tonight, she'd believed he felt nothing for her but friendship.

But no. There was a savagery to his smile, and a darkness in his eyes when he watched her.

He was in love with her. And it hurt him.

~

EVAN HAD TO GET AWAY.

The air in the hall had become overheated. As he'd spoken, Elaine had begun to look at him with something like dawning horror. Her conversation had dried up. And once again, she'd wrapped her arms around her waist, drawing in on herself until she was as closed to him as a locked room.

So. She'd figured it out. He strode down the steps of the hall and signaled to his footman waiting in the drizzle. But there was no way to escape easily; the line of carriages stretched into the distance, and the waiting throng had begun to spill out onto the steps of the hall. He wouldn't be rescued from that crush for at least half an hour.

Instead, he darted across the street to wait. The weather was more fog than rain, but the mist clung to his coat wetly. In the relative haven of the small square, he could pretend to be alone. The crowds across the way were blocked by dense shrubbery; the first tentative spring leaves on trees overhead dampened the carrying conversation. If he could stop up his ears and shut out the persistent clop of horses' hooves, he might imagine himself very private indeed.

He'd made himself give up all hope of Elaine. Most people would have taken such a surrender as an admission of failure—capitulation, by definition, was the very opposite of success. Then again, most people imagined that the successful mountaineer climbed Mont Blanc by persisting in the face of unimaginable peril and privation.

Not so. A mountaineer who kept going when a snowstorm arose was not *successful*. He was dead. Only an idiot wagered his life against the flip of Mother Nature's coin.

That was the first part of climbing a mountain: deciding *not* to die. He'd had to learn that one.

A formal walkway crossed the square; beyond it, a less formal path skirted the bushes. He walked alone in darkness, breathing in air that choked him, and trying to exhale every last frustration.

There was a second part to mountaineering: determining when to make another go at it. Sometimes, the best time to launch an assault was right after a storm, before the snow turned to ice. Sometimes you had to wait until all danger had passed. Evan had always sensed that if he pushed Elaine too hard—if he insisted that she rethink how she truly felt about him—he would lose her.

He stopped walking when the small crushed rocks of the path gave way to springy turf. A fountain, dry and empty of everything but the last remnants of moldering leaves, stood before him. To his right, a statue of William Pitt stood on a stone base. Pitt's cast-metal head brushed the limbs of the trees that ringed the park.

Alone with a politician on such a night. Diana would laugh, if he told her.

And then a stick cracked behind him, and before he could turn to see who had invaded his privacy, he heard a voice. *Her* voice.

"Westfeld?"

He could see her only from the periphery of his vision, but still all his thoughts, so sound and rational, were swallowed up by her presence. He was nothing but a deep abyss of want, and only she could fill him.

He didn't want to turn at the sound of her voice. If he simply stared into the hydrangea for long enough...then he would be a coward. He turned to face the woman who could bring him to his knees.

She approached until she was close enough that they could speak without shouting. Still, he couldn't make out her expression. The new leaves of an ash tree blocked most of the moonlight, save for a few variegated patches that wandered across her cheek.

"Elaine." His voice sounded too gruff, like a tiger's rumble.

"*Evan*," she whispered. It was the first time she'd used his Christian name, and he felt a little thrill run through him at the intimacy.

"What are you doing here?" He narrowed his eyes. "What are you doing here *alone*?"

"My parents are waiting for the coach. Papa is discussing politics with Lord Blakely, and Mama..." She shrugged. "In any event, I told them I wanted to speak with a friend." She took a step closer. "And I do."

She was within arm's reach. He exhaled. "Do not trifle with me."

"Is it trifling for me to say that I enjoy your company?"

"I'll be your friend in daylight. I'll treat you as a comrade in every gas-lit ballroom. But alone, under moonlight, I'll not pretend that I want you for anything but mine."

She didn't say anything. She simply looked up into his eyes.

He reached out and laid one finger against her cloak in warning. "If you don't want to be kissed, you'd better leave."

She'd stolen all the oxygen from the air, and with it, every ounce of his rationality. She was going to run away.

But she didn't. She stayed. He slid his finger up her arm to the crook of her elbow. With the moonlight dappling her face, painting her skin in cream and ivory, she looked like an illusion—a fairy-story princess conjured to life by the sheer strength of his want.

He pulled her to him. They were shielded by shrubbery and trees and the shadow of William Pitt, and even though he could still hear the clop of horse hooves, nobody could see them. There was only so much temptation a man could resist.

He lowered his mouth to hers.

She was most definitely real. She opened to him, warm and irrefutably solid. When he slid his tongue across her lips, she gave a small gasp of sincere pleasure. His arms went around her and he pulled her close. And then he was kissing her in truth, tasting her, unable to stop himself from plumbing her depths. He had the oddest sensation that if he let her go, she would float away. And yet she kissed him back. Her hands slid down his coat. Her tongue found his. Their lips met again and again, melding together until her breath was his, her kiss was his, her soul…

Even in the moonlight, even with her pressed against him, he knew better. Her soul was not his. Reality was the illusion. She'd been maddened by moonlight and taken by surprise. At any moment, she would come to her senses. But until then…

Until then, he was going to kiss her, for no reason except that he loved her and she would let him. He wouldn't let any note of bitterness destroy the sweet taste of her.

He could sense when she began to withdraw. Her hands stopped clutching him closer. Her kiss grew less fevered. Finally, she pulled away from him. Only a few inches, but it was far enough that he could no longer smell her sweet scent. She wasn't a part of him—not any longer.

"Westfeld," she whispered, and with that word—his title, instead of his Christian name—the barriers between them returned in full force. "I—I don't—I didn't know what I was doing."

He couldn't help himself. He molded his hand to her face. "Elaine."

She bowed her head and leaned against him, and he brushed his lips to her forehead.

"It happened," he said. "I understand. I shouldn't—" But he couldn't bring himself to apologize for kissing her. He *should* have kissed her, damn it. He would hold that memory inside him forever—a moonlit kiss, half dream, half solid truth. And so he ran his gloved thumb along her lips, reluctant to relinquish his hold on her.

"Don't speak," he said. "Of all the things I wish for in this world, I want you to find happiness. I suspect you never will have that with me, and I've resigned myself to the matter."

"Evan—"

"Don't feel pity for me. Someday, I'll find someone I *can* make happy—truly happy. I'm sure of it. But for now, I'm perfectly content to have had this one moment with you. I won't ask for anything else."

"Oh," she said. "Evan."

"Elaine," he said softly, "*can* I make you happy?"

The breeze against his collar was light and insubstantial, close to nothing. He felt her cant away from him ever so slightly.

He'd had no hope of her. Still, her silence was a resounding refutation of his every dream.

"There we are," he said, pulling away from her and offering her his arm, polite and gentlemanly once again. "Then I shall settle for making you happier."

~

E LAINE WAS NEVER QUITE SURE how she made her way home. Her mother's happiness burbled over in the carriage, but Elaine barely felt capable of containing the beat of her own heart.

She watched the Mayfair houses roll past, one dark shadow passing after another.

They went by Westfeld's house along the way, a few short streets from her own home. The front windows were alight, and she could imagine him arriving home to his butler and his servants and…and was there anyone else? His mother stayed in the country; he had neither brothers nor sisters. And at this moment, with the memory of his lips still burning against hers, she was all too aware that he was not married. She could see the savage edge of his smile. *I am not going to pretend that I want you for anything other than mine.*

Her hand rose and curled at her throat.

Was that what she had made him do? *Pretend?*

The carriage jolted to a halt in front of her own home. Once she was safely ensconced in her room, the evening ritual required none of her attention. She was washed and undressed. Her hair was combed and then braided. But when she tried to sleep she felt his mouth on hers. The sheets against her skin brought to mind the strong band of his arms around her, the tightly-controlled tension of his muscles. And when she shut her eyes, she could see his eyes boring into hers.

He loved her. He loved her still.

Sleep eluding her, Elaine pushed out of her bed and threw her window open to the night air. The wind against her shoulders was as cruel as a cold exhalation.

She could look into his eyes forever. She tingled when he was near. She had stopped scoffing in disbelief at his pronouncements months before. Instead, when he'd told her all would be well, she had wanted to believe him.

His kiss had been as soft as breath itself, and nearly as vital. When had *that* happened? When had he begun to light a room by entering it? When had she begun to look for him when she first arrived at a party? When had she started to think of him first when she heard something amusing?

Over these last months, she'd altered, too. She no longer held back, hiding her head in the sand like some stupid creature. If she had hated him for what he'd made her into all those years before, she had come to love herself. Whatever resentment she'd harbored had blown away.

He loved her, and it hurt him.

He was close, so close. She could trace the route to his bed down streets lit by dim gas lamps. As she leaned out her window into the chill, the row of three-story houses vanished into the murky night before she could identify his. Ten years ago he'd hurt her. But today...

Elaine took a deep breath of cold air and held it in her lungs, held it until her chest stung.

He'd told her he could move the world, if only he had a lever long enough. Of course there was no need for him to identify a place on which to rest it. Over the last months, he had become her fulcrum: an immovable bulwark in which she could repose all her trust. He loved her.

She loved him back.

The realization folded over her, silent as the city street beneath her window. Two streets down. A mere handful of houses.

She could wait until she saw him next. She might signal her change of heart to him through any number of methods—fans, touches, even a whisper in his ear when next they were together. But no. All of that felt wrong.

She thought of him alone tonight with his bitter, savage smile. They had caused each other quite enough pain for a lifetime. If she was to make him happy, she wanted to start *now.*

Elaine took a deep breath, closed her window, and then rang the bell for her maid.

CHAPTER NINE

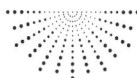

S LEEP ELUDED EVAN.

In point of fact, he hadn't yet tried to succumb. After retiring for the evening and dismissing his yawning valet, his bed had seemed too empty and white to contain him. He'd retreated instead to the low fire of his library and poured himself a half tumbler of brandy.

Tomorrow, he'd berate himself for his idiocy. Tomorrow, he'd ascertain whether he'd completely ruined his chances. But for tonight —hell, tonight, he'd kissed her, and she'd kissed him back. Tonight was time for *celebration*. He raised his glass in the direction of her home and took a hefty swallow. The spirits burned his tongue, but slid down smoothly.

He set the glass on a table, and the hushed clunk it made seemed to echo in the night—as if that quiet tap had repeated itself behind him. He paused, cocking his head in confusion.

The sound came again—not the echo of glass hitting wood, but the low, firm sound of the knocker on the door being struck. He stood and hastened to the front before the noise woke one of his servants. Somehow, he knew what—*whom*—he would see awaiting him before he fumbled open the bolted locks.

Still, when he threw the door back, he felt as if he might have been dreaming. Elaine stood on his front stoop, a heavy white cloak wrapped about her. The moon, high overhead, illuminated her pale hair with an ethereal glow. She seemed so bright against the darkness of night that, for one moment, he thought himself snow-blind in a mountain pass, dazzling light reflecting off her.

But this was no dream. The cold air of the night was giving him gooseflesh. Besides, if he'd dreamt of Elaine on his doorstep, he'd have wanted her naked, and damn the remnants of winter. He also would have conjured her up by herself, and she'd brought an entourage with her. A maid and a footman stood behind her.

"I hope," he said, nodding in their direction, "that their purpose is to ensure your safety, and not to serve as propriety."

A small smile crept across her face, and she glanced down the empty street. "It's past midnight. Propriety has long since gone to bed."

He moved aside in a daze and she entered. Her skirts brushed against his legs as she did, and cold night air or no cold night air, he found himself coming to attention.

"Might I send them back to their beds?" she asked. "I have something to say to you, and—"

"Something that couldn't wait until morning?" he asked hopefully.

She paused, turned to him. "No. It couldn't wait another hour. Evan…"

"Yes?"

She took a deep breath. Even under that thick cloak, the movement of her bosom had him catching his breath.

She touched the hollow at the base of her neck, and he could help himself no longer. He reached out and took her hand, tangling his fingers with hers. A blue ribbon held her cloak in place. Gently, he pulled on the ends until the bow was undone. Her cloak slithered from her shoulders and fell to their feet in a puddle of warmth.

He'd only touched her hand at this point, but it took all his force of will to keep from sliding his hands down the vision she presented. She wore slippers and a gown so thick it might have offered some modesty, had it not clung so to her form. Her very lovely form.

"I have something very important to say." Her eyes were wide and luminous.

He cupped her cheek in his hand. She was warm; as he touched her, she leaned her head to cradle against his palm.

He didn't remember leaning down to her, but somehow, his forehead touched hers and their lips were almost level.

"What have you to say?"

"I…I…"

He didn't know how it happened, whether it was she who tilted toward him or he who was drawn into the kiss by the feel of her warm breath. Still, his mouth met hers, and the only words her lips formed were kisses. Long kisses, languid kisses. He might have lost himself in kissing her.

"I had hoped you wanted to say that," he whispered into her ear. "Now might I repeat it louder?"

He took her mouth again. She tasted of cinnamon. She yielded in his arms as he drew her closer. His hands crept up her side, and found nothing but soft fabric and softer flesh underneath.

No corset. She wasn't wearing a corset. She let out a little sound as his hand rose to her breast, and lust surged through him. He could feel the point of her nipple rising against his palm. His hips pressed forward, seeking hers—

"Ahem."

Evan froze, his hand on her breast.

The tone behind them was unmistakable. "That will be *two* weeks' leave, then, my lady?"

Elaine burrowed her nose into his neck. "Three," she said.

He would have felt mildly embarrassed, had it not been so marvelous to hold her. Still, he waited until the pair of servants had shut the door before he returned to the task of discovering her.

"Will they talk?"

"James and Mary have been slipping out together for years." Her breath was ragged as he kissed her shoulder. "I've not informed the housekeeper, and so—ooh."

He cupped his hand around the solid warmth of her breast, the weight heavy in his hand. "What was it you wanted to tell me? You never did say."

She reached up and pulled a pin from her hair, and all that pale expanse fell past her shoulders. His mouth dried. He wanted her right now. Instantly. *Sooner* than instantly. But he hadn't waited all these months for her acquiescence to rush the experience.

"I wanted to say—"

He leisurely rolled her nipple between his fingertips, and she let out a little gasp. "What was it you wanted to say?"

"I—oh, Evan."

He kissed the side of her neck, and she arched against him.

"Evan, I can't think when you—"

He slid his hand down her side, drinking in the feel of her curves. She felt so right against him, so perfect.

"I was going to say—"

She broke off yet again as he leaned down further and closed his mouth around her breast. Under his ministrations, the nub of her nipple hardened. He could almost feel her body coming to life, recognizing wants that she'd never quite understood before. He could sense her desire in the tension of her fingertips, biting into his shoulders; could discern it in the uneven rhythm of her breathing as he lashed his tongue along the hard tip. She flattened herself against him.

"Evan," she said shakily, "are you doing this on purpose? I can't think, much less speak. And I so wanted to say—"

He set his finger over her lips.

"No," he told her. "Let me say it first. I love you, Elaine. I love your wit. I love your strength." He frowned as he slid his hand around her neck. "I *don't* love these buttons—ah, there we are." He'd loosened her gown enough that he could slide it over her shoulder, until he could expose the naked curves of her bosom.

"I love your breasts," he said honestly. "I really love your breasts. In fact, it's hard to kiss your sense of humor, but these…" He leaned down to taste her again. As his tongue circled her nipple, she gave another little cry. And God, did he love her breasts—and her rounded hips—and her legs, long and delicious, against him.

He backed her against the wall of the entry. His hips pressed into hers and his erection was hard against her belly. By some instinct, she knew to push back. She nipped at his ear, and his own breath stuttered.

"I love you, darling," he said. "But I've just realized that you mustn't say anything back."

He pulled her shift up, his hand seeking the warm haven between her legs.

Still she pressed closer. "But I want to. I lo—"

He cut off her words with another kiss.

God. And here he'd thought that the slick, warm feel of her was more than he could handle. But all his reason was melting into heated slag, like so much scrap metal in a blacksmith's furnace. It was more than he deserved, more than he could possibly imagine. He had her here, body and soul, her skin against his.

"Don't you dare say it," he growled. "Somehow, I'm supposed to keep myself from bedding you before dawn."

Her breathing hitched. And then her hands slid down his back to his elbows. She tilted her face to his. "And why are you supposed to do that?"

If he'd had any thoughts left anywhere, they scattered. He took her hand in his and led her upstairs, lifting her up the last few stairs in his haste. The hall had never seemed so endless; his door had never creaked so loudly. His room had gone completely cold, but he scarcely noticed because she was here.

She looked around her curiously. The dark wood paneling of his room seemed harsh and masculine in the night, but she tinged everything she looked at in an ethereal feminine light. Even the bed, with its straight posts and functional, square frame seemed to take on an elegant look when she ran her hand along the covers.

He shut the door behind them and then turned to her. "I shall need to find my snow spectacles."

She shook her head in confusion. "Snow spectacles?"

"They're of Esquimaux design. You don them when you must walk on the snow in sun. Otherwise, there's simply too much light for your eyes. The world can be too bright."

She must have taken his meaning, because she smiled at him. And then, as he was striding toward her, she gathered up her disheveled gown in her hands and pulled it over her head. Her hair, loose, spilled over her shoulders.

His mouth dried. Her hips were round and full. The hair that covered her mons was only a shade darker than the gold on her head. Her breasts were...oh, God. They were irresistible. Round and firm and even better than he'd ever imagined. Her hips were wide and curved, and her legs... He could imagine them wrapped around him, clutching him to her.

She sat on his bed, and as she did so, she let her limbs fall to either side of her. And if that were not invitation enough, she crooked one finger at him.

"You are the most damnable thing." He managed only a croak. He took two faltering steps to her and then knelt at her feet. "The most damnable, adorable, scintillating thing," he whispered again. He set his hands on her knees, and she grinned at him once more.

Confident. She was so confident. It was what he'd always hoped for from her—her trust, finally given over to him. It was the best thing he could have imagined.

Oh, very well. Second best. But his imagination was turning to reality now, and he could have the very best, too. He slid her knees apart. The rosy folds of her sex unfurled for him. It would have taken a trice to divest himself of his clothing and slide inside her warm depths. But she'd come here because she trusted him. And by God, he was going to prove her right.

So instead of slaking his lust as he desired, he leaned forward. His lips found her inner thigh. She let out a gasp, and her hand went to his shoulder, half in question.

"Trust me on this," he said.

And she did.

He took her sex in his mouth. His tongue traced her folds, already slick with desire. He learned the contours of her, the grip of her fingers against his shoulder, the gasp of her breath as he found the nub of her pleasure. He tasted her want, her sweet feminine musk. And she opened for him, letting him take her, trusting him to bring her pleasure. He could feel when her thighs started to tremble, when her hips rose to meet him. By the time she was bucking beneath his ministrations he was hard and all too ready for her. But he brought her all the way, lashing his tongue against her until she let out a strangled cry. Her fingernails bit into his shoulders. And she came. And came. And came.

He waited until her shuddering subsided. She had fallen back on his bed, her breasts full and round above her. He knelt over her and nuzzled the side of her neck. Forced himself to take in the wild scent of her and not go mad with desire.

"Oh, God," she said. "Evan. Lord above."

"Was that...was that your first, or have you ever done that for yourself?"

She looked up at him, suddenly ducking her chin. "It wasn't my first." A slight blush touched her cheeks. "But *you* will be."

"Yes." The air was suddenly fire around him. "I will."

He trailed his fingers down her neck, feeling almost singed with his own desire. He removed his shirt and waistcoat slowly as she watched. When he pushed down his trousers, her gaze followed. If he'd been hard before, he felt like stone when she looked at him. And when she reached out...

Even expecting her touch, the tips of her fingers against his cock sent a thrill through him. He gasped, and she looked up at him...and laughed. Oh, that laugh. As if she knew his secrets. As if she was lost to propriety. As if she held nothing back—and gave everything to him.

He pushed her onto her back. He wasn't sure how he got on top of her, how his hands tangled with hers. But his mouth found her breasts. Her hips rose up to his. His shaft found her opening, warm and wet.

"Elaine." It was not just her name, but a prayer.

"Evan." Her hand trailed down his back.

She was inviting, spread before him, and he'd been waiting for this for far too long. With one thrust, he seated himself firmly inside her. And God, she felt wonderful around him—hot, tight, her passage clenching around him. It would have been perfect but for the noise she made in her throat—not quite a whimper, not quite a protest.

"Did it hurt?"

She shook her head bravely, but her fingertips bit into his arm. Yes, then, it had. But she wouldn't admit it. He needed to relax, to give her a little time to adjust to the sensation of being filled in this way. He counted sheep in his mind—anything to distract him from the instinct that was overwhelming him.

But then she squeezed him, her muscles contracting about him. He gasped, gritted his teeth. Impossible, though, to set aside the sensation that roared through him.

She did it again. "Do you like that?"

"Yes." He shut his eyes. "No. If you do that again, Elaine, I'm going to—"

"Do it."

He couldn't hold off any longer. He pulled back and then thrust inside her again. She was white-hot friction around him, clamping down on him so hard he could almost see stars. Her hips rose to his. With every thrust, he could feel her breasts—hot and large and lovely, and God, he dipped his head to taste them once more, and she pulsed around him, all heat and tenderness.

She was wet, so wet. He felt as if he were wooing her all over again, tempting her with every brush of his fingers. She was close, so close. He leaned down and pressed his lips to her nipple. It contracted under his kiss. And soon it wasn't just her need that he courted so gently, but his own. Her hips rose to press hard against his thrusts.

He couldn't think of anything but the slide of his body into hers, the pressure, the sensation—and then, deep in the distance, a faint roaring that filled his ears. It was bigger than just him. It was a wave that swept over him, engulfing everything as he pounded his want deep into her.

As he did, her body shuddered underneath his and she made a low, keening sound.

God, yes—she was perfect, totally perfect.

When it passed, he slumped on top of her. "God, Elaine." He kissed her, more gently this time. She was still pulsing around him in little shocks.

It seemed impossible that he could be *more* aware of her, with the edge taken off his want. But when he relaxed on top of her, his hands tangling in her hair, his lips pressing breathlessly into hers once more, he felt as if he knew her as intimately as he'd ever known anyone.

And he never wanted to let go.

~

ELAINE SEEMED TO BE FLOATING ON A DREAM AFTERWARD, a dream where Evan ran his hand down the side of her face, his touch as light as gossamer. It was a beautiful dream. Her whole body seemed to melt away in utter relaxation. She felt as if she'd walked fifteen miles: her whole body throbbed with the ache of past exertion, but now she had nothing to do but slip into lassitude.

His lips brushed hers, touched her forehead. His hand slid down her ribcage and then his fingers entwined with hers.

Somehow, in the months of their friendship, he had become dearer to her than anything she could have imagined. She adored his wit. She was rather impressed by the muscles of his chest, covered with curly golden-brown hair.

But most of all, in the white-columned hall earlier that evening, he'd looked at her and told her what intimacy meant to him. She had wanted to be that person for him. She'd wanted to be the one he could trust.

She wasn't sure how long they lay in the dark, their arms around each other. There was no reason for it, except that she wanted never to let go. Hours might have passed while their breath mingled. Moon-shadows tracked across his body, lengthening as the night drifted by, until in the dark hours of morning the light dwindled to faint starlight. Sleep came and went in fits and starts—warm, comfortable dreams interspersed with the most delicious wakings, to find him holding her, touching her. His fingers curled around her when she slept, and his arms enfolded her when she roused.

It might have been four in the morning before he finally spoke.

"Elaine."

"Mm."

He pressed his forehead against hers. "In an hour or so, the servants will stir, and I shouldn't like you to become the object of gossip. We'd best get you back."

Back. It was only two streets away. But her house seemed to belong to another lifetime.

For just one moment, she imagined herself staying there in his arms. The consequences seemed insubstantial. The gossip wouldn't matter so much, would it? It was easy to avoid all thought of impending reality with his arms around her. She screwed her eyes shut and burrowed against him. "Don't want to."

She could almost feel him smile against her cheek. "I'll seek out your father on the morrow." Another smile. "I suppose I mean later today. We'll have the rest of our lives to hold each other."

She lifted her head slowly at that. It wasn't morning that dawned; it was a lifetime of this—not just kisses and warmth and the feel of his arms around her, but of finally, *finally* feeling safe. She'd come home.

"Yes." She wondered at the words. "We'll have that." Certainty felt new to her, so fragile that she feared it would steal away like fog if he so much as lit a candle.

But there was no need for illumination, not in the dark gray before dawn. He helped her dress, found her cloak, and then slipped into his own clothing. It wasn't so far back—a ten-minute walk with his arm about her for warmth. He paused when they reached her doorstep.

"You've a way in, I presume?"

She nodded.

He reached out and tipped her chin up. Nobody was about. Still, when he kissed her in the open street, it felt like a proclamation shouted to the skies. Perhaps it was her imagination that the night lifted and the sky lightened. Perhaps it was him. He lifted his head from hers and drew a line down the side of her face.

"Elaine," he said, "I—"

But his head shot up. A door had opened across the street. And then…

"Westfeld?"

Slowly, Elaine turned. She hadn't needed to see the speaker to know who it was. Lady Cosgrove stood on her own doorstep, her eyes wide in disbelief.

"What is she doing here?" Elaine heard herself ask.

Lady Cosgrove's eyes grew larger and more murderous. "I *live* here," she hissed, starting across the street with long, swift strides. "Do you suppose I would be oblivious to a matter that concerned my own cousin's welfare? Do you suppose me so stupid as to let you inveigle him into a match so far beneath him? Truly, Evan, it's a good thing you *consulted* me, because—"

"You *told* her?" The words slipped out of Elaine's mouth before she could think them through. "How *could* you?"

His hands bit into her shoulders. His face was gray, washed of all color. He took a step back as if she'd slapped him.

And…and she had. Just not with the palm of her hand. His lips pressed into a thin white line. He pulled away from her and turned to his cousin.

"Diana," he said tightly, "have the goodness to talk directly to me, if you are going to discuss my welfare. And Elaine…" He paused, took a deep breath.

She winced, waiting for the words she knew she deserved. *If you don't trust me now, there's no point in proceeding any further.*

But he didn't say anything about the hurt in his eyes, and somehow his silence cut all the deeper.

"We'll talk later," he said. "Now go, before the servants wake."

CHAPTER TEN

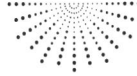

"A NOTE FOR YOU, MY LADY."

The folded paper that her maid slid into Elaine's palm seemed as light and flimsy as her whisper.

Mary didn't need to say that the missive had arrived via a clandestine route. Had it come by way of the front door, a footman would have brought it up. But then, had it come via the front door, news that Elaine was corresponding with a bachelor might have spread about town.

Hardly the worst gossip that could circulate, after last night.

She could be ruined. Oh, it wouldn't herald a complete end to her good reputation. Evan wouldn't let anything so dire happen. They would marry.

Still, when she shut her eyes, it was not her reputation that she thought of, but the expression on his face when she'd accused him of telling Lady Cosgrove. Never mind the impossibility of her accusation. It didn't matter that she'd been tired and the woman had seemed to threaten her newfound happiness. With those thoughtless words, she'd banished the relaxed trust she'd seen earlier that night. His eyes had gone wide with hurt and the tips of his ears had turned white. She could hear the pained gasp he'd given. And the look on his face, when she'd assumed that he had spoken of her—it had skewered her through.

Of course he'd been hurt by her words. Her first panicking impulse had been to shy away from *him*. After everything he'd said and done, she still hadn't trusted him.

She knew what Evan wanted from her. Not mere desire, not just friendship. He'd said it himself: he wanted someone who would hold onto him and never let go. But at the first sign of danger, she had shoved him away.

Her hand clenched around the note in her hand. The paper crackled. Elaine sighed and unfolded it.

Elaine, the note read. *Don't worry about Diana. I'll manage her. It may take some time, though—I might not be over this afternoon to speak with your father, as we'd discussed. Perhaps we shall see one another at the ball this evening. Yours, W.*

So formal. After last night, his note seemed stiff and impossible. And how was he to *manage* Lady Cosgrove? For God's sake, the woman lived across the street. He would come and talk to her and not visit with Elaine? Not even stop by for fifteen minutes?

She bit her lip hard and thought of what she ought to say to him, how she should respond. She had a sudden vision of her turning pointedly away from him that evening. And wouldn't *that* occasion talk, after their months of cozy friendship? The whole situation made her want to weep.

She was tired. She was overset. And she was imagining a life without him over a note that he'd dashed off in a hurry.

"It's nothing," she said to herself.

But it wasn't nothing. After all these years, she was still waiting for him to hurt her. She'd not thought of it in months, but she'd been holding on to the pain of her past, always expecting the worst.

He'd hurt her. He'd made her feel awful.

But he hadn't plunged her head underwater. She'd done that to herself.

And if she continued to flinch at every good thing that came her way, she would do it again and again and again, drowning everything she could have. He'd known it too. She didn't need to forgive *him*. She needed...

"Enough of this." She spoke the words aloud, slicing her hand through the air as she spoke.

"My lady?"

Elaine glanced behind her in surprise. Mary was still waiting behind her, stifling a yawn.

When Elaine had been hurt in the past, she had retreated inside herself. It was time to make a change.

"Mary," Elaine said, clambering to her feet, "we have only a few hours, and I'm going to need a new gown."

$\sim$

EVAN WAS TRAPPED BY PILLOWS. The afternoon sun filtered through his cousin's sitting room. The room was papered in resplendent gold and green; Evan felt rather out of place in his sober brown. A profusion of tiny cushions, embroidered in cunning patterns, flocked about him. If he moved, he would knock them to the floor.

Diana sat opposite him. They'd exchanged only the most inconclusive of greetings. She'd ushered him into the room and had rung for tea, and they'd sat in awkward silence until the tray arrived. Only the faint lines gathered about her mouth suggested her distress.

She had scarcely spoken with him since that evening at the house party last summer. She had informed him at a family gathering in the autumn that he would soon come to his senses. Two weeks later, she'd asked him to drop his friendship with Elaine. He'd refused, and since then they had exchanged only stilted words when their paths crossed.

Now, even with the servants departed, they clinked their teacups at one another. Evan contemplated how to proceed.

But Diana set her saucer on the table next to her and turned to look out the window. "You know, Evan," she said softly, "I would never say or do anything to hurt you."

He leaned to place his cup on a nearby table. As he shifted, a forest-colored pillow tumbled to the floor. "I know. But—"

She waved her hand. "I know what you're thinking. I would never spread rumors saying that I saw your precious Elaine in the morning with an unknown man, either. I wouldn't think of it."

He simply met her eyes levelly. She snorted.

"Very well. I considered it for a few moments, but no longer. If I did any such thing, you'd simply tell everyone it was you, and you would marry her instantly."

"You know me too well."

Her lips pressed together. "I do." She reached over and took his empty cup. It was a familiar ritual to have her refill it and then add a half-spoonful of sugar. She handed it back, almost unaware of what she'd done. "But I hardly see how this matters. You're going to marry her in any event."

Yes. He was. But she'd not asked a question. She hadn't needed to do so.

"Don't." She adjusted the teapot on the tray. "Please don't."

"If you tell me I can do better than her, this conversation is at an end. Besides, after last night, I haven't any choice in the matter. Even if I'd wanted one."

Diana lifted her head, but only to look out the window. "Don't," she repeated. "Please. You're the brother I never had. I've missed you these last months. But how can we be friends with her around? She will never forgive me. If you marry her, I shall lose you forever."

He swallowed.

"I knew you…you were interested in her. I guessed it quite some time ago. Do you remember that time, when you asked me if we mightn't stop laughing at her?"

He nodded jerkily. It had been a few months into Elaine's first Season. He'd broached the matter, speaking lightly, as if it were a joke. Diana had brushed him off, and he'd never said another word.

"That's when I suspected. And I knew that if you stopped teasing her—if she came to know you—of course she would fall in love with you. How could she help herself? And when she did, your loyalties to her would soon outweigh your friendship with me. Evan, she hates me. How could she not?"

She forgave me. But he couldn't grant Elaine's forgiveness to Diana. And when Elaine had pulled from him this morning, he'd been left wondering whether he truly *had* received her trust.

"You could try being kind for a change," he said mildly.

Diana gave him a sad smile. "After all that I've said? If I retract the claws, all of London society will devour me. It is either kill or be killed. If you're not the wolf, you're the rabbit."

"There are no wolves. There are no rabbits. We're all just human. I think you will find that if you treat people decently, they will respond."

"If I were starting anew? Perhaps. But I can't escape myself, Evan."

He knew what that felt like. He could remember it all too well—the sick feeling in his stomach, the certainty that no matter what he wanted, he was *forced* to continue on. If he stopped being an ass, people would laugh at him. If he changed, they would turn on him. He'd run away, but she'd not had that option.

Diana's eyes glistened. "I can't stand myself," she said, choking. "If people did not fear me so, how could anyone tolerate me?"

He knew that feeling, too. But that kind of regard was as false as a thin crust of snow, hiding a bottomless crevasse.

"It's quite simple," Evan said. "You'll have to choose between accepting yourself and having others accept you."

She wrapped her arms around herself. "Oh."

Once, long ago, they'd vowed never to let each other be hurt. What they'd done with that pledge had been ugly. But the promise itself…

"There is one thing you should know."

"No need to even speak it. If I hurt your Elaine, you'll have nothing further to do with me."

"That wasn't what I was going to say."

She raised her head, and for the first time, she met his eyes. She looked weary and ragged.

"You were my first true friend," he said. "I have always known that you would never purposefully wish me harm. You're the sister I never had, and if you think I will turn my back on you, you gravely mistake me. Friends do not let go of other friends. Even if matters become difficult. Even if the road becomes rocky. Even if it seems as if there is no other choice."

She sniffled. "And what if you marry a woman who must certainly be my mortal enemy?"

"Even then." He stood and pillows scattered about him. "But I think you'll find that most people can be remarkably forgiving."

She looked up at him, her eyes wide and sad. "Even you?"

He crossed to her and knelt beside her. "Especially me," he said. And when she leaned against him, he hugged her, hard.

CHAPTER ELEVEN

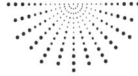

U NTIL ELAINE WALKED INTO THE BALLROOM THAT NIGHT, she had not realized how much of herself she had locked away. She had always stood on the side of such rooms, dressed in colors that drew no attention.

Tonight, for the very first time, she wore a ball gown of red satin. It hugged her waist and then flared out over a multitude of petticoats. The neckline skimmed the top of her corset, flirtatious without quite crossing over into the realm of provocation. The cut was simple—so simple, it had been fitted together in a matter of hours. The hem was still pinned in place, rather than sewn.

It was simple, and yet when she'd looked at herself in the mirror beforehand, she'd been unable to look away. *This* was who she could be. For years, she'd had one purpose at gatherings like this: to make everyone look *away* from her.

Tonight she wanted them to look *at* her. She stood on the edge of the polished wood floor, feeling like a ship clinging to the shore. Out there, amongst the crowd, there were waves and storms and *monsters*. Here at the edges there was safety. Her first step toward the middle of the room was the hardest. The second came more easily. With the third, people had begun to look at her and whisper behind upraised fans.

Lady Elaine Warren didn't wear red. She didn't walk into the center of the room. She hid away everything about herself.

Not any longer. For once, those whispers did not make her falter. They made her lift her chin and take longer strides. The fourth step was the easiest yet, and on the fifth…

On the fifth, she saw Evan. He was standing against a wall, dressed in dark brown. His golden, curling hair was tamed, but when he turned toward her, something just a little wild entered his expression. His gaze dropped, and perhaps—she could not keep herself from grinning—so did his jaw. Just a little. By the time his eyes met hers, his smile matched hers, broad and unstoppable. He started toward her.

She could not run. Not with these slippers on her feet. If she ran, the flowers would fall from her hair, and the straight-pins holding her hem in place would come undone. But her steps grew faster. She made no effort to hide her destination. They met in the center of the crowd. He reached his hands out to her, and she took them. He pulled her close—and then, with everyone watching, he kissed her. Hard.

There might have been tongue involved. Eventually, he pulled away from her.

"Evan," she said, "I'm so sorry—this morning, I—"

He set his fingers across her lips. "What did I tell you?"

"You said when danger threatened, you were looking for someone who would hold to you and not let go. And I—"

He glanced wryly down, where his hand still held hers. "You're letting go, are you?"

"No, but this morning, I—"

"Elaine," he repeated, "*are* you letting go?"

"No," she whispered. "No. I love you."

His smile broadened and he leaned down to her. "Over the years, everyone stumbles. That's why I'll be here for you—and you'll be there for me. I don't expect perfection. I want *you*, and you're a thousand times better."

Her heart was pounding. She was looking up into his eyes. The room was quiet with an expectant hush—

Wait, the room was quiet? For the first time since his hands had joined with hers, she glanced around her. The crowd around them had indeed gone silent—and had drawn in quite close. Everyone was looking at them. *Everyone.*

And why wouldn't they?

Evan's smile simply broadened. "I love you," he said, just loud enough to send a murmur rippling through the awaiting crowd. And then he tucked her hand behind his elbow and gestured to the crowd. "Clear the way," he said, his voice commanding. "If I don't find Lord Stockhurst and ask for his daughter's hand in marriage in the next five minutes, we'll have a scandal on our hands. And none of you want that."

Evan wasn't the only one smiling, now. All around them, people were grinning. And then, one by one, the members of the crowd began to clap.

~

A CROSS THE BALLROOM, DIANA HELD HER HEAD HIGH, willing herself not to tear up.

No matter what Evan said, she didn't believe that they could remain friends—not if she continued on as before. Strange; she'd never felt nervous before in a crowd. But right now, she could sense her own vulnerability. For the first time, she was the rabbit. And lo, here were these many wolves.

She caught sight of Miss Maria Wollton along the side of the room. Miss Wollton had pots of money, but it had all come from trade. When she spoke, she displayed a well-informed, intelligent mind. And so last month, Diana had called her a presumptuous little bluestocking. The appellation had stuck. It had been so easy to push the girl to a corner of the room.

Diana crossed the room to her and dipped a little curtsey. "Miss Wollton."

"Lady Cosgrove," the younger woman returned warily.

"That…" Why should this be so hard? "That shade of peach is quite lovely on you," Diana said, all in a rush. "It truly brings out the blue in your eyes."

Miss Wollton frowned in confusion. To her left, Diana could see the crowd gathering about Evan and Elaine, offering their congratulations. Soon, she would join in. She would have a great many things she would need to say to the two of them.

But for now… Diana drew a deep breath and did the hardest thing she had ever done in her life.

"Miss Wollton," she said, "I owe you an apology."

EPILOGUE

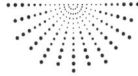

Two months later.

THE CHAMPAGNE HAD BEEN POURED in generous toasts. A dizzying multitude of friends and family had gathered around and offered the young couple congratulations. Elaine's mother had scarcely been able to contain her happiness throughout the wedding breakfast, and so Elaine had barely managed to escape her parents' home. A carriage decked with every spring flower had taken her away—all the way to Evan's house, all of two streets' distance.

Despite the beat of nervousness in her belly, she'd been introduced to his staff and he'd taken her on a leisurely tour of his home—*their* home now, to fill with an entire life together. He'd shown her to her chambers.

"The bed," he said, quite seriously, "is the finest that money can buy. I had it made new for you, you know. I hope you…sleep comfortably." A wicked smile danced on his face, and he glanced out the window at the afternoon sky.

Evening was still a depressing number of hours away.

Perhaps marriage *did* make you of one mind, because when she sighed, he winked at her.

"I was thinking that after our arduous day, we might consider retiring early."

"What an excellent idea," she returned, doing her best to keep her face straight and serious.

He stepped outside and gave the orders. The majority of the servants disappeared as silently as they'd come, heading to their own revels below.

Mary scarcely had time to divest Elaine of her formal white gown and replace it with an inappropriately virginal wrapper before a tap sounded at her door.

"His Lordship is eager," Mary said.

"Mmm," Elaine replied.

"And how could he be? After all, just last night, you were—"

"Mary, don't you think you'll need to pack? You have three weeks' leave coming to you during our honeymoon. I should want to get started, were I you."

Mary smiled and withdrew.

His Lordship wasn't the only eager one.

But when he entered, he did not fall on her and ravish her immediately. Alas. He stood in the doorway, the light of afternoon painting his gold hair in hues of orange. He'd shed his formal coat and waistcoat; the tails of his shirt were untucked.

"Well, Lady Westfeld," he said finally. "Are your accommodations to your liking?"

"Why so formal?"

He took a step toward her. "Formal? I'm just savoring the sound of your name." Another step. "Lady Westfeld." Another step, and he slid a finger under her chin. "Lady Westfeld of mine," he whispered.

"You'll just have to be my Evan," she said in response.

"With pleasure."

And then, step by step, he drew her into the center of the room for a kiss—and another one—and another one after that. She took hold of his arms, and she didn't let go.

TALK SWEETLY TO ME

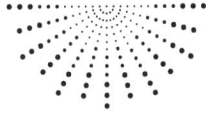

Nobody knows who Miss Rose Sweetly is, and she prefers it that way. She's a shy, mathematically-minded shopkeeper's daughter who dreams of the stars. Women like her only ever come to attention through scandal. She'll take obscurity, thank you very much.

All of England knows who Stephen Shaughnessy is. He's an infamous advice columnist and a known rake. When he moves into the house next door to Rose, she discovers that he's also wickedly funny, devilishly flirtatious, and heart-stoppingly handsome. But when he takes an interest in her mathematical work, she realizes that Mr. Shaughnessy isn't just a scandal waiting to happen. He's waiting to happen to her...and if she's not careful, she'll give in to certain ruination.

For Lucas, my partner in crime, clock-breaking, and quantum mechanics.

CHAPTER ONE

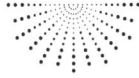

Greenwich, November 1882

THERE WAS NO WAY FOR Miss Rose Sweetly to set down her packages. All six of them were balanced precariously under one arm while her free hand fumbled through her pocket. Her fingers encountered used pencil nubs and a letter folded in half; her burdens shifted slightly, sliding away... If that dratted key ring was not in this pocket, and in the opposite instead—ah!

Thumb and forefinger met cold metal. Rose was withdrawing her find in triumph when a voice interrupted.

"Good afternoon, Miss Sweetly."

The sound of Mr. Shaughnessy's voice—that lilting velvet—set the inevitable in motion. First the book wrapped in paper slipped; then, as she grabbed for that, her notebook began to fall. She could compute the physics of it in her mind, a cascading avalanche of packages resulting from too few hands and too much gravity. Rose had time to make only one decision: save her slide rule or save the shopping?

Her slide rule won. She grabbed hold of the leather case with her fingertips just before it hit the ground.

Her other burdens were not so lucky. *Splat* went the book. The shopping landed with a more complex sound—one that smacked of breaking eggs. Three oranges escaped the bag entirely and bounced crazily down the pavement.

Mr. Stephen Shaughnessy stood two doors down from her. His eyebrows rose at this minor catastrophe, and Rose felt her cheeks heat. But there was nothing to do now but brazen it out.

She gave him her most brilliant smile and waved her slide rule case. "Good afternoon, Mr. Shaughnessy."

The case slipped slightly, but she managed to catch it before an even greater disaster ensued.

Mr. Shaughnessy had taken the house just down from her sister's three months ago. In all that time, she'd never managed to shake the nerves she felt around him. He had never done anything to warrant that nervousness, unfortunately; he was unfailingly polite.

As proof, he didn't abuse her for her clumsiness now. He didn't even remark on it. He simply came toward her. He took three steps forward—and she drew back one—before she realized that he only intended to pick up her oranges.

Any other reason he might have drawn close to her? That was all in her imagination.

She set down her slide rule carefully and picked up her shopping bag. It was canvas, and most of the contents hadn't spilled. The meat, wrapped in waxed paper, was still at the bottom. The eggs…well, she'd check them once they were inside, but she had a sneaking suspicion that she and her sister would be having omelets for dinner tonight. Only the fruit had truly gone awry. She picked up an apple, not looking in his direction.

But she didn't have to look directly at him to be aware of him. Mr. Shaughnessy was a young man—scarcely a few years older than she. He was tall and built on lovely, well-muscled lines, the sort that young ladies who intended to stay innocent were not supposed to notice. He had a friendly smile, one that made a woman want to smile in response, and the faintest hint of an Irish accent. He had dark hair, dark eyes, and a much darker reputation.

But he picked up one of the offending fruits and smiled in her direction. "Why is it that the oranges bounced, but the apples did not?"

His smile felt like an arrow, one that struck her straight in the solar plexus. And so Rose adjusted her spectacles on her nose and said the first thing that came to mind.

Unfortunately, the first thing that came to mind was...

"It's Newton's Third Law. Upon collision, the apple exerts a force on the pavement, and so the pavement must exert an equal and opposite force on the apple. The structure of the apple is inelastic and so the apple bruises. The orange, by contrast..." She swallowed, realized that she was babbling, and shut her mouth. "I'm sorry, Mr. Shaughnessy. I don't think that's what you meant to ask, was it?"

He straightened. Oh, he was dreadfully handsome. He put a casual care into his appearance, and it showed. He was clean-shaven, even though it was three in the afternoon. His cravat looked as crisp as if it had been pressed just now, not at six in the morning. Nothing about Mr. Shaughnessy suggested that he was a degenerate of the first order. Nothing, that was, except his line of work and the persistent gossip in the papers.

"You don't need to let me natter on when I get distracted that way," she told him. "Everyone else stops me. In these parts, it's considered polite to interrupt Miss Sweetly when she's on a tear."

"Nonsense," Mr. Shaughnessy said. He took a step toward her, and then another. Her chest constricted—he was standing so dreadfully, deliciously close—and then he held out the oranges he'd gathered.

For one moment, as she took them from him, their hands brushed. Neither of them was wearing gloves: she, because she couldn't have found her keys while wearing them; he because...well, the heavens alone knew, and she was not about to ask. His fingers were warm and pale against hers.

"I would never interrupt you," he told her. "I love it when you talk Sweetly to me."

She yanked her hand away. "You mustn't say things like that, Mr. Shaughnessy. Someone might overhear and mistake your meaning."

His eyes met hers. For the briefest second, she imagined a spark in them—as if some imp inside him whispered that anyone who heard what he'd said would understand it perfectly. He'd intended to flirt, and he knew precisely how he'd flustered her.

But he didn't say that. He simply shrugged. "We wouldn't want anyone to misunderstand."

If there had been an ounce of sarcasm in his voice, she would have walked away right then and there. But there wasn't.

"So let me say it better. If I didn't want to hear you talk about your opposite and equal reactions, I wouldn't ask about your star charts. What are you computing this time?"

"Oh, it's not star charts, not today. It won't be star charts for months. It's the Great Comet now, and it'll be the transit of Venus after that."

His eyebrows rose. "There's a great comet?"

"Do you not read any scientific papers? It may be the brightest comet ever observed. You can still see it with the naked eye against the sun itself."

He glanced upward at the sun overhead, unobscured by any cometary tail. "If you can see it with the naked eye, how is it that I've never caught a glimpse of it?"

She huffed. "Because London is not in the southern hemisphere. The visibility here is not as it is in Melbourne, for instance."

"Ah."

"In any event, Finlay in Cape Town wired his measurements to Dr. Barnstable, and he's set me to do the computing."

"So what does it look like?"

She got out her notebook, opened it to the appropriate page.

"Here we are. The comet transited the sun a little more than a month ago."

He stared for a moment at the column of numbers she was pointing to, and then gave his head a shake. "Right."

She felt herself flush again. But before she could manage to work up a good case of embarrassment, he had interrupted her, pointing to an orange in her bag.

"So let's say that is the sun. Then where is the comet?"

"Don't be ridiculous, Mr. Shaughnessy. If that orange represents the sun, we here on Earth would be standing seventy-one feet away."

"Seventy-one?" he asked mildly.

"Seventy-one point five eight three, by the last measure of the distance between the earth and the sun, but I try not to be pedantic. It makes people laugh at me." Rose pointed to a dot on her notebook page. "Imagine that *this* is the sun. Then we are a speck of unimaginable smallness here." She indicated a spot some inches away. "The comet, then, traveled along this path..." Her finger, dark against the white page, etched an elliptical curve. "But that's not the exciting part. You see, anyone can calculate the path of a comet given enough data."

"Not anyone," he murmured.

She waved this away. "From all accounts, the nucleus of this comet split sometime after perihelion. Dr. Barnstable believes that we can predict the path of each piece—and since they're so close to each other now, it will be no simple matter. It's a three-body problem, which means it's impossible to solve with equations. He's asked me to work it out for him." She beamed up at him.

He smiled back. "That's brilliant, Miss Sweetly."

"Of course," she started to explain, "we'll be wrong, but it's *how* we're wrong that is most exciting. You see—"

The door opened behind them. Rose jumped again. This time, she managed to keep hold of her shopping bag. She turned to see her sister standing in the doorway. Patricia had one hand on the door handle; the other was placed in the small of her back. She was wearing a voluminous pink gown and a matching kerchief covering her hair. Her eyebrows rose at the scene in front of her, but her dark eyes sparkled in amusement.

"And here I thought I heard you at the door ages ago," Patricia said. She gave her a head an exasperated shake, but Rose was certain—mostly certain—that she smiled as she did it. Patricia stooped as best as she could. Her heavy belly made her awkward, but she plucked Rose's key off the ground. "Ah. I see that I did."

"I...dropped some things," Rose said, flushing all over again. "I was picking them up."

Patricia looked at Rose's notebook, open in her hands. She looked at Mr. Shaughnessy, standing not two feet away. And then she glanced at the pavement, where Rose's other packages—the mail, the paper, the wrapped-up book—still lay scattered. "Yes," she said dryly. "I can see that. That explains everything."

"I'll let you go, then," Mr. Shaughnessy said. He tipped his hat. "Miss Sweetly. Mrs. Wells."

"Mr. Shaughnessy." Rose nodded her head. "I would curtsey, but the apples cannot withstand another inelastic collision."

Beside her, Patricia made a noise in protest. But she held out her hands, gesturing. Rose gave her the book and her slide rule case. While Mr. Shaughnessy disappeared around the corner of the street, she picked up the last of her scattered things.

Patricia did not berate her immediately. She did not, in fact, berate her at all. She would normally have offered to help Rose, but she was eight months pregnant, ungainly and awkward, and bending over did not come easily to her. When they'd gathered everything, they retreated inside the house—Rose at a walk, Patricia at a waddle.

Patricia did not say anything as they traversed the front drawing room and went into the back pantry. She didn't speak until Rose had the shopping spread out in front of them.

"Rose," Patricia said quietly, "have you considered going back to Papa?"

Rose had not. Her stomach clenched at the very thought. "How could I leave you, when Dr. Wells will not return from his tour of duty for more than a week yet? I *promised* him."

Patricia's husband was a naval physician. He'd been sent to Sierra Leone around the time Patricia had realized she was with child, and Rose had come to attend her sister in his absence. But it wasn't just her sister's welfare that had Rose worried. Their parents lived in London—so close, and yet impossibly far from the Royal Observatory. At her father's house, there would be no computations, no comets.

No Mr. Shaughnessy to set her nerves on edge.

"You know," Patricia said, "you *know* that he is the most incredible rake." She did not say who *he* was. She didn't need to.

Rose set the oranges in a bowl, refusing to look at her sister. "He's never once offered to seduce me. I don't even think he's thought of it."

"He's thought of it," Patricia said dryly. "And frankly, Rose, the way he's talking to you? I don't think he'll even need to offer."

Rose let out a long breath and shut her eyes. It was, unfortunately, true. Mr. Shaughnessy was…well, he just *was*. His name had been on all the ladies' lips since Rose was fifteen, when he'd earned renown— or infamy, depending on who was speaking—as the first man to write a column of advice for the *Women's Free Press*, a radical paper that Rose should not have enjoyed nearly as much as she did. In the five years since his first column, he'd only built upon that reputation. He'd published four novels. His books were called "masterpieces of satire" by some, and "dangerous rubbish that was best burned unread" by others.

They had, by all accounts, sold well—and those who harrumphed about setting bonfires with them were the ones most likely to furtively purchase them in brown paper packaging.

Mooning after Mr. Stephen Shaughnessy was foolish. She knew how they looked, sketched to scale. Socially speaking, if he were an orange in Westminster, she was…an elderberry, somewhere in the vicinity of Tanzania.

"I love you, Rose." Patricia sighed. "And I know you'll make a good marriage, one as brilliant as mine. But you have to remember that most of the men who look at you won't be seeing *you*. They won't see that you're clever and amusing." Her sister came forward and took Rose's hand in her own. "They'll see *this*." She rubbed the back of Rose's hand. Dark skin pressed against dark skin. "It doesn't matter how respectably you dress or how much you insist. Most men will see only that you're black and they'll think you're available. So please take care, Rose. I don't wish you hurt."

Rose polished the last apple with a towel. "Don't worry about that," she said softly. "I won't do anything foolish."

She didn't say anything about getting hurt. There was no point worrying about that. She thought of Mr. Shaughnessy's smile, of the wicked gleam in his eye. She thought of him asking her about oranges and comets, of him looking at her and saying in that dark, dangerous, lilting tone *I love it when you talk Sweetly to me.*

She'd also seen the notes about him in the gossip columns. He was utterly outrageous, and no matter how he made her feel, the last thing she needed was an outrageous man.

No, there was no point worrying about getting hurt.

At this point, pain was already inevitable.

CHAPTER TWO

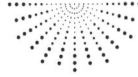

O F ALL THE WAYS that Stephen Shaughnessy had ever
decided to torment himself, this one had to be the most
diabolical.

There was a slight musty smell to the offices a few streets from the
Royal Observatory, as if the windows were not often opened. The
books on the shelves around him ranged from an ancient set of
Newton's *Philosophiae Naturalis Principia Mathematica* to a report on
something called spectroscopic observations; the walls were a
yellowing whitewash over which charts had been tacked year after
year, until only a few spots remained bare.

The room was, in short, little better than a dingy pit, the only
decorations a celebration of mathematics—a subject he had never
excelled at, and, until recently, had never found interesting.

Which was precisely what made his next sentence so shocking.

"Yes," he heard himself saying aloud. "It is a real pleasure to meet
you, Dr. Barnstable. I'm terribly impressed by your work."

Even more shockingly, the statement was true.

"No, no. The pleasure is assuredly all mine." Dr. Barnstable caught
Stephen's hand in his and gave it a few enthusiastic pumps. "I cannot

believe you've heard of me—and that you follow astronomy." He smiled bemusedly. "Truly, I feel dazed by the prospect."

He could hardly feel as dazed as Stephen himself. It had taken him almost a month to realize what was happening and another four weeks to succumb to utter madness. Or mathematics; he wasn't sure there was any distinction at this point.

Dr. Barnstable was an older man in his sixties, with six inches of white beard as proof of his age. But there was nothing fusty about him; he shook Stephen's hand with a firm grip.

"Your paper on the orbit of double stars is a true classic," Stephen said.

The point when Stephen had read it, searching for any hints of Miss Sweetly's contribution to the piece, was the point when he'd known that it was over. It had been like a newspaper headline printed in two-inch type: *There's no use struggling, Stephen. You're well and truly caught.*

"My wife is an absolute enthusiast of your work." Barnstable's eyes sparkled. "She reads me pointed bits from your column. I ought to take you to task—giving away all our masculine secrets—but ah, well." That last was delivered with an amused shake of his head.

"They're not secrets," Stephen explained. "Women already know everything I say. The only reason anything I say is amusing is because a man is saying it."

"Ha!" Barnstable jabbed Stephen's shoulder in a friendly fashion. "You're just as clever in person as you are on paper. Well. I can't say I disagree. Times are surely changing, and for the better. You have no idea how much easier some of those recent advances have made my work."

Stephen actually had every idea. One of those "advances," he suspected, was Miss Rose Sweetly—and from what little he could tell, she'd done very well for Barnstable indeed. The man had better praise her.

"But never mind that," Barnstable said. "We can talk politics some other time. What can I do for you?"

"I'm doing research on astronomy," he said.

"For your next novel? Are you writing about an astronomer, by chance?"

Stephen considered this and decided it was as good an explanation as any other he could offer. "Yes."

He'd made something of a career of speaking outrageous truths, but there was a time and a place for outraging people. Even he knew better than to admit what was really going on. *No, I'm just fascinated with a woman, and I want to know everything about her* would not go over well.

Barnstable nodded thoughtfully. "What would you like to know?"

"Oh dear." Stephen sighed. "I've tried to swot up on my own with woeful results. I need help with every detail, starting from how to calculate astronomical distances by parallax, on up through Kepler and the theory of planetary motion."

Barnstable blinked. "That is…quite a lot."

"Oh, I don't expect you to instruct me yourself. I'm sure you're too busy for that. I had imagined you would fob me off on someone else," Stephen said. "An assistant or a student—someone who wouldn't mind a little extra income."

"Ah." The man's expression cleared momentarily, but then he shook his head and frowned. "Hmm. My student is in the Bermudas at the moment—he's observing the transit of Venus, lucky boy. Were it not for my knee…" Barnstable trailed off, shaking his head. "That leaves only my computer. And…" He hesitated delicately. "She's a woman."

"Your computer?" Stephen asked with studied nonchalance. This was what he'd hoped for, after all. "What's that?"

"Precisely what it sounds like: a person who computes. Absolutely necessary for those of us engaged in any sort of dynamics. All those calculations come to a dreadful mess; if I had to do them all myself, I'd have no time to think of anything. And yes, my computer is a woman." He cleared his throat. "A woman of African descent. Those of my colleagues who are prejudiced on that score only deprive themselves of Miss Sweetly's assistance."

"Surely you don't think I would share their prejudices," Stephen said. "Your wife has been making you read my work, yes?"

Barnstable's smile became pained. "It isn't that. Or it isn't only that. You see, she's a woman. And you..."

"Oh." Stephen smiled. "That. I suppose I do have something of a reputation."

It was hard-earned, that reputation. Occasionally inconvenient, but it was what it was.

"Yes," Barnstable said apologetically. "That. And Miss Sweetly is, alas, a very young woman. She's not quite of age yet. I've an arrangement with her father—my wife must be with her at all times in the building. He'd not like to see anything happen to her, and quite selfishly, I'd not like to lose her, either. She would be ideal if only she were a man. But..."

Stephen wouldn't be here if she were a man. He still couldn't quite believe he'd come.

"Maybe she could manage a lesson or three? Just something to get me started until your student returns. Your wife might stay in the room with us, of course, to avoid any impropriety."

"I don't know..." Dr. Barnstable rubbed at his beard.

"Ask her what she thinks," Stephen suggested. "After all, 'not quite of age' for women often means we'd send younger men into battle. Or to the Bermudas to watch the transit of Venus."

Barnstable nodded thoughtfully at that.

"And I do have a reputation. I won't pretend I haven't earned it. But I've never seduced an innocent before. In truth, I do more acquiescing than I do seducing. So unless you fear that your computer will seduce *me...*"

Barnstable snorted. "Well. I suppose a few hours with her, with my wife present, could not hurt. If she agrees, that is."

The older man left, and Stephen paced to the window. From here, he could see bare tree branches and grass, once a brilliant green, now fading to a less vibrant color.

He really wasn't sure what he was about. He *wasn't* planning to seduce her, not really. It would be a terrible thing for a man like him to do to a woman in Miss Sweetly's position, and he had a very firm rule that he did not do terrible things to people in general, and to women in particular. Liking a woman—even liking her very well—was more reason to adhere to the rule, not less.

As far as he could tell, he *was* just tormenting himself.

A noise sounded in the hall; he caught the low murmur of voices, and then the office door scraped open. Stephen turned from the window to face the newcomers.

Barnstable stood in the doorway. Behind him were two figures. The first was a heavy silhouette of an older woman with a substantial bustle; the second figure, far more familiar, hid herself behind the other woman's bulk. She was scarcely visible in the dim hall light. Still, Stephen felt his pulse begin to accelerate.

He stood and addressed himself to the first woman. "You must be Mrs. Barnstable."

"Mr. Shaughnessy, this is my wife, Mrs. Barnstable." Dr. Barnstable stepped to one side.

The woman behind him moved into the room, all smiles. "Oh, Mr. Shaughnessy! It is such a pleasure to meet you. After all these years of reading your words! I adore—absolutely adore—everything that you write."

"Of course you adore what I write," he said. "You must be a woman of excellent taste. I'm delighted to make your acquaintance."

"I shall have palpitations of the heart," Mrs. Barnstable announced. "Listen to me, going on like a green girl. I sound like a chicken, squawking away. What must you think of me? I'm not silly. I'm not. It's just that I've been reading your work for years now. Can you…" Her lashes fluttered down. "Can you do the *Actual Man* thing?"

The advice column he wrote was entitled "Ask a Man"—and women wrote to him in droves to do just that. He signed every column almost precisely the same way.

"If you'd like." Stephen looked into Mrs. Barnstable's face.

The woman's eyes grew wide; a hand drifted up to touch her throat as if to touch nonexistent pearls. He let his voice drop down a few notes and imbued his next words with all the wicked intent that he could muster.

"I'm Stephen Shaughnessy," he said. "Actual Man."

Mrs. Barnstable let out a wavering sigh. "Are you as wicked as the gossip papers say, young man?"

He didn't *feel* wicked. "Oh, no," he said, lowering one eyelid in a lazy wink. "The papers don't know the half of it."

"If you're that bad, then I mustn't introduce you to my charge."

In direct contradiction to these brave words, Mrs. Barnstable turned around. She took Miss Sweetly by the elbow, drawing her into the room. "Miss Sweetly, look who it is! It's Stephen Shaughnessy— and I know how you delight in his column."

That was not a proper introduction. It wasn't even an *improper* introduction. It left Miss Sweetly at a horrendous disadvantage, after all, putting her directly into the class of enthusiasts like Mrs. Barnstable.

Miss Sweetly was many things, but effusive she was not. She dropped him a little curtsey. "I do read your column, Mr. Shaughnessy." Her voice was quiet and subdued in comparison with Mrs. Barnstable's.

When she looked up at him, though, she seemed anything but subdued. Her dark hair, just a little frizzy, had been tamed and wrestled into a bun. She wore a demure gown—not one of the fashionable creations that a lady might wear, but a sensible, high-necked muslin, a thing of long sleeves and buttons that his fingers itched to undo. The fabric hinted at curves of breast and hip; her bustle, less pronounced, could not quite hide her figure.

Her eyes were dark and still, and he felt as if he'd been struck over the head—as if he were looking up into a night sky, bright with stars.

He gave her a little bow. "Miss Sweetly."

"Oh, yes," Mrs. Barnstable said, shaking her head as if she had just now remembered her duty. "Mr. Shaughnessy, this is Miss Rose Sweetly, Dr. Barnstable's computer. She is very young, although I suppose to a thing like you, she'd not seem so. But she's ever so clever."

"I'm always happy to meet clever young ladies," Stephen said. "They're my second favorite kind."

Miss Sweetly grimaced at this in embarrassment and lifted a hand to adjust her spectacles.

She had no idea what that simple motion did to Stephen. It made him want to do the same himself—to run his fingers up the line of her nose, slowly tracing that elegant curve. To hook his finger under the bridge of her glasses and slide them down her face, and then…

But Miss Sweetly did not ask about his favorite kind of young lady, and the answer that he'd come up with to that obvious question went to waste. Over the months of their acquaintance, she'd always forced him to deviate from his usual responses. When he was around her, he had to think, to pay attention—because she never said what he expected.

She did not mention that she knew him. She did not, in fact, say anything at all. She simply looked over Mrs. Barnstable's shoulder, out the window, as if she had more important things than Stephen Shaughnessy on her mind.

It had always been like that with her. The first day he'd met her, he had run into her on the street—quite literally, as they had both been distracted, and neither of them had been watching where they were going. He'd asked what had her so deep in thought, and she had told him.

It had been the most intense experience of his life, seeing her transform from a shy, nervous miss into a magician who intended to coax secrets from the sky. He'd never found mathematics erotic before that day, but watching her lips form the words "parabola" and "Newtonian step" had been utterly riveting. He had been riveted ever since.

"Mr. Shaughnessy wants someone to show him around a slide rule," Mrs. Barnstable was saying to Rose. "And teach him a few tricks. It's for his next book. And he's even offered to pay—what was that again, Mr. Shaughnessy? Three shillings per lesson? Is that what you said? Isn't that generous!"

He hadn't said anything of the sort, but he had to smile at the effrontery of the woman. Three shillings per lesson was downright exorbitant.

"Of course," Mrs. Barnstable said, "most of that fee will go to you, Miss Sweetly, but as I will have to chaperone, I'll expect sixpence per lesson, and another sixpence for my help in the negotiations."

No, Mrs. Barnstable was not the fluttery mother hen she made herself out to be. But right now, it was not Mrs. Barnstable's approval or her heart, mercenary though it might be, that he cared about. It was Miss Sweetly's.

"Are you going to do the *Actual Man* thing to me, too?" she asked, not looking up at him.

"No," he said with a shake of his head. "You sound apprehensive about it, and I try to do that only where it's appreciated."

She sniffed.

"Don't look so disbelieving, Miss Sweetly. I'm a simple man. I like being appreciated."

"At three shillings a lesson," Mrs. Barnstable put in, "you could appreciate him a little."

Miss Sweetly shut her eyes.

"Oh, dear." Mrs. Barnstable said. "That did come out rather unfortunately. I didn't intend…"

But she couldn't even say what she hadn't intended. Normally, watching others struggle with the ridiculous strictures of propriety was one of Stephen's favorite pastimes. He usually waited until all the feathers were smoothed and everyone was on the verge of sighing in relief. Then he'd come out with something utterly inappropriate—blasting all the careful wordings and euphemisms to bits with a brazen determination.

Now, however, he held his tongue. It was an unfamiliar skill, as rarely used and as poorly understood as his mathematics.

"You don't have to appreciate me," he said to Miss Sweetly. "Just teach me to use a slide rule and explain a few basics, and I'll appreciate you."

She looked over at him. For a long while, she seemed to contemplate this. Finally, she nodded. "I suppose I might. If Dr. Barnstable would not mind."

Permission being granted all around, she escorted him to a smaller office, one that was even dingier than the last, which he hadn't thought possible. A typewriter sat at one desk; Mrs. Barnstable sat behind it, fussing about her piles of paper, before settling on one and picking it up.

Miss Sweetly's familiar portfolio graced the other desk; she gestured him to a chair next to hers. He sat.

"Miss Sweetly," he whispered in a low voice, "I know I've rather trapped you into this, but if you'd prefer I leave, that I not bother you, you've only to say the word."

She looked up at him. "But we speak on the streets all the time. Is this so different?"

It was not so different; it was simply an escalation.

"If you wish for a more robust chaperone than Mrs. Barnstable, I'm happy to find someone else." He met her eyes, holding her gaze for a long, fraught moment, before adding, "Only if you wish it, of course."

She raised an eyebrow and glanced behind them. "Mrs. Barnstable," she told him in a low voice, "falls asleep at her desk in the afternoons. She means well, but she *is* sixty-three."

"Oh, no." He leaned forward and pitched his voice even lower. "How dreadfully unchaperoned that will leave us."

She pursed her lips. "The door is open. Chaperones are for ladies; I'm a shopkeeper's daughter. So long as I have recourse if you forget yourself, whatever could happen?"

"Whatever indeed?"

She had looked back at him as he spoke; now she was looking into his eyes, swaying in place a little, almost mesmerized. He felt the slightest twinge of conscience.

He didn't *intend* to seduce her. But he expected he could; it wouldn't prove too difficult. But he didn't want this to end with her guilt and self-recrimination. In point of fact, he didn't want this to end at all.

"If you're going to write a book that touches on astronomy, we had better teach you the basics. Let's start you off with multiplication." Her voice, when she finally spoke, was a little squeaky.

"Naturally," Stephen said, pitching his voice too low for Mrs. Barnstable to hear. "It's a Biblical command, after all: Be fruitful and multiply."

She did not look terribly impressed by that. Instead, she undid the metal fastenings of her slide rule case and took out the instrument.

"I should let you know," he went on, "I've managed to avoid being fruitful thus far. But I *do* enjoy a good session of multiplication."

She swallowed. "Mr. Shaughnessy," she said reproachfully, glancing over at Mrs. Barnstable.

But the older woman just smiled at them, oblivious to the improper turn of the conversation.

"Ah, was that too much?" he asked. "I can hold myself back, if I must."

She looked down at her hands. They were poised over her slide rule, her skin contrasting with the pale, graduated celluloid of the instrument. "Hold yourself back from the Bible, Mr. Shaughnessy?" She smiled faintly. "Why would I want you to do that? I imagine you need all the godliness you can muster."

"I imagine I do. Let's multiply, then."

She gave him another level look. But instead of reproaching him, she moved the slide rule between them, caressing it with a light touch.

"This is the slide." Her long, slender fingers demonstrated, moving the middle bar in a motion that he could not help but find analogous to another act. The thought of her fingers touching him in that slow, steady manner sent his mind whirling down another path altogether, one that left him feeling uncomfortably aroused.

"The left index," she said. "The right index. This metal window is called the cursor."

He nodded and tried to think of mathematics.

"So to multiply two numbers—let us say three and two—you move the left index to the three and set the cursor on the two." She demonstrated, her fingers working with a swift, practiced precision. "Then you can read the answer from the bottom scale."

He looked down. "Six," he said.

"Excellent." Her tone was almost brisk and business-like—almost, but for that slight hint of a quaver in it. "Now I shall write out a few problems. I expect you to calculate them using the slide rule."

She took out a piece of paper and began writing numbers down the side—lots of numbers, as if he were a child tasked with working problems. She wrote swiftly, in a clear, defined hand and slid the page over to him.

He knew he had an effect on her—the same effect he had on most women. He could dazzle her temporarily. But she did not stay dazzled, and he was not used to being so flummoxed in response.

"Let me know when you're finished," she said.

He looked at the paper. "You're not going to multiply with me?"

"No," she said somewhat severely. "You're going to multiply on your own. But I'll make you a wager. If I can finish my calculation of the projected cometary trajectory without the use of my slide rule before you can multiply a few piddling two-digit numbers..."

He took the paper from her. "What will I win, then?"

"Another lesson on multiplication."

He laughed softly. "And if I don't?"

"Then we'll head straight to division," she said briskly.

So saying, she opened her portfolio. He saw a bewildering column of numbers—interspersed with a few Greek deltas and epsilons—before she bent her head over them.

He'd heard her talk about her work. She'd occasionally done complicated long division in her head as she explained something to him on the streets. He'd known she was a genius—she spilled genius all around her without even having to think of it. But watching her work was one of the most astonishing things he had ever witnessed.

The paper was divided into five columns, each carefully labeled. She had to have been multiplying nine-digit numbers in her head without a moment's hesitation, marking them down on the paper as swiftly as she could write. He vaguely recognized something that he thought might have been the gravitational constant, if only his woeful knowledge of dimly recalled physics meant something…

"You're not multiplying," she said severely. But she didn't look at him. Instead, she adjusted her spectacles on her nose.

"Miss Sweetly, why on earth do you even have a slide rule?" he asked in amazement.

She still didn't look up. "There are trigonometric functions on the reverse of the slide. And occasionally, I need it as an aid to correct someone who believes I might be wrong." She frowned. "Mostly, though, I find it comforting."

He shook his head and started on his multiplication.

She did not finish before him—even though she'd filled four pages of calculations and had marked a cometary path about ten degrees further along. It was obvious that she had not intended to finish before him. She'd made that little wager as a sop to his pride. Boasting that he had finished first would have been like a child sketching a line drawing of a man, and then crowing that it had taken less time than it had taken Michelangelo to complete the Sistine Chapel.

He sat and watched her figure instead.

He knew Miss Sweetly was charmed by him. She was too nervous in his company not to be. When they talked, she winced as she spoke, sometimes shaking her head as if to contradict her own words. It was only when she talked mathematics that he could see this side of her— sure and steady, swift and beautiful, as if when she was surrounded by numbers, she forgot that she was supposed to be shy.

Behind them, he could hear Mrs. Barnstable snoring. Precisely as Miss Sweetly had predicted.

She looked up after a moment and noticed that he was done. She glanced over his paper with a practiced eye.

"That proved easy enough," she said.

"What is next, Miss Sweetly? You did promise me more multiplication."

She nodded. She had lost that air of uncertainty; she was in her mathematical element now, and it showed.

"Let us calculate a very small number," she said. "How about a probability? Do you know much of probabilities?"

"A little." He made a motion with his hand.

"Well, then. I'll make this one simple. What do you suppose the chances are that I will be foolish?"

He looked over at her. "Shy?" he asked. "Or stupid?"

She winced a little at that, but didn't look away. "The latter, if you please."

"Then I'd put it at no better than one in a thousand."

"Very well, then. Multiply that by the possibility of our meeting while alone—let us call that one in four—and that by the chance that you will be charming."

His interest was piqued now. He had no idea what she was computing, but he'd be happy to find her alone and charm her into whatever number she wished. He leaned forward. "Tell me. What *is* the chance that you'll find me charming?"

"I'd approximate it as…" She looked across the room thoughtfully, her finger tapping against her lips. "I suppose I should be generous; you are paying for these lessons. So let us say forty percent."

"A mere forty percent?" Stephen clutched his chest dramatically. "A knife to the heart! You slay me, Miss Sweetly."

Her finger did not stop tapping, but she smiled as shyly as if he'd offered her a compliment. "You misidentify the weapon. It's not a knife."

"No?"

Miss Sweetly shook her head. "It's a double slide rule from Elliots, and I have found it extremely useful in dispatching all manner of men. Especially the ones given to excess histrionics. Now shall we continue the calculation?"

He sat back, smiling faintly. "By all means. I can see where this is heading. I have always wanted to be abused with numbers."

She huffed. "The chance that my father would not discover the whole thing before it proved too late is one in ten, and the possibility that I should be hit on the head with an anvil, or a similarly heavy item, is perhaps one in a million. Tell me, Mr. Shaughnessy, what is the probability of all those things occurring in conjunction?"

"Ah..." He had to use paper to keep track. "That would be...a chance of one in...a hundred billion?"

"Ooh." She winced. "That's a very small number. I'm exceedingly sorry for you, Mr. Shaughnessy."

"It is." He looked at the figure. "What, precisely, was I calculating?"

She looked up at him. For one moment, he thought she was going to be shy again—that she would move away and shake her head rather than answer. But even though her voice was low, she still said the words.

"That," she told him, "is the chance that you'll be able to seduce me."

His mouth went dry, and he coughed heavily. "A slide rule to the heart," he heard himself say. "Ouch. Is that what you think of me? That I'm trying to get you alone so that I can seduce you?"

She met his eyes. "What else am I supposed to think when you show up at my place of work, pretend not to know me, and inveigle lessons with me from my employer? What else would you be trying to do, Mr. Shaughnessy?"

He blinked. He opened his mouth and then very slowly closed it again.

"I don't know."

She scoffed.

"I don't know," he repeated. "But coming here, lying to Dr. Barnstable, lying to you just to seduce you—that sounds like a sinister plot. I don't have sinister plots, Miss Sweetly; they take too much work. I'm here because I would like to spend more time with you, and because I love listening to you talk about mathematics. Nothing more villainous than that."

She clearly didn't believe him. Her nostrils flared ever so slightly; she turned away, setting her hand between them.

"Speaking of mathematics," he said, "why did an anvil appear in the midst of that calculation? I've done a great many things and even I have never had call to use an anvil."

She looked up into his eyes. "How else was I to acquire amnesia?" she asked shyly.

He blinked in confusion, then burst into laughter as he realized what she meant.

She frowned. "I'm not attempting to amuse you. I would need to forget not only my own moral sense, but my work, my family, my future—everything I would give up if you succeeded in such an aim."

"In that case," he promised, "let me set your mind at ease. I hereby adopt a strict no-anvil policy. If I ever have you in my bed, I want you to remember yourself. I like you. There's no point having your body if you're not included."

She should have smacked him for that, or at the very least, ordered him away. Instead, she touched her slide rule, moving the metal cursor back and forth.

"Then there's no point at all," she whispered.

Behind them, Mrs. Barnstable gave a snort. They both jumped, but the older woman only turned her head from side to side before subsiding once more.

"Haven't you been listening?" he asked in a low voice. "This—talking to you, just like this—is already the point. I like you. I like talking to you. If you don't like me, send me off."

She raised an eyebrow at him. And then, without answering, she began to write another set of numbers on a sheet of paper.

"Let's practice division," she said.

Anyone who heard her patient explanation might have thought her cool and earnest. Stephen knew better. She *hadn't* sent him off, and no matter what she was saying, the message was clear. She liked him—unwillingly, perhaps—but she still liked him.

He waited until he'd started on the problems she'd set for him, until she had picked up her pen and restarted her own calculations, before he spoke again.

"I have another question about that last probability."

She set down her pen. "Go ahead."

"You are always very exacting about the numbers you use. When you said I was forty percent likely to be charming…"

She blinked up at him. "I haven't done an accurate calculation, but yes. About forty percent. If you wish, I could collate—"

He shook his head. "I don't need a list. It's just to satisfy my own curiosity. Why only forty percent?"

She looked down. "My personal tastes—nothing you should worry over, really—"

"If I have not made it clear, Miss Sweetly, I take an avid interest in your personal tastes."

She let out a long breath. "I don't trust you," she said simply. "If you had half a chance, you'd take me to bed."

He could have denied it. But truthfully? He wasn't trying to shove her in that direction, but would he say no? Of course he wouldn't.

"Ah." He picked up the next sheet of problems she'd written out for him, found the next number on the slide. "Then you have nothing to worry about, not according to your calculations. You could find me charming all the time, and according to you, I'd still only have a chance of…of…" He fumbled.

She took pity on him. "One in forty billion."

"There, you see? I don't have half a chance. I'm not even within spitting range of a hundredth of a chance. So there can be no harm in your allowing yourself to be charmed by me all the time." So saying, he gave her a brilliant smile.

It affected her. It obviously affected her. Her hands tangled in her lap; she glanced down, not in demure deflection, but as if to avert her eyes from the sun. She rubbed the bridge of her nose, as if her spectacles chafed.

"You're trying to charm me with mathematics," she said.

"Is it working?"

She looked up at him. *Yes,* said her dark eyes, shining at him. *Yes,* said the part of her lips, the fingers that drew up to brush her hair. *Yes,* said the tilt of her body in his direction.

"No," she told him with a firm shake of her head. "It isn't."

CHAPTER THREE

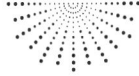

THAT NIGHT, ROSE DREAMED that a column of numbers was chasing her through some odd, non-Cartesian landscape, a vista of lines and swirling colors. In the distance, someone was laughing—not a cruel laugh, or even a laugh at her expense. Just a friendly, welcoming laugh.

The numbers caught her, taking hold of her shoulder. She jerked away, but they held her fast.

How did numbers *grip?* She turned to them, fascinated…and very groggily came awake.

The room was dark; the only illumination was a pale stripe of moonlight, filtered through an inch-wide gap in her curtains. No sound rose from the street; it was the dead of night indeed.

But there was a hand, warm, on Rose's shoulder. It gave her a little shake.

"Rose," Patricia whispered, "are you awake?"

"Patricia?" Rose turned to find her sister sitting on the bed next to her, her form dim in the night.

"It's started." Her sister's voice crackled with excitement, but the hand on Rose seemed tense, almost fearful.

Rose didn't need to ask what *it* was. There was only one *it* in the household these days.

She sat bolt upright in her bed. "What? Already? It's too soon."

"Thirty-six weeks, by Doctor Chillingsworth's count. It *is* too early —but I felt a most definite contraction. It's starting."

"It can't start. Isaac is—"

She cut herself off. Her sister's husband was not yet home. They'd been so sure he would have returned by the time the baby came. They'd charted the remaining weeks of Patricia's pregnancy against the expected return of his ship with a sigh of relief.

When they'd found out that Patricia was with child—days before Dr. Wells was scheduled to leave—he'd been upset at missing the majority of her pregnancy. Rose had promised to write to him, to tell him the day-to-day occurrences.

"Take care of her for me," Dr. Isaac Wells had told her in return. "If I can't be there, you'll have to stand in my stead."

Rose was the younger sister; Patricia had always taken care of her. But somehow, that solemn request, made by a brother-in-law that she liked, had only firmed her resolve. If Patricia had always taken care of Rose, that only meant that Rose now had a chance to return the favor.

And so she wrote to Isaac regularly, telling him everything that transpired. She'd reported faithfully every morning when Patricia felt poorly. She'd described the baby's first tentative flutters, barely detectable, up through the more recent kicks that had drummed against Rose's hand. She'd told him all...but it didn't change a thing. Patricia wished her husband would come back before the baby was born, and Isaac wanted the same thing. He was a little more than a week away now. To have the baby come so close to his arrival would be...

...A blessing, Rose told herself firmly. No matter when it came.

So she swallowed what she had been about to say.

"Have you sent for Chillingsworth?" she asked instead.

"Josephs left a few minutes past. He should be back soon."

Mr. and Mrs. Josephs were the married couple that kept house for Patricia—Mrs. Josephs as the maid-of-all-work, and Mr. Josephs as an all-around handyman. In their neighborhood, having two servants was considered an enormous expense; she'd heard someone whisper that Patricia was putting on airs above her station. But then, Patricia's husband was away, and she herself was pregnant.

"Are you scared?" Rose asked. "What does it feel like, a contraction? I did promise to tell Isaac everything when he returned. You have to tell me."

"Oh, I'm not having the contraction any longer—now I just feel...I don't know, a little odd." Patricia gave a deprecating laugh. "Like a bloated duck on the verge of being popped. But that hasn't changed since last night."

"Can you walk?"

"Of course I can. How do you think I got to your room? Even bloated ducks can manage a good waddle."

Rose smiled. "Well, labor hasn't altered your sense of humor. It's still dreadful."

"Wait until I have another contraction," Patricia said. "Then I'll have no humor at all. Come and wait with me downstairs?"

Rose dressed swiftly and held her sister's hand on the way down the stairs—even though Patricia tried to wave her off, saying she was perfectly able to walk on her own. Once she'd ensconced her sister in pride of place on the sofa, Rose ran around, lighting lamps, pushing away all the shadows of the night. It was lovely to have something to do. She bustled about, fetching and carrying for her sister—slippers, a warm blanket, chamomile tea, and a crumpet that she toasted over a fire and then piled high with butter and currant jelly.

"Mmm," Patricia said, closing her eyes. "Won't you have one, too?"

"I was already having the oddest dream when you woke me," Rose said. "I don't need to upset my digestion any further."

"Dream, eh?" Patricia's eyes narrowed. "You weren't dreaming of—"

"I dreamed I was being chased by a heap of numbers," Rose intervened.

Patricia choked, almost laughing. "You would."

Yes, someone had been laughing in her dream. Almost like that.

Friendly laughter, the mirthful burble of someone who knew all Rose's faults and loved her anyway.

It had been too deep a laugh for Patricia, and not merry enough to sound like her mother. Her father's laugh was more of a rumble. And yet it had seemed familiar.

The answer came to Rose as her sister took another bite of crumpet. Mr. Shaughnessy laughed like that.

She'd been avoiding thinking about him. Despite his protestations, she knew exactly what he was doing. This was how men like him seduced women like her: step by careful step, wearing away at her inhibitions one by one.

She had no illusions that her innocence would protect her; innocence was for a different class of women altogether. Rose was a shopkeeper's daughter; she was a woman who worked for a living herself. The well-to-do men who could command society's respect usually thought that women like her existed to serve in whatever capacity they were desired.

She didn't know why she hadn't sent Mr. Shaughnessy on his way. Stupidity, surely. Misplaced romanticism. But this wasn't the time to berate herself.

As her sister took yet another bite of crumpet, the front door opened. Mr. Josephs entered.

Behind him came Doctor Chillingsworth. The physician's coat was wet with glistening rain; he set an umbrella in the umbrella stand, frowning at it as if it had no business being wet. He took off his gloves and chafed his pale hands together for warmth. Then he looked over at Patricia—seated on the sofa, wrapped in wool blankets, trying not to drip red jelly down her chin—and his expression froze in something that looked alarmingly like a sneer.

The back of Rose's neck prickled. But the doctor shook his head, and that hint of a scoff disappeared from his face.

Maybe she'd imagined it. Maybe he simply didn't like jelly.

Chillingsworth was a tall, elderly fellow. He always had an air about him that Rose disliked. It was not exactly disdain; it only smacked mildly of disapproval.

She tried to tell herself she was seeing things that weren't there. He'd come so highly recommended after all. Before he'd retired to civilian practice, he'd spent thirty years as a naval physician. Maybe that air of his was nothing more than residual military discipline.

Patricia's husband didn't have that air—but then, he was only thirty-two. Maybe, she thought dubiously, it took years to develop.

Chillingsworth took off his galoshes, an outer coat, a scarf, and finally, a blue-striped hat. He came forward.

The examination was brief, almost cursory. Patricia's eyes squeezed shut and her breath hissed when he set his stethoscope against her belly. The metal must have been ice cold. But she didn't complain.

The doctor straightened after he'd finished. "Well," he said. "I was roused from bed for nothing."

Patricia blinked.

"Mrs. Wells is having false labor pains," he announced.

At first, Rose had no idea who he was addressing—the room at large, perhaps?—until she followed his line of sight to Mr. Josephs, who was doing his best to wipe up the water that had splashed in the entryway when they had arrived.

How odd of him to talk of Patricia's health with the servant. But then, people sometimes made that mistake. Mr. Josephs may have been a servant, but he was the only man—the only *white* man—in the household, and people often got confused or uncomfortable as a result. It never did to make a fuss about it. They'd all feel better if they just imagined Chillingsworth making pronouncements to the room.

"It is not yet her time," Chillingsworth said. "The baby has not even turned, and she is not dilated. Women like her are often given to dramatics. Next time, make sure the contractions are coming closer together before sending for me in the middle of the night." He glanced back at the entrance. "In the cold rain."

"Yes, Doctor Chillingsworth," Patricia said contritely. "I'm sorry. It's my first time, and I don't know what to expect."

"Humph."

"Would you like a cup of tea to warm up?" Rose offered.

"I'd like my bed," Doctor Chillingsworth said curtly. He stalked back to the entry without looking at her, stamped into his heavy galoshes, and gathered up his things. He muttered to himself as he wound his scarf about his neck. Then he picked up his umbrella, tapped it against the floor—sending droplets of water all over the entryway—and left.

"Dear." Patricia stared after him. "That went...not so well as one would hope."

"That was rude," Rose pointed out.

Patricia waved this away. "Nobody likes being woken in the middle of the night for no reason."

Then maybe he shouldn't be a physician, Rose thought with annoyance. But she did not say that. Instead, she helped her sister to her feet.

"There we are," Patricia said cheerily. "It looks like the bloated duck is here to stay for a few more weeks. And thank God. That means Isaac will be home after all."

~

MISS SWEETLY HAD MOVED their lesson outside on the next day. Stephen didn't know if she'd done so to cool off his imputed ardor, or if she'd just thought it a good idea. Either way, she'd brought them out along the river past the docks. They stood on the water's edge, in the lee of a lamppost that provided not one whit of shelter from the wind.

The people who made their way past reminded him why he had moved to Greenwich. Here, he wasn't the lone Irish interloper in a hoity-toity neighborhood. The nearby docks brought visitors from around the world: lascars from India, midshipmen from the West Indies, swarthy sailors from Portugal...and yes, a goodly number of Irish toiling on ships and in warehouses.

Here, an Irishman standing with a black woman might get an idle second glance, no more. Stephen caught sight of a dock-laborer that he knew from church and gave the man a nod.

The wind gusted around his collar as he did so, bringing in a damp chill off the Thames. Stephen's nose was cold; his hands were going numb. But Miss Sweetly stood beside him, looking as if she were comfortably warming her hands over a fire instead of holding a metal disc in her gloved hands. If *she* didn't feel the cold, he wouldn't, either.

Mrs. Barnstable, by contrast, had given up in the first five minutes. She'd decamped to a nearby tea shop, promising to keep up her vigil from the window.

"To make a measurement by parallax," Miss Sweetly was telling him, "you must be able to determine angles and distances. You can obtain angles on land most simply by using a prismatic compass. Hold the compass—"

He held out his hand; she dumped it unceremoniously into his palm. The metal was cold; he'd been taking notes, and one could hardly wield a pencil while wearing gloves. His breath hissed in.

"Now look through the eyehole, and adjust the prism until the wire contacts the object you are measuring. Read the magnetic angle here."

Someone else might think those words devoid of emotion.

But when she said the word "prism," her lips formed almost a kiss. She reached out and adjusted the compass in his hand, her fingers brushing his palm. And when she looked up after her explanation, she glanced into his eyes and the flow of her words tumbled to a halt. She stood in place, her fingers on the compass, and her eyes widening.

He fascinated her. He was *good* at fascinating women; he didn't even really try to do it. The only difference was that Miss Sweetly thought him both fascinating and frivolous, all at the same time—and he was fairly certain that she was right.

He pulled his hand away and made the measurement, focusing on the building she'd chosen, lining up the wire, making a notation of the angle in his notebook.

"Now to make a second measurement. It must be from a different angle, and a known distance away." She adjusted her spectacles on her nose.

He wondered if her nose was cold. It had to be; they stood in the same wind. But she didn't seem to flinch at all from the weather. He paced off a distance and measured the angle without saying anything. He made a diagram in his little notebook; she came to stand behind him, looking over his shoulder.

"Having you watch me calculate is like…" He paused, searching for an appropriate analogy. "It's like having Beethoven attend a child's first recital on the pianoforte."

She gave a little snort behind him. "I shouldn't think so. There are a few salient differences."

"True. Beethoven isn't female. Beethoven isn't lovely. You're far more disconcerting."

"Mmm. You're not thinking this through. You see, Beethoven isn't alive. I imagine it would be rather more alarming to be visited by the corpse of a composer."

"Does that make him a decomposer?"

She let out a startled choking noise.

Stephen smiled to himself. "I suppose the analogy does rather break down upon examination." He subtracted the magnetic angles and started on the calculation of the triangles. She watched him in silence for a little longer.

"I don't understand why you want me to teach you about astronomy," she said.

"I don't want you to teach me astronomy." As he spoke, he flipped the slide and consulted the trigonometric tables. "I want you to teach me to see the world the way you do."

"How do I see the world?" she asked in puzzlement.

"If I knew, I wouldn't need to learn, would I?" He shrugged. "But I know how you see me. You think I'm an outrageous flirt, a frivolous fellow who thinks of nothing beyond the next joke."

"And you're going to tell me there's more to you?" She sounded dubious.

"If there is, I can't see it myself. But I do wonder sometimes if you might." He shoved the slide over a few inches, read a number off the bottom scale, and marked it down.

"Are you trying to intrigue me by hinting at hidden depths, Mr. Shaughnessy?"

He shrugged. "Why would I? I don't even have hidden shallows. I am very much as you see."

"No hidden traumas, no childhood disappointments, or lingering resentments?"

"Not a one. Oh. Wait. I suppose I do have one. When I was twelve, I was whipped at the stake for rabble rousing."

She turned to him, blinking. "How dreadful."

He dropped his voice, beckoning her closer. She leaned in despite herself. "Do you want to know what I thought when the lash landed? Shall I disclose the solemn vow I made?"

She made no answer, but her eyes sparkled with the light of curiosity.

He bent his head to hers. "I thought: Ouch."

She waited, holding still, as if expecting more.

"That's it. I'm finished. 'Ouch.' Never get whipped as punishment if you can help it, Miss Sweetly. I don't recommend it."

"Thank you," she said solemnly. "I'll keep that in mind." But she bit her lip as she spoke, and he could tell she was suppressing a smile.

He lined up the last numbers on the slide. "It's two hundred and fifty-seven, by the way," he told her.

"Two hundred and fifty-seven what?"

"Feet. To that building over there."

She blinked, as if only now remembering that she was giving him a lesson. "I had judged it at two hundred and fifty-four," she said slowly.

"Ah. Drat."

"But given that your measurement of distance was done by pacing off the length, your answer is certainly within the margin of error." She smiled at him. "Well done. Now should you like to try something difficult?"

"That wasn't difficult? There were sines. And arctangents. I didn't think any problem should be thought easy if it involved arctangents."

"Hush, you great big baby." She shook her head, but she was

smiling at him. "All you had to do was look up a number in a table. Was that too difficult for you?"

"A great and mighty table, ringed by fearsome logarithms, with their terrible, terrible…" He trailed off. "Oh, very well. Set me another problem, Miss Sweetly. My resolve is firm and my angles are acute. But beware—if I have to draw another diagram, things may become graphic."

She raised her hands in surrender. "No more mathematical jokes," she said in horror.

"Why? Afraid we might go off on…a *tangent?*"

"It's not that." She bit her lip. "Mathematics are a serious business, for one. And your jokes are terrible, for another."

"I can't help myself." He winked at her. "I was born under an unfortunate sine."

One hand went to her hip. "Mr. Shaughnessy, must I eject you from the pier?"

"Oh, I should think not. Not unless you make me use calculus. I'm afraid my calculus jokes are derivative."

She groaned. "Does your adoring public know that Stephen Shaughnessy, Actual Man, makes truly terrible puns?"

"Sadly, no. I keep trying to put them in my columns, but Free—my editor; that's Frederica Marshall-Clark—keeps taking them out." He made a face.

"Have you finished your little spate of jocularity, Mr. Shaughnessy?" Her words might have sounded harsh, but she was suppressing a smile. "I had intended to set you a problem, if you recall."

"Of course. Go ahead."

"Do you see that ferry?"

"The one in the middle of the Thames?" It was surrounded by choppy waters.

"That very one. Figure out how far away it is, if you please. But here's the catch—this time, no pacing off the distances. In fact, you're not allowed to move your feet at all. You may move your hand a quarter of an inch—no further."

"But the ferry's moving."

"So it is."

"Very well, then." He took out the compass, peered through it...

"May I move my feet over to the railing, just to set the compass down?"

"No," she told him with a calm smile.

It was impossible to hold his hand steady enough.

He blew out a breath. "But the needle in the prism is vibrating. I can't get an accurate read on the angle, and if I can only move my hand a quarter inch, I shall need a very accurate read."

As if to emphasize this, a cart rumbled past and the needle trembled.

She smiled at his dismay. "So you can't do it."

"Did I say that? I can. Of course I can."

He tried stabilizing his hand against his other arm, then holding the compass between thumb and forefinger. The wind picked up, making his grip all the more tenuous—and his fingers even colder. He managed to get an almost decent read once—he thought—but by the time he'd moved his hand the allowed quarter inch and tried to stabilize the needle once more, the ferry had moved so much that the first number was useless.

She watched his struggles with a beatific smile. And that was what finally tipped him off. If the problem were *possible,* she'd be aggravated that he was doing it wrong.

"Miss Sweetly," he said straightening, "would you set me an impossible problem just to watch me struggle with it?"

She put one hand over her heart. "How could you say such a thing? You must think me needlessly cruel."

"No. Of course not. But—"

She smiled. "Good. I should hate you to be deceived as to my character."

He let the compass fall to his side. "Miss Sweetly. You're mocking me. I'm absolutely delighted."

And he was. Every day he spent with her brought her more and more out of her nervousness. The more he saw of her, the better he liked her, and he'd hardly needed to like her better.

She looked away, with a little smile on her face. "Let's go join Mrs. Barnstable. I could use some tea; I'm a little cold."

A little cold. Just a little cold. He shook his head. She set off in the direction of the tea shop and he followed.

"I actually wasn't trying to be mean," she told him as they walked. "I was trying to illustrate a point. The closest stars are trillions of miles away. Even if we took our observations of a star from opposite sides of the globe, we'd only manage a few thousand miles of distance between the two points. I was generous giving you a quarter inch to measure the angle."

He nodded and opened the tea shop door for her. Welcome warmth from the coal stove inside hit him.

But she stopped just inside the shop, and he realized that her glasses had fogged up. She took them off, cleaning them carefully, and then set them on her nose once more. She gave him a suspicious look, as if daring him to laugh at her.

Not a chance. He was taken with a sudden fantasy of fogging them himself, of leaning into her and…

Mrs. Barnstable waved to them as they entered, but she was already seated at a table with another woman, with whom she was gossiping.

Stephen gestured Rose into a seat at the table next to Mrs. Barnstable. "So how is astronomical parallax calculated, then?"

Her eyes brightened. "If we measure the angle of a star in the sky twice yearly, taking into account…" She trailed off, waving her hand, then resumed, "…all the various factors we must consider, then we can have two measurements that are far more than a few thousand miles apart."

"Ah. That is clever."

And it was. A year ago, he'd never have guessed that he would find it all so fascinating. That was before he'd seen her get excited about it. Her eyes lit; her hands gestured. She looked like…like…

Why had he never realized how inadequate all analogies were for women in the throes of utter fascination? She looked like a woman talking about astronomical parallax, and that made her brilliantly beautiful.

"So it really is the same concept as measuring buildings from across the Thames, more or less," she told him. "If I gave you two such measurements, Mr. Shaughnessy, could you determine the distance of a star?"

"I think so."

She rattled off a pair of numbers. He began to calculate—and realized that he'd boasted too soon. He looked up to see her watching him with that same beatific smile on her face. A girl came with tea and biscuits; Miss Sweetly poured, but didn't say anything else.

"Miss Sweetly."

"Yes, Mr. Shaughnessy?" she said innocently.

"I spoke too soon. I can't do a thing until I know the distance between the two points of measurement."

"Ah," she said with a long, drawn-out sigh. "That's so."

"It's twice the distance between the earth and the sun—but how is one to measure that? Let a giant piece of string trail behind the earth as it passes, and then reel it back in? I have no idea. I think you must enjoy setting me impossible problems."

"I'm merely making you comfortable with the notion of failure," she told him, looking down. "When it comes to me, you should expect to fail. Often."

He set his chin on his hands. "I'd rather fail at you than succeed at anyone else."

She went utterly still. Her jaw squared; she glanced to one side, ascertaining that Mrs. Barnstable was not listening, and then she looked back at him.

"Too much," she told him. "When you say extravagant things like that, I remember that this is all a game to you. You'd do much better if you used less effusive praise."

"I'll remember that, if I ever decide to seduce you." He picked up his teacup and took a healthy swallow of warm liquid. "But it's rather ironic, don't you think? You were about to tell me how to measure the distance between the earth and the sun without using string. You can imagine numbers larger than I have ever dreamed about. And yet you can't grasp hold of the possibility that maybe, just maybe, you really have brought me to my knees."

She pulled back, giving her head a fierce shake. "Don't be ridiculous. Women like me don't—"

He set his hand on the table, interrupting this thought. "My father was a stable master," he told her. "My mother was a seamstress. I've done very well for myself, but don't imagine that I'm one of those gentlemen who look down on you."

She looked away, dropping a lump of sugar into her tea.

"As for women like you… I don't believe I have ever met a woman like you. Tell me, Miss Sweetly. How did you become the sort of woman who calculated cometary orbits?"

She picked up a teaspoon. "I've always been exceptional at maths. I do mean always. When I was four, we still lived with my grandfather in Liverpool. He owned a shop there, and one day, a man came to the register with a basket of goods. I knew what the total would be, so I said it aloud." She shrugged. "My grandfather made a game of it. I could add a basket at a glance. Grown men would come to watch. A great many of them. By the time I left, there would be a crowd there every day."

Her lips twitched as if she'd tasted something unpleasant.

"Miss Sweetly, that sounds like a hidden depth."

"Unlike you, I have never claimed not to have them." She dipped the teaspoon in her tea and slowly stirred the brown liquid. "It made me uncomfortable, all those people watching. And the things they would say… I was very glad when my father came to London to start his own emporium. I wasn't on display any longer, not until my father tried to have me learn deportment." Rose smiled. "It didn't work so well—I didn't like the idea of performing in society. Eventually, on Patricia's advice, he bribed me to pay attention by offering me tutoring in higher mathematics."

She was still stirring her tea even though the sugar must have long since dissolved.

"So you see, it's nothing, really. Just a little trick I do, something that brings me some amusement."

"Right," he said skeptically. "Just a little trick. Tell me, Miss Sweetly. How *does* one calculate the distance between the earth and the sun?"

She looked up, her eyes brightening. "Oh, so many ways. But there's really only one astronomical event that allows us to make a truly accurate measurement. We can observe the exact time it takes for Venus to cross between the earth and the sun. Two such observations taken at different latitudes would give the most exact distance possible."

"You sound as if this has not yet been done."

"It was attempted before, but there were difficulties…" She caught his eye. "Never mind the difficulties. The entire astronomical community has been preparing for this upcoming transit. Britain alone has twelve stations manned around the world for just this event."

"A lot of to-do about one little number," he teased.

"But I've already told you!" She sounded shocked. "It's not just one little number. It is the only yardstick we have to measure the universe with, and we don't know how long it is! If we knew that distance accurately, we'd know not just how far the stars were, but we could deduce the distance of all the planets in the solar system. We'd then know their mass, which would allow us to test our measurements of the gravitational constant, see if this so-called ether exists…" She trailed off once again, looking up at him. Slowly, the light drained from her eyes. Watching her slide back into self-consciousness was like watching a candle flame flicker in a sudden wind and then go out.

"Oh," she said in a small voice. "You were teasing me."

"No," Stephen said. "I was proving a point."

She flinched. "What, that you can set me to babbling?"

"You keep looking for dark, complicated reasons, Miss Sweetly. I don't complicate. I'm simple. I like hearing you talk about the solar system. If I didn't like it, I wouldn't ask."

"You can't pretend you're a mathematical enthusiast. I've seen you wrestle with an arctangent, Mr. Shaughnessy, and I wasn't sure you would win."

Stephen leaned toward her. "It's because your enthusiasm is a contagion. You look at the sky and see not pretty little lights, but a cosmos to be discovered. If I could listen to you talk and *not* smile in appreciation, I would be an unfeeling brute. And you think the praise I give you is over-extravagant? One of these days, you'll realize how much I'm truly restraining myself."

She stole a glance over at him—one that was both wary and hopeful all at once.

"So tell me," he said. "When will Venus next intervene between us and the sun? The way you were speaking, it sounds as if it will be soon."

Her fingers fumbled with a teaspoon. "It's just days from now," she told him. "On the sixth of December at almost precisely two in the afternoon."

"And naturally, you'll be observing this event."

"Oh…" She looked down again. "From here in London, only about half of the transit will be visible, and that only weather permitting. The sun will set before it's finished. I have a piece of smoked glass that I'll be using to observe—which is hardly ideal, the planet is so small, and…" She trailed off.

"And I don't understand. You work at an observatory. Surely you'd have access to better observational tools than smoked glass."

"I'm not one of the astronomers," she said in a low voice. "I'm just a computer. There's only so much space, and everyone else wants to see it."

Just. She still didn't believe him.

"Well, then." He gave her his best smile. "Next time, you must attach yourself to one of the scientific teams going to…where was it you said? Bermuda?"

But she was shaking her head again. "No, no."

"You think you can't?" He paused, considering her. "The fact that you are female poses some difficulties. The race, I assume, is also a hindrance?"

She nodded.

"But then, those must be overshadowed by the utter brilliance of your mind."

She smiled, but it was a shaky, wavering smile. "It's not that, Mr. Shaughnessy. I mean, it *is* that, but in this case, it wouldn't help." She swallowed. "You see, the transit of Venus is a rare astronomical event —exceedingly rare. There is no next time, not in my life. It won't happen again until June of the year 2004." She gave him a sad shake of her head. "So yes, Mr. Shaughnessy. I'm not one of the people who will watch this happen in all its glory. Women like me will have to content ourselves with glimpsing the phenomenon in smoked glass."

Stephen hadn't known what he intended when he first approached Dr. Barnstable. But looking at her now, her head bent, disclaiming all importance... Now, for the first time, he knew what he wanted.

CHAPTER FOUR

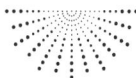

"**R**OSE," PATRICIA SAID THE NEXT MORNING, "I particularly think you should read this." She slid a paper across the breakfast table to sit alongside Rose's teacup.

Rose looked up from her toast to see the *Women's Free Press* opened to Mr. Shaughnessy's latest column.

"I thought you didn't want to encourage me in this."

"This isn't encouragement," Patricia said gravely. "It's a reminder of who he is, what he is. He's flirting with you…"

Rose felt her cheeks heat. Patricia didn't know the half of it.

"…and at the same time, he's carrying on like this, in public. In a *newspaper.*"

Rose had read a good number of Mr. Shaughnessy's columns. She had an idea of the sort of things he wrote. She doubted anything he could write would shock her—and if Patricia only knew the sorts of things he was saying to her face, she'd know that she would need a more powerful arsenal than a few lines in a newspaper. Still, Rose dutifully picked up the paper.

Dear Man, she read. *I am sorry to say that I have spent the last five years in a madhouse. My uncle and guardian had me put there when I refused to marry my cousin. I passed my time in that horrible place by making a list of all the things I would do if ever I were released. Now he is dead and I am free, but I find I cannot bring myself to do even one of them. How does one go about setting oneself free?*

—Not Mad.

Rose swallowed hard and read on.

Dear Not Mad,

Normally I approach my columns with a certain amount of jocularity. (Never tell this to my readers; they would never believe it.) But your situation has moved me to seriousness. You must work yourself up to your desires, bit by bit. Before you can dance on your uncle's grave (I assume this to be on your list), you must first visit it and stand upon the grass. On the next visit, be sure to tap your toe and hum a ditty. Before you know it, you'll be waltzing in the cemetery.

Should you need a dancing partner, consider yours truly.

Sincerely,

Stephen Shaughnessy

Actual Man

"You see?" Patricia said. "He's flirting—publicly—with another woman. That's the sort of man he is. Just keep that in mind the next time you encounter him." She nodded as if she had proven a point.

Rose shook her head. It wasn't flirting, no more than the time he'd done the *Actual Man* thing to Mrs. Barnstable had been flirting. It was…kind of him, in a sweet, outrageous sort of way. It hurt to read it, not because she thought him unfaithful, but because she could hear him in it, all of him.

I don't have hidden shallows, he'd told her. Maybe he didn't. She suspected that if she judged him by his column, she would see…

A man who offered to dance with a woman who had been badly wounded. A man who mocked other men when they made too much of their own importance. A man who wished to make others laugh, even when they suffered. She had never looked at him and seen a bad man, and the more she looked, the deeper she fell.

That, perhaps, made him the most dangerous specimen of all.

He liked people. He liked *her.* She suspected he'd told her the simple truth: He wasn't *trying* to seduce her.

He was just succeeding at it.

~

"THIS WILL BE OUR LAST LESSON," Rose said, when Mr. Shaughnessy had settled himself into her office two days later. "There is only so much you need to learn, and after tomorrow I shall be flooded with work. We'll have data from the transit of Venus—and once we have that, there will be star charts to update, and I shall be up to my ears in calculations. I shan't have time for you any longer."

Mrs. Barnstable looked up at that, but she had a report to type for her husband, and the noise of the typewriter drowned out their conversation.

The truth was that Rose should never have made time for Mr. Shaughnessy. He was… *Charming* was the word she'd used, but charming sounded so sweet, so innocent. And by nature, Mr. Shaughnessy was never innocent.

He was not watching her innocently now.

That was the problem. She knew precisely what was happening to her. She could feel him coaxing her along the path to seduction. He made her forget herself every day she was with him, and one day, she would cross an uncrossable line. So long as he was around her, he would lead her astray.

His lips thinned, but he nodded ever so slightly as if he were accepting her edict.

"You'll still tell me what you're doing when we meet on the street," he said. "And now I'll understand it better."

She shook her head. "I don't think I should."

No; that was too wishy-washy. The clattering of Mrs. Barnstable's machine was beginning to annoy Rose.

"In fact, I know I mustn't."

"Aw, Rose." He looked into her eyes. "You know I love it when you talk Sweetly to me."

Her throat seemed to close at those words. She felt hoarse, almost ill. Her heart was pounding and her head seemed light. But this was no illness; she wanted more of it.

Therein lay her problem. He'd told her that her enthusiasm was contagious.

His lack of innocence, then, was a raging plague, and she was infected. The smallest glance in his direction sent her into an internal tizzy—the flash of his eyes, a glimpse of his wrist when one of his cuffs pulled up. The sight of him gave her ideas, and she didn't need to be having *ideas* about him.

Once she had it in her head that he might do things to her, she could not help but imagine those things. Kisses, and not just on the lips or the hand, but on her neck, her inner wrist, up her elbow. He might give her caresses, too—slow, languid, full-body caresses. He didn't have to seduce her; she was doing all the work of seduction on her own.

"Come, Mr. Shaughnessy," she said briskly. "I'm sure you dream of more important things than listening to me ramble on. I don't wish to be a way station on your way to bigger and better." She looked down. "I have enjoyed—rather too much—spending this time with you. But I think I'll be better off if our time together draws to a close."

He took this in silence. His lips compressed into an almost angry line, and he looked away.

"Here," she said. "I've set you some...some problems to work. Just a little parallax." She actually choked as she spoke, as if she might cry over mathematics.

Better that. Better to cry over maths than a man, especially a rogue like this one. He'd scarcely even exerted himself and already she found herself watching his fingers, hoping he might crook one of them at her...and fearing that if he did, she'd come running.

He took the sheet from her and began to work.

"You know," he said, "I realized last night that you were granting me a signal honor when you let me use your slide rule. Thank you."

He didn't sound as if he were making fun of her. She glanced suspiciously at him.

"I don't dream of bigger and better," he said, making his first notation on the page. "I told you: I'm appallingly simple. There is no grand design."

"You're a novelist. And a columnist. There's nothing simple about you."

"Yes," he said. "I'm exceedingly clever and exceedingly outrageous. But that doesn't make me exceedingly devious."

"But you must have had some plan in order to ascend the heights so swiftly."

He smirked. "Here is the extent of my planning. When I was fifteen, I realized I was a poor Irish Catholic in England, a country with an excess of poor Irish Catholics. My only real skill was a talent for outraging others. Either I had to stamp out my only source of genius in order to have a go at making a living in the most menial fashion, or I had to indulge it to the fullest and hope for the best." He shrugged. "Here I am. For the next few years, I shall be in demand enough to command a thousand pounds per book from my publisher. By the time that's dried up—and the public's capacity for any brand of outrage always dries up—I'll have enough saved that I won't have to care. See? There is no grand plan. No meteoric dreams. Just a dislike for manual labor and a talent for annoying others."

She sniffed.

"You, on the other hand…"

She shook her head. "We are not talking of me."

"You, I wager, do not dream timid dreams. You walk with your head in the clouds."

"Oh, no. The clouds are in the troposphere. My thoughts lie well beyond the mesosphere."

"Precisely. So tell me, Miss Sweetly. What is it *you* see for yourself, after you send me on my way? What is your grand plan?"

Behind them, Mrs. Barnstable changed a page in her typewriter. Rose flushed and looked away. "There is no grand plan. My father is on the board of the *African Times*. It has been their mission for the last decades to see to the elevation of the race. They've sponsored a number of medical students in their work, starting with Africanus Horton." She couldn't look him in the eyes. "Patricia—my sister—

married one of those students. They met over dinner, took one look at each other...and that was the end of it. Everyone expects that I'll marry one of the two students arriving in the next year." Rose traced a trailing vine on her skirt. "I suppose I do, too."

"And is that what you want?" he asked in a low voice. "To marry a medical student on scholarship? To have his children and to keep his home?"

"I am not opposed to marriage. And yes, I should like children." She still couldn't bring herself to look at him.

"Will your husband let you spend your days in computation? Will he listen to you talk of parallax and the transit of Venus? Or will he expect you to subside into compliance, to set your slide rule aside until it is dusty and warped?"

Her chin went up. "How do you suppose I met Dr. Barnstable? He's also on the board of the *African Times*—he was stationed in Cape Town, and didn't like some of the things he saw. He heard about this ridiculous talent I had, and next thing I knew, he was pleading with my father to let me work with him. I know for a fact that there are men in this world who will allow a woman her interests."

"True. But would they adore you for yours? Where others see numbers and charts, you see a universe, vast and mighty. You can see the face of the cosmos in a few dancing lights. You shouldn't have to trade the stars in the sky for a home and a marriage and babies."

She let out a shaky breath.

"I admit," he said, "it took me longer than one look at dinner. It took me five or six looks. But then, I cannot see five trillion miles away."

Her heart was pounding heavily. "Mr. Shaughnessy."

"I'm a clever fellow," he went on. "I know I'm not your heart's desire. I'm too outrageous, too frivolous to be the sort of man you dream about."

She couldn't speak. She didn't dare tell him what she truly longed for. If she did, he'd use it against her.

Mrs. Barnstable, oblivious to this entire exchange, pulled the last page from her machine. "Miss Sweetly, I'm just running these down to Dr. Barnstable, if that's all right with you."

No. Rose needed to say *no*. She couldn't be alone with Mr. Shaughnessy, not even for so much as a minute. Especially not now.

"Of course, Mrs. Barnstable," she heard herself say.

"I know I'm not your heart's desire," he said again in a low voice as soon as Mrs. Barnstable had quitted the room, "but I can still give you yours."

She looked up. "What do you know of my heart's desire?"

Looking into his eyes was a mistake. He gave her a smile—not a low, cunning smile, or a clever smile that hinted at seduction. It was a warm, welcoming smile—the sort that made her think she had come home.

"I know what you want. It shows."

She wanted him, impossible rake that he was. She wanted him in love with her, faithful to her. Even she knew that was too much to ask.

"It shows?" she asked in a low voice.

"It does." He gave her a duck of his head. "Miss Sweetly, I beg of you—that you will accept from me this one thing."

Her heart pounded.

He stood. She looked wildly around the room—but with Mrs. Barnstable gone, there was no one to see. Nobody would see him coming toward her. Nobody would detect the look in his eye, that bright light that froze her in her seat.

He got on one knee before her. She couldn't think, couldn't imagine what to say or how to say it. He wouldn't really ask her to marry him—not now, *ever*, and even if he did, surely he wouldn't mean it. Men promised things to women like her all the time, and never meant a word they said.

But the thing he took from his pocket was not a ring. It was a bit of card stock, printed with a decorative border. He handed it to her; she took it. Stamped on the front were the words *Admit One*. Beneath that, there was only an address.

"What is this?" she asked in confusion.

"That?" He smiled smugly, as if he had just done something very clever. "That is your heart's desire, Miss Sweetly: a ticket to the best viewing in all of Greenwich of the transit of Venus. Courtesy of... Well, that would be *me*."

If anyone had asked Rose about the things she wanted, watching the transit of Venus would assuredly have been on her list. Not the first item there, nor the second...but high on the list nonetheless.

But it wasn't the thought of astronomy that had her breath catching in her lungs. It was that he'd obtained this as a present. It was the most thoughtful gift she'd ever received. And he'd been the one to think of it.

"It's a very exclusive viewing," he said, "from one of the highest points in Greenwich itself. There will be a great many steps up, and there won't be a fire in the viewing room for warmth, so take that into account when dressing."

There was one thing wrong with this. "People will talk if I arrive at an event like this with you."

"Ah." His eyes glittered. "It's a very exclusive gathering. I assure you, nobody will speak of you. Nobody at all. As for me? I promise not to importune you."

Watching the transit of Venus with a handful of people she didn't know would be interesting. Delightful, even. But her heart's desire, even if it was only for an afternoon...

...was to have him truly care for her. It might be temporary. It might be foolish. But if he'd gone to this length, she was more than a whim to him.

He's seducing you, she told herself.

Just this much, she pleaded in return. *Just this far, and after that, I'll venture no further.*

"Oh, very well," she said. But when she looked in his eyes, she couldn't stop from smiling.

Heavens, she was a fool.

∾

S HE WAS A FOOL, Rose told herself for the twentieth time in as many hours. She'd been arguing with herself ever since Mr. Shaughnessy had issued his invitation.

She'd argued with herself silently as she told her sister she'd be home the next day no later than four-thirty because she was observing an astronomical event. She had argued with herself all through her computations the next morning. She argued with herself now, at half past one, heading to the address on the card he had given her.

She knew what Mr. Shaughnessy was about; she knew better than to accept an invitation to any event with him, no matter how intellectually engaging it was. She really ought to have insisted on bringing a companion—why hadn't she thought of that earlier?

Oh. Because she was a fool.

But every time she told herself she was a fool, she also remembered what he'd said. *You do not dream timid dreams.*

The address he had given her was not so far from the Royal Observatory; it stood on that same high ground. She wondered, idly, if one of Dr. Barnstable's acquaintances would be present at this viewing party.

He'd promised people wouldn't talk, but how could he know? How could he stop them?

There was a part of her, scarcely buried, that dreamed that he was in love with her. Who thought that no matter how different they might seem in comparison with each other, they would get on well together. She could see them fitting into each other's lives so comfortably. He lived near the Royal Observatory; she could continue going in the mornings. In the afternoons, they might walk together, and he could tell her about his work for a change. And at nights…

That was where it all broke down. She could imagine their nights alone all too well. But whenever she tried to make herself imagine going out in company with him, she remembered who she was and how she'd be received.

You do not dream timid dreams.

She didn't *want* to dream timid dreams. She just knew the truth: She didn't belong in his sphere, and women like her were not invited to join men like him in matrimony. The only way she would have a man like him was if he did seduce her. They could deal with each other very well alone. It was only when she imagined...oh, anyone else at all around them that it all fell to pieces.

The address he had given her was situated on Crooms Hill. When she was almost there, she realized that he was not directing her to a rooftop viewing at a stately, private home; there was only one place high enough for viewing the transit of Venus.

That place was a church. Not just any church, but a Roman Catholic church—a place she had often passed but never entered. If he'd been invited to view the transit of Venus there, he must attend regularly—regularly enough that they'd know him.

Somehow, that thought seemed entirely incompatible with the Mr. Shaughnessy that she knew. The Mr. Shaughnessy she knew was outrageous. He took part in all sorts of immoral acts. He wrote columns that hinted at things that Patricia had refused to explain, and that she'd had to figure out as best as she could on her own. And that was nothing to the gossip that linked him to woman after woman.

It was impossible to think of him as a regular churchgoer.

And yet he'd invited her here. She came up to the graceful building roofed in slate and dressed in Caen stone. A tall spire wound its way up to the heavens, terminating in a cross.

Even Mr. Shaughnessy would not seduce her in a church.

Would he?

She was staring at the church in something like dismay when he came out the front doors and strode to her side. "There you are," he said.

"Here I am," she heard herself repeating. "You *did* promise not to importune me, didn't you?"

"Ah, but I'm sure you've already determined the loophole in that." He winked at her. "I never said anything about what you could do to me. Come along."

He did not take her into the chancel. She caught a glimpse of a marble statue of a lady, a gold-plated ship beside her, before he conducted her into a back way.

"Mr. Shaughnessy," she said, balking a little. "Where are we going?"

"Up the turret, of course," he said. "We're ascending the spire."

He stopped in front of a wooden door and took out a key ring.

"Where did you get that?"

The door swung open onto a dark, stone staircase.

"Father Wineheart," he said. "He likes me."

She had nothing to say to that. There was something odd about this, something dreadfully strange about that darkened staircase...

"Mr. Shaughnessy," she said, "do you mean to tell me that there is nobody else watching the transit of Venus with us? Nobody at all?"

He stopped, raising an eyebrow at her. "I did tell you it was very exclusive, and that nobody would talk."

She had thought he meant that the party was discreet. Maybe she hadn't let herself dwell on it overmuch. Maybe that had been purposeful. She *was* a fool. If she had thought more clearly, she would have known. And if she had known—even as foolish as she was being now —she wouldn't have come.

"Mr. Shaughnessy." She put her hands on her hips. "I had assumed there would be mixed company, that I wasn't going to be alone with you as the sun set. It would be horribly improper for me to follow you into...this."

He paused and looked at her. For a moment, his nose wrinkled. She wished she knew what he was thinking. She almost wanted him to charm her into compliance, to convince her to go up with him. She could imagine the whole thing unfolding. How *did* rakes make women lose their minds? Champagne? Madeira?

He'd offer her a glass. She would...

Drat it all. She would say no. But if she let this happen now—if she let him take her alone into a dark spire—she'd let it happen a second time, and then a third. Maybe the fourth time, she'd say yes to the Madeira. By the fifth time, it would be more. She knew how rakes seduced women, and she knew she was more than halfway there. She'd promised herself that she'd only go this far and no further...and if she didn't keep that promise now, she might as well give up and give in.

She swallowed hard and looked away. "I'm sorry. I'm truly sorry. But I can't go alone with you into a deserted turret."

"Aw, Rose."

No. He couldn't plead with her. He'd break her down.

"Not even for the transit of Venus," she said. Her voice broke.

But when she looked over at him, he wasn't looking at her beseechingly. He was looking at her with another expression on his face—one she couldn't understand.

She didn't want to let herself understand. "I'd better go." She turned to do just that.

"Wait. Rose."

Against her own better judgment, she stopped. She knew she shouldn't. She knew he'd make her laugh, that he'd put her at ease. He scarcely had to convince her at all; she wanted to be convinced so desperately.

He took a step toward her, and then another, standing so close that he might have set his fingers on her chin. She could feel herself opening to him, her eyes shining up at him. He could kiss her right here, in view of the chancel, and she might let him.

But he didn't. Instead, he pitched his voice low. "Do you think I would do that to you?"

"I don't think you'd have to try too hard." Already she was trying to persuade herself without any effort on his part at all. She had only to keep quiet, to keep her distance. She might watch the transit; then she'd go down the stairs, and nobody would ever be the wiser. If she never did it again...

No. That sort of thinking was precisely how girls like her ended up ruined.

His gaze slipped to her lips. "That isn't what I meant." He inhaled sharply, and then held out the key ring. "Right, then. The door to the spire is opened by this little key here, the copper one."

She blinked at him in confusion.

"You've got twelve minutes until the transit starts. There's a great many stairs, but if you hurry, they shouldn't prove to be much problem. There's an excellent view of the river once you get to the turret."

She shook her head. "What are you saying?"

"This is a rare astronomical event," he told her. "It won't happen again until the year 2004. Do you really think I would let you miss it? If you can't go with me, go by yourself." He leaned against the wall. "I'll wait here. I need to get the keys back to Father Wineheart when you're finished."

"You're really not going to come?"

"Did I not just say that? Go. Hurry. You don't want to miss it."

He gave her a wave of his hands, urging her through the door onto the dark staircase. She started up. The stair was cold and just a little musty, but she couldn't think of that.

She had come, expecting him to wear down her every defense—and hoping, almost, that he might succeed.

And…he hadn't even tried. No jokes. He'd taken no little jabs at her when she'd balked. He'd just handed her the keys and told her to go. He hadn't tried to wheedle or charm her, and if he'd made even the slightest effort, he could have brought her around. She knew it all too well. And Mr. Shaughnessy, Actual Man, expert that he was with the human female, must have known it, too.

It was almost as if he cared what she wanted. She came to the topmost landing on the stair turret. Her calves were already a little warm from the exertion; the air around her had become colder. She could see out the little rectangular window, down onto the river, over to a sun dipping lazily in the sky. Clouds far away over London threatened, but they'd not be here in time to block her view. She took the key ring out, found the copper key, and put it reluctantly in the door that led to the spire.

Eight minutes until the transit started. Eight minutes until she stood, watching it alone, with her heart still back down the stone stairs.

Rose inhaled. And then—stupidly—she started back down the stairs, slowly at first, and then faster and faster, until her shoes pattered heavily against the stairs, taking them two and then three at a time. When she reached the final landing, she was going so fast that her feet skittered against the smooth stone. She held up her hands to stop from slamming into a wall, and then she pushed off once again.

She went out the little wooden door. He was sitting on a bench nearby. He had a little book out and he was reading.

"Stephen." She'd never called him by his Christian name before, and hadn't intended to do so now. It had simply slipped out.

He looked up. She hadn't understood herself why she'd come back. Not until she saw his face. He caught sight of her. His eyes widened and he burst into a smile, a lovely, brilliant smile that seemed to cast light throughout the darkening corridor. She felt an answering smile spread shyly across her face.

"Rose," he said. "What are you still doing here? There's a transit about to start."

"I can't watch it without you," she said. "I won't enjoy it."

He looked at her.

"Come now," she said. "Hurry. If I miss this because of you…"

He stood. And then, very slowly, with a broadening smile, he came toward her.

CHAPTER FIVE

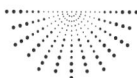

R OSE WAS SWIFT. She had a head start on Stephen, darting up
the stairs. By the time he'd entered the stair turret, he saw
only a swirl of pink skirts as she turned, already on the
landing ahead of him. He followed after, his mind a maelstrom of
confusion.

She stopped halfway up the next short flight of stairs and turned
to him. Her eyes were shining from the exercise—and then she
reached back to him, holding out her hand.

"Well?" she said. "Come along."

He stopped dead. For a moment, he wasn't sure what she intended.
Slowly, he climbed the steps that separated them until he stood just
below her. That brought him on eye-level with her.

He held out his hand, palm up.

She took it, folding it in her own. "Hurry up," she said.

Then she took off again. He was jogging up the stairs beside her,
hand in hand. She had a smile on her face. Her fingers squeezed his,
and he squeezed them back.

They came to the top of the turret. She fumbled the keys out,
unlocking the final door. There were no easy stairs up the spire.
Instead, a wooden ladder sat at the base, climbing to a final platform.

"Climb quickly," she told him.

He did. He could feel her on the ladder behind him even though he couldn't see her—feel her in the vibration of the ladder, sense her in his tingling nerves.

He came to the top, pulled himself onto the platform, and crouched down and held out his hand. She took it, and he helped her up.

There were two windows in the spire. One faced northeast; the other—the one he'd spent all morning setting the apparatus up in—faced south and west. She dropped his hand, inhaling, going to that one.

"Mr. Shaughnessy." Her voice shook. "Did you do this?"

He'd had to talk with Barnstable about how to manage it.

"Well. Yes. I did."

One couldn't look at the sun directly, not without risking damage to the eyes. But with the proper telescope lens, it was no difficulty at all.

"You've mounted an entire theodolite telescope in the window. How did you get…" She shook her head in wonder. "No, never mind that. I can tell how. No one who owned a theodolite telescope would willingly loan it to you, not with the transit today. Never say you bought it just for this."

"As you wish." He smiled. "I won't tell you that I bought it. But…"

She shook her head. "And were no doubt charged treble in light of the transit." She reached out and touched the base lightly, almost reverently.

"Do you have a telescope, Miss Sweetly?"

"No." Her voice was low and reverent. "I don't."

"Well, then. Do you want one?"

"Yes, Mr. Shaughnessy." She bent over it, set her eye to the eyepiece. "I want one very much. But we both know you cannot make a present of this to me. It is too dear."

"Then I won't."

"It seems an extravagant purchase on your part," she said.

He'd had years of scrimping and saving before he'd come to

prominence; it was not in his nature to make pointless expenditures. But when the shopkeeper had quoted him the cost of the telescope, he hadn't even blinked.

She was enraptured. The light from the window illuminated her figure, casting a golden glow all around.

"It was worth it," he told her. He would have purchased a score of telescopes just to see the look on her face now.

"But to buy such a thing for a single use… I suppose you can sell it." She trailed her fingers longingly down the tube.

He'd never intended the use to be singular. She adjusted the inclination, her head bent like a woman in prayer.

One day. One day, he hoped she'd look at him with half that amount of emotion, that wonder. One day he'd make her feel just a little breathless.

Today, though…

"I don't understand you," she said, still peering into the telescope. "Surely after going through all the trouble and expense of setting this up, you expected some return on your investment."

"Oh, I have it already," he said nonchalantly.

She glanced up at him.

"I told you," he said. "I just want to give you your heart's desire." Their eyes met, the moment stretching.

She looked back down with a shake of her head. "It must be about time."

He didn't speak. He could see her excitement in the tap of her gloved fingers against the scope, in her breath catching. "It's starting," she said.

Somewhere, a clock tolled the two o'clock hour.

"Come here." She gestured to him.

"I don't want to take your time…"

She made an impatient noise. "It will never again happen in our lives, and you don't want to see it? Don't be ridiculous."

The telescope, fitted with a solar filter, showed the image of the sun clearly—a bright disc the size of a sixpence. A dark spot, the merest speck, had just broached the edge.

He'd never stood so close to her. He could smell the sweet fragrance of rosewater, of something else he couldn't identify, something enticing and lovely. Her shoulder brushed his. If he turned to her now…

He'd distract her, and she'd never forgive him. "How long will this last?"

"Until the sun sets just after four or the clouds intervene."

"Well. Then maybe we can take turns." He gestured her back to the telescope.

She took her place once more. But after a few moments of staring into the eyepiece, she spoke again. "However did you convince Father Wineheart to let you set this whole thing up?"

"He likes me," Stephen said. "Even though he hears my confessions —which I must admit are shocking—he likes me."

"That's not what I meant. Why did he agree?"

"The same reason that Barnstable did. I told him I was writing a book about an astronomer, that I needed a little experience." Stephen shrugged.

She straightened and glanced at him. "When are you going to tell him that you were using that as an excuse to try and seduce a woman? I would not think that a man of the cloth, no matter what his denomination, would acquiesce in such a scheme." Her words were severe, but her tone was light and teasing.

"I told you already. I'm not trying to seduce you." But he couldn't help but smile. "If it happens, it will be a happy side-effect."

She raised an eyebrow.

"But he'll find out when he hears my next confession."

She shook her head, and leaned down once more. "I can't do what you do, you know."

"What do I do?"

She waved a hand—a very general hand-motion that he decoded as *I don't want to say, and I'd be obliged if you inferred it without any more effort on my part.*

"Do you mean that you couldn't write novels?"

She snorted.

"That you couldn't write my columns? You're right, Miss Sweetly. I think you're a little too earnest for them."

"No. You know that's not what I mean. I mean, how do you…do the things you do with women and not fall in love?"

"Ah."

He pushed away from her and looked out the window. The sun was a dusky gold; with his naked eye, he could see no hint that anything extraordinary was taking place.

"That's easy enough to answer. The first time, I did."

She did look up from the telescope at that.

"I was nineteen, which according to some, is rather late to start on such matters. But I'd been concentrating on my studies, and, well…" He shrugged. "I had just started writing for the *Women's Free Press,* and there was some gala event that I was invited to. I met this woman. She was ten years my elder, widowed, and absolutely lovely. I was charmed, delighted, seduced, and I promptly fell head over ears in love." He put his hands in his pockets. "I think it took me a week to propose marriage. She kissed me on the cheek and laughed at me. You see, I was not the sort of man that a woman like her would marry. And she told me why in great detail. I hadn't any money, any station. I was Irish and Catholic. I was too young and far too radical. Women would adore me, she said—and I could offer them a great deal—but I shouldn't expect to marry them."

She did not look up from the telescope. "Mr. Shaughnessy," she said slowly, "that sounds suspiciously like a hidden depth."

He let out a gasp. "You're right. It is!" She wasn't looking at him, but still he played it for all it was worth, setting a hand over his breast. "I *do* have a secret trauma—my many prior love affairs. There can be no sharper pain then to make love to a vast number of women—but I have masterfully accepted it as my due. I soldier on under the burden."

She shook her head. "Are you ever serious?"

"I suppose some other man might have been wounded by that. But I'm like a cashmere jumper: comfortable, soft, and as fabric goes, not much given to wrinkling."

"No wrinkles? Not over even one of them?"

"Aside from the obvious, it was all to my advantage. If one wishes to be a grand, outrageous name in society, one must do a few grand, outrageous things. Absinthe is too dangerous; gambling is too expensive. Opium is a dreadful habit—one has only to look at those in an opium den to know the effect. No; if I was going to be an outrage, I wanted the safest, least expensive vice I could find. So women it was."

Rose inhaled. "Are you telling me that you seduce women as a calculation?"

"It's been mutual. And I don't seduce women—at least not the way you mean it. The Countess of Howder wanted an affair with me to let everyone know she was out of mourning and didn't intend to be a pattern card of propriety. I'm an outrage, and the women who are so placed as to wish to be outrageous, well…" He shrugged. "And besides, I *like* women. I like them a great deal."

She straightened. But instead of upbraiding him, as he'd expected, she gestured to the telescope. "Come take a look."

He did. It was unnerving to not be able to see her—not after what he'd confessed. The dark spot had begun to traverse the sun's disc.

"Aren't there dangers in using women that way?"

"There are. There are also ways to minimize those dangers. Technically, they're also forbidden to me, but…"

A longer pause. "Do you confess those ways to Father Wineheart as well?"

"I confess all my sins."

He could hear her behind him, but with his eye on the disc of the sun, he could not see her. He had no idea if she was outraged or interested, if he'd disgusted her forever or set her mind at ease.

"I can't imagine that. You tell all these salacious details to Father Wineheart, and in turn, he lets you put a telescope in the spire."

"I only moved to this parish three months ago, Rose." He shrugged. "I met you almost the first day I was here. I've had nothing to confess since that moment."

She inhaled behind him, sounding almost shocked. "Nothing at all?"

"Nothing but lust, which he rather expects from a man my age." He straightened, gesturing her back to the telescope. "You'd better take it back, Rose. The clouds are coming in—I'd hate to have you miss anything."

She held his eyes for a long moment. He didn't know what she was seeing, didn't know what she was thinking. She bent back down.

She had to adjust the telescope yet again to track the sun in its descent. She didn't say anything for a while, but he could see her hands nervously tapping against the optical tube. Her breath was uneven.

"Tell me, Mr. Shaughnessy. Is that what you had hoped for from me? To…" She stopped briefly, swallowing, and then continued. "To seduce me and then not fall in love?"

"No," he told her. "I'm tired of having to remind myself that the women who are after me wish only an experience or a reputation and not a lifetime. I'm tired of holding myself back. I'm tired of having to flatten all but the barest hint of affection."

Her breath caught.

"I'm tired," he said, "of not letting myself fall in love."

She didn't say anything for a long time. "They're idiots," she finally said. "Complete idiots, the lot of them."

"No," he replied. "They aren't. I don't tend to hold idiots in affection."

"No?"

"Of course not," he said. "Why do you think I like you best of everyone?"

She didn't say anything. He could see the clouds coming closer now, dark swells creeping across the sky.

"I am not outrageous." Her voice was small. "I don't wish to be outrageous."

"I know," he said. "And I've forgotten how to be anything but the most flagrantly outrageous man ever."

She drew in a breath. "This was supposed to be the last time I saw you."

"It's the only sensible thing to do. We sound like the most ridiculous match; I know we do. But I can't help but think, Rose, that if we could get over this awkward beginning bit—if we could just get to the part where you tell me about mathematics over breakfast and I buy you telescopes and we spend half the evening kissing—"

She made an annoyed noise.

"Too much? A quarter of the evening kissing?" he amended.

"No." She straightened from the telescope. "The sun's gone behind the clouds." She glanced at him. "We've lost it for now. Maybe the weather will clear up." She glared out over the city.

He didn't put the chances high. The clouds had gone even darker; they stretched as far as he could see. She rubbed her gloved hands together briskly, and he realized that she was almost certainly cold.

He was, too—his hands and feet were uncomfortably chilled. He just hadn't noticed, because…he'd been watching her. Hell, he'd been spilling his heart out to her, such as he did these things. He'd just told her he hoped to marry her, and he wasn't even sure if she had noticed.

"An eighth of the evening kissing?" He looked over at her. "I can go lower if necessary."

She shut her eyes. "Stephen." That single word, long and drawn out. It was neither yes nor no; he wasn't sure what it was.

"Every time I'm with you," she said, "I tell myself I must beware. That this is what you do—make women comfortable, make us forget ourselves, principle by principle." She rubbed her forehead and slowly opened her eyes. The light in the spire was waning even as she spoke, and yet for some reason, it seemed to find her, glinting in her eyes, reflecting off the warm brown of her skin. It caught a faint tilted smile on her mouth.

"So why is it," she said, "that I have just now noticed that you've only ever come to me about me? You've asked about my work, my thoughts, my wants. You set this up for me, and when I balked, you handed me the keys and walked away. If you wanted me to forget myself, you wouldn't keep reminding me of who I am."

"Rose, love," he said in a low voice, "I think you know why that is."

She inhaled and spread her hands against her belly. Then, very slowly, she walked closer to him—close enough that her skirts touched his trousers, close enough that he could have drawn her to him. She swallowed; he could have set his fingers against the hollow of her throat and felt the movement, so close was she.

She looked up into his eyes. "I don't want to dream timid dreams." Her voice was soft, with just a hint of a catch in it. "I want to dream large, vivid ones. I want to dream that you'll fall in love with me. That..." She bit her lip, but continued on. "That I could dare to reach out to you, that I needn't fear what would come."

She lifted her hand tentatively. He had thought that she might brush his cheek. But she didn't. Instead, she took his hand. They were both wearing gloves; he should not have felt a thrill at the brush of cloth on cloth. But he did, and it swept him from head down to toe, settling particularly in his groin, warming him in the cold air.

"But I do fear." Her hand clasped his. "You're clever and never off balance around others. You're handsome and sweet and outrageous. You could hurt me so badly, and I'm afraid to let you do it."

He swept his thumb along the side of her hand. "Sweetheart, if you don't trust me yet, there's no assurance I can give you that will put your mind at ease. All I can do is keep on not hurting you, and keep on, until you know in your bones I never will."

Their fingers intertwined, their hands coming together, palm to palm. He was enchanted, enraptured. She let out a long slow breath and slowly reached out with her other hand. This one she set on his shoulder. His skin prickled through his coat, his whole body tensing with her nearness. She drew a finger down his collarbone and then laid her palm flat against his chest.

He couldn't move.

"I trust you." Her voice was low, so low. "God knows I shouldn't—but I trust you."

She stepped even closer, skimming her hand down his arm, his elbow, and then bringing it back up to his shoulder. She took another step in, now, bringing her body even closer to his, warming the channel of air between them. He could feel the heat of her breath, the tension in her hand against his chest.

"Truthfully?" Stephen leaned down to whisper in her ear. "I can't pretend I'm fit for a decent woman—but if the question is whether I'll hurt you? No, Rose. Never. I adore you."

She took another step in, ducking her head as she did so, as if she did not want to look into his eyes. But her hand slid around his shoulder, drawing him full-length against her body.

Cold? It wasn't cold in the spire. How silly of him to think it had been. The air seemed almost hot around them. His whole body was coming to life with her against him. He put his arm around her—it seemed fair game, as she was pressing against him, and it was either that or hold it out awkwardly to the side. But she didn't protest at all. Instead, she set her forehead against his chest. Her hand slid down his back; his arm came around her shoulder.

She lifted her head. They were both breathing heavily.

"I don't think I should have touched you," she said shakily. "It's—it's…"

"It's nice." His own voice came out like gravel.

"It's too nice."

"It gets nicer."

She leaned against him. "How is that even possible?"

"Ah, well. I promised not to importune you, or you'd discover it. If I hadn't, this might be a little less chaste."

"Chaste?" She let out a shaky breath. "This isn't chaste. It's utterly wanton."

"On a scale of wantonness that ranges from…" He paused, trying to think of a suitable analogy. "From multiplication to astronomical parallaxes," he said, "embracing someone you care about while fully clothed ranks at about the arctangent level."

"Oh, dear. And I'm already so overheated."

A wave of his own heat washed over him at that, and he groaned, pulling her closer. "God, sweetheart. You're killing me."

She reached up tentatively, and set her fingers against his cheek. He stilled.

"May I slay you further?" she whispered.

"By all means," he replied, unable to move. "Kill me now."

His breath stopped. He couldn't do anything but watch her. She stood in place, her hands on him unmoving, as if gathering up the courage to move forward. Then slowly, very slowly, she came up on her toes. Her weight shifted; he could feel her hand against his jaw, her other hand against his chest, pressing all the harder.

Then her lips brushed his. She was kissing him—lightly at first, just sliding her lips against his, then pressing with greater firmness. He set his hand against the base of her spine and kissed her back.

There was nothing else, nothing but her, the weight of her in his arms, the warmth of her breath, the softness of her mouth.

"Rose," he said against her lips. "God, Rose." He shifted so that he could gather her up, so that the curves of her body slid against him.

She must have been able to feel his erection pressing against her, must have felt the tension in his arms as he held her close.

Usually at this point for Stephen, matters would have easily, swiftly progressed beyond a mere chaste close-mouthed kiss. But he'd promised Rose not to importune her—and no matter how urgently his body responded, there was something delicious about the slowness of the pace. He reveled in the sure knowledge that this would not be the last and only time he tasted her. He could slow everything down, enjoy the electric build-up of desire, delight in every gasp she gave.

"Have I earned a quarter of your evening yet, Miss Sweetly?" he murmured against her lips.

"I don't know." Her voice still had a quaver. "I need a little time to decide."

She kissed him again. He could have fallen into a trance, kissing her. Feeling her lips against his, awakening her first ardor with brush after brush of the lips. He wasn't sure when the kiss deepened, when he began taking her lips in his, when he first slid his tongue along her bottom lip. She responded with all the enthusiasm he'd ever hoped for, her tongue meeting his, tentatively at first, and then more boldly. He was lost in the feel of her. The space was close about them, warming to the point that the nearest window fogged over with condensation.

He wiped it clean, verified the clouds were still out in force—and then began kissing her again.

At some point, he simply lost his mind. Her hands had begun to roam and his had, too, cupping her breasts—which fit, so nicely rounded, in his palm. A kiss was one thing; running his thumb along the neckline of her gown, undoing buttons halfway down her bosom, sliding it down and then leaning over and nibbling... That was another thing entirely. A lovely, delicious, wonderful thing. She tasted faintly sweet.

Maybe that was his imagination. Maybe he only thought so because she was making the most captivating noises, little moans in the back of her throat halfway to purrs. He let his other hand drift down, cupping the juncture of her thighs over her skirts.

She made no noise of protest, not when he pushed harder, not when he pressed the ball of his hand against her, rubbing in a slow circle. He took his time about it, easing off and then coming back harder, pulling away and then returning, until she was almost as desperate as he was, until her hips were pressing against his hand, until she came apart against him. He felt her orgasm shudder through her, her limbs trembling. It was an almost electric sensation for him, too, watching her eyes flutter shut, watching her give herself up to him.

Her breath slowed after. She opened her eyes, looked up at him.

"Half the evening, do you think?" He gave her a long, slow smile.

That was when he realized that darkness had fallen while they'd been kissing. From the window, he could see a few beginning flurries falling to the ground, scarcely visible in the lamplight from the street below. He had no idea how long they'd been engaged in such pleasantries.

"Rose?" he said. "Are you...?" But he didn't know what to say beyond that. *Are you in love with me?* seemed too soon. The other words he burned to say—*touch me here, do that to me*—were too brazen. She was still dazed, unsure of herself, and slightly unsteady on her feet.

She still hadn't said anything.

161

"Right, then." He touched his thumb to her forehead, sliding it down the bridge of her nose. "Well. That settles that."

"Settles what?" They were the first words she'd spoken in God knew how long. He couldn't decipher the tone of her voice.

"We need more astronomical events," he said. "Because I am not waiting until the year 2004 to do this again."

CHAPTER SIX

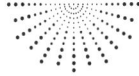

H E KNEW IT WAS A MISTAKE as soon as the words were out of his mouth. As soon as he heard himself and realized that it sounded like an invitation to tryst with him, rather than an offer to spend her life with him. She straightened, pulling away from him.

"Rose." He reached for her.

She brushed his hand away. "Don't. Please don't."

"Rose. I'm sorry. It was a joke."

"I know it was a joke." Her voice shook. "Of course it was a joke. It's always a joke to you."

She grabbed her cloak from the floor, found her gloves in the growing darkness.

"Rose."

Had he not been able to decipher her voice before? He'd not been listening hard enough. Now, now that he'd opened his mouth a moment too soon and spoken just a little too much... Now, he could hear the hurt in her tone.

"Rose. Sweetheart. I never meant to hurt you. You know that. You must know that."

She pulled on her gloves. "I know that. Stephen, I..." Her voice dropped. "You must know how I feel about you. But I don't think you understand. This isn't easy for me, and you aren't making it any easier. I want to trust you. I am trying to trust you. I even trust your intentions." Her voice dropped. "I don't trust your results."

"Rose."

She shook her head. "It's late. I promised my sister I'd be home just after four, and who knows now what time it is. I have to go."

"Rose."

"Thank you." She swallowed. "For bringing me here and arranging for a telescope."

"At least let me accompany you—"

"I think you've spent enough time with me at the moment. Please, Stephen. I told myself I wouldn't—and look at me. I need to think."

He rocked back, feeling as if he'd been punched. But he bit back his sharp reply. He'd hurt her first, after all. He'd talk to her when the sting of his ill-timed words had died down, when he was feeling more like himself—less vulnerable and more in control.

She swung down the ladder. He could scarcely see her descending into the gloom.

"Be careful," he called after her in a low voice.

She didn't say anything in response, not for a long while. But he heard her reach the top of the turret. She didn't move for a long time. He wondered if she was looking up at him, if she could see him in the gathering darkness. He wondered what she was thinking.

"I should have been careful hours ago," she said. "It's rather late for that."

≈

THE HOUSE WAS NOT DARK when Rose returned; the lamps on the bottom floor were all lit. Rose could see a silhouette moving against the front window.

She thought back uneasily to the last toll of the clock. It was now… who knew how long after six?

The door was not locked. Her stomach hurt as she turned the

handle, but it swung open on easy hinges and she walked into the light.

"*Now.*" Patricia's voice was hoarse and ragged.

It took Rose a moment, standing there blinking in the blinding light, to understand that her sister was not talking to her. Patricia sat on the sofa in a robe. Her hands were on her knees; she grimaced as she spoke, her whole body tensing.

Doctor Chillingsworth sat on a chair before her, looking at a watch.

Rose could see the tension in her sister's face, the grit of her teeth, the faint sheen of sweat at her temples. Rose stood in place, unsure of what she was observing.

The doctor, however, raised an unimpressed eyebrow. "Really, Mrs. Wells," he said reprovingly. "Do you really think that you can falsify a contraction and convince me?"

Patricia's hands gripped her knees. "Falsify? I wouldn't lie about such a thing."

Chillingsworth met this with a wave of his hand. "Exaggerate, then. The too-prominent grinding of teeth, the low noise in your throat—Mrs. Wells, you are a doctor's wife. It does not behoove you to behave in this fashion." Chillingsworth stood. "There is no cervical dilation; the, ah, *contractions,* as you call them, do not seem particularly intense. And the baby still has not turned. You've at least three weeks remaining by my estimation. This is false labor once again, Mrs. Wells. Try to sleep, and do make an effort not to bother me with trivialities until it is truly your time."

Patricia's face was a mask. Rose stepped forward, all the heat rising to her face. "Doctor Chillingsworth, my sister does *not—*"

Patricia interrupted this defense with a swift shake of her head. "Thank you for seeing me, doctor. I'm much obliged to you for putting my fears to rest. Now that you've explained what I must look for, I shall be sure not to bother you again until it is time."

"See that you don't." Chillingsworth ran a hand through his hair and glanced at his pocket watch once more. "Right in the middle of dinner," he muttered. He dropped the gold disc into his waistcoat pocket and gathered up his bag.

Patricia did not say anything until after he had left. For that matter, she didn't say anything immediately then. She simply sat on the sofa looking at Rose, while Rose stood in place, afraid to speak.

"I've been frantic," Patricia finally said. "Waiting for you to come home. I was afraid something had happened to you. I looked all over —up and down—I went to the Observatory myself, and they told me you weren't there. I was so frantic, and then I thought my contractions were starting."

It didn't matter what Stephen's intentions were. It didn't matter what he wanted. It didn't matter how sweet or how gentle he had been. It didn't even matter how much she loved him, how much she still yearned to run back to the spire and fall into his arms.

He hadn't made her forget herself; she'd just forgotten her sister.

Rose came in and sat on the chair Chillingsworth had vacated. "I'm so sorry, Patricia. But the transit of Venus…"

"Would not have been visible after sunset," Patricia said. "Or with the clouds that rolled in. I *do* listen to you. What were you doing?"

"I know it looks bad, but—"

"It *is* bad. I'm responsible for you, and you disappeared out from under my nose. Being out past sunset—that does not look good, Rose. Please tell me that you were with Dr. and Mrs. Barnstable the whole time, celebrating…whatever it is that astronomers celebrate."

Rose swallowed. "Um."

"Please tell me that Mr. Shaughnessy was not with you."

Oh, she could see it now. Patricia was right. It didn't just *look* bad. It was bad. What was she to do, lie to her sister for the rest of her life? Tell her she was marrying a man who would carry on in such a fashion? Their father had scraped and worked so hard to achieve even the barest measure of gentility. Was she to give it up so easily?

Rose examined her knuckles. "Did I…" She swallowed. "Did I not mention that I've been tutoring him in the methods of calculating astronomical distances?"

Patricia's eyes grew wide. "No. You know very well you did not mention any such thing."

"He may have set up a telescope in the church spire. So I could observe the transit."

"Together?"

Rose nodded.

"Alone?"

Another nod. Rose felt her cheeks burn in mortification.

"Did he hurt you?" Patricia demanded.

"No. He wouldn't." Not the way Patricia meant it anyway. "And don't look at me like that—I don't know what you must think of him, but he wouldn't hurt me." He would tell her that she was beautiful and brilliant. He would say that he liked her. But in the end, it would always come down to this—that if anyone found out that he was pursuing her, they would instantly think the worst.

"Oh, Rose. What am I to do with you?"

"How should I know?" Rose asked bitterly. "*I* don't know what to do with me, either."

Patricia didn't hesitate. She held out her hands. Rose stood, going to her, wrapping her arms around her.

"Sometimes," Rose said, "I can make myself remember that we live in two different worlds—he in his, and me in mine. Other times, I think that we live in the same place—one world, so much better because he's in it. I think I could fall in love with him, if only I dared." She swallowed. "But I can only dare to do so many things at a time." Her voice was thick. "And now, daring to do this one... I left you."

"Oh, Rose. You mustn't worry about me."

So like Patricia, to insist she needed nothing for herself.

"How can I not? I promised Doctor Wells I'd be here for you, and I wasn't."

"Shh. You're here now. And I do understand. Hypothetically speaking, I might have been willing to sneak out at night to see Isaac, when I was your age."

Rose smiled wanly. "Why, Patricia. We *are* speaking hypothetically, are we?"

"Oh, shh. Then say it's realistically speaking, too. Just…don't meet a man alone at night unless you're sure he'll marry you."

Rose sighed.

"And, ah, even then… Don't let things go too far."

"Whatever do you mean by that?" Rose asked innocently.

Too innocently, apparently, because Patricia gave her shoulder a slap. "Hussy. You're not that naïve. If you feel like falling asleep afterward, you've done too much."

"Oh, dear. I feel like falling asleep now," Rose told her, shutting her eyes.

"Cuddling with your sister doesn't count," Patricia said severely. "*I* don't have designs on your virtue. All I ever want to do at this point is sleep. Use the chamber pot and sleep."

"How indelicate."

"Anyone who thinks that ladies are delicate has either never been pregnant or has put the experience from her mind out of sheer horror."

Rose snorted. For a long while, they did not say anything. Rose held her sister's hands, her head resting against her shoulder. She could almost pretend that they were still young, that she was a child and Patricia not much older, that she was once again falling asleep to the sound of her sister's heartbeat.

But they weren't. Rose was twenty. Her sister was pregnant, and she had to take care of her. She had not thought anything would ever make her forget that…but then she'd underestimated Stephen Shaughnessy for too long.

He made her think this would all be easy—that all she had to do was love him and then all her problems would disappear. They wouldn't, though. They would multiply: his problems with hers. All he could do was what he'd managed tonight: He could make Rose forget herself long enough for real danger to threaten.

Rose buried her head in her sister's shoulder. "I'm sorry," she said. "I'll never leave you to worry like that again. I promise."

"I know."

After a long while, Patricia's hands squeezed her shoulders—not hard, but long—five seconds, then ten. Rose turned and looked at her. Her sister's breath came ragged; her jaw squared. Eventually, though, Patricia relaxed and glanced at the clock. "Forty-seven minutes," she said calmly. "They were forty-seven minutes apart."

"You had another contraction?" Rose sat up even straighter. "We should go get—"

Patricia shook her head. "False contractions, remember? Doctor Chillingsworth was just here."

"But—"

"Even if they are real," Patricia said, "which I doubt—they're still forty-seven minutes apart. They'll have to come much faster before it's time. We can fetch him then."

CHAPTER SEVEN

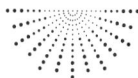

R OSE HAD EXPECTED TO SEE Mr. Shaughnessy on her walk
into the observatory the next morning, but she did not
encounter him. She wondered all day if he might come by,
asking for another lesson—an excuse, of course, but she'd not have
expected him to balk at inventing an excuse to see her—but every
time the door opened, it was not him.

She was beginning to think that her worst fears had been right—
that all he'd ever intended was a seduction, that he'd never wanted
anything more—when she encountered him on her way home. She
saw him, his scarf flapping in the wind, his hands in his pockets. He
paced along the pavement, his face solemn. She did not know what to
say to him.

He caught sight of her and gave a little shake of his head—not
denial; by the tension that seemed to leave him, it rather looked like
relief.

He came up to her. "Rose." His voice was low. "Before you send me
on my way, let me be as clear as I can be. I love you. I have loved you
for months, and I don't wish to do without you. I want to marry you. I
want to buy you telescopes. I want you to have my babies. I want you,
Rose. You and only you."

Oh, how it hurt to hear those words. She had suspected they must be true, even if part of her hadn't been able to make herself believe it.

"I love you," he said. "I didn't say it directly last night, and I ought to have. I love you. Marry me."

"Listen to you." She gave him a sad smile. "Have you given any thought at all to what this would mean? Given your reputation, it will be a terrible scandal if—when—you marry. Everyone will assume the worst of me."

"At first. It will blow over, though," he said confidently.

"Stephen. *Think.* Have you considered what it would mean for us to have children together?"

His eyes softened. "At length."

"No, you beast. I don't mean the begetting of them. Have you thought about what it would mean to have black, Irish, Catholic children?"

He blinked, slowly, and frowned. He really hadn't thought about it.

"You told me the awkward, difficult bit will only be the beginning," she said. "But it won't be. It'll be difficult in the middle, over and over. It'll be difficult at the end. It will never *stop* being difficult, and the only reason you don't know that is that you haven't considered the possibility. At some point, Stephen, you'll realize this is not a joking matter."

He spread his hands. "Maybe. But I'm not a worrier, Rose. It's not in my nature to fret about the future. Things happen as they do."

"Yes, and four years in, you'll realize what you've landed yourself in. You'll discover that it's not all kisses and telescopes. I give you credit for good intentions, Mr. Shaughnessy—but I don't think you're serious."

He spread his hands. "I'm not grave and sober, Rose. But I *am* serious about you. I know who I am and how I feel—and I'm not going to walk away from you simply because things may prove difficult. I don't worry about the future not because I'm blind to it, but because I don't see the point."

"Don't see the point! How can you want me if you don't even bother to think about what marriage to me would entail?" Her hands were shaking. "How can you say you love me and want to marry me, when you haven't even considered what that would mean?"

"At least I've said it," he snapped. "You haven't said what you mean at all, and I wish that you would. It's not that you think it will prove too difficult for *me*. You think it will be too difficult for *you*."

"My life is going to be difficult no matter who I marry." She raised her chin. "That's why I need to find someone who takes it seriously."

He leaned down to her. "There. Now you're saying what you mean. Finally. If you want a man who takes things seriously, you don't want me."

She opened her mouth to deny it…and then shut it. Her heart was breaking. She *did* want him. She wanted his laughter, his terrible jokes about mathematics. She wanted him handing her the key to the spire and telling her to go up alone. She wanted his practiced hands on her, coaxing her, seducing her, while he murmured in her ear. She wanted everything about him except…him.

"You don't make me forget myself." She shut her eyes. "But you make me forget who I have to be. You don't need an anvil, Stephen. You *are* the anvil. And you're right; I can't marry you."

His lips thinned. He looked at her, his eyes wild and fierce. And then he turned his head away and shrugged. "So be it. I'm an amusing fellow with no hidden depths. There's always some reason why I'm not suitable. I won't fret over it." He straightened, casting her a look. "I never do."

"Stephen…"

He shook his head. "Tell me if you change your mind, Rose. I won't alter mine. I may be frivolous—but I'm not faithless, and I'm not fickle."

"Stephen."

She didn't know what to say beyond that. She reached out and took his hand in hers. She couldn't bring herself to say words, didn't know what she could say even so. She just squeezed his fingers, not wanting to let go. Not being able to hold on.

"Be careful, Rose," he said with a nod of his head. And then he was drawing his hand away.

His thumb brushed hers briefly—but it was as temporary a warmth as his presence in her life. He smiled at her. "If you see me about," he said, "do talk Sweetly to me." And on that, he touched his hat and left.

~

ROSE SHUT THE DOOR behind her. Her hands were shaking; she felt sick to her stomach. But she had done it. She'd cut ties with Stephen Shaughnessy—and she'd survived it. She looked about the entry and frowned.

The house was dark. The sun had not yet set, but it was close enough to evening that a few lights ought to have been on. There were no lights in the front room, the dining room, the back pantry.

She frowned and tentatively called out. "Patricia?"

A door opened upstairs. A few moments later, Mrs. Josephs put her head over the railing.

"Your sister is not feeling so well, Miss Sweetly."

Rose frowned. "Has she seen the doctor?"

"Not since last night," the older woman said. "She says it's just more of that false labor again. She doesn't want to bother him."

Rose felt a pit of foreboding open in her stomach. "Didn't he say that false labor pains are supposed to stop? How can she be sure that it's false labor, and not something else?"

Mrs. Josephs shook her head. "I've never been blessed with a child, Miss. Really, I don't know a thing about it."

Rose shook her head and then carefully ascended the stairs. Her sister's room was dark, but Patricia was not in bed. She was walking a figure eight pattern on the carpet.

"Rose." Patricia looked up as her door opened. "You're back. Don't worry about me; I'll feel well soon enough. In fact, I don't feel so badly now." She managed a creditable smile.

"Should you lie down?"

"I feel better walking."

"What's wrong?"

"Nothing really," Patricia said. "Just more of those false labor pains, that's all. And they're not coming particularly swiftly—they're still only twenty-three minutes apart."

Rose felt cold fingers clutch her heart. "You're still having labor pains? They've gone on all day? They're coming closer together?"

"*False* labor pains." But Patricia sounded as if she were trying to convince herself. "It's too early for real labor. I...sent over another note to Doctor Chillingsworth at noon, and he replied that I had nothing to worry about from my description, that the only thing I needed to do was calm myself."

"I do not like Doctor Chillingsworth," Rose said passionately.

"He makes me a little uneasy, too," Patricia said, far too nicely as always. "But I don't want to bother him with a triviality. If I do, maybe he'll not come when it's urgent. So for now..." Patricia smiled. "He's only five minutes away, less if Josephs runs. It's doing me no harm to wait. And if I'd rather walk, it can't be that bad, can it?"

No need to frighten her sister, no matter how Rose's heart pounded or what scenarios her imagination invented. "No, of course not," Rose said. "You'll feel better tomorrow, no doubt. For now, do you want me to walk with you?"

"Yes. That would be lovely."

Rose took her sister's hand and paced with her along that four-foot strip of carpet. Patricia's steps were slow and hesitant, but her voice was as welcoming as ever.

"Did you have a good day today?"

Rose hesitated. She could talk about her calculations, about the story Mrs. Barnstable had told her. But Patricia would see through her false humor in a moment. She was already peering at Rose, a frown on her face.

"I told Mr. Shaughnessy I couldn't see him any longer," Rose said swiftly.

"Oh, Rose. I know you had to do it—but I'm sorry you did."

Rose shook her head. "It's for the best, really. But..."

"But you liked him anyway, even though he's a rake."

"But I wish I were someone else," Rose heard herself say instead.

"Someone who didn't have to think so hard about marrying an outrageous fellow without risking anything."

"Marry?" Patricia turned her head to look at Rose. "He wasn't talking marriage, was he?"

They made another circuit of the carpet, her feet falling on flowers, before Rose felt ready to respond. "He was," Rose said softly.

"Did you doubt his future fidelity?"

Oh, she should have. All of England would doubt his future fidelity —all of it but her.

"No," Rose said, her voice on the verge of breaking. "No, not that. But I'd be in all the gossip papers. They'd sneer at Papa for being in trade. And that would be only the beginning. It would be hard. Every day would be hard, and he simply won't admit how hard it would be."

"Oh, Rose." Patricia's hand clenched in hers. "I love you. But sometimes you have to do what you most want in life. You can't hide from everything."

"I don't *hide*," Rose said, stung.

Patricia didn't speak for a moment.

Rose thought of her portfolios, her columns of numbers. She thought of the transit of Venus, of her ducking her head and insisting she'd never be attached to a scientific voyage.

It's not that you think it'll prove too difficult for me. *It will be too difficult for* you.

"I don't hide," she said, more slowly this time.

"You do. A little. And you have ever since you were small. It's why Papa broke with Grandpapa all those years ago, you know."

"What?"

"When Papa moved to London from Liverpool? It wasn't just to set up that first import store. It was because he didn't like what Grandfather was doing to you—putting you on display, having you do your little adding trick with the basket in front of the crowds. You *weren't* shy before then. After that... Papa wanted it to stop, but Grandfather said it brought in customers." Patricia shrugged. "So Papa and Mama left instead."

Rose swallowed. She hadn't realized they'd left for her. She had thought… Well, she'd been too young to think of reasons. She had simply thought that her parents wanted to strike out on their own.

All she could remember when they moved was a feeling of gladness—that she could stop feeling ashamed of the best part of herself, that she could sit and revel in her talent without everyone's eyes on her. She had stopped belonging to other people.

She had always thought it a happy accident. It hadn't been; it had been a gift from her parents.

"So I worry about you sometimes." Patricia squeezed her hand. "I worry about you a lot, in fact, ensconcing yourself in a quiet office with nothing but numbers to keep you company."

"It's not just numbers," Rose said. "I like astronomy. It's exciting. And it feels so…safe. Nothing else is about for millions of miles."

But she hadn't felt alone last night. Last night, when she'd taken his hand and kissed him, she had felt brave. Not afraid that the world would laugh at her, not with him at her side.

Patricia squeezed her hand again—but this time in a hard, lengthy clench. It was only because she stopped walking that Rose realized she didn't intend it as a comforting gesture; she was having another contraction.

"Patricia," Rose said, when she finally loosened her grip, "I really think we should send for Chillingsworth."

CHAPTER EIGHT

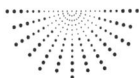

ROSE HELD HER BREATH as Doctor Chillingsworth frowned. It had taken Josephs hours to find him; he'd been with another patient when Josephs had first set out. The doctor had come only reluctantly; he seemed tired now, his left eyelid drooping asymmetrically.

He'd turned the lights on full bore and felt Patricia's belly with a clinical detachment.

"Thirty-seven weeks along," he said with a shake of his head. "Thirty-seven weeks, if that. The baby's not yet turned. There's no dilation to speak of. Mrs. Wells, it is still not your time."

At least he was actually addressing Patricia now. Not that he had any choice; Mr. Josephs had not come up to the bedroom.

"But I'm having contractions," Patricia said. "Regular contractions, coming closer and closer together. The time between them has fallen from forty-five minutes last night to nineteen just now."

Chillingsworth looked at Patricia. He let out a long, long sigh. "And yet you are...*mistaken,* I suppose I shall say charitably. There are a great many changes that occur in the human body during a period of gravidity. No doubt you are experiencing gas."

"Gas." Patricia sounded shocked. "No. It's not gas."

"Your husband is absent," Chillingsworth said, "And no doubt you find yourself in want of attention. I have observed it all too often in women in your state. But you are worrying yourself needlessly and no doubt causing more harm than not. Rest assured that it is not your time. I do not need more dramatics from you." He shook his head. "I'd have a little more patience with a new mother's antics—but I was called here at eleven in the evening after an exceedingly taxing day. Please show some consideration for others, Mrs. Wells."

He packed up his things. Patricia's lips had thinned considerably; her hands clenched together. She didn't speak a word, and Rose couldn't blame her.

Dramatic? In want of attention? *Her* sister? There was not a chance in the world of it. Patricia had never done a thing to draw attention to herself.

Rose wanted to talk to the man sharply.

But Patricia simply said, "Yes, Doctor Chillingsworth. I'm sorry to have disturbed you."

If Patricia didn't want to make a fuss, Rose wouldn't make one for her. After all, wasn't that the way of the world? Rose rarely made a fuss for herself; it was seeing the people she loved be treated unfairly that made her angry.

Rose sat with her sister long after Chillingsworth had left, holding Patricia's hand, not saying a word, trying not to count the minutes that elapsed between squeezes.

She fell asleep in her clothes, trying to convince herself that the squeezes were not coming closer and closer together.

～

SHE WOKE IN THE DARK, disoriented and bewildered.

"Rose." Patricia was shaking her. Her voice was a little ragged. "Rose, my water just broke."

"Oh my God." Rose came out of her confused dreams instantly. "Oh, God. I'll wake Josephs. He can have Chillingsworth here in ten minutes."

"Yes," Patricia said. "Yes. I think that's for the best now."

Rose ran down stairs. She knocked sharply on the servants' door and explained the situation. In no time, Josephs was stomping into his boots and setting off. Rose watched him go out the door into a wild flurry of snow.

A bell tower chimed twice in the darkness; Rose closed the door and ascended the stairs to her sister.

"He'll be here soon," she said. "Mrs. Josephs is fetching towels and putting water on to boil."

She fumbled with a spill, igniting the rolled paper from the coals before lighting the lamp.

Patricia had her hands on her belly. "This is happening." She gave Rose a wan smile. "This is actually happening. How…exciting."

Exciting, Rose suspected, was not her first choice of word. Nor her second.

"Very exciting."

Rose didn't say the other thing on her mind—that at thirty-seven weeks, it was too soon. What happened would happen; if Patricia didn't want to fret, Rose would keep her worries to herself. It would all be well. It would be. And Chillingsworth would be here soon.

"I wish Isaac were here," Patricia said.

So did Rose, and not just because Patricia's husband was a doctor.

"Don't you worry," Rose said. "I'll make sure you're taken care of. I promised."

Five minutes passed, then ten. Patricia's contractions were coming closer now—mere minutes apart, and from the strain on her face, they were getting worse. Fifteen minutes had elapsed since Josephs left, when a third contraction came. Patricia gritted her teeth; Rose held her shoulders. "Shh, shh," she whispered. "It will all be well."

But even after the contraction passed, Patricia remained as she had been, her teeth set, her breathing ragged.

"There, there," Rose said soothingly. "You're doing so well."

Patricia's hand slipped to her belly once more. "Rose?"

"Yes?"

"I've just thought of something."

Rose set her hand on her sister's shoulder. "What is it? I'll make it better."

Patricia let out a shaky breath. "The baby hasn't turned yet."

Rose stared at her sister in horror. For one moment, she couldn't find any words of comfort at all. Every snatch of remembered conversation, every story she'd heard of what might happen in labor floated to mind.

She caught herself before she could recoil in horror. "You mustn't worry," she said. "Chillingsworth will be here soon. We live in modern times. There's a great deal that can be done. I'm sure of it. Don't you worry."

As she spoke, the door opened below.

It was a sign of how frightened she was that the thought of Chillingsworth—self-important, cold, rude Chillingsworth—warmed her through and through. "There," she said soothingly. "He's here now. I imagine he was only delayed because of the snow."

There was some stomping in the entry, followed by footsteps coming up the stairs. "You see?" Rose told her sister. "It will be…"

The door swung open on the lonely form of Mr. Josephs. For a second, Rose waited, watching him in utter silence. It took her that second to understand that something was wrong—that the footsteps she'd heard just now had been solitary, that no doctor followed on his heels.

Mr. Josephs hung his head wearily. "He's not coming."

Rose blinked, trying to comprehend what had just been said. "He's out on another call?"

"No," Josephs said shortly. "He's in. He's just not coming."

Rose felt all her hope slowly drain from her.

Patricia pressed her hand. "What does that mean?"

Josephs shook his head. The thing he didn't say—well, Rose could hear it echoing all too well. Chillingsworth referring to her sister as "dramatic," saying that she was "mistaken" and thinking himself charitable for not calling her an outright liar.

Rose stood. "There's a misunderstanding," she said tightly. "A mistake. He just needs someone to explain what is happening to him."

That had to be it. "We didn't tell Josephs your water broke. No doubt once he hears that, he'll be right over."

"No, Miss," Josephs started to say. "I told him—"

Rose held up a hand, stopping those words. She couldn't accept them. She'd promised Patricia that she would take care of her; she couldn't let her down. Not now. "I'm going," she said. "I'll get him. I'll be right back, Patricia. Right back. Mr. Josephs, have your wife come up and sit with my sister. You'll need to come with me."

It was a good thing Rose had fallen asleep in her clothing. She had only to find stockings and boots—no point doing them up all the way —and slip into her coat. She was winding a scarf about her neck when Mr. Josephs came down to her.

"Miss," he said in a low voice. "Perhaps you need to hear..."

"Don't say it." She couldn't hear it.

"Mrs. Walton, the midwife—she *is* out. That's why I was so long returning. I was checking on her. I can find someone else, but the next nearest physician is miles away, and in this snow..."

"Do *not* say it," Rose warned. "If the next nearest physician is miles away, then we will simply have to get Chillingsworth." She thought of her sister's face twisting in fear. Of her sister trying to be brave as she told her the baby hadn't turned. "We will *have* to get him."

The snow was falling in earnest; Rose could scarcely see more than two houses down. The street lamps were like dull white globes of light, scarcely illuminating their way. Three steps in the snow—now three inches deep—made Rose realize she should have taken the time to lace her boots. Snow slipped in, cold and wet, packing itself against her stockings with every step. But she didn't dare stop. She counted time not in minutes, but in the length of time between Patricia's contractions. She could almost feel the squeeze of her sister's hand in hers as she hurried down the street.

It took two contractions to arrive at Chillingsworth's home. She rapped smartly on the door. In her mind's eye, she could see her sister smiling gamely, trying to put a good face on things.

No, Rose told herself. It was going to be all right. She would make it all right.

The door finally opened. Chillingsworth's eyes fell on Rose; in the flickering light of the streetlamp outside, she could see his nostrils flare.

"Please," Rose said. "My sister's water broke. The baby is coming now. It hasn't turned—"

"Of course it hasn't turned," the doctor said in a cold voice. "It's not her time yet."

"No, it is. It is absolutely her time. She's laboring now, Doctor Chillingsworth, truly laboring. There can be no question—"

"And how many births have you presided over?"

"None, but—"

"Did you *see* her water break?"

"No, but our woman was cleaning—"

"Miss Sweetly, I spent ten years at a naval post in the West Indies. While I was there, I saw a hundred women like your sister, and let me tell you, a more dramatic set of lying malingerers I have never observed. I have gone to your sister twice in the last twenty-four hours. I will not rouse myself for her again."

"But—"

"I shall wait on Mrs. Wells at seven in the morning, which is far earlier than she deserves. No sooner. Tell your sister to stop with her hysterics and behave with some decency."

Rose was too shocked to speak.

"And for God's sake, if you bother me again tonight, I'll not come in the morning, either."

"Doctor Chillingsworth. Please."

He shut the door in her face.

"I tried to tell you, Miss." Beside her, Josephs sounded apologetic. "I did."

He had, and she hadn't wanted to listen. She hadn't *dared* to listen, because there was no one else to be found at this time of night but this man.

This man who had spent ten years in the West Indies. Who had called Patricia dramatic, had accused her of falsifying her condition simply because she craved attention.

I saw a hundred women like your sister, he had said. For weeks she'd listened to Chillingsworth talk. For weeks, she had wanted to believe that when he said *women like your sister* he had meant women who were pregnant with their first child. But he hadn't qualified his comments with a statement about pregnant women. He'd talked about working in the West Indies.

A more dramatic set of lying malingers I have never observed.

It was a punch to the stomach. Rose inhaled. The cold air felt like a knife in her lungs. But she didn't have time to weep over it or to gnash her teeth at the unfairness. She didn't have time to rail at life's injustices.

In the back of her mind, she was still counting contractions—and she knew now that they were coming even closer.

"Josephs." She was proud of herself; her voice was steady. "Find someone. Anyone. Please. I'm…"

She paused. Odd, how times like this made everything clear. There was no room for worry or second-guessing, no space for wounded pride any longer. There was nothing but her sister.

"I'm going to find someone who will help," she said.

CHAPTER NINE

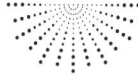

S OMEONE WAS POUNDING on Stephen's door.

It was his first coherent thought upon waking—that hard, repeated tattoo beating in time with an urgency he did not understand, but felt instinctively in his blood.

He came out of bed, put on trousers and a loose shirt, and slipped downstairs.

He opened the door onto a white flurry of snow—and in dark counterpoint, with the streetlight behind her making a golden halo about her, Rose Sweetly. She had a cloak pulled about her, but her teeth were chattering noisily.

"Rose?" He had to be dreaming, but from experience, his dreams of her had never had her so bundled up.

"Stephen." She sounded almost frantic. "I don't know what to do. Patricia is in labor—her water broke—the baby's coming and it's still breech—"

"I'll go fetch someone."

"No." She turned her head away and swiped at her eyes. "Mrs. Walton is out on another call, and Doctor Chillingsworth is...not available. Josephs is off in search of someone farther afield, but there is no time. The baby is coming *now*, and I don't know what to do."

He'd never seen her so upset. Little crystals of ice clung to her eyelashes, to the corners of her eye. Frozen tears, he realized. Her lips quivered.

"Right," he heard himself say. "My father was a stable master. I've birthed dozens of horses, one of them breech. It's not the same thing—"

But she was on the verge of a panic, and she needed him.

"—but I'm happy to come," he finished. "Don't worry. It's going to be all right."

"That's what I kept telling Patricia." Her teeth chattered. "And it just keeps getting worse and worse instead."

"Well, you're going to have to keep telling your sister that," he said. "That's your job now, Rose. You keep telling her that—and we'll make sure it's true. Come along."

He found a pair of shoes in the hall.

"You're coming like that?"

"No point wasting time. You're only two houses down, after all."

Rose nodded. It was cold outside—cold enough for the wind to cut right through the linen of his shirt, cold enough to drive the last remnants of his weariness from him. He followed her to her home. When she fumbled with her key, he took it from her numb fingers, unlocking the door.

"Rose," he said as she took off her cloak in the hallway. "The most important thing is that you must not let her panic. You're her sister. It doesn't matter if there's reason for her to be frightened; we must do our best not to scare her. You're in command. I'm just here to make jokes. Understand?"

She paused looking up at him.

He set a finger on her chin. His hands were cold, but her skin was colder. No knowing how long she'd been outside looking for someone. Her lips parted; for a second, she looked up at him as if expecting a kiss. For a second, he wanted to give her one.

Instead, he took a handkerchief from his pocket and very gently wiped the ice crystals from her lashes.

"There," he said quietly. "That's better. You can do this."

She drew in a shuddering breath. He reached out and took her hand in his. Her fingers were deathly cold; he rubbed them between his palms.

"Come," she said. "Let's go."

As she ascended the stairs, her chin came up. Her jaw squared; he could see her gathering determination with every step.

She entered the room to the left of the small hallway.

"Patricia," she announced. "I've returned."

Stephen followed behind her. The room was warm and comfortable. A fire crackled on the hearth. Mrs. Wells was in bed, her head turned to the side. An older woman sat in a chair next to the bed, watching over her.

He'd only ever seen Mrs. Wells properly attired. Now she was in a loose-fitting gown. Her dark hair was held back by a kerchief. She took one long look at Stephen. "He's not a doctor," she said in a low tone.

"No," Rose said firmly. "Chillingsworth…was otherwise detained. Patricia, you know Mr. Shaughnessy."

"Mrs. Wells." Stephen nodded at her.

"Stephen Shaughnessy." A smile played along her lips. "Actual Man. My. I feel better already."

"Mr. Shaughnessy has presided over many births," Rose said in a commanding voice. "He'll make sure all goes well."

Stephen was not so sure about that, but he tried to look…well, competent.

Mrs. Wells raised an eyebrow at him. "Mr. Shaughnessy. I knew you were an Actual Man, but I had not thought you so…prolific."

"Not my children," he said.

"Oh." She contemplated this. "Not human, either, then, I take it."

"Horses."

"Well, then." Mrs. Wells swallowed. "Do we try to turn the baby?"

He regarded her thoughtfully. "I don't think we can," he said. "At this point in labor? I'm not sure it's possible, and if it is, none of us know how to do it."

"If there are any minor complications," Rose said, "Mr. Shaughnessy will see to it."

"And if there are major ones?" He could hear the strain in Mrs. Wells's voice.

"Then the birth will take a little longer," Rose said matter-of-factly, "and by the time greater expertise is needed, Josephs will have returned with another doctor."

"Yes," Stephen said. "So you're in good hands. The best hands, Mrs. Wells. Your body knows what to do; it is doing it as we speak. Don't fight it; do what your body tells you."

"But the baby is coming breech."

"Hundreds of babies are born breech every day," Stephen said. "Hundreds of babies the world over—many of them without complications or further incidents. It'll be a little harder on you, but you can manage."

It wasn't fast. Rose draped a sheet over her sister for modesty's sake as the contractions came closer and closer. Mrs. Wells began to cry out with every passing wave; when she tried to choke back her moans, Rose encouraged her.

"Yell if you must," Rose said. "You're letting the world know the baby is coming."

Stephen didn't know when he became the one to hold Mrs. Wells's hand. He didn't even know when the room began to lighten from the burnished gold illumination cast by the lamp to the pale gray of dawn. The hours blurred together.

"There you are," Rose said. "The feet are coming. Oh, Patricia. They're the most darling feet."

Mrs. Wells made a noise that might, under other circumstances have been a laugh.

"You're almost there," Stephen said. "You have it, Mrs. Wells."

She gritted her teeth again and let out another cry.

"Patricia, he's a boy."

"There you are," Stephen said. "All your friends will be jealous— they had to birth their babies all the way before they knew the sex. Here you are, beating them out."

Mrs. Wells did laugh at that. "Yes," she said with a shake of her head. "Surely they will all be jealous of my thirty-some hours of labor."

Another push; her hands dug into his arm, hard—but nothing. When her contraction subsided, she gritted her teeth.

"Next one," he told her.

But it wasn't—not that one, nor the one after that. Out the window, the sun had come out. The snow had stopped falling; a little light played on tree branches laden with a heavy white blanket.

Another push came, and it, too, was futile. Mrs. Well's face glistened with sweat; her jaw squared in determination.

"Rose." Stephen gestured. She looked up.

"You need to lend your sister a hand on the next push."

"What—how—should I pull?" She looked dubious.

"No. Have Mrs. Josephs take your place. Come here."

She stood.

"Set your hand here." He gestured to her abdomen. "Feel—you should be able to find the baby's head. A nice round lump. Yes?"

She nodded.

"Good. Then as soon as her next contraction comes, push. Start off gently; push harder and harder as she does, too."

"But—"

Stephen took hold of her free hand. "You can do it, Rose."

It came in the next instant. Mrs. Wells gritted her teeth and let out a moan. Rose squared her jaw and pushed. And then—just a moment later—they heard a low wail.

"Oh." Mrs. Wells's voice was hoarse and ragged. "Oh, thank God."

"He looks healthy." Mrs. Josephs sat at the edge of the bed. "Not that I'm an expert in babies—but he's moving and breathing and crying…"

"Let me have him." Patricia's voice was weak but triumphant.

Mrs. Josephs stood. She wrapped a white cotton towel around dark, glistening chestnut skin. A tiny hand pulled at the air; a foot kicked out. A minuscule face scrunched in protest.

Stephen was not a baby sort of person. They'd always seemed

strange, clumsy things to dote over—human beings that were not yet old enough to be interesting.

But *this* baby might have been the most beautiful thing Stephen had ever seen. Every toe seemed perfectly formed. The whole room seemed bathed with light.

"Excellent work," he heard himself say. It seemed inadequate to the occasion.

Mrs. Wells took her child, holding him to her. Her eyes were shining. In fact, the entire world seemed to shimmer, and Stephen found himself surreptitiously wiping his own eyes.

Rose and her sister were holding each other, speaking in barely coherent sentences, and Stephen realized he was extraneous.

Scarcely a friend. Definitely not family. He'd only been the man who was close enough to help when no one else was around. He hadn't slept; his presence in a woman's bedchamber was entirely improper, and...and...

He stayed long enough to make certain that the cord was cut, the after birth properly expelled.

He wished he could stay longer, wished that he belonged here. But this wasn't the time to demand attention—not now, when the sisters were basking in victory after a hard-fought war. This moment was about everyone but himself.

He smiled at the two of them and then slowly, quietly slipped out of the room.

$\sim$

M RS. JOSEPHS HAD LEFT to fetch some hot water for her sister, who was doing her best to stay awake with little Isaac in her arms, when Rose realized that Stephen was no longer in the room. She absented herself swiftly, ran to the stairwell—and caught sight of him below, staring bemusedly at the door in the entry.

"Stephen," she called.

He turned around, tilting his head up. He looked every bit as

exhausted as she felt. His shirt had long since lost any hint of crisp-
ness; it was unbuttoned past his throat, showing a triangle of pale skin
and dark, wiry hairs.

"I'll be on my way shortly," he said with a small smile. "It's just that
I've realized it's broad daylight—and it will be extraordinarily
shocking if I'm seen walking out of your door. Particularly looking
like this." His hand swept down.

She followed his gesture. His sleeves were rolled to his elbow,
showing a shocking, delicious amount of skin. His trousers were
wrinkled—which only made them mold to his thighs all the more.
Without a coat, the linen of his shirt clung to his shoulders—and if she
remembered the gossip correctly, hadn't he done some rowing at
Cambridge? He looked like he had.

And she could see precisely what he meant. Bedroom slippers;
shirtsleeves. It would be shocking indeed.

"Oh, dear." Rose found herself drifting down the stairs toward him.
"Oh, dear. I see what you mean. If you go out like that, you'll start a
veritable riot."

He blinked once…and then ever so slowly, he began to smile.

"You can't leave without letting me thank you."

"Ah, Rose. There's no need for that."

She descended the staircase. "There's every need. After what I told
you yesterday—"

A sharp rap sounded on the door. Rose frowned—and then realized that Mrs. Josephs was assisting her sister upstairs and Mr.
Josephs had not yet returned. She was the only one who could answer
the door, and Stephen was standing right here, in a shocking state of
undress. Not that she was doing much better; her gown was stained. It
wasn't just wrinkled; it looked as if it had spent the last year wadded
up in the back of the wardrobe.

"Go to the back room," she said to Stephen. "Quickly."

He winked at her and disappeared.

Rose smoothed her hands over her gown, which did nothing at all.
The cause was hopeless, and so she gave up on it and opened the door
anyway.

She really ought not to have been surprised at the man who stood there. He had, after all, promised to come in the morning. But at the sight of Doctor Chillingsworth, all the emotion she'd hidden over the course of the night bubbled to the surface—all her fear, her despair. Every last ounce of impossible worry that she had swallowed came back in one blinding rush.

"Doctor Chillingsworth," she said in a cold voice.

He looked down his nose at her. "I am here as promised."

"You are too late," she heard herself say. "Patricia gave birth an hour ago."

His face did not even flicker at this news. He didn't look surprised. He didn't apologize for his hateful words the previous night.

"Ah, did she?" he said instead.

She felt her hands clench into fists at her sides. "You said it wasn't her time." No. It wasn't despair that filled her. It was a cold fury, one that threatened to overwhelm her. "You said she was a *lying malingerer—*"

He shrugged. "Well, there was some chance I was mistaken—there is always that chance. But I figured there'd be no real harm. Women of her sort are like cows: They scarcely need any assistance when dropping their calves."

He stepped into the entry and took off his coat, oblivious—or perhaps just indifferent—to Rose's splutter.

"I suppose I'll take a look now."

Lying malingerer. Women of her sort are like cows. It was too much— far, far too much.

She took a step toward him. "When Doctor Wells left, he asked me to stand in his stead—to tell him every time I heard the baby's heartbeat, to convey every last kick I felt."

It had not been so long ago that she'd held her sister's hand, had put her hands on her sister's belly and pushed her son's head that last inch. They had not needed this man—but they might have. It staggered her what might have happened had things been even an iota worse. His absence could have meant the baby's life. Or Patricia's. And to him, this was a matter that he could shrug off. She could scarcely think for the anger that filled her.

"On behalf of my sister's husband," Rose said, "this is for you."

So saying, she punched him in the stomach. She felt the blow travel all the way up her arm, stinging in the most gratifying way. His breath blew out; he gave a satisfying grunt.

"This is for her." Rose punched him again. "And this is for *me.*" She made to ram her fist into his belly again, but he caught her wrist this time.

"Why, you little—"

"You'd better let go of her." The words came from behind her. Rose felt herself smile—a beautiful, impossible, gratifying smile.

Chillingsworth froze. He looked up at Stephen, who had come into the entry. "And you are?"

"Taller than you," Stephen said. "Stronger than you. Younger than you. And at this moment, I'm angrier than you, too. Let go of Miss Sweetly and get out of here before I hold you down for her to pummel."

The doctor released her wrist. He stepped back and then shakily took his coat from the hook.

"Get out, then," Stephen said.

He took another step forward; Chillingsworth wrenched open the door, letting in a blast of cold air, and then, as swiftly as he could, he vanished. The door slammed behind him.

Rose could hear her own breathing echoing wildly in the entry. She'd punched a man. Twice. And he'd deserved it.

And Stephen...

She turned to him. He was looking at her with the most intense expression on his face, one that made her whole body tingle from head to toe.

"Stephen." She took a step toward him. "Stephen."

He raised a finger and set it on her lips. "Don't promise anything when your emotions are running high," he said. "Or when you're exhausted."

Tired though she was, Rose had never felt more certain. All her fretting had burned away.

She didn't know when she'd become sure. Not when he'd sat with her sister. Not when he'd agreed to come with her. Maybe it was when Chillingsworth had sent her away, when Rose had not known where to turn...until she had known. She had known that help was not a million miles away, but right next door. That she had only to stretch out her hand and ask, and it would be hers.

She had known. She had gone to him, and he had come.

"Now," he said, "have you a coat I could borrow so that I could look respectable long enough to return home?"

She smiled up at him. "Of course. I have everything you need."

She found one of Isaac's old jackets and a pair of his boots in a trunk and brought them out. He was sitting on the sofa, looking somewhat dazed. He smiled at her wearily.

"Here," Rose said. "Let's get these on you."

They were both too large on Stephen's frame. He let Rose do up his buttons. Her hands trembled as she did. She'd kissed him, let him touch her. But somehow, this seemed the most intimate act yet, the sort of favor that wives performed for husbands.

When she'd done the last button, she looked up into his eyes. She'd expected, maybe, to see a reflection of her own emotion.

Instead, his gaze was hard and utterly unreadable.

"You're exhausted," she said. But that was not all it was.

"I'm contemplating." His words came slowly.

"Here. Let's get you home, where you can rest."

He didn't resist her tug on his arm. Rose put on her own coat, opened the door to the house, and glanced down the street. It was empty but for the drifts of snow.

"Quickly," she told him, "while nobody's about."

She accompanied him. Maybe she needed to make sure he arrived safely; maybe it was because he seemed strangely subdued, and she feared he'd not think properly. He unlocked his own door and then looked down at her.

"You were right," he said. "I didn't understand how difficult things might be for you—not until just now at the very end."

The fear she'd been trying not to feel washed through Rose. He'd stopped her from making a declaration. Of course he had; he'd seen what Chillingsworth had said and done, had understood all the indignities she'd face, small and large. And of course he'd changed his mind. She stared up at him, stricken.

"The Irish are accounted violent drunkards," he said. "Gamblers with no sense of responsibility, and terrible human beings, through and through. But at least we're considered human beings."

Rose would not let her heart break. Not here, not in the snow, not with her sister's new child next door. She would stand here and look him in the eyes. She would…

She choked and looked down.

"But there's something you don't understand," he said. "When I said I loved you, I didn't mean that I would walk away when I realized your life was difficult. The fact that I understand how hard things can be means that I want to stand by you sooner, and try even harder to make it better."

She could scarcely believe it. She lifted her face to his, her heart pounding.

And then he smiled at her, and all her fears took flight.

"I love you," he said. "Let me buy you telescopes and kiss you half the night. And when things grow difficult, let me be make them a little easier."

She looked up at him. She felt dazed, utterly worn out. And so she said the first thing that came to her mind, which happened to be…

"Did you know that Dr. Maro in Italy has calculated the likelihood that the earth will be struck by an asteroid at two hundred and fifty million to one?"

He blinked. "No. I did not know that. Is it…relevant?"

"Yes," she heard herself say. And then she reached out and opened his door, and before her nerve left her, she stepped inside.

He followed her, scratching his head in bemusement.

"Yes," she told him. "It's very relevant. You see, it's one hundred and sixty times more likely that the earth will be struck by an asteroid than that you will seduce me. And yet…" She swallowed, looking up at him. "I find myself seduced. Utterly. The only explanation is that we are all about to perish."

He looked down at her, his breath hissing out. "Rose. Darling."

"And since we are going to die anyway…" Her throat felt dry. "Would you…take me to bed?"

He looked at her. Really looked at her. His eyes were dark; a light danced in them. He leaned over her and drew one finger down her cheek.

"Rose," he said. "I have just one question."

She nodded.

"Does probability really work like that?"

Her cheeks burned and she ducked her head. "No," she moaned, feeling rather ashamed. "It doesn't. I'm sorry—I was going to tell you afterward. And I know that doing such a thing under false pretenses…" She let out a little laugh. "I know it doesn't make sense. But I love you, and…and… I think that if we are to do this, I must learn to be a little outrageous." She swallowed. "And in a few hours my parents will be here, and once we're engaged, it'll be four months before we'll be left alone, and—"

"Four months! No, never mind that for now. Rose, did you just lie to me about *mathematics* to get me into bed?" He laughed. "I don't think I've ever been so flattered." He took her hand. His fingers were warm against hers, and her whole body thrilled at his touch. "Come, Rose."

She followed him up the stairs.

His bed was solid wood, heaped with a quilt of shifting greens. He stopped on the threshold of his room. "Are you sure, Rose?"

Her heart was pounding. "I'm sure."

She wasn't sure what to expect. But he didn't pounce on her immediately. He didn't take off her clothing. Instead, he turned her to him, set his finger under her chin, and he kissed her.

It was a sweet, intense sort of kiss—soothing in it's own way. And yet his hand crept around her. His fingers touched the back of her neck. Her skin felt sensitive all over.

"Hullo, there, Rose," he murmured against her lips.

She smiled and tilted her head back. "Stephen. I love you."

"Ah, good."

His touch was gentle and yet so firm, caressing the base of her neck. She didn't even realize that he was undoing her buttons down her back until she felt the cool air against her skin. But he didn't stop kissing her, and gradually she felt her whole body coming to life.

He lifted his head for one second—just long enough to slide her gown off her shoulders. She felt the fabric pool at her feet. And then he stepped close to her once more. But instead of kissing her mouth, he bent his head to kiss her shoulder. His fingers tangled in the corset laces she'd tied in front, deftly undoing them, loosening them…and then pulling away the boning and heavy fabric.

When he took her nipple in his mouth through her shift, she tilted her head back. Her breath came shorter and shorter. And yet…

She opened her eyes. He was intent on her, his hands gentle on her skin. But she hadn't wanted to simply give herself to him. She'd wanted to be brave and maybe a little outrageous. And so slowly, she reached out and put her hands on the placket of his trousers. His eyes shut; she could feel the hard length of his erection through the fabric.

"God, Rose."

This was what she needed to do—not just to give herself to him, but to take him in return. Her hands were not so practiced as his had been on her buttons, but he didn't seem to care. He pressed his hips against her hand, urged her as she peeled back his trousers. His small-clothes came next, revealing a long, pale shaft, already swelling under her attentions. She ran a finger over the tip; he gave a little growl.

And then she looked up at him.

"There we are," Rose said, feeling her lips curl into a smile. "Stephen Shaughnessy, Actual Man."

He let out a laugh—but before he could say anything else, before she could lose her nerve—she took him entirely in her hand, caressing him from tip to stem. It was the most amazing thing, the male organ—

responsive, moving ever so slightly with her every touch. His breath grew uneven; his shaft pulsed in her hands, growing harder and longer.

"Rose." He set his hand on her shoulder. "Let me have a turn at you, love."

She looked up at him. And then, ever so gently, he pushed her down to the bed. Her heart was beating wildly; she couldn't quite believe she was about to do this.

But then he came over her. He let his weight settle into her, slowly, ever so slowly, until their hips fit together, until her breasts brushed his chest through her last under layer. He kissed her first on the shoulder, then on the chin, and then, tilting her head up, on the lips. That kiss on the lips didn't stop. She let herself sink into it as his body settled against hers. They were hip to hip, separated only by the sheer fabric of her chemise. It was both too much and not enough. Their bodies found a rhythm together, a push and pull like heartbeats, like the tide of gravity between them.

He pulled away from her—only long enough to sweep her chemise up her body, to bare her to the cool air. He took off his shirt, revealing wiry muscles. And then he looked in her eyes. "Four months," he said with a shake of his head. "Truly, we're going to have a four month engagement?"

"It will have to be long enough to forestall all gossip."

"Four months." He made a noise, but he was smiling at her. "Then I'll fetch a French letter and we'll be very careful."

She wasn't sure what to say to that.

He turned from her momentarily, and found something in his dresser. He fitted this to his erection, and then turned to her. "Now it's my turn to prepare you."

He advanced on her. But instead of getting atop her once more, he spread her legs and then very slowly, slid his fingers between them.

"God," he said, "you're beautiful. Beautiful and wet for me. And I can't wait to taste you."

And then he did. He set his mouth to her, and she felt the sure sweep of his tongue. It was the most shockingly intimate thing she'd ever experienced—entirely beyond her imagination—to have him doing this, tasting her, finding that nub there. He slid a finger inside her. Her breath caught. Between his hand and his tongue, she couldn't think, could only experience a sweet pleasure, growing. Her body felt restless. She pushed against him, wanting...

He pulled back ever so slightly. And then, while her body was still desperate for more, he kissed his way up her hips, her navel. His mouth left a warm imprint against her belly, rising up her body rib by rib until he found the rounding edge of her breast.

He took her nipple in his mouth again just as he began to move his finger inside her. Those two points—so deliciously, utterly warm—drove her into a frenzy. She was close to something, so close, and if only he would...

But he didn't. He took his hand away. She almost protested, but he came over her again. This time, he set his erection to her cleft.

"Rose, darling."

She looked up at him.

"I love you," he said.

He slid into her. She'd expected it to be painful and rough, but by the time he entered her, she was already wet and ready for him. There was a pinch—she caught her breath—he stopped...

And she could feel the tip of him inside her, warm and hard, could feel him on top of her, his muscles cording as he held himself back. She reached up tentatively and set her hand on his chest. Very slowly, she drew her fingers down his chest. He made a noise in his throat; his hips flexed, and he slid inside her another inch, and then another, moving slowly until he had filled her completely. Their bodies were joined intimately. She looked up at him...

He smiled, reached down, and brushed her cheek.

"Well," he said. "I had better make sure that you like this. Because four months from now, I'm having you again and again and again."

He moved his hips, pulling out of her and then sliding back—over and over, until that rhythm they'd found before swept them both up. Until her skin seemed to catch fire, and his hands came to her hips. She felt herself come apart around him; he gritted his teeth and then, just as she thought she could take no more, gasped and pounded into her one last time.

They drifted afterward. They'd scarcely slept the night before, and she could not keep her eyes open. She fell asleep to the feel of his fingers against her temples, and the soft murmur of his voice.

"Damn," he said. "Four months."

~

"**F**OUR MONTHS."
It was six that evening, and Rose's parents—who had journeyed hours through ice and snow to see their first grandchild—sat at the dinner table, frowning at Stephen Shaughnessy.

"Four months," her father repeated. "Is there any reason the engagement must be so short?"

They had already interrogated Stephen on his finances and his family. Her father had muttered when he'd said he was Irish, and frowned when he mentioned that he did some work for a newspaper. Rose had thumped her father, urging him to behave...and when Stephen gave a cheeky answer, had done the same to him. But Stephen had actually comported himself in an almost respectable manner.

If someone didn't say something soon, her parents would have the surprise of their lives when they discovered the things she hadn't told them. She really was going to have to show them one of his columns. If her father discovered it on his own...

"In fact," Stephen said, "I should like the engagement to be shorter."

Right. An excellent way to introduce the topic of his reputation to her parents. Rose managed to hide her wince.

Her father stiffened, glaring at Stephen. But her fiancé—oh, how lovely that word was—simply leaned casually back in his chair, as if he'd not announced to the entire room—to both her parents, watching in wide-eyed shock—that he wanted to take her to bed, and soon.

Which, really, her parents ought to have guessed that from the circumstance of his wanting to marry her, but then parents could sometimes be willfully blind about such things.

"You see," Stephen said piously, "my understanding is that Doctor Wells is expected home any day now. Once he's back, there will be no need for Rose to stay here. And once her sister has recovered herself from the birth... Well, I think Doctor and Mrs. Wells might enjoy having some privacy."

"She'll come home to us in London," her father growled. "Of course she will."

"But then how will she work with Dr. Barnstable?" Stephen asked. He reached out and took her hand under the table. "She enjoys her work with him so, and I would hate to see my Rose deprived of something she liked simply because I was loathe to commit to marriage on a reasonable timeline."

Oh, that was clever.

Her father huffed. "Oh, you're good." He glanced suspiciously at his son-in-law-to-be. "A little too good."

"Oh, no," Stephen said angelically. "I'm afraid not. You'll likely hear about it all too soon. It's the only reason I'm agreeing to four months at all—because if I had insisted on three weeks, the gossip would be too fierce."

Rose's father sighed, but before he could say anything more, the front door opened.

Rose heard stomping feet, a dull thud—and then a man stepped into the back room. His dark skin was more weathered than when last she'd seen him. His hair was cut close to the scalp; a light brush of gray at his temples made him seem all the more austere. He wore a scarlet band on his arm over his uniform.

"Rosie?" He blinked, looking around the room in confusion. "What is going on? Where's Patricia?"

Rose let go of Stephen's hand and sprang to her feet, uttering a little cry of joy. "Isaac! You're back. Oh, you're back. Patricia had the baby—"

"What?"

"And she's well—and he is well—you must come see them now."

"Wait," her father was saying. "We're not done here. I haven't agreed yet."

"Papa," Rose said, "don't let him fool you. He's a rogue and an outrage." She winked at her father. "And once you know him, you'll like him very well. I promise."

Stephen met her gaze, and then, ever so slowly, he smiled. "Ah," he said with a shake of his head. "I love it when you talk sweetly to me."

EPILOGUE

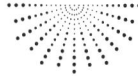

December, 1882

Dear Man,

I do not wish to know what the average man wants in a woman; I wish to know what you want in a woman. Tell me, how is a woman like me ever to attract you?

—Blushing in Bedford

Dear Blushing,

Over the years of my writing this column, I have received literally thousands of letters asking this question. Until now, I have never answered.

I don't ask for much in a woman. I like mathematics, astronomy, and women who can multiply nine-digit numbers in their heads. The difficult part was convincing her to like me back.

You had all better wish her luck. I think she'll need it.

Sincerely hers,

Stephen Shaughnessy

Committed Man

HER EVERY WISH

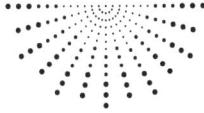

Crash has never let the circumstances of his birth, or his lack of a last name, bother him. His associations may be unsavory, but money, friends, and infamy open far more interesting doors than respect ever could. His sole regret? Once lovely, sweet Daisy Whitlaw learned the truth about how he made his fortune, she cut him off.

Daisy's father is dead, her mother is in ill health, and her available funds have dwindled to a memory. When the local parish announces a Christmas charity bequest to help young people start a trade, it's her last chance. So what if the grants are intended for men? If she's good enough, she might bluff her way into a future.

When Crash offers to show her how to swagger with confidence, she knows he is up to no good. But with her life in the balance, she's desperate enough to risk the one thing she hasn't yet lost: her heart.

For a dog named Lucky.
I wish you were around to hate this book.

CHAPTER ONE

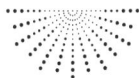

London, England, November, 1866

The crowd stood elbow to elbow, buffeting Daisy Whitlaw about as if she were a slice of bread that had landed in a bucket of slops. No wonder; she suspected she was about to be thrown to the pigs.

A temporary stage had been set up in the square just outside the church. A few dead leaves lay in the gutter as a reminder of autumn, but the trees were bare. The days were growing shorter and colder, but the holidays were too far away to seem real. Perhaps that was why the awarding of the charity bequest felt like such a celebration.

Wooden benches ringed the stage, but nobody was sitting. It was cold, and sitting was freezing work. People shifted from foot to foot, chafing gloved hands, leaning in close to one another. The crowd on this fine Saturday afternoon was jovial. They'd worked their half-day. Most of them had already downed a pint or seven of their favorite ale, and the afternoon's entertainment still lay ahead of them.

Daisy gritted her teeth and popped up on her toes. She still couldn't see.

"Excuse me." She tapped the shoulder of the big, broad fellow who was blocking her view.

He didn't notice her. She was used to this. With a sigh, Daisy jumped atop the bench. From this vantage point, she could see over the man's head. She was five rows back. Close enough, she hoped. Gray buildings enclosed the square, the walls high and grim in the dying light. The noise from the docks was a distant, ever-present roar, layering over the hum of the crowd.

More importantly, the respected, gray-bearded grocer who had been appointed to run the proceedings was already standing at the podium. They were about to start.

Daisy knew she didn't have a chance. She'd been foolish to enter. Still, she'd done it, and there was no walking away now.

"All right, you lot," the grocer at the front bellowed. He was grinning, too, his face flushed with what was undoubtedly more than his fair share of beer. "You all know what we're here for, so let's get started. Sit down, everyone, sit down."

There was a general rumble. The man in front of Daisy started to sit on her feet without looking behind him; she yelped and jumped off the bench, scarcely in time. There was one spot on the end of the row. Daisy slipped into it just ahead of another woman, who gave her a cheerful shrug before retreating farther back.

"We're here," the grocer said as the crowd's noise subsided to a mere rumble, "to settle the terms of the late Mr. and Mrs. Wilding's bequest. They've left fifty pounds to be given to one promising individual who attends services at St. Peter's."

"Hear, hear!" called someone in the crowd.

The grocer paused for a nod at the vicar before continuing. "In the month since the initial announcement, we've received proposals of business from forty-seven young people, all of whom wish to start a trade."

Daisy had her letter of acceptance in her skirt pocket. She'd scarcely believed her luck when it had arrived. Good news rarely came her way. Letters came from creditors, not charity committees.

But she'd labored over her proposal. Every spare hour she had, and then some, had gone into it. She couldn't fail now.

She folded her hands in front of her as the crowd slowly quieted. A ridiculous figure of speech, that. A stupid one. Clearly, she *could* fail now. Failure was expected. Failure was a given.

Every time she reached for her dreams, someone slapped her hands away. Still, she kept on reaching. She wouldn't have the best proposal; she knew it. Men who had studied business had no doubt entered. She didn't know why she kept trying. She just knew that she did.

"We've selected the ten finest proposals that were put before us," the grocer was saying. "Those ten promising young people will deliver a preliminary description of the business they wish to enter today. Each of the five judges will choose the best of this lot. Seven days hence, we'll hear their perfected proposals. The most promising one will receive the full fifty pounds."

That was what the bequest had said. Daisy had read the announcement posted on the church wall over and over to be certain. *The most promising proposal.* Not, *the* man *with the most promising proposal.*

Daisy's position at the flower shop was secure—assuming Mr. Trigard, the owner, didn't hear about this little excursion on her part. With the little extra her mother earned for her lacework, they made do.

She wasn't starving. She had no reason to enter this competition. None, except that she hoped to win.

"And so, without any further ado," the grocer declaimed, "I should like to invite our first candidate up to present his proposal. Mr. J. Batting, please come up."

The crowd applauded, and a man near Daisy let out a sharp whistle. Daisy knew Jonathan Batting. He was the blacksmith's second son, about three years her elder. He lumbered up to the stage and started explaining the plan he had for a new business making straight pins.

She'd expected something stupendous from him. Pins? Factories made straight pins these days, and in far greater quantity, at far lower cost, than any individual man could manage. But the judges nodded gravely as Batting spoke. They asked how he would compete with factory goods.

"Quality," Batting said, with the placid intellect of a cow contemplating its cud. "I'll deliver superior quality."

Superior-quality pins. Had there been any chance anyone preferred handmade straight pins, pin factories would not have driven pin-makers to the poorhouse. Daisy shook her head. She wouldn't win, but maybe her chances weren't so terrible.

Mr. Edwin Diggle spoke about his proposed business as a copyist. Mr. Allan Ebler had a plan to sell fish from a cart. Mr. Arden Flisk intended to own a dry-goods store. He'd need more than fifty pounds to amass a creditable store of dry goods—had nobody done any research? By the time the judges had worked through Misters Glowter, Hargo, Manning, Porget, and Walder on their way down the alphabet to Whitlaw, Daisy was beginning to feel an unreal sense of hope. *None* of the ideas were as good as hers. They wouldn't toss her out, even though she was—

"Our final candidate. D. Whitlaw," the grocer announced. "Mr. D. Whitlaw, if you will."

Daisy stood and started up the aisle.

The grocer frowned and scanned the crowd. "Mr. D. Whitlaw? Is Mr. D. Whitlaw here?"

Daisy drew in a deep breath. "Sir." It came out a squeak.

He glanced at her down his nose and looked away. In that moment, she saw herself as he must see her: skinny, pale, almost ghostlike, standing in the aisle. Her best gown was dark brown. Once, the flowers imprinted on the cotton had been yellow. Now they might charitably be described as beige.

She'd let out the hem as far as it would go. It went...not quite far enough. That extra black stripe at her ankles proclaimed that this was a gown she'd made over and over again. Daisy's Sunday finest was much like her hopes: worn to threadbare weariness, not quite dire enough to be discarded.

"David Whitlaw?" the grocer asked hopefully. "Or maybe Damien? Darius? Daniel?"

"Sir." Daisy spoke a little more loudly. "Sir. I am D. Whitlaw."

The grocer frowned at her, his eyes shifting away, then returning. He rubbed his forehead. He adjusted his spectacles, squinting in her direction. Finally he spoke. "Is the entrant your brother? I hope he's not ill. The rules are that he must speak on his behalf in person."

She squared her shoulders and raised herself up to her full height. "Sir," she repeated. "I am D. Whitlaw. D is for Daisy."

He stared at her in utter confusion, as if she were a fish who had announced her intention to stand for Parliament. Behind her, she heard a high titter of amusement.

"You." He licked his lips. "Where's your brother?"

"I don't have a brother." Daisy raised her voice as loud as it would go. "I'm D. Whitlaw. I'm the tenth candidate."

The frown on the man's face intensified. "But you're a woman."

"The bequest is for the best proposal." Daisy stood ramrod straight, clasping her hands behind her back. "Not for the man with the best proposal. I have a proposal."

The grocer pulled back a step. "Manhood is generally understood to be a prerequisite. The bequest is assumed to be for a man."

Daisy stood in place, refusing to leave. She'd planned out an argument, something about the law and presumptions and whatnot. Now, with him glaring at her, she felt her throat go dry. Her argument evaporated.

She had no words any longer. She felt ungainly, unwanted. Everyone was watching her. She should just sit down and apologize.

Her legs wouldn't move.

The grocer's lip curled. "Feisty, are you?"

Cats were feisty. The word he was looking for was *hopeful.* Perhaps *unrealistic.* Daisy didn't say anything. She stood stock still, looking at him.

He sighed. "Well, I suppose it's the thing these days for women to ape men. We shouldn't be surprised that it's happening here. What do you say, gentlemen? Shall we give *Miss Daisy Whitlaw* the chance to show how women compare to men?"

Nine men to one woman. The odds were entirely unfair. They were also no worse than any Daisy had faced in the past.

"Come on up, then," the grocer said with a smile that was definitely not kind.

She ascended the steps, her knees stiff with the effort of not knocking together. It felt very cold on that high platform. Without the crowd to shield her, the wind seemed to slice through the fabric of her gown. Still, she marched to the front where the other candidates had stood.

"Tell me," the grocer said with a smirk. "Tell us all what sort of trade a woman wants to engage in."

"I'll take her in trade!" shouted a man from the back.

Daisy looked over the gathering and swallowed back an exclamation.

As a single member of the crowd, the people around her had seemed an overwhelming sea of indifferent waves. Even when she'd addressed the grocer, she'd not had to look at anyone else. But now she stood in front, and every face was turned to her. The gathering felt hostile. All those eyes bored into her. Every person seemed to murmur to one another.

She imagined their whispered conversations. *Look at that stupid girl. She'll come in dead last.*

She started speaking anyway. "We have fish carts. We have flower shops. We even have copyists. We don't need any more of them."

People stared at her in sullen disapproval.

"We don't have any of what I propose." Daisy had practiced her speech often enough that she could launch into it despite the dryness of her mouth. "Daisy's Emporium will be a small shop of carefully selected goods. Durable, beautiful, and inexpensive. Designed for—" *Women,* she had been going to say, but she was speaking too fast. And looking out over those disapproving faces...

They didn't want to hear about women and their wants.

She inhaled. "I propose a business in a central location, one where—"

"Speak up, girl," the grocer said. "Nobody can hear you."

She tried again a little more loudly. "I propose a business in a central location, one—"

"Can anyone hear the girl?" the grocer asked.

"Yes!" shouted a man in the back.

"Because all I hear," he said, "is something like the squeaking of a mouse."

Daisy's face flushed hot. She turned to him. *"I propose a business in a central location,"* she bellowed at the top of her lungs. *"One that provides inexpensive items designed to lift spirits, beautify homes, and teach relevant skills."*

The grocer looked upward. "How like a woman. Screaming like a fishwife already."

She was not going to let him bait her. Daisy took a deep breath and recalled her place in her memorized speech. "The cost of all this—"

"Oh dear," the grocer said. "Please stop before you get into the figures. We know what happens when women attempt mathematics."

"I have to do the figures." She could not keep the hopelessness out of her voice. "It's part of the bequest." She turned back to the crowd and tried to put on a smile. But if that mass of faces had looked unfriendly before, it seemed downright hostile now.

"The cost of all this," she made herself say, "is, as an initial outlay, fifteen pounds per annum in rents as determined by…" She was stumbling now, the words she'd practiced so many times sounding rote and boring. The people in the back could no longer hear her; they were turning away.

A man at the back stood. At first she thought he was going to leave. Instead, he stepped into the aisle and hurled something at her. She watched the brown blob come sailing in her direction, watched it in confusion, scarcely able to move away as it hurtled toward her. She stepped aside just as it landed on the wooden platform with a disheartening plop.

Horse dung.

It took the words right out of her mouth. She looked at the man. He smiled at her, a cruel, ugly smile.

Before she had a chance to say anything, another man materialized at his side. The new fellow took the man by the elbow and spun him around lightly. She could only tell that he'd wrenched the man's arm by the sudden squeal the thrower let out.

The newcomer leaned down, whispered something in the man's ear, and then pushed him to the ground before raising his face to Daisy.

She'd known who it was from the moment he had stood. Crash stood out in any crowd. It wasn't just the color of his skin—a pale brown—nor the brightness of his smile. He had an air about him, one that always attracted attention.

"Go on, Daisy." Those were the words she thought his mouth formed. Or maybe he'd said, "Go to hell, Daisy." Either was equally likely from him.

Once, she'd loved Crash's attention. Every moment he'd given her. Every wicked smile. Once, she'd believed that…

But none of her wishes ever came true. It wasn't fair, but it was her life, and she was used to it.

"So." She swallowed. "These are the figures." She'd spent so long gathering them; now she felt herself deflating like a child's broken toy. She stumbled through the end of her speech.

Nobody applauded her.

"Well," the grocer said. "The men have presented their ideas. The woman has…tried. Now the judges will confer. They will each pick one candidate to advance to the final proceedings."

Daisy was left standing stupidly on the stage.

The grocer looked at her. "Go join your fellow…ah, candidates."

Daisy stumbled to the seats at the back of the stage.

None of the other men looked at her except Mr. Flisk, who turned around and whispered to her. "You took a spot from a man who might have needed it. A man with a family to support. You should be ashamed of yourself."

Oh, she was. What did you call someone who refused to learn? Who kept reaching above herself?

The judges stood one by one, coming to the front. "I choose Mr.

Flisk," said the first judge. "Hargo," said another. They named Manning and Porget next.

They were the ones Daisy would have picked out of the proposals she had seen. She supposed that Mr. Diggle would be the last one chosen. Stupid or no, his proposal had been the most sound out of the remaining candidates.

The fifth judge came to the front. He didn't look at any of the candidates. He just looked out over the audience. He wouldn't choose her. Daisy knew it, the way she knew that snow was cold and winter turnips were bitter. She knew it in her chilled, numbing hands and her growling belly.

She'd reached. They'd slapped her down. It had happened to her often enough that she was almost used to it by now. One day, she'd learn to stop wasting effort chasing foolish dreams. One day. Just…not yet.

The final judge faced the crowd and said one word. "Whitlaw."

Daisy jumped. A well of hope started up inside her. There was a moment of utter silence from the crowd. Maybe the strain had finally driven her mad.

Maybe he hadn't said it. It couldn't be true.

But Mr. Flisk turned to look at her with venomous eyes. The crowd murmured more loudly.

"Well," the grocer managed after a meaningful pause. "We'll see you all next Saturday. And it looks like we have our entertainment in order. After all, we've just lined up the jester." He gave Daisy an exaggerated waggle of his eyebrows and let out a great, braying laugh, one that explained precisely why she'd been chosen.

CHAPTER TWO

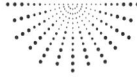

D aisy tried to sneak away.

It should have been easy; nobody would look at her, let alone talk to her. Yet somehow, the crowd seemed to have more elbows on the way out. People stepped in her way as if she were not present. Feet stamped on her own. And no apologies were made.

After she had the wind knocked out of her a third time by an "accidental" blow that nobody else seemed to notice, she gave up on fighting her way out of the square with the crowd. She simply waited, stamping her feet to keep them from freezing, until everyone had left.

Almost everyone. A small knot of women remained on the street corner, clustered in the growing darkness under an unlit lamp.

She didn't want to go past them. She knew who was at the center of that knot, knew it before she could see him. Before she heard his voice.

"I was wondering," one of the women was saying. "I have always so wanted to ask you…"

"Yes?" Daisy recognized Crash's voice, even though she couldn't see him through the crowd around him. It felt like a shock to hear him even after all these months apart.

A flush of heat—shame and excitement all mixed together—rushed through her. Speak of wishes gone awry.

"By all means," Crash said, "ask me anything you like."

The woman giggled, and Daisy felt a kind of sorry kinship for her fellow sufferer. She did her best to slink past the little gathering. That poor woman might have been a flirt, but Crash was an incorrigible charmer. He flirted with anyone and everyone who gave him the opportunity, men and women alike. Everyone had to learn not to play with fire in her own way, and Crash had been as good a place for Daisy to learn that lesson as any.

Enjoy the ride, Daisy wished the girl as she slipped past. *I hope your heart can withstand what comes after.*

"It's this," the woman said, wide-eyed. "What *are* you?"

Ah. Daisy felt a little less sorry for her. *That* had to be the worst way to flirt with Crash.

She caught a glimpse of him through the ring of women.

Crash took off his rounded hat and smoothed back black, lightly curled hair. Daisy had spent long enough staring at him to know that he looked like nobody she'd ever seen. In those heady months when she'd thought of nobody else, she'd spent a great deal of time looking at him, then at the rest of the world. Sailors, woodcuts of foreign delegations—it hadn't mattered. She'd searched for his features everywhere and found them only in him.

Those wide, dark eyes angled ever so slightly. His light brown skin never paled in winter. His hair never straightened. His cheeks took days to turn to patchwork stubble, which she knew only because he rarely bothered to shave.

"What am I? What sort of question is that?" She could imagine his smile—just a little tilted. "I should think that was clear enough."

Daisy ducked her head, proceeding down the steps. She couldn't help but glance at him as she slipped past.

"I am not a pineapple." He made a show of looking down his body, checking himself. Of course he drew attention to his own figure in the process. Crash was slim, lithe, and muscled. He had long fingers, slightly callused, square at their tips. Once, he'd held her...

She gave her head a shake and pointedly turned her face away.

But Crash was hard to ignore. "I am not an elephant, nor a mouse, nor an oak tree. I seem to land firmly in the human category."

"Yes, but..." The other woman's voice was trailing off behind Daisy. "What *sort* of human are you?"

"That much is apparent at one glance," Crash said. "I'm one hundred percent pure perfection. Now, if you'll excuse me?"

Daisy wouldn't look back. She wouldn't let him know she was paying attention.

"But—"

"Business calls," Crash said.

"But couldn't we—"

"I'm afraid not," she heard Crash saying.

"I haven't even said—"

She could just imagine the cocky smile Crash must be giving the woman. "It wouldn't have mattered," she heard him say. "Now run along."

Daisy could almost hear the sound of a heart breaking. She knew that sound all too well; she'd heard it in her own chest. She couldn't even really blame Crash for it; he'd done nothing but tell her the truth. It was her own fault that she'd wanted lies.

She didn't look behind her, but she could hear him following. "Excuse me," he said. "Pardon me."

There followed a set of gasps and a burst of applause. No doubt he'd done something ridiculous—something foolishly Crash-like, like doing a backflip off the steps to escape his hangers-on.

She'd spent enough time watching him to know what he could do. She wasn't going to look. She wasn't.

"Daisy," Crash called behind her.

The word sounded like a warning. Once he'd said her name very differently, almost reverently. As if she were not some kind of joke. But she couldn't allow herself to dwell on that *once*. It wouldn't help.

The snow underfoot had changed from delicate white lace to the disgusting, dingy slush of well-trodden streets. Icy water seeped through the seams of her shoes. A cold wind tugged at her, and she cinched her scarf around her neck. She didn't look back. She wasn't foolish.

"Ahoy, Daisy."

She wouldn't turn. That little skirling breeze coming up behind her would make her eyes water, and she was not—she absolutely was *not*—going to let Crash see her cry. Not even if her tears were merely wind-induced.

But Crash had never been deterred by…well, anything, Daisy suspected. Certainly not anything so mild as someone purposefully failing to hear him. He came jogging up to her, settling into a walk at her side.

At least he wasn't on that terrible contraption he'd taken to riding about everywhere. What did he call that two-wheeled unbalanced monstrosity? A velocipede?

Ha. An accurate description; it made her think of some monstrous twenty-legged thing, rushing about. One of these days he was going to crack his skull when he fell from the dratted thing, and she…

She wasn't going to care when he killed himself, not one bit.

"Daisy," he said. "You rushed off far too soon."

She made the mistake of meeting his eyes. Crash was a man who had mastered the speaking glance. *This* one could have been an epic saga. It was the unshakeable look that a farm lad gave to his sweetheart when she was sentenced to be fed to a dragon. *Don't worry,* it promised. *I'll save you. I've a plan.*

It was the kind of look that would have that blushing farm girl spreading her legs for her love in the barn the night before she was condemned to die. She'd give up her virginity, her trust, her love, her future in one trembling hour. When she bid her swain farewell through tears and kisses, she would believe in her soul that he was going to kill the beast. She'd believe he would save her until the dragon crunched her between its teeth.

Even now, even knowing Crash as she did, a flush of heat blossomed along the back of her neck.

Daisy's mind knew all about Crash, even if her body pretended ignorance. She'd already given him everything. She'd had that trembling hour. All these months later, Daisy had no virginity, no trust, no love, and her future was chock-full of dragons.

"Aha," Crash said, coming to a temporary halt. He snapped his fingers. "Right. Of course. I forgot. I'm to address you as Miss Whitlaw now."

He gave her a teasing smile, arranged the cloth at his neck into a mockery of a cravat, and shifted his tone. When he spoke, he sounded almost proper—the way Daisy's mother sounded at her most querulous. The way Daisy spoke when she wanted people to take her seriously.

"My dear Miss Whitlaw," he said in that distinctive, plummy-sounding voice, "I know you've little desire to speak with me at the moment. But I have a business proposition to put before you."

"You may recall," Daisy said severely, "that I do not care for your line of business."

That smile on his face flickered. "My line of business is the business of making people happy."

Ha. "Yes," she said. "A great *many* people."

"A great many people," he agreed, instead of getting angry at her implication like a normal person would. "I'm here to offer my services."

"I had your services once," Daisy snapped. "I don't need them any longer."

"Services," Crash said with a slow grin. "Is that what we're calling it, now? It's a good thing you don't need them any *longer*. You couldn't find services any longer—or thicker—or harder than mine."

Her cheeks flamed in memory of *long* and *thick* and *hard*. "Crash. *Please* don't say things like that."

He shrugged. "It's simple. I saw what happened back there. They're planning to make a joke of you, you know. All they want is to laugh."

"I know," Daisy said through clenched teeth.

"You should give up now."

"I know." Her teeth ground against each other.

"But you won't."

He knew that, too. His knowing things about her had fooled her thoroughly. She'd thought she was special. She had thought he actually cared. She'd been such an idiot.

As these things are reckoned, you are a complete waste of a woman. That was what she had to remember him saying. Her teeth gritted.

"And since you won't give up," he said, "then you cannot leave them with one single thing to laugh at. You know that's how it works, yes?"

"I know," she whispered.

"You will have to be brilliant to win." He looked at her. "You won't be able to hesitate. You'll have to make them believe that nobody will be able to survive without your..." He frowned. "I couldn't actually hear. Your...emporium, was it?"

She was not about to be inveigled into a conversation with him.

"That means you will have to practice."

"I know all these things," Daisy muttered. "It doesn't matter. I'm not going to win."

"You'll need an audience to test yourself against," Crash continued on as if she hadn't spoken. "Not your friend the marchioness nor your mother. You need to practice in front of someone you hate. Someone who makes your stomach curdle. Someone who will ask questions while you want to smash his face in. If you can impress *that* man, you can impress anyone."

She frowned at him. "I'm not going to win."

"Aren't you?" He took off his hat and gave her a flourishing bow. "I am, as ever, at your service."

He straightened and set his hat back on his head at an angle that might have been called rakish. No, not rakish. Mere rakery was never good enough for Crash. He adjusted it to something altogether promiscuous.

Daisy eyed him suspiciously. "Stop flirting with me."

His eyes widened in *Who, me?* innocence.

"I'm not going to win. I have a sweetheart." She'd told him that before. She had nothing of the kind. But right now, a man—an honest man, a solid man, one with prospects and morals—seemed as good a talisman to hold up as any. She needed to remind herself why she'd cut ties with Crash.

"Of *course* you do," Crash said in a tone that dripped with treacly, disbelieving sincerity.

He had seen her just now. In public. He'd been the only one to stand up, such as it was, on her behalf. If Daisy had a sweetheart, he was the most delinquent, useless sweetheart in the existence of romantic entanglements. Either that, or...

"He's a sublieutenant in the Royal Navy," she invented. "He'll be promoted any day—in fact, I expect he's already been promoted, but you know how the mails are at conducting letters written overseas." She was saying too much. He would notice she was lying. "Once he's back in port, we'll marry. I'm not going to win. I don't *need* to win. And I certainly don't want your help."

Crash rolled his eyes. "Come now, Daisy. You should know me better than that. You think I offered to help you because I wanted to interfere with your sweetheart? Nothing could be further from the truth."

That sounded actually sincere, not overly so. She narrowed her eyes at him suspiciously. "What do you want, Crash? What do you really want?"

"Ooh." He scratched his chin. "So many things. Ten million pounds, a large house, three carriages—oh. Wait. You mean what do I want from *you?*"

She exhaled. "You're being obtuse."

"One of my greatest talents." Crash ducked his head as if she'd given him a compliment. As if she'd mentioned the only modest bone in his body. "I'm flattered that you realized. But you were asking me a question. What do I want with you?"

He looked up, and her skin prickled under his attention. It was just her luck that she was susceptible to him. To the dark entreaty of his eyes, the way he adjusted his hat on his head.

"What do I want with you?" He shrugged. "Come, Daisy. You know I take odds."

Among so many other things. If there was an occupation that

skirted the edges of legality, Crash was involved in it. She'd seen him organize a spot of gambling at the slightest provocation. The bestowal of the charity bequest had turned into a pageant for the entire parish. There might as well have been a banner floating over her head: *Place wagers here.*

Stupid to feel disappointment that he didn't want anything else from her. "I should have guessed. Of course you're gambling about the competition."

He reached into his pocket and took out the little book where she'd seen him record his bets. "Think on it, Daisy." He waved the leather-bound book at her before tucking it away. "After that little catastrophe on stage, do you imagine that *anyone* placed money that you would win? No. Everyone wanted to put odds on Hargo or Flisk. Imagine the purse I'd collect if you prevailed."

She let out an exhale. That was all she was to him at this point—a wager to be won. He looked at her and heard shillings rattling in his pockets.

"I'm not going to win," she informed him.

"Aren't you?" His eyes bored into her. "The Daisy I once knew would never have said that."

She didn't want to be reminded of the person she had been. Gullible, naïve, and optimistic. She'd believed him when he said that he loved her as much as he breathed. That of course, had been *before* he took her virginity.

"As you are, you're not going to win. There's no chance of it. You need someone who will teach you how to swagger," he said in a low voice. "To ignore the shouted insults, the thrown horse droppings, and to shout out your confidence to the world. It's the only way you'll have a chance."

She folded her arms and glared at him.

He went on as if she'd issued an invitation for him to make a speech. "Make them believe that no matter how they posture, no matter how they bluster, you have nothing but victory in you."

Statements like that had drawn her to Crash. He could make the entire world disappear. He could make her forget how cold her feet were, how little money she had. She could look into his eyes and believe that she could prevail despite everything.

He was right. If she floundered about a week from now the way she had just now, she was not going to win.

She was not going to win with his help, either.

But some part of her, some foolish part, had never quite managed to give up all her naïve confidence. She had a brief vision of herself, standing on the stage in front of the crowd. Of the grocer calling her name as the winner.

She shoved it away.

She *wasn't* going to win, no matter what she did. But if she did her utmost… Maybe, maybe this time she'd finally learn not to waste her effort trying.

"Very well." Her voice came out a little too high. "I accept."

"An excellent choice. To us prevailing, then." He held out his hand as if he expected her to shake it.

She looked at his fingers. They were encased in wool gloves. She wouldn't have to touch his skin. She would scarcely even feel him. But she remembered too much about Crash, and *scarcely* was already too much.

Daisy put her hands behind her back. "No," she said. "No hand-shakes. There will be no touching of any kind. This is just business."

He gave her a sardonic smile. "We're nothing but business, you and I."

Her cheeks flamed and she turned away. Her legs could not move fast enough to get away from him and the memory his words sparked in her mind. Once, he had—

No. Absolutely not. She was *not* going to think of what she'd let Crash do.

"I'll see you Monday," he called after her. "At three, when I've done my rounds, outside the general store. You should be finished at the flower shop then, yes? Wear skirts that allow a good deal of movement."

She knew better than to let Crash get under her skin; really, she did. Still, she whipped around. "Don't talk about my skirts!" she hissed. "It's not proper."

He simply laughed.

God, what had she agreed to do?

~

Crash's aunt—and his uncle, when the man was in England—lived in a flat over a cooper's shop. At night, with all the customers departed and the apprentices off, the neighborhood was quiet. As quiet as anything ever was here, a quarter mile from the eternal hum of the St. Katharine docks.

He stepped close to the door and detected the muted sounds of spirited voices.

His aunt had guests over. She often did; her husband was the first mate on a trading vessel, and in the months when he was away, she entertained.

He knocked and waited. The door opened, and a brilliant dazzle of light met him. For a moment, his aunt was nothing but a dark silhouette lit by the oil lamps from behind. Then she moved back a pace and the palette of her skin shifted from midnight to umber.

She tried, oh, she tried, to frown at him disapprovingly. Alas. His aunt was terrible at disapproval, particularly where he was involved.

He embraced her. "Aunt Ree."

She gave him a grudging pat on the back in return.

The other two women seated at the card table smiled at him over Ree's shoulder, as if the evening's entertainment had just arrived. Three white-haired women looking at him with that particular expression might have put another man off, but Crash knew them better.

Harriet Cathing had been his aunt's friend since before he was born. She'd been a laundress then, before she married a ship's lieutenant. Now she was... Well, technically, she was a laundress married to a ship's lieutenant.

May Walsh hadn't married anyone—at least not in a legally

binding ceremony. She swore by the strategy to any of the young girls who would listen to her. She had a strong jaw and dark freckles spattering brown skin.

Once, Martha Claving had been the fourth whist player in their little quartet, and May's longtime partner and companion. A little pencil sketch in a black crepe-draped frame marked the place she would have taken.

His aunt was shaking her head at him. "Crash," she said, "Crash, Crash, Crash. You know Saturday night is whist night, and still you chose to invade. Ladies, you all know my scapegrace nephew. Crash, do try to be respectable."

It was a bit of a joke between them, that word.

Crash gave the gathering a sweeping bow. "I am *always* respectable. If anyone chooses not to respect me, however…" He gave his aunt a low grin. "There's very little I can do about that, is there?"

"Pish-tosh," Miss Walsh said. "I so hate when men are respectable. It usually involves rather too much posturing."

"Nonsense. You remember old Barnabas Tucker? Well, he…"

And they were off, as they so often were, on the sort of conversation that would have offended the more proper households three-quarters of a mile to the north.

"Speaking of Barnabas and his unfortunate predilections," Miss Walsh said, "have you all heard what happened at Redding Copy House?"

The other two women shook their heads and made little tsking noises.

"Badly run," Harriet said. "Staff constantly embezzling. No discretion in the clientele. I was certainly not surprised when it closed."

"I am so glad to not have to labor in my advanced age," Miss Walsh was saying. "It leaves me free to pursue leisure activities in my final years. Like—"

"Cheating us all at cards," Ree put in.

Yes. That was their favorite pastime of a winter evening: playing whist and cheating wildly. Cheating was the unspoken rule of the game. Cheating, in fact, was the *only* real rule of the game, and the competition was cutthroat.

Much of England would have summed up these three women with one word: whores. They'd won that epithet by virtue of the poverty they'd labored through, the men they'd associated with, and the color of their skin.

It wouldn't have mattered if they'd never sold sexual services on the streets. They'd been poor. Aunt Ree and May Walsh were too dark to be considered anything other than unacceptably foreign; Harriet Cathing's mother had also been what the uptight middle class would call a whore.

They had never been seen as respectable by England's rules. The rules had written them out of the game centuries ago.

Crash set his bag down. "I've brought rum, milk, bread, spices, potatoes, and eggs. It's cold and you're almost out of everything."

Harriet beamed at him. "How utterly darling. He brings rum. Ree, I must get myself a nephew like him. How ever does one obtain one?"

Ree rolled her eyes. "Don't let the rum fool you. It's scant penance for all the woe he's brought into my life. Fortunately for us all, Crash is one of a kind."

Crash waggled his eyebrows at his aunt. "You know you love me."

She glowered at him. "Unfortunately."

"I've always meant to ask. What sort of a name is Crash? Is it a first or a family name?" Miss Walsh frowned at him. "That can't be your real name, can it?"

"His Christian name is Nigel," Ree put in, "but we started calling him Crash at a very young age, and it stuck so well that we've just decided to forget there was ever anything else. As for family names, we don't deal in those. It's a bit of a tradition. But if you feel better calling him Nigel—"

"Refer to me as Nigel again," Crash said with a raised finger, "and I'll start calling you Catriona."

His aunt made a face. "You don't want him," she explained earnestly to her friend. "He talks back. And he only brings enough rum for a little glass here and there. He's hardly worth all the bother."

But she gave him a proud smile.

And oh, he *had* been a bother. Never sitting still, always moving. Once, when he'd been a child scarcely old enough to learn his letters, he'd lived up to his assumed name. He'd dashed around a corner in a store and had run headlong into a display of canned goods. They'd toppled to the ground with a resounding crash.

The shopkeeper had grabbed him up, shaking him viciously, calling him a good-for-nothing hell-bent bastard who would end his days in a noose.

"Just like your father," he'd said. "But then, you don't even know who that is, do you, you worthless little mongrel?"

His aunt had taken Crash's hand and conducted him out of the shop.

"Don't you listen to him," she had said, her voice shaking. "He can't see you, not as you are. So don't you listen to what he says. You're good for anything you want to do. You'll have to try harder, and you'll have to do it a little differently—but don't you ever listen to him."

Twenty-six years of *don't you listen to him.*

Every time someone crossed the street at the sight of him. Every time someone spat in his direction. When the vicar announced at Sunday service that unnatural attractions to men were a sign of moral turpitude. The morning when a well-meaning woman had sought him out in a crowd and earnestly explained that foreign heathens like him needed to learn of Christ and seek divine forgiveness.

For twenty-six years, his aunt had told him not to listen to any of them. After all she'd done for him, a little rum was the least he could offer.

"You know," Miss Walsh put in, "if we could get this fine young man to play Martha's hand for us, nobody could use her to cheat."

Three faces considered this contemplatively. Crash was fairly certain that all three women were considering the many ways he might choose to play Martha's hand.

"Speak for yourself," Ree said piously. "I never cheat. I win by skill."

This was met with the raucous laughter it deserved.

Ha. She'd give up cheating the day she... No, he didn't want to think such morbid thoughts. His aunt was fifty-four; she had decades left in her, God willing. She'd taught him everything he knew about cheating. Cheating was the only way to win, and so she did it assiduously.

He sat and dealt.

"He won't do for a fourth," Harriet said. "But you know, May…"

May frowned. "I know. It's been a year. We should…consider a replacement now."

"I am not available on a permanent basis," Crash said smoothly. "My innocent young ears would burn off if I had to listen to more than an evening of your conversation."

They all laughed good-naturedly.

"Young man," said Miss Walsh, "you do realize that we know you?"

"Who?" he asked. "Me? You must be thinking of Nigel."

Ree had taught him to cheat, too, with everything he had in him. When the rules were stacked against you, cheating was a moral necessity.

A moment earlier in the day flashed in front of him—Daisy looking up at him in disapproval.

Stop flirting with me, she had said.

As if he *wanted* to flirt with her. Every time he saw her, every time she threw her so-perfect fiancé in his face, he became more and more certain that he'd had the luckiest of escapes. All those months spent worrying while he was in Paris…they'd been for nothing. He'd hoped for a letter. A telegram. A single word.

Not a damned thing had come. He'd not thought her the sort of person who would treat him like a shameful secret, one to be hidden as soon as possible. He was done flirting with Daisy.

She could have her emporium and her sweetheart. He'd learned long ago not to waste tears on anyone who pushed him away. Not shopkeepers. Not stablehands. Not even sweethearts he'd once intended to marry.

He smiled and poured little jiggers of rum for the women who had raised him. They had told him not to listen when the country shouted that he was nothing. They had taught him to walk with his head held high, to act as if he meant something even though nobody else would agree.

He wouldn't spare a thought for the woman who'd decided he meant nothing. He didn't want her back. He didn't care how she felt about him.

All he wanted was for Daisy Whitlaw to realize how wrong she'd been and to regret her stupidity. He wanted her to marry her stupid sublieutenant and have equally stupid children and look out her stupid window and think occasionally: *I suppose Crash was right after all. I made a mistake.*

Aside from that? He didn't care one bit. He wouldn't let himself do it.

CHAPTER THREE

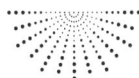

D aisy was always going to feel like an interloper on her Sunday visits to her best friend. She'd resigned herself to that fact.

It didn't matter that Judith ushered her into a front salon as if she were regular company. The walls of the luxurious room were covered in a white-and-gold damask silk. The table Daisy sat at was laden with goodies: biscuits, sandwiches, scones.

Once, Judith had lived just across the street from Daisy. At first Daisy had felt she was the luckier of the two. Her father might have failed as a grocer, but he'd had a bit of an annuity, and her mother had been frugal enough, and genteel enough, to teach Daisy everything she had needed to know. Then Daisy's life had jagged down. Her father had died; his annuity had disappeared. Her mother had become ill. Alongside that, Judith's luck had jagged up, and then up again. She'd married a wealthy, powerful man she had known from her childhood. Now, instead of exchanging bread recipes and household tips, the two women sat at a table where three years of Daisy's labor would not pay for all the china.

"Here," Judith said with a smile. "Would you care for a roast beef sandwich?"

"Of course I would," Daisy said with a smile.

Once, Daisy and Judith had gone shopping together and joked of purchasing kid gloves with diamonds. They'd talked about adding gold leaf to their meager meals. It had been silly, ridiculous—and utterly necessary for Daisy's peace of mind. Their little game had provided perspective on her wants. *Your wishes are silly. Be happy you have soup bones, Daisy. You could have less.*

"How goes the flower shop?" Judith asked.

"It prospers." Daisy gave her friend as confident a smile as she could muster. "In fact, I've been awarded additional compensation for my valiant efforts. We're positively flush."

Not a lie. Five pence more a week—it had gone a long way. She and her mother were actually saving money in winter now, not bleeding it slowly away in coal bills.

Judith smiled, as Daisy had known she would.

The sad thing was, their friendship was already over. Judith just didn't know it yet. There was the literal distance between them—four miles, difficult for Daisy to manage on her own unless Judith sent a carriage, as she'd done today.

There was the way the maid's eyes cut toward Daisy as she placed the tea on the table, as if Daisy were a bit of refuse that she longed to sweep from the room. There was the fact that Daisy suspected Judith's servants earned more in a week than the owner of the flower shop bestowed on Daisy. Daisy would have been lucky to scrub floors for her friend.

"Tell me all the gossip," Judith said. "I don't want to miss a single story."

Daisy went through all their former mutual acquaintances: Fred Lotting and his wife, Mr. Padge, Daisy's mother... She talked of everyone but herself.

Daisy was lying to herself, she realized as they spoke and laughed. They *were* still friends. They still had those years of poverty binding them together. Judith had been her support, the shoulder she cried on when everything went wrong. In turn, she'd held her friend through every reversal.

They were friends still, fragile though that friendship was. Their hours together felt like spider silk—ready to dissipate with one good sweep of a servant's broom. One day it would break. One day. Still, it held. Spiderwebs tended to remain in place if you held your breath when you were close.

Daisy was trying not to breathe.

"Is there anything else?" Judith asked.

Daisy almost told Judith what she'd done about the charity bequest. She almost told her of entering the competition, of the grocer mocking her because she wasn't a man.

She didn't, though.

Daisy's Emporium was a dream that was as unattainable and unrealistic as gold leaf on radishes. Deep down, Daisy knew it would never come to pass. Dreaming was one thing. Entering a competition she couldn't win? That was a little worse.

Telling her friend about it? That would make this serious. *Real.* Judith would want to hear the details. She might even offer to help. And if she did…

Daisy would end up another one of Judith's servants, running a storefront for her. And if the store failed the way her father's store had…?

She did her best not to breathe on the attenuating cobwebs of their friendship.

"No," Daisy said instead. "That's all there is. All this about me, and we've scarcely spoken of you. How are you? How are the terrors?"

The terrors were Judith's younger brother and sister.

Judith laughed. "I'm well, as you can see." She gestured around the room. "Theresa's being fitted for dresses at this very moment. Imagine her in silks, if you will."

Daisy couldn't imagine that sort of transformation. Judith's younger sister was a hellion at the best of times. She'd rip a silk gown in a minute flat. She'd smear grease on the skirts.

But of course, the cost of repair would no longer matter to her friend. And who knew how a deportment teacher might have changed the girl she remembered from a few months ago?

"We're well," Judith said. "Very well, and I'm glad to see you. I miss you. A few stolen hours here and there are hardly enough."

"I miss you, too." A few hours was all Daisy had. "But I need to go back to my mother."

"I know, dear." Judith patted her hand. "Is there anything you need?"

Daisy could have laughed. *Everything.* She needed everything.

"Gold leaf," she said instead. "Gold leaf and diamonds at my hem, and with that, I should be splendid."

Judith smiled at her.

It wouldn't be much longer until their friendship diminished to nothing. Until that moment, though, Daisy would let the servants frown at her. She wouldn't flinch when they kept too-careful an eye on her as they conducted her to the door, hoping to catch her in the act of stealing the silver.

Daisy took her leave, her smile plastered firmly on her face. She kept it there for three whole minutes before the reality of her life set in again.

She'd entered a competition she couldn't win. She'd agreed to let a man she didn't like assist her in her preparations.

Of course she hadn't told Judith. Judith knew she was poor; she didn't need to know that she'd gone witless.

⁓

Crash was already late. Five minutes ago, the clock had chimed three. Daisy still found herself waiting in front of the general store. She was exhausted from her day at the flower shop, the wind was cold, and her patience was running thin.

Late was perhaps a little unfair. She knew he was around somewhere because his velocipede was leaning against the side of a building. But he was not present, and she'd not so much free time that she could afford to waste a moment of it.

Especially not if he had arrived on his velocipede. Just looking at the thing made her palms itch. She had done her best *not* to learn about the contraption when he'd first started riding it a few months back. She had been certain that he was going to live up to his name and crash into something.

That was because Crash on a velocipede belonged in a circus act, one that should have been paired with lions and flaming hoops. If she'd had any idea what a velocipede was when he first mentioned the thing, she would have protested. He'd called it a vehicle. Some vehicle it was; it couldn't even stand upright on its own. It was nothing but two wheels, one in front of the other. Nothing to stabilize it. No sticks to keep him upright.

Worse, Crash turned those wheels not by propelling himself with his feet on the ground. The wheels turned by means of little pedals attached to the front axle. A seat three or four feet above the ground might not seem so high, but he went flying past as fast as a horse could gallop.

She had to hide her face every time she saw him. She kept imagining him overbalancing. Or underbalancing. Or hitting a wall. She imagined him smashing into hard bricks at that speed...

She didn't care about Crash, not one bit. But just because he'd broken her heart didn't mean she wanted him to crack his skull.

Daisy was not the only one who had noted the velocipede's presence; three other women had observed it, and were standing—lolly-gagging, really—outside the store. Now she could see him inside through the dirt-smeared windows. A cap covered his hair; he'd unwound his scarf so it was loosely looped around his neck, long enough to dangle enticingly just past his hips. He was gesturing, describing something to the store owner.

The storekeeper was laughing, ducking his bald head in amusement. Crash was *good* at making people laugh. He took nothing and nobody seriously, she reminded herself.

She wasn't the only one whose eyes drifted toward Crash's dim silhouette in the storefront. The other women ranged in age from sixteen-year-old Molly Jenkins, whose eyes glowed with the sort of unrequited worship that young girls needed to be warned about, to thirty-seven-year-old Martha Pratt, who really ought to have known better.

Daisy refused to join those three. They were doing their best to pretend they were just talking on the street corner. Talking, indeed. Talking out here in the cold, shifting from foot to foot and rubbing hands together, waiting, hoping that Crash would come out and warm them up.

Daisy had no such expectation. She'd already been burned.

She drifted a few yards down the pavement, letting her eyes stray to the pastries in the bakery window. Gingerbread men with iced pantaloons and colored buttons smiled vacantly onto the street. Cinnamon loaves, braided and laced with sugared nuts and sultanas, were laid in an enticing row. The air outside was laden with sweet and spice; she could almost taste that flaky crust. Buttery-looking scones flecked with bits of orange zest and currants made a mouthwatering pile.

It had been a very long time since breakfast.

Her stomach growled as the door to the general store opened behind her in a ring of bells. She wouldn't turn. She wouldn't look.

"Well, look who it is." She heard Miss Pratt speak. "It's Crash. What mischief are you up to today?"

"I've been looking for two items." Behind her, Crash's voice was low and velvety. "I procured the tinned ham. The carbolic smoke ball, however, was nowhere to be found."

These prosaic errands were met with a moment of disappointed silence.

"Oh." Miss Pratt let out a burst of laughter, as if nothing could be more amusing than oversalted pig meat in a metal container. "I *see*. Tinned ham *indeed*."

Daisy wasn't going to turn around.

Young Miss Jenkins was not to be outdone. "Is this for your supper? Why, Crash, I've just realized. You don't even know who your people are. You must be very lonely. Aren't you positively *starved* for proper company?"

Crash laughed. "Someone has been feeding you poppycock. Who told you that? I can trace my lineage for generations."

"You can?" The girl was startled into momentary quiet.

It was a very short moment.

"That is to say, I had thought that...um..."

Daisy heard the rattle of metal. That was Crash taking his velocipede from the side of the building. "Don't spare a moment of pity for me, Miss Jenkins," he said. "I come from a long, illustrious line."

"You do?" That was Miss Pratt again, trying not to sound dubious.

"I do." A note of infectious laughter touched his voice. "I'm proud to say that I'm the scion of three generations of dock whores and sailors."

He was so utterly impossible. Daisy choked into her handkerchief and couldn't help looking behind her. Crash was standing, his hand outstretched as if he were declaiming some kind of poem. Only Crash could say he was descended from prostitutes with that flair, as if it were a thing to be delighted about. Only Crash could carry the thing off so perfectly, smiling beatifically. He acted as if everyone whose birth had been legitimized by something as prosaic as marriage was somehow less fortunate than he.

Crash looked as if he'd never had horse dung thrown at him. As if nobody had ever told him to behave in a manner comporting with his station. As if he'd never harbored doubts, as if he expected at any moment to be informed that he'd been made mayor of all London. She felt a brief tickle of jealousy that he should be so free of all the rules that bound her. Daisy turned back to the bread again.

She could scarcely pretend those fine, sugared confections held her interest.

"Oh," Miss Jenkins managed in a strangled voice.

"Really," Crash said, "do you think I'd want a carbolic smoke ball for myself? I'm young and in excellent health. It's for my aunt. She's a little older, and with winter coming on, I don't want her to take sick."

"Oh." That syllable was also a little strangled. "I'm sorry to have asked."

"Don't be," Crash said cheerfully. "I daresay my family is more interesting than yours. I merely wanted to inform you that there's no need to squander your pity on me. I surely don't need it."

If Crash could bottle his arrogance and sell it to the masses, English society would crumble within a decade. They'd never be able to govern their empire, not with talk of ruling by right of blood. The peers of the realm would renounce everything, mount their velocipedes, and ride into the ocean en masse while he looked on and laughed.

"But... Don't you ever wish for...for..."

"What?" Crash said. "Are you asking if I ever hope that maybe one day, a lovely young lady of good breeding and decent education might take pity on me, and I might give up all my wicked ways? Do you think that maybe I yearn for someone to transform me? Someone who will turn me from my path of sin with one speaking look?"

None of the women answered. Daisy imagined they were all silent, caught in the thralls of lust. He must know she was listening.

"Wonder no more," Crash said. "I'm just looking for someone to share my..."

He paused, and the women sighed.

"What?" whispered Molly.

"My potted meat," Crash said, exaggerating the word *meat* so there was little doubt that he was referring to something other than ham in tins. "What else?"

She couldn't bear it any longer. Daisy turned to him. "Crash, stop tormenting those poor souls. You're like a cat with a butterfly—you never can stop playing."

"Allow me to defend myself, Miss Whitlaw." Crash winked at her. "I wasn't tormenting them. I was tormenting *you*. Did I do a proper job of it?"

"You don't do proper jobs." She sniffed. "*That* was always the problem."

Crash inclined his head, as if granting her that point. "Ladies. I must be off." He held his velocipede by the handles and walked toward her. "Come, Daisy. We've much to discuss."

She shouldn't have agreed to this. She shouldn't have come here.

As he stalked toward her, her stomach turned. Oh, she wished it were nausea.

She folded her hands. "We do," she said. "Let's start with this. You should have been more punctual."

Crash folded his arms. "I've spent the day looking for a space for my shop. There's little available, none of it in the right location. Find the right location, and the space is wrong. One place was perfect, but twice as large as I need." He glowered in her direction, as if this were her fault. "On top of all that, I've been trying to obtain a carbolic smoke ball. So yes, Daisy, I do apologize. My future and my aunt's continued health should have taken second place to your minor discomfort."

"Thank you. I take your apology for precisely what it is worth." Daisy knew how she ranked in his estimation. "Your shop? What are you selling?"

He didn't look at her. "You remember. I'm not in the mood to pretend otherwise."

So he still intended to sell his damned velocipedes. Idiot plan. Only a fool would want them.

He was probably going to make a fortune. There were always idiots out there willing to pay money to kill themselves. Crash had never had any problem obtaining *his* wishes.

A little steering column was attached to the front wheel of his velocipede. He took hold of this and began guiding the contraption down the street, walking next to her. Thank God he wasn't riding. She'd have had to crane her neck to look at him, and she felt uncomfortable enough in his presence.

It had been one of those days. She had been up since four that morning, tying bouquets.

He didn't say anything. He didn't tell her where they were headed or what he had planned. The wheels of his velocipede made a curious staccato sound as they passed over the cobblestones.

Crash's silence had once been welcoming, for lack of a better word. He had kept silent the same way another man might stand up from a seat on an omnibus. It used to make her feel as if he were making room for her.

This quiet felt disapproving.

"Oh, shut up, Crash," she said, even though he hadn't said anything at all. "I'm sure you had a jolly day making wagers on my eventual public embarrassment and searching for your...balls."

He made a little choking sound. "My carbolic smoke ball, you mean?"

"I spent *my* day at honest labor." Her voice shook. "Honest labor where every man who found me alone felt it was his right to pinch my behind."

"So why is getting your behind pinched considered honest labor, while—" He cut himself off. "Never mind. I'm not arguing with you." He glanced at her and shook his head. "Walk faster. We're almost there."

She trotted after him. They turned a corner and traversed a street. He dragged his velocipede through the mud of a park before he turned to look at her.

"Where are we going?" she asked.

He gestured to an abandoned gravel footpath that followed the line of a canal. The waters were brown and stagnant, running sullenly through the gray warehouses on either side. "Here."

"Here?" She chafed her hands together. "What are we doing *here?* Could we not go somewhere warmer?"

"No." He gave her a not-quite-friendly smile. "We can't. You see, I'm going to teach you how to ride my velocipede."

For a second, she had an image of herself hurtling into the canal at full speed. She flinched back. "Oh no. No. There isn't a chance of it. That is not at all what I had in mind."

He pushed the contraption toward her. "Oh, yes," he countered. "You are going to learn."

She shook her head more violently. "First, your stupid veloci-whatever has nothing to do with the competition. Second, I could not walk on a fence rail without falling off, ever. I have no balance to speak of, let alone enough to manage that—thing. I'm not here to ride your da—your dratted veloci…tastrophe. You said you were going to help me win."

"I did," he said. "And this is how you're going to do it. You're going to—"

"Let me guess: I'm going to wear a revealing outfit, come flying through the crowd on a velociclysm, hurtle through a flaming hoop, and land on the stage to tumultuous applause."

He blinked and looked at her. "Well, that would be *one* way to manage it. But I had quite a different idea in mind. See, there's a trick to riding a velocipede."

"You have to be a lunatic." Daisy sniffed.

"Correct," Crash said. "You have to be a lunatic, although that is rather unkind to the lunatics, don't you think?"

She made a noise in her throat in response.

"Here's the trick: you have to not care. Our bodies learn motion from walking. When you're walking, you learn to balance on your feet, to stay upright as you move. Height frightens us; speed more so. But all the rules we've told ourselves must be true about motion in general? They're wrong when we're on a velocipede."

He was warming to his subject matter. He leaned the contraption against a bench and began to use his hands to demonstrate.

"On a velocipede," he told her, "you don't need to balance."

"How do you stay upright?"

"The faster you go, the more stable you are."

She snorted in disbelief.

"I know it sounds unlikely, but it's true. When you turn, you might be afraid that you'll fall. You won't—but to make sure, you should lean into the direction you're turning."

"Poppycock." She swallowed. "You're trying to get your revenge. You're trying to kill me."

He gave her an unreadable look. "You never did believe me, Daisy. No matter what you think of the other times we disagreed, *this* time I am simply right. The velocipede is a simple application of the principles of natural law. You've spent your entire life learning lessons. *Stupid* lessons. Keep quiet if a man pinches your bum. Don't speak loudly, or you'll turn heads. Express yourself in the mildest possible terms, so that no one can have any objection. There are reasons you have to act that way on a daily basis. But if you want one damned chance at success at this competition you've entered, you're going to have to forget them all. You can't forget *some* rules and hope for the best."

She swallowed. She looked at the machine leaning peacefully against the bench. "But I could *die.*"

He didn't call her overly dramatic. He didn't roll his eyes.

Instead, he raised an eyebrow. "Daisy," he said slowly, "I assume you entered the competition to establish yourself. Because you wanted lasting financial security. At present, your future rests entirely on other people continuing to provide you with gainful employment. What do you think would happen if that stopped?"

He didn't need to ask her to imagine what would happen if she had no money. If she were tossed from her rooms, if she couldn't afford bread, if her mother…

Daisy didn't want to think of her mother. She swallowed. "I'm… I'm not going to win."

"Ah, ah." He held up a finger. "None of that. My only point is that there's no way around risk." He gestured her forward. "That is precisely why you're learning to ride a velocipede. If you're going to risk your life, you had best risk it properly."

She frowned. She was fairly certain there was a flaw in his logic. He'd always been able to convince her of anything and everything. Wagers? They were harmless, so long as nobody bet money they couldn't afford to lose. His prior liaisons with men and women? Well, so long as he was honest about what happened, and hadn't lied to anyone, who was hurt by it? She'd been so turned around that she'd accepted it all. Even now, she was certain that he had been wrong. She just wasn't sure how.

"One more thing." His eyes met hers. "It's called a *velocipede*. Or a bicycle. You're not stupid, so use its proper name. Call the product I will be selling a *velocitastrophe* one more time, and I will…"

They watched each other for a long moment.

"You'll what?" she asked. "Push me over?"

His lip curled in distaste. "I'll make polite conversation. Like this: How is your fiancé, Daisy? When did you last hear about him? Was his last letter everything you hoped for?"

His eyes were dark and narrowed, looking down at her, and Daisy felt a little shiver slide up her spine.

She swallowed. It was an excellent threat. "Him?" She hadn't even given him a name. "Why would that bother me? I would gladly talk about...Edwin."

"I'm sure you would. He sounds like quite the stick-in-the-mud. The two of you no doubt get along splendidly."

CHAPTER FOUR

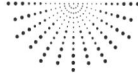

For a second, Crash thought Daisy would turn away. Instead, her chin went up. Her fingers, clothed in dark gray wool gloves, clenched at her side. Her eyes glittered like shards of blue glass.

"Go ahead," she said. "I'm not afraid of you or your threats or your velossacre."

"Velossacre?"

"I'm making this up as I go along." She glowered at him defiantly. "It's derived from massacre. If you kill me with that thing, at least you'll hang for my death. I take what scant satisfaction I can find in this cruel world."

Damn it all. He didn't want to remember why he'd once liked her.

He simply tsked instead. "Daisy, you know that my slightly less-than-legal activities are chosen so as not to harm anyone. I'm a reprobate, not a villain. Veloci-probate hasn't the same ring."

Her nose wrinkled. "No. That sounds like an exceedingly swift Court of Chancery."

"Ugh. Nobody wants that."

She almost smiled. Almost. "Very well. How does one even get on this…monstrosipede?"

He wasn't going to take the bait. Instead, he guided her to a bench, one where she could hop up and reach the seat of his velocipede. It was a simple matter to brace the machine against his hip and gesture her forward.

"So," he said. "Get on."

"What, with you holding it?"

"Yes." He rolled his eyes. "With me holding it. Do you think I'm going to let you fall?"

She gave him a dark look. Her nose twitched. "You might."

"I might," he said, returning her dark look. "That's one of the risks you'll have to take."

She glared at him for a long moment before gathering her skirts to the ankles, awkwardly straddling the metal top bar, and lowering herself gingerly to the seat.

She shut her eyes instantly, clutching the handlebar. "Oh, God. It's very high. And *extremely* wobbly."

"Well, then," Crash said sarcastically. "I suppose our lesson is done. We'll leave the having of trades to men, and you can keep on getting your bum pinched in your flower shop."

Her eyes flew open.

"That's better," he said. "Yes. It's high and wobbly. That's because you're not moving. Now I'm going to come around to the side, and you're going to put your feet on the pedals. Understand?"

"But…"

He moved without waiting, and she winced as the machine lurched beneath her.

"You're touching me," she said as his hand landed against her spine. "I said, no—"

He pulled his hands away and held them up in the air. The velocipede faltered, tilted, and—

"Touch me!" she shrieked. "I lied! I don't mind!"

He calmly took hold of her before she fell. "Come now, Daisy. I'm not touching you for my pleasure. If you die, I hang, and hanging is not in my plan. Besides, you have a sweetheart. I won't do anything that your dear Edwin won't approve of. My promise."

She gave him a baleful glare.

"So," he said. "Feet on the pedals. Push first on the top one. No, not to the side—down, smoothly down. Like that. Now the next."

It took her a few revolutions to get the gist of the motion. She went slowly; he paced beside her. They started along the canal at a snail's pace. He kept one hand on the seat, the other on her spine, steadying her as she moved.

"A little faster," he told her. "I can keep up."

A little faster meant there was a bit of wind as they moved. The breeze whipped her bonnet off her head and left it trailing behind her, held in place only by bonnet strings. The wind stole little tendrils of pale hair from Daisy's braid. A little faster meant that his hand was no longer steady against her spine. His palm jogged with his pace, up and down, up and down.

The cold lent color to her cheeks. Her determination gave fire to her eyes. God, he missed Daisy.

It wasn't the first time he had missed her.

It happened at odd intervals. When he heard an amusing story and thought of telling her. When he had an idea he wanted to share with her. When he saw her on the street and accidentally smiled before he remembered.

He didn't *really* miss her. He missed the woman he'd once believed she was.

But he missed that woman now, almost intensely. He missed the way she gritted her teeth as she concentrated. He missed the way she kept trying, no matter what life threw at her. The way she gripped the handlebar, as if holding on more tightly would save her from a fall.

He missed the way she'd once trusted him, the way she had used to look at him.

"See?" he told her through even breaths as he ran alongside her. "Keep going. You're still very high up, but you're less wobbly, aren't you?"

Her teeth gritted. "Maybe."

"You can go faster."

"But if I do?"

"I'll be right here," he lied.

She went faster.

It wasn't hard to get to the point where he couldn't keep pace with her on the velocipede. She had her gaze trained ahead; she didn't even notice when it happened. He let go and she kept on pedaling. For one moment, then two. Her grip relaxed. Her teeth stopped gritting together.

Her expression began to soften into exhilarating wonder.

It lasted for precisely one second. Then she realized that he was no longer supporting her. She looked around, jerked the handlebar—

Crash winced as she toppled to the ground. He jogged up to where she lay on the path, a tangle of skirts and pedals and indignation.

She pushed herself up on her hands, brushing gravel away. "You said you'd hold me up!"

"I lied," he said succinctly.

She unraveled her scarf from the mess on the ground and unwound her skirts from the pedal where they'd tangled. "I ought to have known."

"It was worth it," he said. "You had the feel of the velocipede for one second. For one second, you understood. All you have to do is go fast enough, and you don't wobble. You fell because you *stopped*. Not because of me. That's how it works. Don't stop. Don't question. Go faster."

She brushed debris from her skirts and stood. "What has any of this to do with Daisy's Emporium?"

"You let fear stop you," he told her. "You stood up in front of the crowd and lost your nerve. I know you, Daisy." And he did, a little. "Your figures are no doubt sound. Your plan is well thought out. You've likely researched every last item you want to sell in your shop. You know how much you can purchase it for in quantity and how much it will sell for. None of that matters, because nobody will ever know how good you are if you lose your nerve. That's what you need to work on, Daisy. Not your speech, not your facts. Your nerve. You will be high up in front of everyone with no support, and when you get scared, you can't falter. You need to go faster."

"You…" Her jaw squared and she looked at him with suspicious eyes. "You think my plan is well thought out?"

"I'm not going to repeat myself."

One of the things he'd once loved about Daisy was this. She looked down at her skirts, now decorated with a liberal smear of muddy snow down the side. She shook gravel from her gloves. Her jaw squared and she lifted her chin.

"Very well. I'm getting back on."

It took Daisy an hour to achieve the minimum skill she needed to pedal down the footpath. An hour of wobbling and catching herself. An hour during which she fell twice. Her gloves tore. Her gown ripped. Daisy gritted her teeth and kept going.

An hour of Crash watching her, his heart aching for what they had almost been to each other. It was an hour until he steadied the velocipede against the bench one final time. Until he took her hand to keep her from falling as she dismounted and almost didn't want to let go.

"Tomorrow?" he asked. "You need more practice."

She shook her head. "The next day. I need… I need…" She didn't say what she needed. She stood on the bench she'd used to disembark and looked down at him with wide, hurt eyes.

"Why?" she asked finally. "Why are you really doing this?"

Of course she knew it wasn't about the damned wagers. If she'd talked to anyone at all about him, she had to know he'd refused to take any bets about the charity bequest at all.

"Because." His voice came out a growl. "Because I want you to understand for once. I don't get to stand still—if I do, I will fall. Unlike you, I never had a choice. If I start to wobble, I have to go faster."

She flinched. "I *said* I was sorry."

"I recall that you said you forgave me." At length. That unwished-for absolution still rankled.

"And that's why you're still angry? I've seen you brush off harsher insults a thousand times."

He held up a hand. "No. That's where and why this ends. Tell yourself I could have lived differently all you wish. I can't stop you; you are remarkably good at lying to yourself."

She stared at him.

"I am *good* at going fast," Crash said. "So good that sometimes all anyone sees is a blur. Insult me all you like. Deep down, though, you know better. You know who I am."

Her eyes glittered back at him. "I know you very well, Crash. *Everyone* knows. You make a point of it."

His teeth ground together. "But don't lie about me when I'm standing right here. I don't need your holy dispensation to exist."

"Just as well," Daisy shot back. "You don't have it."

∼

Daisy unwound her scarf and set her ruined gloves in a wad on the entry table. Her body ached from the exertion and from the falls. She'd be sore the next day.

How fitting. Crash had a tendency to leave her sore in the morning.

The single room that she shared with her mother was still warm, a good sign. She always had to tell her mother to burn coal and never mind the cost. Winter was hard on her, and heat was one of the few things that kept her mother's pains away.

Today, her mother had actually listened.

"Mother?" Their flat was a scant two rooms—one, really, but they'd rigged a curtain. Somehow, two tiny rooms seemed more luxurious than one small one. She peered around the fabric into the alcove where their shared bed stood. "Mother?"

She could smell something delicious—crisp jacket potatoes and something savory that might have been fish. But there was no answer.

Good. Her mother wasn't here. Daisy found a rag and scrubbed at the mud on her skirt. The hem needed repairing, but it could be fixed. For now, a pin or two would manage.

She'd hastily tacked the fabric in place when the door opened behind her. Daisy turned guiltily. "Oh, Mama. There you are."

Her mother removed her own scarf and gave Daisy a bright smile. "I'm feeling better today. I was thinking that perhaps I'd take on a little more lacework instead of just the two pieces a week we agreed upon."

It was always a delicate balance. The more her mother earned, the easier it was to purchase coal. The more her mother worked, the worse her rheumatism became.

"Mama." Daisy stood and set her hand on her mother's shoulder. "The last time you tried, your rheumatism had you laid up for weeks. It's not worth it."

Rheumatism. That's what they assumed it was. Years ago, they had spent money they didn't have for a physician. When he'd come, he'd examined her mother for a cursory three minutes. Then he'd pulled Daisy aside.

"There is nothing wrong with your mother," he had told her in a quiet voice. "Women of her age don't get rheumatism. She is malingering. She wishes to stay in bed, and so she's invented aches and pains to do so. She doesn't need compassion or medical treatment. She needs someone to insist that she work."

Daisy had wanted to slap the man's supercilious expression off his face. Instead, she'd paid his fee. So much for physicians, then.

"I have supper ready," her mother said, "and I cleaned up a little—it does look nice, doesn't it?"

"It does."

"Sit," her mother said. "Eat."

They sat.

"Tell me about your day."

Daisy looked over at her mother. Her hair was beginning to go white in wisps. Daisy still thought her pretty. She had a lovely smile. But speak of unrealistic wishes. Here was one. A single woman could hardly support an aging mother on her own.

Daisy knew it. The doctor had known it. Her *mother* knew it. Her friends tried to hint at it, to tell Daisy that she should—gently—do her best to disentangle herself.

Daisy held on through sheer stubbornness. They would make do as long as Daisy had good work. As long as neither of them got sick. As long as nothing bad ever happened, she could manage it all.

She couldn't think of her mother, and her mother's future, without feeling a little ill.

She didn't want to talk about her day. She considered all her possible responses.

"I did some research," Daisy said instead.

"What sort of research?"

"Research into the sorts of new businesses that are opening shortly." Daisy frowned and speared a bite of potato.

"Oh? Anything interesting?"

Daisy considered the white lump on her fork. "There's a shop that is selling...um. Velocipedes."

"Whatever is a velocipede?"

"It's..." How to even describe the thing? "A metal frame. With wheels. Difficult to describe." She trailed off, mid-twirl of her fork, and looked at her mother's pursed lips.

"That's a thing that people would purchase? Why?"

Now that she'd ridden one, she could understand. There had been a moment of exhilaration. A sense that she could fly.

Daisy shrugged. "It's not much stupider than, say, a carbolic smoke ball."

"A *what?*"

"Another thing." She frowned. "For invalids. It's supposed to prevent influenza."

"Fools and their money." Her mother sighed. "Fools and their money. Drat it, why don't we know more fools?"

Daisy smiled. "I shall have to expand the circle of our acquaintance."

Her mother turned and contemplated Daisy. "You know, Daisy, it's probably time that you start looking for a fool."

Her heart sank. "You mean so that I can sell him a carbolic smoke ball?"

Her mother reached out and touched her hand. "To marry."

Daisy looked away. She felt raw. Unready for this conversation.

"Youth won't last forever," her mother said. "I know you're telling yourself that you have time..."

Daisy's fingers lay quiescent under her mother's while her stomach churned. *You are remarkably good at lying to yourself.* Crash was wrong; she knew perfectly well how things were.

"You have to take care of yourself," her mother was saying. "Establish yourself. Have you seen a girl working in a flower shop above the age of thirty?"

Daisy shook her head.

"There's a reason for that." Her mother's grip tightened subtly on Daisy's hand. "It's like those flowers you sell. Nobody wants them after they've begun to wilt. I know I sound terribly mercenary, but Daisy, dear, you don't have to *love* him. You just have to be able to pretend well enough."

Here was the thing: Daisy wouldn't be marrying for herself, and her mother knew it. On her own, she might support herself indefinitely.

The person she could not support was her mother. Her emporium was a dream. No, worse; a distraction. It was a plaything she held up to pretend her future might be different than it was.

But this was the stark reality she faced. She needed to find a fool who wouldn't mind—or notice—her lack of virginity. If she didn't, one day she would have to walk away from the woman who had raised her because she could no longer afford her care.

It didn't matter how little Daisy wanted that to happen. It didn't matter how sick she felt at the thought. Coins didn't lie.

Daisy could only hope she hadn't ruined her chances at marriage. If she couldn't marry, if nobody ever wanted her…

She couldn't think of that.

She *had* to think of that.

Crash was right. Daisy was remarkably good at lying to herself. One day, she'd stop hoping to come to her own rescue. One day, she'd recognize that there was no escape. She'd do her best to find herself a fool of a fiancé, because she knew she wouldn't leave her mother. She couldn't.

When that happened, when she smiled at some man with half her sense, Crash would think the worst of her. He'd call her a liar and a cheat and more. He wouldn't be wrong.

There were some things one could not say to one's mother.

I cannot marry yet. There's this man I hate—incidentally, the one who took my virginity—and he would poke fun at me.

No, it was time to grow up and face the truth. She couldn't care what Crash would say.

She smiled at her mother instead. "I know." Her cheeks hurt, holding that false expression.

Today was Monday evening. On Saturday, the judges would award the bequest to someone else. They would crush her dream. They'd make it clear that she'd told herself lies. At that point, she would have to accept what she had to do. She would *have* to stop hoping for an escape.

It was as inevitable as her mother's rheumatism.

"Sunday," Daisy said. "This Sunday. That's when I'll start looking."

CHAPTER FIVE

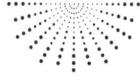

Daisy was glad for work early the next morning, even though she woke with every muscle in her body shrieking in protest at their ill-usage the day before. Work gave her an excuse to wash quickly and hide the bruise on her hip before her mother noticed. Work allowed her to leave before the sun rose.

She didn't have to think of her presentation or what would come after she lost. She arrived at the shop in the early morning hours and lost herself in her work, bunching together little bouquets of forced violets and tying them with ribbon. It was quiet work, comforting work; she didn't have to talk to anyone while she was doing it. She could just match flowers together and tie them with cord. White and purple; pink and lilac. Each little bouquet was a bit of happiness that she put together for someone else.

Today, though, she couldn't entirely lose herself in the activity. Her mother's words came back to her.

It's like those flowers you sell. Nobody wants them after they've begun to wilt.

Bouquets of temporary happiness. Purchased for a penny; discarded the moment they became inconvenient.

She could almost imagine Crash leaning close to her and whispering in her ear. *You are remarkably good at lying to yourself.*

She shoved her mental image of him away.

At least she enjoyed her work. She made people happy. She made them smile.

The shop bell rang and a woman peered in. She was wearing a sober workingwoman's skirt of dark wool and a dingy gray shirtwaist —likely once white—with ink stains on the cuff.

Daisy summed the woman up with a single glance. She was likely one of the unmarried women who labored in the backroom of one of the nearby shops. Daisy had talked to many such women. She probably lived in a rooming house with dozens of other women. She saved her coins, one by one, dreaming of another life, a better life.

It would never come. Women never worked their way up. They started their life near their pinnacle and had only to fall from there.

Daisy had been instructed to shoo women like this away when she first started.

"They're trying to poach our heat," Mr. Trigard, the owner of the shop had grumbled. "They know we must warm the place for our flowers, and they're looking for a handout. They'll never purchase a thing."

For the first month, Daisy had done as Mr. Trigard said. Then he'd started trusting her, and he'd stopped coming in.

It turned out that inhospitality was not one of her talents. She'd given up and started making them bouquets in her spare moments. Not the exquisitely put-together sprays of baby's breath and rosebuds that she constructed for the gentility. Instead, she made little things, pretty things, with leftover bits: flowers cut too short, extra sprigs of leaves, scraps of ribbon that would otherwise have been discarded.

Her creations could be purchased for a halfpenny.

The woman looked from bucket to bucket, her lips pursed.

That was the thing about working in a flower shop. One learned to assess customers. A maid in crisp, brown livery buying for an entire household didn't want to dilly-dally over her purchase. She wanted Daisy to tell her what was available right away.

A woman who wandered in, glancing about timidly, was exactly the opposite. If Daisy launched herself in her direction the instant she entered the room, she'd disclaim all interest and slink away.

Give a customer a little time to start imagining a flower in her life, though, and she'd take it.

The woman stopped at the violets in a little metal tray filled with water, brushing the velvety green leaves with a single finger before biting her lip and moving on.

It was November; the wares were much denuded. But then again, it was November, and so was the world. A single forced tulip could bring color to any room these days.

Daisy concentrated on tying ribbons and watched her customer beneath her lashes. The woman removed knit gloves carefully. She glanced at the hothouse rosebuds, looked at the golden lilies with wonder in her eyes, and then gave her head a little shake.

Time now for Daisy to intervene.

"Are you looking for a buttonhole or a bouquet?" she asked cheerily.

The woman jumped. "Oh. I hadn't thought."

Daisy pointed to her own buttonhole—a bright pink dahlia, smaller than usual, just over her right breast.

"Me personally, I prefer a buttonhole. They're not so expensive as a bouquet, but I can carry one around with me all day. That way I always have a little beauty close by."

The woman looked away. "Pardon me for saying so, but it seems extravagant. Flowers are for…" She gestured outside, at the rest of London. "Not really for someone like me."

Someone like *her*.

Maybe it was her conversation with her mother, but Daisy felt a kinship with the woman. This was who she would be in ten years if she didn't marry. Alone. Cloistered in a backroom, thinking that a halfpenny expenditure was too extravagant.

"Nonsense," Daisy said a little too sharply. "Whoever said that flowers aren't for you?"

The woman blinked.

Daisy knew the answer to that question. *Everyone* said that flowers weren't for her. The woman wasn't married and likely wasn't going to be. She worked for a living. She didn't have servants. She was supposed to be satisfied living a drab little life, just because everyone thought she was a drab little woman.

Drab women didn't get flowers. They didn't deserve beauty.

The woman glanced down. "It's such a luxury. I don't see..."

She had stopped in front of the yellow flowers. Daisy reached out and picked out a creation she'd made of a forced tulip that had snapped off its stem—nothing more than the brilliant yellow bud and a spray of green leaves.

"Here," Daisy said, holding it out. "It's a halfpenny. Tell me, Miss..." She trailed off.

The woman inhaled. "It's missus, actually." Her eyes shut. "Mrs. Wilde. My Jonas passed away five years ago, and..."

"Mrs. Wilde," Daisy said softly, "is there anyone who believes you're worth a halfpenny of beauty any longer?"

The woman shook her head.

"Well, then." Daisy gave her a nod. "Maybe the person who needs to believe it is you."

Daisy had done this before, convincing a reluctant woman to bring a little beauty into her life. She'd never felt guilty about it—but now she did. She could almost imagine Crash standing behind her, whispering in her ear.

My, you are *good at lying to yourself. Listen to you.*

She wasn't lying to herself. She wasn't. She *did* bring a little beauty into these women's lives; if she didn't, why did they all come back? Why would they bring their friends?

"I shouldn't." But Mrs. Wilde hadn't relinquished the tulip.

"Where do you work?"

Mrs. Wilde sighed. "The apothecary down the way. I weigh and measure for him and track his receipts." Her mouth pinched. "I keep track of whatever fine remedy is in vogue, make sure it's ordered and on the shelves. This month, it's the carbolic smoke ball."

Those damned carbolic smoke balls again.

"So you help hundreds of people take their medicine and get well," Daisy said.

"That's…one way of looking at it."

"I'd never tell you to spend money you don't have," Daisy said sympathetically. "But if you're saying you don't *deserve* this, with all that you do…?"

She let her words hang.

Mrs. Wilde looked at the tulip. She glanced down at her hands, out the door, and then back to the tulip. Then she gave a fierce little nod.

"Here." She opened her purse and removed a coin. "Take it before I change my mind."

It was worth it for the smile she saw on Mrs. Wilde's face as she left the shop. Daisy *was* selling happiness. Temporary happiness, very likely, but was there any other kind? Poor women deserved flowers as much as rich ones—more so, in fact. They had that much less beauty in their lives.

Daisy went back to making bouquets, but bouquet-tying was delicate work, and her fingers jerked the twine a bit too hard. She wasn't lying to herself, and she hadn't lied to Mrs. Wilde. She *hadn't*. Rich women were taught that their every wish would be granted. Women like Daisy? Like Mrs. Wilde? They were allowed nothing. They weren't even supposed to properly wish, not for anything worth having. They were allowed to subsist, and then only if they were lucky and useful.

Daisy wasn't lying to herself. She was just making it possible to get through one day and then the next, to find the little moments that made it possible to not dread her future.

That future loomed closer than ever.

Sunday. She'd promised her mother to start encouraging gentleman on Sunday. The very idea left her cold. No wonder she was wasting time submitting applications for a charity bequest. She wanted to believe she had a chance to get away.

She wasn't that naïve.

Daisy stared at her violets. They were just as pretty and just as purple as they'd been a few moments before.

"I don't lie to myself," she told them. "I know the truth all too well."

They looked up at her. Purple petals faded to white in the center, with a dot of yellow. Flowers couldn't really *look.* They didn't have eyes. So why did this batch seem to glower at her in disapproval?

She switched from making bouquets of violets to working with tulips. Putting a good face on things wasn't lying. She told herself the truth with scrupulous regularity. She was running out of time.

Running out of time to establish herself, running out of time to save her mother, running out of time to be anything except another drab woman in a drab occupation telling herself she didn't deserve so much as a halfpenny flower.

So she took a moment to make sure her dreams were well and thoroughly crushed before accepting the inevitable. What of it? Crash was wrong. She didn't *lie* to herself.

But then Crash had said that she'd lied about *him.* That was what rankled. She'd thought of that moment when everything had gone wrong between them over and over.

It had been after…after…

No, if she wasn't lying to herself, she could use the proper words.

It was after they had sex.

Speaking of stupidity. What sort of idiot was Daisy? He'd told her he needed to leave town. He'd said he would be gone to the continent for months. She'd thrown herself at him.

She was a first-class fool, and her face burned in memory.

But he'd been sweet, and it had been lovely, and… And then it had been over. They'd been in bed together, holding each other. She'd been naked and vulnerable and too much in love to realize she ought to have been scared.

"You know, Daisy," he had said. "I told you, you shouldn't have a thing to do with me. Look here. I've corrupted you." He'd kissed her.

"You never told me any such thing. Not seriously."

"True."

She'd kissed him back. "I don't mind being corrupted, if it's by you."

Now, she could flinch at her gullibility. Then, she'd leaned into him with complete trust.

He had sat up in bed. "I haven't explained to you why I'll be gone yet. I've a plan to turn…well, not respectable. But." He had shrugged. "Something like. I've taken risks, but I can't keep doing that, not with a wife and a family."

Her heart had thumped wildly at those words. *Wife. Family.*

"I need to go to France," he told her. "There's a craze building there for velocipedes."

"What are those?"

"They're metal vehicles. With foot-pedals."

"With what?"

"One pushes the pedal with one's foot, and it turns a wheel…" He'd gone on.

It turned out there was no way to describe a velocipede, not with any number of words. She'd stared in confusion.

"It will all make sense when you see one." He'd given her a cocky grin. "They're on the verge of becoming a phenomenon in France. Give it five years, and they'll be the rage here, too. I'm going to have the premiere velocipede shop in all of London. But I'll need to visit factories, learn how to repair them… I'll be gone a while. Months, at least."

Her hands entwined with his.

"The way I see it," he said, "you could marry me and come with me."

She had inhaled.

"Or we could wait two months for me to go in order to be certain that nothing comes of what we just did. I would return to you as soon as I could."

That dose of reality had made Daisy stop and think.

"Crash." Daisy had leaned her head against his shoulder. "I can't leave my mother for months on end, and I can't see her traveling to France."

He'd kissed her. "Wait two months it is, then. That is, assuming you'll marry me despite my terribly checkered past. Will you?"

In the time since that night, Daisy had examined her response over and over.

"That depends," she had said teasingly. "Precisely how many checks does your past have?"

"Maybe one or two." His eyes had glinted wickedly.

"You can't fool me." She'd leaned in and kissed him. "There must be dozens. I know about the gambling."

"That? That's not really a check at all—just illegal." He had given her a cocky smile.

Daisy had heard this from him a great deal in the past months. In some ways, it had felt like Crash had suspended her good sense.

She'd started arguing his side to herself.

Who do I hurt if I kiss him? If I let him put his hand there? It can't really be wrong, not if it feels so right.

She'd told herself that so often that she'd almost completely believed it. Almost. She was already making excuses for him.

That had brought her to this moment, naked in bed with him.

"Really," he mused, "the only true check in my past was the time Jeremy and I robbed Mr. Wintour. But he deserved it, and everyone does stupid things when they're young…"

All Daisy's explanations had failed her at that moment. Her stomach had roiled uneasily, and the *almost* she could not quite dispel returned with a vengeance.

"You did what?"

"Oh, did I not tell you about that?" He'd given her a brilliant, unashamed smile. "Actually, it's an amusing story. Mr. Wintour, see, was Jeremy's employer at the time—you recall Jeremy, yes? In any event, he accused Jeremy of thievery. Which was…" Crash had shaken his head. "Stupid and wrong, and in any event, Jeremy was sacked without his wages. Taking matters into our own hands was a matter of justice…"

Daisy had scarcely heard the account that followed.

Who does it hurt? He had always asked her that question. He'd given her his magical smile, and she'd gone along. His magic had finally failed.

Who does it hurt?

Here, there was an answer. Never mind his earnest confession. Never mind that it wasn't that much or that Mr. Wintour had deserved it. Crash could only alter Daisy's sense of right and wrong so far, and stealing was wrong. Under all circumstances. It was wrong, demonstrably wrong.

Maybe he'd been wrong about everything else.

"It was nine years ago," he finished. "I was seventeen and stupid, and, well…"

And he was sorry now. She clutched at that. It had just been the once. Boys did stupid things.

Her thoughts might have been rationalizations, but she held tight to them. She had reached out and taken his hand impulsively.

"It doesn't matter," she had said. "I love you. I forgive you."

He'd frowned down at her fingers twining with his.

"You forgive me," he had finally said in a low tone. "Why do *you* forgive me? I didn't steal from you. What are you forgiving me for?"

"For everything," she had said earnestly. "I forgive you for *everything* you've done."

"Everything." The pleased animation had slipped from his face. The next words came slowly. "You forgive me for *everything*. Not just the one-time theft. Pardon me; I should like to have your *everything* spelled out."

She'd felt confused.

He pulled his arm from her. "Do you forgive me for taking wagers?"

"Of course."

"You forgive me my former lovers, I assume."

"Naturally."

Instead of appeasing him, each answer of hers made his face even more dangerous. "You forgive me for being a bastard, I suppose."

"You know I do."

His voice was low and cutting. "Next, you'll forgive me my aunt and my mother. You'll forgive me for not having English features, for the color of my skin, for—"

In the months since, she'd come to understand that she'd misstepped. She had said the wrong thing, precisely the wrong thing.

At the time, she'd thought she was reassuring him.

"Yes," she had said desperately. "I do. All of it."

"Then you surely *forgive* me for having the stones to believe I'm worth something."

She'd stared at him in confusion. "How can you doubt it?"

He had pulled away from her, standing up, hunting in their clothing piled together for his trousers. "Very well. Do you want me to forgive you for your mother? *She'll* be a burden, that's for sure. Shall I forgive you for working in a shop? I know you flirt with the men who come by."

"Only a little—it doesn't mean anything, just enough to puff up their esteem—"

"Don't worry." He made the next words sound ugly. "I forgive you." His voice dropped. "I forgive you the fact that you were raised to think yourself better than you are."

She had gasped.

"I forgive you your impertinent and unwomanly desire to be more."

She had been beyond gasping.

"I forgive you your utter ignorance in bed," he had continued, "and your maidenly qualms. Hell, I'll forgive you your very existence in return. Even though, as these things are reckoned, you are a complete waste of a woman."

She felt as if she'd been flayed. As if she were as sore in her spirit as she'd been between her legs. She'd pulled the sheets about her.

"What are you saying?"

"What does it sound like I'm saying? I forgive you, Daisy. I forgive every miserable thing about you."

She had choked back tears, but his words hurt. Not because they were lies; they were all the truth. The truth she'd hoped he didn't see. The simple facts of her, laid bare.

She *was* ignorant about lovemaking. She *was* impertinent. Her mother *was* a burden.

"I'm only saying what you said," he told her. "I forgive you."

"Maybe I didn't say the right thing the right way." She'd struggled to understand. "But there's no call to hurt me like that. Good heavens, Crash, it's not like I wounded you."

Even now, even months later, it still hurt to remember his words. So she had said the wrong thing. What should it have mattered to him? She'd seen him shrug off worse insults, and her remarks had at least been kindly meant. His response... Now *that* had been truly unkind.

"Of course you didn't wound me," he had said. "I never feel pain. Why should I care if you do?"

She had been too devastated to think. "Get out." She'd scarcely managed those words.

"These are my rooms."

"I don't care." She turned away from him. "I can't look at you. I can't talk to you. Get *out.*"

He'd hesitated. Perhaps at that moment, he had realized that he'd said too much. "Daisy."

"Don't." If he talked to her, she would remember all the lies she told herself. She'd remember thirty minutes ago, when he had said he loved her, when he'd kissed her and entered her and talked to her and made her laugh. She'd remember that, instead of what he had just said.

"Daisy. Wait."

She had looked over at him. "For what?" she had said viciously. "For me to *forgive* you?"

He sat beside her. "I lost my temper. I have a— Oh, God, I have more than a little chip on my shoulder about some of this. And, well..." He had looked over at her. "I know everyone thinks I don't care. I can't let them know when I do. But I thought you understood me."

She had thought she had, too. "Did you mean it? Any of it, some-where—did you mean it?"

He had inhaled. He'd looked away. There had been a long moment where she'd scarcely been able to breathe. His knuckles had turned almost pale, clenching so hard. Very quietly, he'd spoken. "Yes."

One word, and it had ended everything. All her lies. All her wishes. All her dreams.

Crash had been the lie she told herself.

Who does it hurt?

Her. It hurt her. It had stabbed her so deeply she thought she might weep blood.

"Don't wait two months." She had shut her eyes. "Go to France."

"But—"

"There are telegrams," she had told him. "If I have need of you, I will let you know. Go to France. We shouldn't see each other any longer. Now get out."

He had left the room. She'd dressed, her hands shaking, and let herself out.

Part of her had hoped that something would come of that single time together. She'd woken at night, her fingers probing her stomach, not sure if she feared a pregnancy or wanted one. If she'd been with child, she would have been forced to speak with him again, forced to lie herself back into love. But that wish, too, hadn't come true.

She hadn't seen him for months.

He had come back, wild as ever, smiling, with that damned velocipede and his damned plan. He hadn't been hurt at all. But every time she saw him, she still bled.

He was right. His words had only been harsh and painful because they'd been true. She was, as these things were reckoned, a complete waste of a woman. No money. No family. Nothing to give to a marriage but a beauty that would fade in a matter of years.

Crash reminded her of the truth. Of course it hurt to look at him.

And what had she done to deserve his cutting words? She'd forgiven him.

For taking wagers.

For that.

You forgive me for being a bastard, I suppose.

She stopped, coming back to herself from her reverie. She was in the shop where she worked. The day was winding down, slowly, surely. She had only a handful of flowers left, sitting forlornly in empty buckets.

You know I do, she had told him.

You surely forgive me for having the stones to believe I'm worth something.

Yes, she hadn't delivered her sentiments properly. Who could choose the perfect words at a time like that? But Crash was invulnerable. She'd heard him laugh at constables when they'd shoved him against a wall.

He was arrogant, full of himself, confident, audacious...

And she could see him as he had been yesterday glaring at her.

I am good at going fast, he had said. *So good that sometimes all everyone sees is a blur.*

He was right. She *had* known that. She'd known beneath that brash exterior that he was kind. Devoted to his aunt. Boastful, yes, and ambitious, but he'd caught her up in his ambitions, making her feel she could do anything.

Yes, she'd heard him laugh off far worse insults. He'd always laughed the hardest at the cruelest ones. His laughter, like his wickedness, was a persona he put on. He never let anyone know how he really felt.

Anyone, that was, except her.

All this time, she'd felt her own hurt. It had been so all-encompassing that she hadn't heard his.

She had forgiven him for existing, and when he'd complained, she told him he couldn't be hurt by it. How must that have felt? To have had Daisy shrug off his pain as inconsequential simply because he was good at hiding it?

All she'd seen was the blur of speed. The illusion of him that he cast. She'd thought that his laughter made him invulnerable. She hadn't seen him, not really, not even in the moments when he'd stood still for her.

Daisy exhaled and felt the world around her coming into sharp relief. For the first time since Crash had walked away from her, she understood why.

CHAPTER SIX

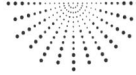

C rash stood at the narrow window of his aunt's flat. Aunt Ree was bundled up in her seat, her feet warmed by bricks, her eyes narrowed on the street in front of them.

"Did that man just hug a goat?"

Crash found the person she was speaking about, a tall, thin man. "Ah, that's George Mirring. And no, I suspect it wasn't a hug, knowing his habits. It was likely more of a glancing embrace. He tends to be private with his affections."

"Hmm." Her eyes narrowed. "You're making this up."

He didn't let so much as a smile touch his lips. "That goat saved his life once."

She turned to look at him. "Did it?" Her words conveyed the utmost disbelief.

"Here's a little known fact. Goats are excellent watch-creatures. Better even than dogs."

"Crash," Ree said with a shake of her head, "are you capable of speaking without making up a story?"

"I wasn't!" Crash smiled at her. "This is the truth. Mirring got the goat because its nan rejected it. Everyone had given up on getting it to eat, and he raised it from a bottle and a rag. After that, the goat followed him around everywhere. They were nearly inseparable. One day, a man tried to cosh him over the head. The goat grabbed hold of his would-be assailant's coat and held him back."

"And did you see this?"

"No," Crash admitted, "and the goat ate the coat, so there isn't any evidence. But—"

A knock sounded on her door, and they both turned to look in its direction.

"You have a visitor," Crash said slowly.

"How exciting." A glimmer of a smile showed on Ree's face. "Maybe it will be a goat. My very own personal watch-goat. Since they are so very much in vogue these days."

Crash went to the door and opened it. There on the other side stood Daisy.

She looked weary. She looked beautiful. Her eyes were wide, her hair slipping out from under her bonnet. She must have been awake since the early hours of the morning.

She looked up as the door opened, and when she saw it was him, she gave him her shopgirl smile—the one that occupied her lips, but not her heart, the one that was all faked politeness. It was the smile she'd give a man who was dallying in her shop at the end of the day.

It was an act. She'd always fooled him with the way she looked: so carefree, with that smile that said she was up to mischief. He'd let that lead him astray. He'd let himself make no such mistakes any longer.

"Ah." He met her eyes. "How appropriate. We were just speaking of goats."

He really shouldn't goad Daisy. He knew he oughtn't. He knew it was unkind, unfair—every *un* he should avoid. But he'd waited and waited for her. He'd expected that telegram in France every day for months.

I'm sorry. I need you. I love you.

He'd come back to discover that in his absence, she'd found another sweetheart.

So yes, he was annoyed with Daisy Whitlaw. Annoyed, frustrated, and…

Her chin squared. There was no mischief dancing in her eyes now. Just a fierce determination. She cradled a brown paper package in her two hands.

"Here," she said. "I hope you'll excuse my calling on you without a prior appointment, but Mr. Lotting said that you were here with your aunt. This is for her."

His eyebrows rose.

She pushed the package into his hands. "You were right," she said simply. "I feel terrible. I was angry about everything you said to me. I never thought through what I said to you. I…" She paused, then the false smile fell from her face. Her tone lowered. "I told you that I would forgive you for who you were, for what you did. That was unfair. It wasn't even true. I *didn't* forgive you. I was still sniping at you about those other things, even last week, which I oughtn't have done if I had actually forgiven you." She frowned and looked down. "I thought nothing could hurt you. I didn't realize that I could."

Crash could not have been more stunned.

Her cheeks were pink with emotion; she wouldn't meet his eyes. "I think I am discovering that I'm something of a horrid person who lies to herself. You were right about that, too."

"Daisy."

"No, don't stop me. I can't stop, or I'll fall." Her words came out in a rapid stream. "I lie to myself. I lie to myself all the time. I would apologize, but I don't know how to stop. Women like me don't get wishes granted. Instead we just keep making them and making them and making them, and what else am I to do…" She trailed off. "So." She shook her head. "In any event, there. I'm sorry."

His fingers closed around the package as she unceremoniously dumped it in his hand.

"Good-bye." She turned to go.

He reached out and took hold of her elbow. "Wait. Daisy. That's all. Really?"

"Really." Her cheeks turned an even brighter red. "Now, if you'll excuse me, I'm going to go…" She pointed out the door.

"You're going to go where?" He felt somewhat stupid.

"Out there," she said. "Just because you were right doesn't mean I want to spend time with you. I may be a waste, but I'm *my* waste, thank you. Good-bye." She said that last in a tone that brooked no denial. "I'll see you for our appointment tomorrow, still, because I haven't stopped lying to myself. I can't appear to give up on anything."

He let go of her, and she turned and marched down the stairs.

He stared after her, his mind whirling. Of all the things he'd ever expected to happen, having Daisy apologize to him…

"What on earth was *that?*" Ree asked behind him.

Crash sighed and let the door close. "That was…a woman."

"A woman." His aunt said the words with care. "And does this woman have a *name?*"

"Daisy," he muttered. "Daisy Whitlaw."

"Ah. *That* woman. The one you said I should meet."

"I…possibly, I…" He looked over at his aunt, who was watching him with her head tilted.

"It's like this," he said. "I was smitten with Daisy for a while." He still felt stunned. "She is clever and kind and funny, and she never made me feel that I was beneath her. Not until…" He looked upward. "In any event, I thought we were of like mind. We were taken with each other. Then the inevitable happened, and after that, she found out about some of the things I'd done in the past, and she…"

Ree was watching him with a frown.

"To make a long story short," he said, "we argued. She made it clear what she thought of my past, and I told her she was…" He couldn't say those words. Not to his aunt.

"I heard what she said." Her voice was cold. "You told her she was a waste?"

He'd heard that voice before. Not for years, but that warning tone could still make him shiver. "Aw, Ree. Not like that. It was more in the context of—"

"The context of the *inevitable* happening?" Ree frowned at him. "Do you mean that you had sexual intercourse with her?"

"I…" He frowned. "Yes."

"And she's been brought up to be a good little English girl, hasn't she? Don't lie; I can tell from her accent."

"Yes, but—"

"So that was the context you refer to, then? 'I know I just took your virginity; terribly sorry, but it was a waste of my time.'"

"Oh, for God's sake." He winced. "It wasn't— I didn't— *She* was the one who overreacted in the first place."

"Think of it from her point of view." Ree folded her arms. "She has gentility in her background."

He gave her a curt nod.

"So all her life, everyone has told her the only thing she has of value is her virginity. That she must guard it; that it's the only thing she can sell to safeguard her security. And here you come. You over-whelm her."

"I didn't—"

"Oh, shut up, Crash," his aunt said. "Don't be stupid. Of *course* you overwhelmed her. She told you she loved you, I wager."

He looked down. "Maybe. But I said it back, and—"

"And," his aunt continued inexorably, "you idiot, you removed her of the one thing she'd been told had value, and you went right ahead and made her think everyone else had been right. That without it, she was a waste."

He stared at her, appalled. "It wasn't like that," he said. "It wasn't. There were other things that happened first. I offered to marry her."

"Crash," Ree said, "do shut your mouth and listen. Do you know how *hard* it was to raise you to believe you could be more?"

He stopped.

"Every day," Ree said. "Every moment we had. Your grandmother, your uncle, my friends… Every day we had to sit you down and tell you. 'He doesn't know who you are; he's accusing you of stealing because he can't see you.' Every damned day we had to drum it into you until you believed it."

He put his hands in his pockets.

His aunt wasn't finished. "Do you suppose anyone told her she was worth anything?"

He paused, and for a moment, he didn't know how to answer. "But... She..."

"I'm sure she never had anyone think her a thief just by looking at her," Ree said. "But men have thought her a great many other things. Including a waste."

He had nothing to say to that. His aunt was right.

"So tell me," she said. "Why did you pay attention to Miss Whitlaw in the first place?"

Crash swallowed. "The first time I saw her, she was defending her mother. Her mother has pains." He indicated. "She tries to work, but, well..."

Ree nodded.

"Someone was accosting Daisy. Telling her that if she didn't confront her mother about her malingering, she'd end up walking the streets." He could almost remember that moment. "Daisy threatened to punch him in the kidneys to see if he could work while in pain."

He could still see her, her hands on her hips. *Do you know my mother, or do I? Then stop telling me what she's doing. If you felt pain the way she did, you'd never leave your bed.*

He shrugged and looked over at his aunt. "I...liked that. I wanted it. I wanted someone who was so loyal to me that she'd punch a man. And then I started talking to her, and she was..."

He stopped again.

"She was trying," he said. "So hard, with so little, and I thought, this is someone who can understand what it was like to be me. Finally. To have to try so hard, and to not let anyone know how hard I was trying. And she understood. I thought she did."

"Crash," his aunt said quietly. She didn't offer advice. She didn't tell him he was wrong. She just looked over at him.

For a long moment, neither of them said anything.

He'd been holding on to his anger—righteous anger!—for so long.

Daisy had forgiven him his existence, damn it all. She'd been as bad as that lady, telling him he was a sinner because…

No. She hadn't been that bad. He frowned. He had this to complain about. She'd sent him away. She had found someone else.

He had told her she was a waste.

Maybe… Possibly…

Damn it. Under the circumstances, he'd have sent himself away, too.

He exhaled and looked at the package in his hands.

"There," she said. "Now what do you have?"

He didn't know. Slowly, he unwrapped it. Inside was a glass flask labeled *carbolic acid.* An india rubber ball was attached to a tube. He turned the ball and found a little opening.

She had found him a carbolic smoke ball. He had read an advertisement. This was supposed to rid a room of the fumes that caused pneumonia and influenza. He'd looked for one for days.

And Daisy had obtained one for him as an apology.

Oh, God. What was he doing?

~

D aisy was angry with him. Crash could tell by the way she smiled at him when she saw him the next evening—a cold, glittering smile that came from the quiet reserve of strength she always kept.

She came up to him at the bench near the canal. "I understand how it is supposed to be now." She looked over at his velocipede leaning against a wall. "If you fall," she said, "you get back on and go faster." Her eyes were dark and steady. "You don't think I can do it. Well, if this is my one chance to secure my fate, I should try to go faster."

She'd leave him behind.

"Daisy."

Her eyes cut to him. "I prefer Miss Whitlaw."

"I owe you an apology," he said.

"You owe me at least two." She looked away from him. "Don't

worry; that's one debt I don't intend to collect. Now, are we going back to the velocipede?"

"No. I wanted to show you something else today." He gestured. "Come. Walk with me. We'll get cold otherwise."

She looked at him a moment, as if considering walking away. Finally, she took a few steps toward him. It was enough. They started down the gravel path, a sedate two feet apart.

"There's a trick my grandmother taught me," Crash said. "She got it from her mother. She told me to imagine I had a bubble around me. When someone said something about me—something harsh and untrue—she told me to push out on my bubble, to shove those words away. Someone said I had shifty eyes and was up to no good? That was *his* thought, not my reality. I had to push it away. I looked like the devil's spawn? That was *their* belief, not my truth. It wasn't inside my bubble, so I could push it all away. Don't let anyone else's rubbish inside your bubble, she would say."

Daisy didn't look at him.

"It was a good trick," Crash said. "And when it became hard to believe that I was good for something, when everyone told me I was destined for the gallows, I just pushed harder. She taught me to let my mistakes just be mistakes. Not an indictment of my character."

"Is that what I need to do?" Daisy asked. "Learn to push those thoughts away?"

"Yes," Crash said. "And...no. Not yet. You see, you got inside my bubble. Back when we were something to each other. You said things, and I reacted the way I always had. I pushed. Hard. I pushed those thoughts away from me the only way I knew how."

She didn't look up at him.

"I sometimes forget how much of me is truly invisible. People have assumed I was wicked since before I could spell my name. They wouldn't hire me on for respectable work, so I decided to use what they thought of me, and make a name for myself as fashionably unre-spectable."

Daisy nodded imperceptibly.

"People look at me and think only the devil will care about me. So

I laugh off all their insults with my best devil-may-care attitude. I give the impression that nothing can ever hurt me, because that way..." He shrugged. "That way, fewer people try."

She looked up at him. "I didn't understand. I hadn't thought it through. And..." Her eyes glittered just a little. "I think yesterday was the first time I understood that I hurt more than your pride. I *am* sorry."

"So am I." He wanted to take her hand. To tip her chin up. "I was at least as wrong. You didn't have a bubble. You've never had anyone telling you what thoughts you could push away. Yes, you made a mistake. But so did I. All your life, they've been tossing rubbish at you, telling you that you had to believe it. Blaming you for not under-standing it was rubbish. That was my mistake. I should have trusted you enough to explain, instead of dumping more garbage on your head."

She bit her lip. "Explain what?"

"You're a woman. Your ambitions are..." He paused, waiting for her to finish his sentence.

Her fingers clamped together and she looked away. "Unwomanly," she said in a quiet, choked voice. "Unattractive. Unappealing."

"There. That's *their* rubbish. Push it away, Daisy. Your ambitions are a fire that will keep anyone worthwhile warm."

"But—"

He held up a finger. "No buts. Push it away. That's theirs. You don't need to keep hold of it anymore, thank you."

She exhaled. "Crash. I don't know."

"They'll hand you a sack of rubbish and then make you apologize for holding putrefying refuse. They act like their rules are holy and moral, but their only rule is that people like me—people like you— must lose."

She looked up at him. "But we *do* lose."

"Not always. Try another one. Tell me what you fear."

"I'm..." She let out a shuddering breath. "I'm only worth anything now because I'm pretty." Her voice shook. "I'm ten years from being too old, too ugly, too *everything,* and if I don't establish myself now, I'll have to leave my mother."

To have a sell-by date, as if she were a notation scrawled on a can of potted meat. To feel that responsibility.

"Push it away. That's false. That's their rubbish. Can you see the truth?"

She didn't say anything, not for a long while. He waited, letting her think.

"In ten years, I'll be just as clever. I'll be me with more experience. Beauty need not matter."

"Almost right. In ten years," Crash said, "you'll still be pretty. Don't let them tell you that youth is a woman's only beauty. That gray hair and wrinkles will rob you of your appeal. It's a load of rubbish. You should meet my aunt. She's beautiful. Push it away, Daisy."

She shut her eyes. "I'm not…worth anything because I'm not a virgin," she said in a low voice.

"Oh, Daisy." That one stung to hear. He did touch her then, setting his hand on her shoulder.

She raised her eyes to his. A sea of hurt reflected in her pupils.

The thing about being raised as he had? He'd thought of what he would do if she were with child. He hadn't given one thought to the fact of her virginity. It was not something his aunts and her friends thought important, except as an afterthought.

"You don't become less for caring. For loving. For existing, for being a person who does all those things."

She looked over at him.

"Push it away," he said. "Push it all away."

"How?" Her hands fluttered once in front of her. "How? How, when everyone says otherwise, do you…" She swallowed.

"Do I what?"

"How do you smile when people say these things to you? How do you laugh and say that you're proud of your background, when…"

Crash looked Daisy in the face. Her chin was tilted down, her eyes turned to the side. "When what?" His voice seemed dangerously low to his ears.

"When you cannot be," she whispered.

Long ago, he'd heard similar words from her as condemnation. He hadn't heard them as a prayer for mercy, nor as a plea for help. But that was what they were.

"I say that I come from a proud line of dock whores and sailors," he said in a low voice, "because I *am* proud."

She swallowed.

"Nobody except my family takes pride in what we are, so we've had to invent it ourselves. I don't know what race I am. I don't know if the question makes any sense. But I know where I come from. My grandmother was born a slave on the island of Tortola. She accompanied the trader who held her on his voyages as…never mind. One day, a mile from the shore of England, she jumped overboard."

"Why?"

He managed a short, frowning glance. "Because slavery was not recognized in England," he said shortly. "She couldn't swim. She made it to shore anyway. At the time, she was pregnant with my aunt."

Daisy looked up at him.

"When people hear 'dock whore,' they imagine some poor specimen of a woman who wanders up and down the wharf, thinking of nothing but her next john. My grandmother took in laundry. She sewed. She did all these things for sailors, and one of them fell in love with her. How could he not?" He smiled. "The only people who called her a whore were ladies who had no other words for a poor woman with a prior bastard child. My grandfather was an Indian lascar who had been abandoned in London by a shipping company because he had injured his knee. No clergy would solemnify their marriage. It didn't lessen the affection in it. The gentry saw her as nothing but a prostitute. But those of us who knew her? She was an extraordinary woman. I was ten when she died, and the crowd at her funeral wouldn't fit in the tavern."

Daisy let out a long breath.

"My mother, they told me, was sweet. She worked for a seamstress and lived with my grandmother. And yes, I suppose she was a whore, too, in the sense that she took coin in exchange for intercourse from more than one man. But nothing is simple. The life of a sailor is hard. They see no women for months on end; they're expected to be tough as nails all the time. My mother was the shoulder they cried on, the woman they imagined during the worst storms. She was the one who held them and reminded them that they were human, that they mattered. Men would give her everything they had—not to purchase her favors, but because she *was* everything they had. She died when I was two. I have no memory of her, but I remember men coming to our flat for years after, asking after her. I remember them weeping inconsolably when they were told she had passed away." Crash shrugged. "More than one of those men claimed to be my father. He was probably from China, but there was a man from Portugal, and a French fellow... Well, never mind. Three men claimed they were my father, and every time they docked, they'd come see me. They brought me toys and books. They'd leave their earnings with my aunt for my care. They taught me to cheat at cards. They all knew about each other, but they didn't care."

She was watching him with wide eyes. Listening.

"So there you have it, Daisy," he said. "My grandmother was a woman so strong of will that she threw herself over the side of a ship, not knowing how to swim, because she would be free. My mother was a woman so loved that she gave me three fathers after her death, not just one. And my aunt was the one who told me about them—story after story when they had passed away. Every time someone told me to keep my head down or slapped me for thinking myself above my station, my aunt was there. Holding me. Whispering to me that they were wrong, that the blood in my veins was every bit as red as theirs. That I was worth something. Anything."

Daisy looked down.

"I am descended," Crash said, "from a line of dock whores and sailors. Men and women who were told they were nothing. They refused to accept the label. Yes, Daisy, I'm proud."

She exhaled.

"I should never have called you a waste."

Daisy was still considering her feet. "Now what?" she said. Her eyes drifted to the dingy water of the canal. Her question encompassed not just the next hour, but...more. "Now do I get on the velocipede and ride fast?"

"Now," he said, "now you give the speech you intend to deliver at the final competition in a few days. This time, you don't waver. You don't stop. You don't apologize. You believe that you're right, that you can win, that you *deserve it.* And you don't let up."

CHAPTER SEVEN

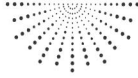

It should not have been so exhausting to deliver a speech Daisy had already memorized to an audience of one. But with Crash listening, Daisy heard her words with a new ear.

Everything she said came out sounding stilted and wrong. She could hardly make it through a sentence without an interruption.

"Even though women—"

"You're apologizing," Crash told her. "Stop apologizing for having a store for women."

She swallowed. "Because women are the main clientele, I expect loyalty, word-of-mouth sales, and…" She trailed off. "And a savvy eye for bargains?"

"Reasonable," Crash said, "but why are you asking me a question?"

Her hands curled into fists. Two sentences later…

"Although the main clientele will be—"

"Although?" Crash folded his arms and raised a disapproving eyebrow. "Don't apologize. Start over."

By the time she'd run through it all once, she wanted to scream.

"Good," he said. "Now do it again, this time without prompting."

At the end of the second time through, she wanted to pull out her hair.

"Excellent," Crash said. "Now do it, imagining that you're on a velocipede. All arrogance; no hesitation. Start."

By the fifth time around, she wanted to pull *his* hair out. Even Crash had begun to look weary. His eyelids drooped a little.

She looked at the flickering streetlamps. "I must be going," she said. "You've done enough. You must be exhausted."

He gave her a tired smile. "Don't worry about me. I'm game for another five rounds. Never let anyone say I'm anything other than indefatigable."

"But I have to go now."

"Tomorrow, then." He frowned. "No. Tomorrow I've appointments to see more space for my velocipede shop. Friday, although that's cutting it rather close."

"Friday. And now my mother will be wondering where I am. Good heavens. You must really want to win those wagers."

He frowned at her and looked away. Then he gave his head a tired shake. "I didn't take wagers, Daisy."

Her mind went blank. Of course he had taken wagers on the competition. His entire point in assisting her was to make a little money. He had to… She couldn't… Feelings swarmed her, assailing her from all sides.

"You said." The words came out all choked up. "You *said*, you told me, that people placed bets on the competition."

"Technically," he said, looking upward, "I merely *implied* they had done so and let you come to a false conclusion."

A hard lump formed in her throat.

"But we've never much been technical, have we, Daisy?" He gave her a weary half-smile. "Yes, if you want to put it that way. I lied to you. Of course I didn't make wagers. It would be wrong for me to take bets as if I were an independent observer and then try to influence the outcome. You should know that."

She couldn't help herself. She was exhausted, emotionally drained, and… She began to laugh. "Most people would say that it was wrong to make bets where a woman was involved. That's your reason why you didn't? You have the strangest version of morality I have ever heard."

He looked honestly confused. "Is it supposed to be a *compliment* for me to say that I'd not risk my money on you? I didn't wager because… Oh, for God's sake, I'm not going to explain it now. I just didn't." He shook his head. "English morality is utterly ridiculous. It doesn't make a lick of logical sense."

Talking to Crash about morality was like talking to a wall. You could never talk the wall down, and no matter how you bounced things off it, it always stayed right where it was. Immovable. Unchanged. After an hour of shouting, one was left with the distinct impression that the wall was probably in the right place to begin with. Crash made the rest of the world seem utterly mad in comparison.

Maybe it was.

They stood in silence, Daisy not wanting to speak. She had too many questions. *Why didn't you take the bets? If it wasn't the wager, why did you intervene? Why are you here?* It was the last question she most wanted answered, and he wasn't talking.

"Why?" She made sure her voice didn't shake. "Why did you…"

"Why did I lie to you?" He shrugged. "Well, that's easy. I was fairly certain that if I told you the truth, you wouldn't want my help."

"Crash." She tried to imbue the single syllable of his name with the deepest reprimand.

"Daisy." He didn't mirror her tone. He said her name quietly. Once before, he had used to say her name like that. Like her name was a precious thing, an important thing. Like those two syllables were an honor on his lips.

She couldn't look at him. "If you knew I didn't want your help, you should have…"

"What," he said, "done nothing? I suppose I should have let it go. But I am notoriously terrible at letting things go."

She understood precisely what he was telling her. She'd walked away from him, and nobody had ever done that. He wanted her the way she'd once been—silly, unwise, willing to throw over all good sense when he tossed a smile in her direction. And she, fool that she was, could feel herself falling back into her old ridiculous yearning.

This is not going to happen. This was the moment when she should bar her shutters and wait out the storm.

She was tired.

"It was simple," he said. "If you want to know why I did it, it's because of your sweetheart."

This brought her up short. She turned to him, frowning. "My *sweetheart?*"

"Yes, your sweetheart." He looked in her eyes. "I wanted to... Well, that is..." He frowned. "Maybe I wanted you to miss me a little. I used to imagine him forgiving you for who you are. It made me angry. I wanted you to know you were wrong. That neither you nor I needed forgiveness."

She felt her throat close.

"What are you talking about?" she finally managed to say.

He frowned at her. "You must be exhausted." He sounded patient. "We're talking about your fiancé, Daisy. The man you're supposed to marry? How hard is it to understand that I want you to be happy? That I think he should care about you?"

She felt utterly stricken. She had no fiancé, and the one she would eventually try to acquire would, by necessity, not know her at all.

What came out of her mouth was this: "Crash. You *idiot.*"

"What?"

She took a step toward him.

"You colossal, stupid, ridiculous—" She'd run out of adjectives, but she still had nothing to say to him. "Don't pretend to be a fool. You know."

"What do I know?"

She snapped off the next words. "You *know* I made him up. There is no sweetheart. There is nobody waiting for me. There isn't anyone who cares what I do aside from my mother."

He stared at her in such dazed incomprehension that she wanted to slap him.

"You knew it," she told him. "I told you, and you looked at me just like that, and you said, 'Of *course* I believe you.'"

"Of course I said I believed you," he said stupidly. "Because *of course* I believed you. Why wouldn't you have a sweetheart? Why wouldn't some officer out there"—he jerked his thumb in the vague direction of what might have been Portsmouth—"dream of you every night, and want you to be his? It sounded perfectly reasonable to me."

"Look at me." She gestured. "Oh my God, Crash, *look* at me."

"I am." He frowned at her. "I have. And I know you hate to admit it, but we've known each other quite a long time. You're lovely. You're loyal. You're funny, and you always put the best face on anything bad that comes your way. Who wouldn't want you?"

"You must think I'm the most gullible woman on the planet."

"Wait one moment," he said. "Are you honestly telling me you *don't* have a sweetheart?"

It took her a moment to realize that he was serious. That all this time, he'd thought… He had actually thought…

He was frowning now. "I returned. I sought you out. You thought you had to *lie* to me about having a sweetheart to keep me away? Did you not think I would listen to you? Did you not trust me? Were you afraid of me?"

"Always," Daisy said. "Every day. Every time I saw you."

He looked surprised. "Daisy, I was an ass. But I would never force myself on you. If I have somehow allowed you to believe otherwise—"

She couldn't listen to him any longer. "I was afraid," she said, "that I would do this." She stepped close, wrapped her hands in his coat lapels, and drew herself up.

One instant, when she felt his shocked breath against her lips. One crazed instant, where she wondered what she was doing—and why—and then she imagined herself on a velocipede, heading pell-mell down the street at top speed.

So she kissed him. She didn't hold back. All the months of hurt, of pain, of loneliness poured out in her kiss. In the feel of his chest against the palms of her hand, his body, radiating warmth against her.

His arms wrapped around her, holding her close. His mouth opened to hers.

God, she'd missed kissing him. Missed the taste of him, that mix of coal-smoke and spice. The all-encompassing feel of his hand on her spine, drawing her in.

She'd missed the brush of his lips, the way he drew her bottom lip in his mouth and bit it, lightly, before he descended on her again. She'd missed feeling beautiful and strong and desired.

She'd missed feeling his heart beat faster, knowing that *she* was affecting him. She'd missed him, and they'd hurt each other so much, and maybe…

She pulled away. He was looking down at her, his eyes dark with desire. Their kiss had turned into a question, the question she hadn't answered yet for herself. Letting this moment linger on would make her response irrevocable. She was tired and upset and…

And she needed time, time to think it all through.

"My mother is waiting," she said.

"I know."

"I'm sorry—" She bit off that apology. "No, never mind. I'm clearly in need of more practice on that front. Let me start again: I refuse to apologize for kissing you."

The corner of one lip tilted up. "Nicely done, Daisy."

"Good day, sir." She stepped out of the circle of his arms.

"Friday, then?" he called after her. "After you finish at the shop? You need to practice more, and…"

He paused. How was it that she could *hear* him smirking in silence?

"And you should spend more time not apologizing to me, I think."

Daisy let out a long breath. "Crash, you're terrible."

"No, I'm not," he said, sounding amused. "I'm brilliant at everything. And if you would like to not apologize to me in that particular manner once again, I'll be happy to accommodate you."

She tossed her head. "Go smoke your head. I believe you have the medical apparatus for that now."

His laugh chased her down the street—warm, inviting, and not the least bit apologetic.

~

The sun had set by the time Daisy arrived home. Her skin was numb from the cold; she rubbed her hands together in the dark hall before her door, peeling her gloves away, stamping her feet until the feeling returned.

Her lips still tingled. And her heart...

Just as well her mother wasn't home; her face would give away all her secrets. She opened the door into darkness and reached for the matches.

"Daisy." Her name came from the bed.

"Oh, Mama." Daisy let the wooden match fall back into its box. "I didn't know you were home."

"Just getting a little rest." Her mother started to sit up.

Daisy rushed over. "There's no need to stir on my account. I'll manage supper for you tonight."

"You do too much for me."

Daisy didn't answer as she sliced and buttered bread.

Deep down, sometimes she agreed. She had told herself she was a good daughter. But as she set the teakettle on the hob, she wasn't sure anymore.

The future was coming. She ought to have felt a pit of dread in her stomach at that. Maybe, tonight, she was too weary to worry.

Or maybe she was thinking of Crash.

How can you be proud? she had asked Crash. And he'd answered. Oh, how he'd answered.

She'd never asked that question of herself.

How can I be proud?

"You taught me to read when I was five," Daisy said slowly.

Her mother frowned at her in the gloom. Daisy walked over to the bed and sat down. "You taught me how to jab a man who brushed up against me on the omnibus with a hat pin when nobody was looking."

Her voice was shaking. "You drilled me in proper speech because you told me I'd have better prospects if I could sound genteel. You make dinner and handle laundry and do more than your fair share of lacework."

"Daisy. What are you saying?"

Daisy took her mother's hand. "You taught me to never stop. To always try one last thing. To keep hoping through the bleakest of times."

Daisy had not let herself truly want to win the competition, not until this moment. Or maybe it was that deep down, she had always wanted to win. She'd wanted it so much, with every aching fiber of her being, that she hadn't let herself know the ferocity of her desire. She had told herself she couldn't do it instead to cushion her heart from the blow.

Now she thought about what her emporium would mean. If she succeeded, she'd have not just financial security and a lasting position. It would be a place where her mother might help, as much as she could, with no employer to scold her when her rheumatism took a turn for the worse. She could have a chair in front of the fire on bad days, and Daisy could work and still see to her needs.

Daisy had not let herself feel her desire until this moment. Now, she wanted. She wanted the shop in her imagination fiercely.

"Daisy," her mother said. "What are you saying?"

Daisy's voice trembled. "Papa gave up when he lost the store all those years ago. You? You never did. You are the reason I am here. Alive. Well. Taking care of you."

Her mother said nothing.

"And so nothing more of the future," Daisy said. "If you please. *Whether* I marry, I promise you, Mama, you will always have a place with me. No matter how hard I must try. No matter how many times I have to stretch for plans outside my grasp. No matter how many times I am told no. I am proud of you. I'm proud of who you made of me. And I'm not going to stop being proud, no matter what the future brings."

"Daisy." Her mother took her hand.

Daisy couldn't win the competition. She had told herself that for so long that she had made herself believe it. But Crash had been right. The grocer's certainty that she would fail? That was his rubbish. The reason she kept reaching was because she could not stop dreaming.

She wouldn't.

"Daisy." Her mother's voice was small. "I'm proud of you, too."

Daisy's chin went up. "Good. Then watch what I can do."

CHAPTER EIGHT

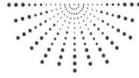

D aisy was counting out the final coins in the till two days later, going through her speech for the competition on the morrow, grimly preparing herself to do her very best. The door opened. A gust of cool wind swept in, and she looked up.

The momentary annoyance at a customer arriving right at closing was swept away when she saw who it was.

"Crash." She tried not to smile. "I didn't expect you to meet me here."

"No?" He slid his gloves off and sauntered toward her. And oh, did he saunter. Nobody could saunter like Crash, with those languid steps, that slight roll to his hips. She hadn't known what a saunter truly was until she'd met him.

The fact that it left her staring inadvertently at his crotch…

She swallowed and dragged her gaze to his face.

He came up to her, so close that he could reach out and touch her. And he did. He set his hand atop hers where it rested on the till. A little thrill ran through her.

"You need to practice your speech again," he said in a matter-of-fact tone.

A strangled noise escaped her.

"Yes," he said in a low, warm voice. "You do. I know you're exhausted and I know that two days ago, I tried my damned best to rattle you. Now you need to do it one more time—once when I *don't* try to rattle you. You need to do it perfectly once, so you know how that feels."

"Crash." She should say no. Spending time with him was dangerous; it always had been. "It's so cold today. The thought of trying to be perfect while my hands freeze next to the canal…"

Speaking of hands. His hand twitched atop hers. "Luckily," he said in a low voice, "I have a perfectly warm set of rooms. With tea. And I can obtain pastries."

"I will not be won over by baked goods." Daisy folded her arms.

"Yes, but what about pastries *and* tea?" He waggled an eyebrow at her.

"No self-respecting woman would…" She paused and listened to her own words. Come to think of it, why wouldn't a self-respecting woman go into a room with a man she wanted to be alone with? Especially with pastries. She was tired; she couldn't think straight. And she was always ravenous after work.

It didn't sound like a terrible idea.

He waited, watching her.

"You know," she said severely, "this whole questioning of societal mores thing… It's entirely self-serving on your part, I've just realized."

"Come to my side," he murmured. "We have baked goods and tea."

"That's a terrible argument. The side of proper English morality also has pastries and tea. They practically invented it."

"They stole the tea, and they certainly never baked the biscuits. In addition, I know fifteen ways to give a woman an orgasm."

Daisy choked.

"Which is rather antithetical to their position. So which do you prefer, Daisy. Pastries and tea? Or pastries, tea, and, orgasms?"

"I'll have tea," Daisy said, "and…a baked good or two." She felt her cheeks burn. "But if we are going to be precise about the matter, your presence is not necessary for me to have any of those things. I can manage all three on my own."

His eyes met hers and he let out a long breath. "Bravo, Daisy." He pulled his hand away. "Now there's an image. Damn."

She locked the shop and gathered the final remnants of flower stems. "I have to take out the rubbish."

He slid ahead of her and picked up the basket. "Toss it out, then."

She gave him a look. Oh, she tried to make it a warning, repressive look, but her smile got in the way. "Don't think I'll be won over so easily. I value myself more than a biscuit or two."

"What do you want, then?"

"What do you think?" Daisy shrugged. "To get on your velocipede, and to aim straight for the walls. As fast as I can go." She took the rubbish bin from him. "You can sit in one place and listen to my speech."

~

They stopped at the bakery. Crash chose little twists of puff pastry laced with cinnamon; Daisy asked for currant scones. They went back to his rooms in good cheer. She smiled at him the whole way.

This is what it would be like, his mind whispered. *This is what it would be like if we were together. If...*

No. When.

Daisy gave her speech. He didn't interrupt. He wished her all the best in the world, pouring every ounce of good will into his smile.

"You're brilliant," Crash said when she finished.

"No," Daisy started to say. Then she paused. Crash could see her inhale. She tilted her head. Then she gave him a glowing smile. "I *was* brilliant, wasn't I? At first, I thought I couldn't be any good in comparison. Now I think I'm excellent. What are you doing to me?"

"Nothing. You're amazing on your own, you know. You've always known, deep down, that you deserved more. Now you want others to believe they deserve it, too. That's what you're really selling in your emporium."

There was something about having her stand above him as he sat

291

in his chair. His head tilted back and his body came alive. Stirring. Wanting.

She looked at him for a moment, then gave a slow nod. "That *is* what I'm selling."

"And I," Crash continued, "for one, bow to your genius."

One of her eyebrows rose in a perfect arch. She took a step toward him. "Do you, now?"

"I positively genuflect to it. In fact, I—"

Daisy held up a hand. "All talk. I've had tea and scones. You didn't promise me adulation, Crash. You promised…"

She trailed off, and Crash found himself holding his breath, waiting for her to say the word.

"You promised…"

"I promised you an orgasm? Oh, no." He sat back in his chair and folded his arms. "You declined. I recall you promising to see to your own."

Her eyes narrowed. "Are you asking me to leave?"

He paused. He considered. Then he crooked a finger at her. "On second thought… Come here."

She took a step toward him, then another, until she stood next to his chair. He sat watching her. Wondering what she would do. Hoping…

She didn't reach out. She didn't lay a hand against his cheek. She looked at him with solemn blue eyes. He wondered, then, if she was remembering what had happened the last time they'd been in this situation—alone together, their bodies humming, reason taking its leave.

There had been nothing quite so vulnerable as that moment after they'd had each other, when passion was sated, when the future had opened up before them as a vast unknown. They'd wounded each other deeply then.

"Not again," he said slowly.

She looked at him.

"I promise," he said. "Not again. No matter what happens. I will never again lash out at you in anger. I will never tell you the words that other people would say. I will never say you're less because I've been hurt. I promise."

"I promise," she said. "I will never again see you with anyone else's eyes. Just mine."

Their eyes met. Those promises settled on him like a comforting weight. They felt like a velvet cloak in the middle of a winter night, shielding him from winds and cold.

"I'm sorry," he said, "that I hurt you. So much that you shoved me away."

She reached out and took his hands. "Make it better, then."

He wasn't sure if he pulled her onto his lap or if she came to settle there on her own. This time, when he kissed her, he kissed her for all his hopes, all his wishes. For the future he'd built. For the things he wanted for him. For *them*.

His hand slid up her spine. Gently.

She moved to straddle him, her thighs settling against his hips. Even through layers of petticoat and skirt and trousers, he could feel her body press against him. Against his cock, which slowly came to life.

They'd done this before, kissing, touching, exploring until they were both afire. This time, though, it felt... fragile, like a plant thought dead, poking new leaves through the soil after a freezing winter. Fragile and yet strangely robust, as if the roots had grown deep during their dormancy.

He kissed her gently, nurturing every unfurling leaf.

The gasp she made as he kissed her. The lift of her head as he pressed his lips to her neck, turning her face up like a flower to the sun. The parting of her lips as his hand found her nipple.

"There you are, Daisy," he whispered. "There you are."

Her hands slid down his ribs. "Here you are." Their lips met once more.

"Here." His hands slid up her skirt, skimming the soft flesh of her knees, her thighs. "Let me help."

She was wet; when he slid his thumb between her folds, her breath caught momentarily. That little catch nearly broke him. He kissed the side of her neck, wanting more. She tilted her head back.

"There?" he asked.

"Yes." The word came out in a hush. "There."

"Wait."

"Wait? I can't—"

He bodily picked her up, holding her close. "If I set you on the bed, I can use both hands instead of just the one."

She nodded, and he brought her there. He could smell her desire, the wet, intoxicating musk of arousal. He set her down, lay beside her, and kissed her again. A kiss on the lips; a brush of his hand back between her legs. She opened for him, mouth and body alike. Her hips moved against his touch.

"This is why I need my other hand." He unlaced her bodice, freeing her breasts.

She froze when his lips found her nipple, but then exhaled and moved against him. They found a rhythm like that, her beside him, his hand between her legs.

Her breath grew faster, then faster still. Then she let out a little choking noise.

God, he'd missed her. Her fingers clamped on his arms; her passage clasped his fingers, and her hips moved in time with him. She came apart in his arms.

He wanted more. All of her. That dazed look in her eyes, that soft, sweet smile that she gave him. He wanted to do it all over, to go back to the last time he had this, to do it right this time.

Her skin was warm; her mouth was soft and inviting when she kissed him.

More. His body was hard and all too ready. *Don't think. Act.*

"Daisy." His voice was low. "Darling. We have to talk of what comes next."

"No." She smiled up at him. "We don't."

"We haven't decided anything. We should—"

She reached up and pulled him to her, and all his *shoulds* went up in smoke. There was nothing but Daisy, her hands pulling the tails of his shirt from his trousers. Her fingers ran up his chest, and it became imperative that he disrobe. That they touch each other. That the next kiss, when he took it, be skin to skin with nothing between them.

He shed his clothing and slid back against her. He could feel the curve of her hips against him, the nubs of her nipples against his chest. His cock nestled against her, hard and wanting, and he could not help that tiny thrust of his hips. God, he needed to think.

He pulled away six inches.

"Crash." Her hair was spilled on the sheets; her eyes were wide and inviting.

"Daisy, dearest."

He'd been here before, with her. Wanting her so badly. *Needing* her.

Now he wanted to redo it. To take that hurt he'd given her last time and turn it to pleasure. Nothing but pleasure for her from here on out.

Even now, even with his blood insistently thrumming in his veins, with his desire riding high, he wanted to cuddle her close, to build a fortress with his body to keep the world from getting at her.

He couldn't shield her from everything. He hadn't even been able to shield her from herself.

She smiled and curled her finger at him, beckoning him closer.

And in that moment, he was helpless. He leaned his head down to her. "Daisy. We shouldn't."

She laughed. "Who are you," she said, "and what have you done with my Crash? You sound like someone who cares about such things as propriety and manners. We should, and you know it."

They should.

He knew it.

He kissed her again, longer this time, lingering. He let his hands slide down the sides of her body, let his knees nudge hers further apart. Her breath scattered.

He slid inside her.

"Oh, God." The words fell from her lips.

"Sweetheart."

She surrounded him, all warmth and tight surrender. He took her, slow sweet inch by slow sweet inch, waiting for her breath to loosen before he went further. She opened to him slowly. Perfectly.

Until they were together, until he was buried deep inside her, her legs wrapping around his hips. Until she smiled up at him, and he wanted this, nothing but this, forever, and he drove into her, gently at first, then harder still. Until the world began to break apart. He held that line, waiting, bringing her with him, until they both dissolved in pleasure.

He held her afterward. He didn't ever want to let go. He felt soft and vulnerable and almost afraid of what might come next.

But they had to disengage. They had to lie next to one another.

They had to look in each other's eyes. He had to stroke her cheek and say the words that he most feared. "Daisy, darling. We have to talk of the future."

She exhaled, leaning her forehead against his. "The final round of the competition is tomorrow. I don't know how to think beyond it."

And yet beyond it was where they had to go.

The truth, sometimes, was a weapon. He didn't want to wound her, but…

He exhaled. "We both know you should win. We know it."

But. That last word went unspoken.

She looked him in the eyes. "We both know I won't."

He shut his eyes.

"I'm not stupid," Daisy said. "Just ambitious."

"If we'd found ourselves here together, earlier," Crash said, "things might be different. I'd saved money, you know. But I've already committed what funds I have to a first order of velocipedes. They'll arrive in two months, and what I have left needs to be spent on a lease. If I had known then, I might have made different choices. But if tomorrow goes as…"

He couldn't make himself say it.

Daisy sat up. "You were right," she said. "You were entirely right when you told me I lied to myself."

"No, Daisy…"

She didn't look at him. "I've spent all these years telling myself I won't get my wishes. My little game with Judith saved me from disappointment. It let me label my every wish as foolish and insubstantial. Impossible. A game. A dream of things that would never come to pass. I believed I would never get anything I wanted."

"That won't happen. I won't let it happen."

She folded her arms around her legs.

"No. *I* won't let it happen. This wish, Crash?" Her voice shook. "This one? This wish for Daisy's Emporium? I tried not to let it sink its hooks into me. I tried not to want it too hard. But it's too late. I want it. I want it so much I can taste it."

He slid toward her, putting his arm around her.

"You were telling me that I can believe in you," Daisy said. "That you'd never hurt me. I know you won't. What I don't know is…" Her voice shook. "Is whether I can believe in myself."

"Oh." He hurt, looking at her. "Oh, Daisy."

She gave a little sniff and looked at him. That determined look came into her eye—the one that he'd seen when they'd first met. He'd fallen in love with her then.

"But I will." Her chin squared. "I need to. I need to believe that I can do this. That if I just pedal fast enough, I won't fall. Not this time."

"Daisy."

She set her hand on his shoulder. "I won't come to you feeling myself a failure. I want to prove that I can do this. Ask me what our future holds after I've won my own destiny. Ask me after I've accomplished everything I never believed I could really prove."

He felt a hint of panic. She was walking away. Again. Telling him he wasn't good enough, that he couldn't be enough for her…

"I need to go fast," she said. "I need to pedal with all my might. I cannot go as fast as I need if you are there to hold me up."

"Are you saying that I'll hold you back?"

She looked back at him, not saying a word.

He inhaled, swallowed the indignant response that leapt to his lips. Swallowed the pain. The part of him that wanted to argue, to make her listen, to…

To do what he'd done last time.

He blew out a breath instead. "I think," he said after a moment, "that you also need to know." He swallowed. "Last time we found ourselves here, talking of the future, things went...badly."

Her eyes darted to her hands.

"I think you need to know," he said, "that I won't hurt you again. That this time I'll listen."

Her eyes widened a moment, and then shut. "Maybe. Maybe that, too."

He slid his arm around her. He didn't want to say the next words. Not with all they could entail. But he had to do it. "I'll never hold you back. Never. Not even if it means letting you go."

He didn't let go, not right away, and she didn't move away. Not for minutes. He did his best to memorize the scent of her, the complex smell of lavender soap and something sweet beneath that. He committed the feel of her skin, smooth and soft, to his store of thoughts. He learned the shape of her in his arms by heart. Just in case.

They sat there, holding one another, until the last bit of sun disappeared from his window, cloaking them in darkness.

"Go, Daisy," he finally said. "Go fast. Don't stop. I'll see you tomorrow after the competition."

CHAPTER NINE

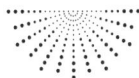

Daisy woke on the day of the final presentation in the hours that were too dark to properly be called morning. The world seemed preternaturally still. When she peered through the curtains, the street she looked out on was cloaked in fog.

She could almost pretend the building across the way had vanished. That her entire uncertain future had been swallowed in mist. There was nobody but her, her and her mother. In that moment, winning seemed possible.

Likely, even.

I could win. The thought threaded through her like the bright ribbon she wove through her hair. *I could win.*

This irrational hope did not vanish. Not as the sun crept to the horizon, spilling pink mist down the street. Not as she dressed, doing up her buttons, making sure she looked like a respectable, sober woman who could start a business and succeed.

I could win.

She felt as if she were on a velocipede, the wind whipping around her face as she pedaled with all her might. She felt as if her arms were wings. If she raised them, she might take flight. As long as she went fast enough, she'd never fall.

I could win.

She nurtured her treacherous, dangerous hope as she marched down the streets to the gathering. Those who were headed the same way saw her and whispered behind their hands.

She invented a conversation for them.

Look. That's Miss Daisy Whitlaw. She could win.

When one of them let out a burst of explosive laughter, she smiled and nodded at them. They were laughing because they knew how ridiculous the other men would look when she won.

I can win, she told herself as people filled the square, sitting first on benches, then bunching in groups along the edges. The crowd grew large, then larger still, its noise a hum that tried to slide under her skin.

I can win.

I can win, she repeated as the grocer introduced the contenders. He lingered before introducing her.

"Finally, Mr. Daisy—" He stopped, pausing for the ugly laughter that erupted from the crowd. "Right. It's *Miss* Daisy Whitlaw. Our favorite female."

I can win. She wouldn't let that little witticism destroy her confidence. Not this time. Not again.

I can win, she told herself as the other contenders gave their final speeches. The proposals were much improved over the course of the week, she had to admit. Viable, even. She applauded each one politely. But deep down, she knew the truth.

I can win.

No, more than that.

Mine is better. I should win.

The grocer called her to come to the front, and she squared her jaw.

I will win.

Daisy stood. As she did, the man next to her set his hand on her wrist. Her heart was already pounding; her throat was dry. She looked down at the fingers clawed into her cuff, followed the arm back to the glaring face of Mr. Flisk.

"There are men here with wives and children," he hissed at her. "You're making a spectacle of yourself with your selfishness."

For a second, her throat dried. *Selfishness. Spectacle.*

Then she remembered how to ride a velocipede: look forward and pedal faster. She imagined his words bouncing off a glittering ball that surrounded her. And Daisy pulled her sleeve from his grasp and proceeded to the front.

The crowd seemed a hostile force, more so even than the time before. She looked over the sea of faces. A man in the front sniggered. Behind him, a woman sat with a stony face, her arms crossed in disapproval.

This time, they'd known she was going to be here, and they were prepared. A low murmur of unhappiness rose like a susurrus from the crowd.

It was not all that rose. She saw it coming as if in a dream. A potato flew through the air to splat rottenly on the boards in front of her.

"For shame!" someone called out. "For shame!"

Her stomach gave an involuntary lurch.

But there was nothing to do except go faster. Harder. She inhaled and rolled her shoulders back. Her chin went up an inch. Let them all hate her. She didn't care. Except…

In the first row, a little girl with bright red curls was seated on her father's lap. She was watching the stage, and at the sight of Daisy standing up front, her eyes widened. She tugged her father's sleeve, whispering urgently.

Her father shook his head, but the little girl waved her hands in excitement and gave Daisy a gap-toothed smile.

There, at the very back, Daisy's mother sat, bundled in scarves, smiling as best as she could. Crash stood against one of the back walls, watching her intently.

To the right, in the third row, a young woman gave Daisy a tremulous smile. Two rows down from her sat Mrs. Wilde, wearing a tulip in her buttonhole and leaning forward.

Daisy wasn't entirely alone.

She could win. She *would* win.

She wasn't going to apologize for her existence. She didn't need to be forgiven for her ambition. She wasn't going to pretend she didn't matter to assuage their fears.

Let them throw their rotten produce. Let them tell her she was nothing. Let them call her selfish for wanting the same chance as any man. Daisy didn't care; she was going to win.

She squared her shoulders, reached down, and picked up the potato. It was a slimy, shattered mess.

"Women." She said the word loudly, projecting her words to the entire crowd. She held the potato up. "We all know it's an ugly world out there."

That disapproving murmur faltered just a little bit, and Daisy bulled her way into the temporary silence.

"You have been told all your lives that you are a part of the ugliness," Daisy said. "That your only value is to others. That you must labor on piecework, or bend over a desk copying words, or work a loom in a factory. You've been told your only value is what you make for others. You've been told that you'll lose your beauty and once you do, there's nothing more to you."

"For shame!" someone in the crowd yelled.

Daisy ignored him and went on. "Daisy's Emporium of Hand-picked Goods is more than a general store. It's more than a bookseller, or a flower shop, or a tea shop. We'll sell fresh-cut flowers, chosen for their lifespan, so that for a mere halfpenny a week, you'll have something pretty in your life. We will have scarves and gloves that are designed to be splendid as well as serviceable. All these years, you've believed that society has given up on you. And all these years, you've refused to give up on yourself. Daisy's Emporium is for you."

The murmurs had not stopped, but Daisy continued.

"We will have not just goods, but gatherings. For no cost at all, you'll be able to attend a course that will show you how to use a few ribbons to beautify a space, how to make curtains that will make your rooms both warmer and brighter. For those who can't attend, we will sell halfpenny booklets on those same subjects."

Daisy wasn't going to stop now. She was going to win.

"Men." She addressed the crowd. "You are no doubt thinking you have no place at Daisy's Emporium, and I'll grant you the goods I have will be chosen with women in mind. But many of you may wonder about curtains as well, and you'll not be shamed for attending. Daisy's Emporium is for you, too." She took a deep breath. "Now let me lay out the financials of Daisy's Emporium."

"For shame!" someone called again, but repetition had eroded those words of their hurt. This time the call seemed muted.

She went into detail: The cost of goods. The estimates she'd received. The work she would need to do. Where she'd print the booklets. What sort of courses she had planned, and how they'd pay for themselves with sales of tea and goods while still providing additional income for the local women who might teach.

She talked about the number of unmarried women on the parish rolls, and how few of the main businesses on the commercial street were intended to meet their needs.

"I believe," Daisy said in conclusion, "that this is an opportunity to not only establish a business, but to better the surrounding environment. I hope that Daisy's Emporium is chosen for us all."

There was a moment of silence as Daisy gave her final curtsey.

She looked over the crowd—at the little girl in the front, still beaming up at her. At Mrs. Wilde, who gave her a tremulous smile. At the woman in the second row who had stopped frowning and was now looking thoughtfully into the distance.

"Thank you." She turned and swept back to her seat.

"For shame!" someone yelled halfheartedly, but there was a good amount of applause, too. Loud, and more than would come from one or two people being polite.

She'd done well. She knew she had.

Daisy was going to win. She had to believe that to keep the smile on her face. To walk calmly back to her seat with her head held high. She was going to win. Nobody else had gone through parish records to talk about the demand for their business, nobody but her. Nobody else had official estimates from suppliers. Nobody else had a plan anything like hers, and damn it all, if they weren't going to award her the prize, she wanted them to at least be embarrassed by their stupidity.

She sat facing the crowd and smiled. Let them call for her shame; they could call forever. She had no shame in besting everyone else.

She had to stay like that, frozen in place, smiling, for long minutes while the judges conferred. The murmur of the crowd grew to a dull roar as people argued over their favorites.

She'd done well. She *would* smile. She had already won; the only question was whether they would award her the victory or steal it from her hands. She wouldn't let any of them see the slightest crack in her composure.

She sat in place, her hands clenching because her teeth should not.

Finally, the grocer came to the front. "Ladies and gentleman," he said, "after much deliberation, we have reached a near-unanimous decision."

Daisy would not lean forward. She would not scoot to the edge of her seat. She would not hold her breath.

The man turned to gesture at the stage. "Our winner is…"

He let his sentence trail off suggestively, and oh, that was cruel.

Because her imagination slid her name into that gap. *Miss Daisy Whitlaw.* Every fiber of her being yearned to hear that. *Miss Daisy Whitlaw. Say it. Miss Daisy Whitlaw.*

She felt as if she were watching him in a dream. He gestured expansively and spoke. "It's Miss Daisy Whitlaw!"

Her world seemed to fade. It *was* a dream. It had to be. He'd said her name. He had actually said her name.

But it couldn't be a dream. In a dream, his pronouncement would have been met with thunderous applause. Now, the crowd simply murmured in confusion. Someone started clapping madly; Daisy wasn't sure who. But it was just one person.

She didn't care who applauded her or how few. That had been her name. Her name. She'd won. She had really won. It had worked; she had actually won.

Her hopes jumped high, so high. Her heart hammered in her chest.

It wasn't just the money. It wasn't just that she'd won against impossible odds. It was that she'd been brilliant, and they'd been forced to recognize it. She'd fought for her wish, and she had prevailed. The impossible had come to pass.

Daisy felt light-headed. She was not going to faint; she wasn't. She was going to accept the award graciously, sweetly, fairly. She'd make sure they never regretted it.

She started to stand. She'd scarcely stood up from her chair when the grocer let out a loud, wheezing laugh.

"Just a little joke, ladies and gentlemen! I do so love my jokes; I hope you'll forgive me that one. We all know that this esteemed panel could never err in so grotesque a fashion."

Daisy's behind hit her seat. For a moment, she could scarcely breathe. Little spots swam in front of her. The edges of her vision darkened. She swayed in place.

She had to force herself to take one breath, then another. She wasn't going to faint on stage. The cruelty of the man. Raising her hopes up, only to smash them into the ground. Calling her dreams grotesque in front of everyone.

She was not going to cry in front of them all. She *should* have won. She could have won.

She hadn't.

She steeled her chin, planted a smile on her face, and looked ahead. The crowd was a blur.

She scarcely heard the words that followed.

"Mr. A. Flisk," the grocer said, "your plan for a dry-goods store has been selected as the winner of the contest."

Daisy couldn't process the sounds that assailed her. Not the applause, tinged with a derisive note. Not the congratulatory speech the grocer gave, nor the grateful acceptance that Mr. Flisk delivered. She fixed a vacant smile on her face and stared into nothing.

She hadn't won. They hadn't let her.

She waited as hands were shaken, as ribbons were bestowed. She waited until the crowd was dismissed and people began leaving the arena in a great mass.

She didn't want to talk to anyone. Not anyone at all.

She slid behind the stage and slipped through an alley. The street on the other side was bare still; she'd avoided them all. Thank God.

When she was sure nobody could see her, she started running. She didn't stop for a long time.

CHAPTER TEN

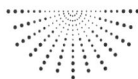

D aisy ended up in a park a mile away, her feet hurting, her lungs complaining, and her hands trembling.

She hadn't won.

She'd let herself believe it was possible. She'd put everything she had into the proposal and the presentation. She'd done well—better than anyone else. She knew she had.

She just hadn't done well enough. There could be no *well enough* for the likes of her.

She hadn't won.

She *couldn't* have won. She felt as if she'd lost not only her chance at a future, but at that short-lived confidence Crash had showed her. How could she go to him now? She'd gone as fast as she could and smashed headlong into their laughter and their jokes. She felt splintered into pieces.

She'd been lying to herself. There had never been any way to win. Not ever. She'd been setting herself up for disappointment from the first.

Now that the future she'd let herself desire was torn from her grasp… Now she had to look clearly at what would happen to her.

She could marry. She could likely marry Crash. It was not the drab, suffocating fate she'd once feared. She'd just started hoping for…more.

She looked up. The park was empty, the branches devoid of leaves. The grass underfoot was brown, a hard blanket of ice encrusting the soil. Brick walls, covered with dead ivy, met her gaze. She could feel the future she'd let herself dream of falling from her grasp.

"I might never have any of my dreams. They might all be stolen from me." The sound of her voice rang out in the quiet.

The words were colder than the winter air. She listened to those words. Tasted them, *knew* them, made herself believe them.

When would she learn? She never got her wishes. She'd let herself believe, and she knew how stupid that was. When was she going to learn to stop wishing? How bloody would they have to slap her hands before she finally learned her lesson and gave up?

Her eyes stung, and she looked up at the gray sky. She should just accept what she had. Things were going well with Crash. That was more than she'd hoped even a week ago.

Loving Crash was easy; she'd fallen back into it with an ease that was hardly surprising. She'd scarcely ever stopped.

Loving herself was harder. How long would she have to wait until she stopped yearning for more?

She exhaled into the wind.

How long until she finally gave up? She waited, listening, yearning for the answer. It came on the next breath.

Until she didn't have hands to reach with. Until she lacked a heart to hope with. Until her every wish had been smashed into dust.

She was not made for giving up. Not ever, and especially not *now*.

She had never needed to prove to herself that wishing was futile. When she fell, there was only one thing to do: Get back on and go faster, and faster still.

Daisy inhaled, stilled her hands on her skirts, and started walking.

❧

The chandelier was just as bright, the damask silk paper just as expensive.

But Daisy had changed. She refused to feel out of place in her friend's home, no matter how expensive the furnishings.

"Daisy." Judith came into the room, followed by a maid who did her best not to frown suspiciously at Daisy. Judith, at least, was smiling.

Daisy's heart was pounding, both from the brisk walk and from fear. But she held out her hands to her friend.

"Judith."

Judith took her fingers and grimaced. "You're cold as ice," she said. "What brings you here this fine Saturday evening? If I had known—"

"I know," Daisy interrupted. "You'd have sent the carriage. But I don't need a carriage." She exhaled. "I need…"

Judith motioned for her to sit. "Is everything well? Your mother? Yourself?"

Daisy set the papers she had brought with her on the table. "I entered a…competition. Of a sort. It started a week ago."

Judith looked at her. "You said nothing of this to me."

"I didn't want you to know." Daisy moved the top paper. "If I had, you would have known how much I wanted to win. And if you had known that…"

Daisy held back a moment. If she had told Judith the truth, her friend would have offered to help. Of course she would have. And Daisy would have felt she didn't deserve it.

"You would have known how desperate I felt," Daisy said. "Everything in your life is…" She gestured, an expansive swing of her arm that encompassed the sparkling glass windows, the oil lamps, the crystal chandelier sending gleams of light throughout the room.

Judith frowned. "You felt desperate? And you didn't tell me?"

"I don't want to be the fly in your ointment," Daisy said. "The person you always worry about. You've achieved everything; you shouldn't be bothered with my complaints. I don't want to be the reminder in your life of what you've escaped."

Judith looked at Daisy, her eyebrows drawing down. Slowly, she exhaled. "Daisy."

"I didn't want to leech off you," Daisy said. "I wanted to feel I had something to contribute to our friendship."

"Oh, Daisy. I'm so sorry, so, so sorry. If I've made you feel—"

Daisy shook her head. "I didn't want to burden you with it."

Judith exhaled. Then she motioned Daisy to lean in, and when she did, she whispered. "Daisy. The servants think I'm beneath them."

Daisy looked at her friend. "Your pardon?"

"Everything I do—how I dress, how I eat, how I plan menus— meets with resistance. 'Are you sure, my lady? The dowager wouldn't.' The servants are unfailingly kind and polite, but the reminder that I don't belong is incessant."

Daisy touched Judith's shoulder.

"The servants have been in the family for generations. They mean well. It's getting better, but…" Judith sighed. "Then there are the children. Benedict has gone from telling me he won't go back to school to saying he has no intention of staying in England. Theresa fights with the dowager marchioness *daily.* And we still have no word of Camilla. What is the point of all this when…?" Judith trailed off, then raised her chin. "No, I know what the point is. It will all work itself out. But the transition is…not easy."

"Oh, God." Daisy bit her lip. "You never said anything to me. Not one word. Why did you never say anything?"

"How could I complain to you? What was I to say? That I was envious of you? That I wished everything might be simple again?"

They exchanged looks.

"And Christian?" Daisy asked in a low voice.

"As wonderful as ever," Judith said. "He's the only reason I haven't given up and set fire to the building. I thought Theresa would do it; no, it's more likely to be me."

"About that competition," Daisy said. "Fifty pounds was the object; the winner with the best plan for a business was to receive the entire amount. They didn't technically *say* it was for men only."

Judith winced. "Oh dear."

"Precisely," Daisy said. "It turned out about as well as one might imagine. But my plan was sound and…" She slid the papers across the table. "Here. I need a business partner. You provide the capital. I'll provide the labor. We'll split the profits." She glanced at her friend. "I'll ask for forty percent."

"Mmm." Judith picked up the pages and started reading. "Daisy. This will not help my social standing."

"Will it not?" Daisy shrugged. "There's something I've learned in the last few weeks. When you feel yourself on the verge of falling, you need to go faster. To not apologize for who you are, what you have come from. Apologies sound like excuses. You're brilliant, Judith, and kind, and funny, and anyone who does not like you is unworthy of you."

"Easy to say."

"I know." Daisy looked at her friend. "But has giving a damn about them changed how they react to you?"

"No."

"Then why bother giving one?"

Judith frowned. She tilted her head. "Yes," she said thickly. "Yes. And I need a friend. A real friend, a female friend. Christian is wonderful, but I can't go forward without you. Daisy, this is…" She trailed off and waved the papers. "This is brilliant. I love it."

For a moment, Daisy almost contradicted her. Then she remembered what Crash would say about apologizing. She lifted her chin and managed a smile in return. "I know it is. They were idiots not to award me the money."

Judith gave her a nod. "We'll draw up the papers. Do everything properly. And it will give me an excuse to get out of this godforsaken gown after all."

"I suggest a work dress," Daisy intoned, "of sheerest lace and rubies."

Judith grinned at her. "Of course. We shall accept nothing less."

~

C rash had tried to make his way to the stage immediately, but Daisy had disappeared in the congratulatory throng that surrounded Mr. Flisk after the competition came to an end.

He'd given up trying to reach her after three minutes attempting to elbow well-wishers aside. The absence of Daisy fed his ire. Didn't any of these idiots know that Daisy ought to have won? Did they not care that the grocer making the award had purposefully humiliated her during what should have been a moment of celebration? That the entire thing was a cruel travesty?

Every congratulatory remark that he heard felt like coals heaped on his head.

Finally, afraid of losing his temper, he backed away from the entire mass of idiots and waited. He waited while the happy cluster of friends and acquaintances slowly dissipated, watching every person who pulled away from that tight, crowded knot, one by one.

After fifteen minutes, it was clear that she had escaped by some other route. He left the square with a quick, sure stride. But she wasn't on the street outside, conversing with any of the other folk. She wasn't around the corner. She wasn't at her flower shop. He tried first one park, then the other, the footpath by the canal, the river walk, her own home, his rooms, and then, just in case he'd missed her, all those locations once again.

He ended up at his aunt's flat. Daisy had gone there once. Maybe she had visited again.

Merry voices rang from inside; they stopped all at once at the sound of his knock.

His aunt answered the door a minute later. She frowned at him.

"Crash. What are you doing here? It's whist night."

"Is, ah, is…" He trailed off.

He'd expected to see the usual three women here, playing alongside the little pencil sketch of Martha Claving. But Martha's picture had been moved to the mantel. Now there were four women.

The fourth was Daisy's mother.

"Ah." He blinked, unsure of what he was seeing. "Mrs. Whitlaw. Um. Is your daughter…"

His aunt just shook her head. "No, Crash, she isn't here. We thought she was with you."

He didn't know what these women were doing together. Why were they discussing him and Daisy? *He* had barely discussed the matter with Daisy.

"Where's the rum?" Harriet asked.

"I don't have—"

"Hmm." She sniffed. "No rum, no entrance."

His aunt barred the door.

"Also, no Daisy, no entrance. What are you doing?"

"What am *I* doing?" He threw up his hands in bafflement. "What are the lot of *you* doing?"

Behind him, Daisy's mother rolled her eyes. "What does it look like they're doing? They're teaching me how to cheat at cards."

His aunt made a shooing motion. "Get out. Go away. We don't need you."

Crash refused to give up; he just needed to regroup. He made his way home, up the stairs to his rooms. He came to the final landing and stopped.

Daisy sat just outside his door, looking as tired as he felt. She huddled on the floor, her arms around her knees. She looked up at him with wide, hurt eyes. Then she smiled.

His heart lifted. His weariness fell away. "Daisy, what are you doing here?"

She met his eyes and slowly—not entirely gracefully—clambered to her feet. "Where have you been?"

"Looking for you." He set his hand against the wall next to her. "Where have you been?"

"Waiting for you." She gave him a smile. A bright one. A brilliant one, in fact, one that warmed him everywhere.

"No," he said. "Never mind any of that. How are you, Daisy? That stage—what happened this morning has been much on my mind. I saw your face. I saw what they did to you." He took a step toward her.

"I wish I had a host of well-fed pigeons to release over their heads. How are you?"

"Truly?" She took a step toward him. "I feel bruised. Hurt. Angry. Sad."

"Of course you do." Then, because she stood mere inches from him, he reached out to her. He cupped her cheek with his fingers, stroking the soft warmth of her skin. "Of course you do."

"I am also," Daisy said, "determined, triumphant, and exuberant. They won't stop me."

There was something in her eyes as she spoke. Something so strong and unbreakable that he wanted to squeeze her tight, just to prove that she was real. "Of course they won't."

"They can't," she said. "They handed me the largest pile of dung a horse has ever dropped on the street and pretended it was my due. That I deserved nothing better." Her chin went up in defiance. "I held it. I *smelled* it. And I'm throwing it back at them." Her eyes bored into his. "When you feel your velocipede slipping, there's only one thing to do."

"Go faster," he said softly.

"Don't stop. Go hard. Pedal. Don't flinch. Maybe you'll still fall, but maybe, just maybe, you'll make it through the other end." Her smile glittered. "I've signed partnership papers. With Lady Ashworth—that's Judith."

He grinned at her. "Have you now?"

"I have. And I was thinking. You told me a while back that you'd looked at a storefront that was too large by half."

"Yes?"

"If you haven't committed to anything yet… Do you suppose we might take it together? We could divide the space in two."

He broke out in a grin. "Yes, Daisy. I think we might. I rather think we might." He paused. "You know, it wasn't just space for a business. There were living quarters above the shop."

"Oh." She looked over at him and a small smile touched her face. "Oh dear. We shall have to argue over who gets them. And I had so hoped that we were done with arguing."

He folded his arms. Two could play at that game. "No arguing necessary. We shall simply divide them down the middle."

"What a lovely solution," Daisy said. "Be sure to tell me which half is yours so I can come visit. I've been told you have scones. And tea. And orgasms."

"God, Daisy." He found himself laughing. "I love you. Will you please stop teasing me and tell me you'll marry me and share everything?"

"I suppose if there are pastries..." She hesitated just a moment. "Then, yes. Yes. I might as well admit that I love you, too."

Their hands clasped. She leaned toward him.

"Wait." He stopped her. How he stopped her when she was on the verge of kissing him, when her lips were so close he could have touched them with his tongue, he didn't know. "Wait. I have some bad news about your mother."

She gasped. "Oh, God. My mother. Is she... Has anything happened?"

He shook his head sadly at her. "You'll never beat her at whist again. My aunt has found her out. She cheats, and she'll teach your mother *everything*."

Daisy smiled. "Good. My mother could use a little cheating in her life."

Ever so slowly, he wound his arms around her.

"So can I," he said.

Her lips brushed his, and he pulled her to him.

EPILOGUE

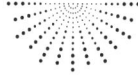

Four months later

There ought to have been some sort of fanfare. Daisy would have settled for a single trumpet playing a few triumphant notes. After months of hard work, the world ought to have announced the alteration of Daisy's life with something more than the chiming of a church bell two streets away.

That was all she had, though. Daisy turned the iron key in the lock on a sunny spring morning and opened the door to her new emporium. The key didn't even give so much as a portentous squeak.

The door swung open onto the cobblestone street. The glass window showcasing Daisy's goods glittered in the sunlight.

It was just another day. Soon this would be prosaic. Daisy danced a little jig of excitement in place and retreated back inside.

Nothing to do now but wait for customers.

Daisy was too nervous to sit. She paced instead—from one end of the store to the other. The mahogany chairs in the sitting area for tea and biscuits gleamed with polish, but she wiped them down anyway. The brightly colored scarves didn't need to be rearranged, but she fussed with them regardless.

That all took precisely one minute.

She glanced out the window, and the bell on the door rang.

In came Mrs. Wilde. In the months since the competition, they'd conversed several times. Daisy had promised her that if she ever needed an assistant, she would ask her first.

The woman looked around and smiled.

"My dear, this is lovely. You've done an excellent job."

Daisy smiled in pleasure.

"I'm here for my buttonhole," Mrs. Wilde said. "Then I'll be out of your hair. I'm sure you'll be busy."

Daisy hoped so. "Flowers. Excellent. We've three choices today. Violets, nasturtiums, and—"

The bell rang again, and Daisy looked up. She didn't recognize the woman who came in. She wore a light green gown with a gold sash, and she smiled and looked about with an air of satisfaction.

"Good day," Daisy started.

But a man entered ten seconds behind her, and Daisy *did* recognize him. He was one of the judges from the competition. The last one, the one who had chosen Daisy to give her presentation. He had set her up for that painful embarrassment.

Daisy winced. She'd be gracious. She *would*. She prepared a smile, however false it was.

"You were right, Benjamin." The woman turned to the man behind her. "She *has* done an excellent job."

Daisy inhaled in surprise.

"Let me look at these hairpieces," the woman said, and the couple walked across the room.

Daisy turned back to Mrs. Wilde. "And tulips," she finished in a voice scarcely above a whisper.

Her mind had not yet recovered from the shock. The judge had thought she would do an excellent job?

She wasn't sure how to credit it.

But after Mrs. Wilde had left with a cluster of tulips, the woman in the green frock picked out a bangle, a set of hairpins with paste jewels on them, and a scarf. Her husband paid for them, counting exact change from a coin purse.

"Thank you," Daisy said.

He met Daisy's eyes. "I voted for your proposal at the end."

She blinked.

He shrugged. "Scant comfort, I imagine, to know the final tally was one against four. But if you want that comfort, there it is."

The bell rang as Daisy stared in stunned confusion. "Thank you," she managed. "And thank you for your patronage."

She didn't have time to say more. The bell rang yet again, and soon her emporium was flooded with customers. The class on dressing hair as a single woman without assistance was filled by eleven; she added an additional day, and *that* was filled by noon. She had to replenish the bangles from the store she kept in the back twice, the scarves three times, and the hairpins... Lord, she'd need to order more of those the minute she had a chance.

If this kept up, she would need to hire a shopgirl. She'd need two.

At ten minutes from closing, the shop was still full. She scarcely looked when the bell rang again.

She saw a man removing a dark hat, a flash of auburn hair. The man was holding a young girl's hand. The child smiled brightly at Daisy, her red hair a cloud of curls around her.

"Can I—" the girl started.

Daisy recognized her; she'd been sitting on her father's lap during the competition.

"Go ahead, pumpkin." The man released her hand. He didn't look at Daisy.

But he accompanied his daughter to the register when she returned in five minutes. The little girl placed a bracelet of wooden beads on the counter.

"Two pence, please."

Her father set two pennies down and looked directly at Daisy. "I wasn't sure about you then. But my daughter was at the competition, and she's been asking me to go to your store." He trailed off, frowning. "I'm *still* not sure."

"Enjoy the bracelet," Daisy said to the young girl. "We'll have new ones in next week, so be sure to stop by."

Her father let out a sigh.

"I will!" promised the child. "Papa, look at my wrist."

"I see it, poppet. It's very pretty. Just like the rest of you."

He was the last to leave, and as Daisy locked the door behind him and drew the curtains, she wanted to laugh triumphantly. She wanted to waltz around the room. And she would, right after she collapsed to the floor in a puddle of weariness.

Footsteps sounded behind her. Then a voice spoke in low tones.

"I believe I promised that you would have tea and pastries, madam."

Daisy turned.

Crash stood behind her. He'd come in through the back door that joined their two shops. He had a tray, one stocked with sandwiches and some biscuits that he must have set aside from her store earlier, because she'd been positive there was nothing left but crumbs.

"I tried to bring you something at eleven," he said, "but you were busy. So..." He set the tray down in her sitting area and waved her to a seat. "Sit."

She did. "How was your day?" Crash had opened his velocipede store over a month ago.

He didn't sit beside her. He knelt in front of her on the floor and very gently removed a slipper. His fingers pressed into the ball of her foot, into sore flesh that had been abused all day. She let out a little moan.

He shrugged. "Delightful. The appointment system you came up with last week has cut down the worst of the arguments. Who knew that the velocipede would prove so popular? One would have to be a downright genius to foresee that."

She took a sandwich and bit into it. She was hungry, and his fingers were pulling all the aches from her feet, her calves.

"*You* foresaw that," she pointed out. "You did."

He looked up at her with a glitter in his eyes. "Ah. So I did. In fact, I suppose my genius is matched only by that of someone who recognized the need for a store catering to working-class women."

"Ah." Daisy smiled. The shop needed to be swept, the shelves restocked, new goods ordered, and the books done... She would never sleep. "Yes. My genius is much overtaxed at the moment."

"I'm greatly pleased," Crash said, moving his hands up stockinged feet, "that my wife is also a genius. There's wine upstairs and dinner."

Daisy sighed. "After. I still have to—"

Crash shook his head. "When I saw how busy you were, I asked Cecilia Evans to come by in fifteen minutes. She'll clean and restock, and you can eat dinner."

"Eat dinner." Daisy smiled at him. "Is *that* what we're calling it these days? You didn't just promise me tea and pastries."

"So I didn't. I know what else you need."

Daisy waited.

"You'll need a good night's sleep." His tone was pious. His look—and the touch of his hand against her knee—was utterly wicked.

"Hmm." She considered him. "Do you know what helps me sleep?"

His smile broadened. "Yes," he said. "Now that you mention it? Yes, I do."

MRS. MARTIN'S INCOMPARABLE ADVENTURE

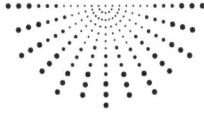

For Yuzuru Hanyu—
the eternal proof that not all men

also a very good source of calming videos
(again the sea of flags from Japan—
what can he produce lying in fifth place?)

.

CHAPTER ONE

Surrey County, England, late autumn, 1867

Miss Violetta Beauchamps had made a terrible mistake. It wasn't the taxing journey from London. Nor was it the coin she'd spent—money she could ill afford—on hiring a cart to come to this large country house that belonged to one Mrs. Martin. Waiting in the parlor for half an hour with her doubts eating away at her certainty had not been a mistake, even though she had spent the entire time wondering if the reason she'd not been offered tea or refreshments was because the target already knew the truth.

No. She was beginning to think this entire scheme had been a very bad idea.

Well. Technically, she had *known* it was a bad idea the moment it came to mind. It had just been the best bad idea out of a truly rotten lot. She should apologize. She should go. She should—

She heard steps behind her, finally, and her circling thoughts fled like a flock of geese rising from a pond at the crack of a shot. She stood slowly, her back cracking audibly as she did.

"Well? What do you want?" The woman who came into the parlor did not look the way Violetta had imagined. She'd expected someone around her age, but stuffier in every regard—her hair, her gown, her corset, her manners. The woman who stood in the doorway had hair of pale white, tugged up into an unpretentious bun. She wore a loose, pink gown, probably silk—comfortable and opulent all at the same time.

Violetta had done her research. She always did. Mrs. Martin owned this massive home and had a fortune in the tens of thousands of pounds stashed in the five percents. Apparently all that money wasn't enough for her to purchase a little politeness. This comfortable woman had the gall to demand what *Violetta* wanted, without so much as an introduction or an exchange of polite talk?

True, Violetta was here to swindle the woman. But Mrs. Martin didn't know that yet.

Violetta considered her options before inclining her head. "And how do you do? You must be Mrs. Martin. I am Miss Violetta Beauchamps, up from London. I hope your morning has been going well."

Mrs. Martin's nose wrinkled at these pleasantries. She acted as if Violetta were some sort of an interloper.

Violetta was not just *some* sort of interloper—she was the worst sort. She was here to put one over on this woman. But from what she had seen of the massive house, Mrs. Martin wouldn't miss what little Violetta would take, not in the slightest.

Mrs. Martin continued the conversation as she had begun it—with an unpleasant huff. "Blah blah blah," she said. "Imagine I just uttered all the greetings that politeness requires. What do you want? Answer *now*, truthfully, or get out."

What did Violetta want? She wanted not to starve. Moralists would undoubtedly tell her that it was too early to turn to crime out of desperation. She knew this; she had done the calculations (impeccably, perfectly—as always) for two nights running. She had spent all her life being careful, and she would not run through her savings for another five years, if she were frugal. She might—perhaps—at the age of sixty-nine find gainful employment once again, at a comfortable wage that allowed her to put aside a small sum on a monthly basis.

Just because she'd never been struck by extraordinary luck before didn't mean it couldn't happen.

The woman hadn't invited her to sit, but then again, Mrs. Martin had told her to imagine whatever pleasantries she wanted. She sank back onto the white and gold damask sofa in this fussy parlor and pinched the bridge of her nose.

Violetta had not made it to this age with the pleasant fortune of having fifty-seven pounds in the bank, with no debts, without being excessively practical.

Mrs. Martin was pretty in the way that conventional, comfortable women often were. She came and sat opposite Violetta with something near perfect posture. Of course. She had no burdens weighing down her shoulders. She had no fears dragging at her future. Her head was held high; her neck was long and graceful.

Violetta had never been pretty, not at any age. She'd always been too round, and one of her eyes had never moved as it ought—"it's disconcerting," a man had told her once. "It's unnatural."

She'd learned not to look at people directly.

Now that she was older, she was even less exciting. Everyone wished she would disappear, and she would be happy to fade into the background so long as she had enough to eat for the rest of her life, thank you.

Nobody was going to hire her again—not for the wage she was used to earning, at any rate. She was sixty-nine and unmarried—one of the so-called *surplus women* who choked up the attics and rooming houses of London. Never mind her experience, her meticulous calculational capabilities, her voluminous memory. She was old and unpretty, and she could either scrape and grow more and more desperate as the years passed...or she could do *this*.

All she had to do was tell one lie. Everything else would be God's honest truth. *One* lie, and if it was believed, she'd be able to spend the rest of her days in her comfortable room, taking nice walks in the park and enjoying the sunshine when it came.

One lie, and she'd have all of that, instead of a slow slide into desperation.

She started with that one lie: "I am here on a matter of business. I own a rooming house in London."

She did *not* own the rooming house in question; she had managed it for Mr. Toggert and his father and grandfather before him for forty-seven years, along with twelve of his other properties. She'd made them a reasonable sum of money. For decades, the reigning Toggerts had praised her diligence, her book-keeping, her careful work. The latest Mr. Toggert had promised her a pension if she worked for him until she was seventy.

He'd sacked her two days ago, eleven months shy of that goal.

Mrs. Martin rolled her eyes, looking singularly unimpressed. "Good for you. I hope you like it."

Violetta pressed on. "I rent rooms to several men, including—"

"Well," interrupted Mrs. Martin. "There's your problem, right there. I have no idea what cockamamie story you're about to tell me, but *don't* rent rooms to men. They get drunk, piss in the corner, and who knows what else? If you'd desist in that one thing, I'm certain your life would improve immensely. There. Problem solved. Are we finished?"

In Violetta's forty-seven years managing Mr. Toggert's rooming houses, men had done every single one of those things. Monthly. She fixed her face in a smile. "Allow me to explain. One of the men who has taken a set of rooms in my house is Robert Cappish."

The look on Mrs. Martin's face changed from annoyed to something far worse. Her nose wrinkled. Her eyes rolled. She looked upward and shook her head.

"Well," she said after a moment. "That's an even worse problem. You have my sincerest condolences on your lack of intelligence in letting rooms to what has to be the worst specimen of humanity on the planet. We do not use that name around here, I am sorry to say. If you must refer to him, you may call him the 'Terrible Nephew.'"

Violetta had not wanted to lease the room to him at all. She had wanted him tossed out *years* ago. Mr. Toggert had insisted. "He has not paid a penny in twenty-seven months."

"That's because he doesn't have any money," Mrs. Martin replied.

"He did his best to spend his mother's allowance when she was alive. After she passed away a decade ago, he ran through his inheritance in a matter of five years, and my patience two years after that. Throw him out on the street. Sell his belongings. Salt the earth behind him as he leaves. What on earth has taken you so long?"

Mr. Toggert had said that if they pressed the matter, they would lose his custom, which would be considerable once Mr. Cappish came into his inheritance. The current Mr. Toggert had insisted they wait, and only make occasional gentle inquiries. Then he had demanded to know why his profits had gone down. Violetta had explained that it had been *his* decisions that had led to the result, but he hadn't listened. He had sacked her.

She had realized, watching his eyes glaze through her careful explanation, that it had all been a pretext. He had *wanted* to sack her and avoid the pension. He'd created the excuse to do so.

"Mr. Cap—" Violetta caught herself at the other woman's ferocious glower. "Your, ah, Terrible Nephew claims you will pay on his behalf."

"He lies." Mrs. Martin sighed. "He is very good at that, you know. I have far more experience denying his creditors than you have in collecting, I am certain."

"But when we let him the rooms, you signed as surety."

"I would never have done so. That was also a lie."

Violetta had never considered this possibility. It had seemed so perfect, the opportunity. Still, she could not give in so easily.

"But..." She leaned down and found her bag at her feet, and withdrew the file she had stolen before she left Mr. Toggert's office that final time. She had a record of payments (few); here, a copy of the lease, signed in Mr. Cappish's own hand. And there...

"Here." She held out the sheet. "This is your signature, agreeing to pay the amount in question if he fails to do so."

"That's not my signature," Mrs. Martin shot back. She stood, waved a maid forward, and—when the woman returned a half minute later with a lap desk—scrawled lazily along a sheet of paper. "That's my signature." She folded her arms. "My Christian name is spelled Bertrice. B-E-R-T-R-I-C-E, not B-E-R-T-E-R-I-C-E. I know how to spell my own name. My idiot of a Terrible Nephew does not."

"But—"

"He forged it, I'm sure," Mrs. Martin said. "He does that. He can't be trusted. Not at all. He truly is terrible. A little forgery is the mildest of his crimes."

Drat. Her plan had seemed so simple—go to Mrs. Martin, apologetically demand payment for the two and a half years due, collect almost seventy pounds, and then disappear with her ill-gotten gains.

Was it a crime?

Yes.

But it should *also* have been a crime to promise a woman a pension and then—after forty-seven years of service—sack her eleven months before the pension came due, for doing precisely what you'd made her do under protest. Two wrongs didn't make a right, but occasionally they did make an escape.

There was nothing for her to do but beg.

She bowed her head before Mrs. Martin. "I am sorry. I ought to have been more zealous in looking over matters."

Mrs. Martin blinked, her eyes narrowing in suspicion. "Why are you apologizing to me?"

"I know you have no obligation to me," Violetta continued, "but I implore you. You cannot leave me with this man in my rooming house, his debts unpaid. I'm old."

"You're not old. You're my age."

"I'm sixty-nine," Violetta said. "I'm weaker than him physically, and I have no way to press the matter, not without risking my own safety. The proceeds from the rooming house are my only income. I beg you, woman to woman. Please help me." She bowed her head. She could hear the hint of her own very real desperation peeking out in the quaver of her voice, and she hoped it would be convincing.

Silence.

Silence was heartening, because Mrs. Martin was not immediately rejecting the idea. She had been blunt enough throughout the conversation; Violetta had no doubt that she'd have scoffed immediately if she were entirely unmoved.

Instead, Mrs. Martin reached out and picked up the file. Violetta's meticulous marks marched down that that first sheet, indicating when he'd paid (the first three months only) and what he'd done thereafter. She'd left little notations of conversations after every encounter.

"Hmph." Mrs. Martin tapped one such notation. "This sounds very like him."

Every month, she'd tallied the amount owing. Interest had been added; the sum had grown larger and larger.

Mrs. Martin flipped to the last page, to that final sum. A little more than sixty-eight pounds. It would be enough to save Violetta.

"You want me to pay *this?*" she asked.

"Please."

Mrs. Martin looked up. "It's such a shame. I have vowed that my Terrible Nephew will never get a single penny of mine, not in any way. You cannot imagine the depths of hatred that I harbor for him. He is a wandering fleshbag of fetid morals, and I would rather encase every penny I have in pig manure and toss it into London Harbor than allow him to have the benefit of a single coin."

"But…"

Mrs. Martin raised a hand. "Give me a moment."

She stood. She straightened, grimacing as she did so, and then leaned on a walking stick. After a moment, her face smoothed.

She left the room with scarcely a limp.

Two minutes later, a maid brought in the refreshments that politeness and hospitality demanded should have provided long before. She laid it all out from a tray—tea and biscuits and sandwiches. For one ridiculous moment, Violetta imagined herself swiping the sugar biscuits into her bag. It had been so long since she had anything sweet at all. Instead, she took one and bit off a corner and let the rich, buttery sweetness dissolve on her tongue.

If *she* had Mrs. Martin's money, there would be biscuits every day.

God. If only she did.

Mrs. Martin returned a few minutes later, sitting herself across from Violetta.

"Sarah," she said, "the ink and paper, please." The maid—who had been standing in the corner since serving refreshments—retrieved the lap desk from where it had been set earlier, removed a pen and a creamy sheet of paper, and set these in front of Mrs. Martin.

Mrs. Martin dipped the pen, a lovely thing of bottle-green, the sort that expensive stores displayed in windows to entice people to enter, and unceremoniously tapped it against the inkwell.

"I have decided that I will do you a favor, Mrs.…. What did you say your name was again?"

"Miss," Violetta corrected. "I am Miss Violetta Beauchamps."

Mrs. Martin started writing.

"'I, Mrs. Bertrice Martin'—note the correct spelling."

She pointed at the page, and Violetta nodded.

"'I, Mrs. Bertrice Martin, do agree to use my best efforts to remove—'" Another frown, and she looked up. "Dear God, if this is to be a legal document, I suppose I must use the Terrible Nephew's actual name." She spoke in a way that practically enunciated the capitals. "What do you think?"

Violetta had no idea what was happening. "Perhaps you could soften the effect by using a sufficient number of adjectives?"

"Mmm. Adjectives. I like the way you think. Where was I? Ah, yes. '…my best efforts to remove the despicable, detestable, disgusting—'" She frowned. "That's not enough, gah, my aging brain—"

"Putrid," Violetta suggested. "Loathsome. Slimy. Beastly."

"Excellent. All of those," Mrs. Martin said, scribbling hastily, "but not beastly. I prefer the company of beasts to men."

"Insect-like?"

"Unfair to crickets."

"Vile, then."

"That will have to do. '…slimy, vile Robert Cappish (hereinafter "said Terrible Nephew") from Miss Violetta Beauchamps's property. In exchange, Miss Violetta Beauchamps agrees to never allow said

Terrible Nephew to lease one of her rooms again, and to assist in such efforts to remove said Terrible Nephew as requested."

That was all well and good, but Violetta needed money. She licked her lips.

Mrs. Martin just looked at her and nodded once, before bending over the paper once more. "'If I am successful in this aim,'" she narrated, "'I promise to give Miss Beauchamps the sum of sixty-eight pounds and 12 shillings for her service, such amount *not* to be accredited to said Terrible Nephew's account because dear God that idiot needs to pay his debts like an actual human being instead of lying like a snake.'" She wrote this out as she spoke.

"Should we be using words like 'idiot' and 'vile' in a legal contract?" Violetta mused. "It seems a bit improper."

"Ah, well." Mrs. Martin frowned at the page. "Maybe you have a point? I don't know. Perhaps as long as we make it clear it's intended to be legal—like this. 'Hereby signed, Mrs. Bertrice Martin.'" She scrawled her signature across the page, then gestured the maid over. "Sarah, you'll witness. The 'hereby' makes it more legalistic, don't you think?"

Violetta was not sure of that. She was not sure about *any* of this. Honestly, she had just hoped for a handful of bills hastily shoved her way. How was she supposed to get the Terrible Nephew to vacate the premises, when she lacked that authority? That would make this *two* crimes, not just one.

But on the other hand... If Mr. Toggert never found out why the Terrible Nephew left...?

It was almost the perfect fraud. Mrs. Martin wasn't asking for his account to be credited; she *insisted* on not doing so, in fact. So the Terrible Nephew would still owe Mr. Toggert the money.

And Mr. Toggert rarely paid attention to his properties. He had not yet hired her replacement; he might not yet for another week. By the time he realized what had happened—and he might never know— Violetta would be long gone, the money with her.

If all went well, Violetta would get something very like her pension and nobody would ever realize that she'd cheated for every penny of it.

She picked up the pen. "Hereby signed," she intoned, "Violetta Beauchamps."

A moment too late, she realized that perhaps she ought not to have signed her actual, legal name to a crime. Ah, well. Some criminal she made. Good thing she wasn't planning to make a habit of this.

She looked over to see Mrs. Martin smiling.

"This is good," Mrs. Martin said. "My physician said I should embark on an adventure. He suggested Bath. Boring. This is much better. I cannot imagine anything more exhilarating and adventurous than making the Terrible Nephew less comfortable in his surroundings. Let's get started, shall we? I can't wait."

CHAPTER TWO

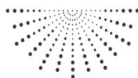

London, early the next day

It was horribly anticlimactic for Bertrice Martin to be standing at her Terrible Nephew's door after having knocked, then waited, and then knocked again. She had built up what was to come in her mind for hours. She felt excitement, yes. Anticipation, definitely. Nerves? Those were old friends, especially when it came to standing up to men.

Her stomach churned with a mix of both fear and delight. To find no immediate resolution at all? That left her rather out of sorts.

The rooming house was clean and bright with new paper. The walls were freshly scrubbed. The wooden bannisters going up the stairs were polished. It looked like a very nice rooming house. Far too nice for the likes of her Terrible Nephew to enjoy without paying.

Miss Beauchamps had removed a key from her pocket—just the one, Bertrice had noted, not a great ring of keys—and unlocked the door below.

It was a rooming house in a part of town that was *just* on the near side of genteel. Miss Beauchamps had explained on the train down that she let rooms to single gentlemen—often those who served in government or law, but who didn't *need* to labor for their income.

"Ah," Bertrice had remarked. "Important enough that they know their own importance; not important enough that anyone else would know it."

The corner of the proper Miss Beauchamp's mouth had twitched at that, and something in Bertrice had felt an exhilarating sense of adventure spark in her at that hint of a smile.

The woman was a bit of an enigma. She'd said more about her rooming house than about herself.

"See here," Bertrice had said, "when I call my nephew the 'Terrible Nephew'—I really do mean it. He is utterly terrible."

The woman had smoothed her skirts and not met Bertrice's gaze. "I *do* know. He lives in my rooming house."

There had been just that flatness to her tone that made Bertrice think maybe she really *did* know. If the notes of her conversation were accurate, he'd threatened to call the constable on *her* if she tried to collect, and that was just what Miss Beauchamps had been willing to commit to writing in her precise, elegant hand.

So Bertrice had spent the remainder of the journey plotting precisely what she would say to that perambulating bag of male pretension and violence when she first had him in her sights. It was rather taking the wind out of her sails to have to wait for the opportunity.

"Is he really not here?" She peered at the door, but it remained firmly unanswered.

Next to her, Miss Beauchamps looked up at the ceiling. "We shouldn't be surprised. It's evening. He's a man of a certain age. He's not going to be sitting in front of the fireplace doing needlepoint, you know."

Bertrice should have guessed. He would be off, doing... *Things,* she supposed. Horrible things. *Man* things. Her nose wrinkled. "Well, damn it. What do young things of his age do, anyway?"

"You do realize that Mr. Ca—your Terrible Nephew is forty-nine, yes?"

"He *is* my nephew. I was present for his birth. I am aware of his age."

"I am only saying that forty-nine is not young."

"Oh, for God's sake. Forty-nine is *extremely* young. If forty-nine is not young, that would make *me* old, and I am not old. I have reached the age of maturity to which all humans must particularly aspire; to dismiss this pinnacle of perfection as *old age* is to demean all of humankind."

Miss Beauchamps did not look impressed. "But you use a cane. And your knee, it looked as if you were favoring the other leg—"

"That can hardly signify." Bertrice rapped on the door one last time just to be certain. "Very young children have difficulty walking, and knee pain is not limited to the elderly. Why, just the other day I met a delightful young woman of thirty-seven whose pain was worse than mine."

"How could you know whose pain was worse?"

"I am entirely certain," Bertrice said, because she had never found it useful to admit that she had no idea. "And don't distract me with irrelevant questions—where is that godforsaken mobile rat's nest that masquerades as my nephew? Have you any idea?"

Miss Beauchamps sighed. "There are two likely options. Most of the men who take quarters in this rooming house do so because the rooms are pleasant and well-appointed, and because it essentially shares a wall with a gentleman's club known as Glaser's. They are the only two buildings on the street."

Bertrice felt her lip curl up in distaste. "Gentlemen. In a *club*. All squashed together. How odious. I cannot believe it is allowed."

"Of course it is allowed. They make their own rules." After a moment, Miss Beauchamps shrugged. "They make ours, as well. In any event, I see it more in the light of putting all the cockroaches in one jar."

"A salient point." Bertrice wrinkled her nose. "I'm not certain why one needs a jar of cockroaches."

"It's better than having them scattered around the house. I would expect that either your Terrible Nephew would be in attendance at

Glaser's, or…" Miss Beauchamps trailed off. "Or," she finished, "he may be in the park."

"The park. Why would he be in the park? It's almost dark. Don't tell me he takes constitutionals for his health. It's hardly his way. He always was the sort to pretend to box for his exercise."

"Ah." Miss Beauchamps's cheeks colored faintly. "That particular park is where the gentlemen of the club find female companionship, should it be wanted."

This was going to take forever if they couldn't use actual words to describe actual things. "Oh. You mean prostitutes frequent it. Stop circumnavigating the conversation. I know what a prostitute is, and so do you. If God didn't intend us to use the words that He made to refer to the people He created, He would have said so."

Miss Beauchamps looked slightly nonplussed. "I'm no lexicographer, but I do not believe God created the English language." Her frown deepened. "Also, most people don't refer to the ladies of the street as God's creations."

"Their mistake." Bertrice gripped her cane and eyed the stairs going down to the street with distrust. Scarcely wide enough, and no fun to navigate at the end of the day. Well, no point waiting; she gingerly started downward. "My husband, God rot his soul, used to bring prostitutes home all the time. After he'd finished with them, I'd serve them tea and double whatever he was paying them."

Miss Beauchamps huffed, sounding faintly outraged at this. Bertrice just concentrated on descending. Down the stairs was harder than up; she had never figured out why. Perhaps it was all in her head, the notion that she might slip. Still, she found herself clutching the rail. She was focused on the descent when Miss Beauchamp's question came from behind her.

"But why would you do that?"

"Why not? It's good sense to be kind to people who are doing work for you." Bertrice didn't think that was so strange a proposition. "It was hard work fucking my husband. Trust me, I should know. *I* certainly didn't want to do it."

She heard Miss Beauchamps slip on the staircase, and turned back to frown at her. "Take care. It's a narrow stair; you mustn't hurt yourself."

She had no idea what the woman muttered in response. By the time they were out in the clear air, though, there was nothing to do except stand in one place, surreptitiously waiting for the deep ache in her knee to subside, and pretend to look about. The sun was setting over the park. No snow here; that was a mercy. Still, it was cold. There was a bit of wind tonight, chilly enough to cut through her combined layers of shawl and thick cape. She pulled her scarf around her neck and hunched over.

She hoped her Terrible Nephew was enjoying himself. It would make it all the more satisfying when she ruined his peace.

"There," she said, gesturing with her cane to the building next door to the rooming house. "That's it, that's the gentleman's club?"

It was a nondescript building of white stone, obviously scrubbed regularly to keep it looking clean-ish on the outside. The better, she supposed, to hide the man-rot within. A plaque on the wall, unreadable from this distance, gleamed in the last rays of the sunset. Steps rose up to an entrance that was trying to appear imposing. Two solid black wooden doors with carved silver lions-head knockers seemed almost gratuitously masculine.

"You know what they say," Bertrice muttered to herself. "The grander the entrance, the smaller the brain."

Miss Beauchamps coughed beside her. "I've never heard anyone say that."

"You should see a doctor about that cough. Maybe it's the beginnings of consumption. You wouldn't want that, would you?"

"No," said Miss Beauchamps mildly. "I wouldn't."

A pair of men stood in front of this melodramatically mannish edifice, jawing about…who knew what? The hair on their chests, maybe. As she watched, a third man came up and greeted them.

Again, that feeling of anticipation mixed with dread roiled through her. Bertrice rubbed her hands together to try to dispel her unease. "There. That's him." She squinted. "I think?"

"Maybe we should discuss how to—"

Discussions never helped anything; they inevitably ended in people begging Bertrice not to do whatever it was she wanted to do. She would then have to waste good effort ignoring them. Instead, she pretended she hadn't heard and started forward at as much of a march as she could manage with her knee aching in the cold wind.

"—The club treasury will withstand a month, maybe two," one of her Terrible Nephew's undoubtedly equally terrible companions was saying. "We have been entirely understanding thus far, Mr. Cappish, and while we welcome men of your quality and caliber at Glaser's, even if you temporarily find yourself unable to pay your membership dues, we must ask that you stop imbibing liquor on credit. I am certain that—"

Now would be a good time to interrupt. Bertrice raised her cane like a weapon and shook it in the air. "Robby Bobkins," she said, because she had to say *something* to get his attention, and she had called him that when he was a very small child and still had the appearance of sweetness, "are you going into a house of ill repute?"

It was, indeed, her Terrible Nephew engaged in a hushed conversation about how he was no longer allowed to drink for free. He whirled to look at her, knocking his hat off in the process.

Oh, he did not look well. There was a certain sallowness to his face that suggested that he needed to stop drinking for reasons other than his pocketbook.

"Aunt Bertrice." He sounded utterly shocked. "What are you *doing* here?"

The man standing next to him perked up. "Ah. This is the aunt who…" The man paused, trying to figure out a gentlemanly way to inquire when Bertrice intended to kick off this mortal coil, and how much money she planned to leave her Terrible Nephew when she did.

God, being a gentleman must be a colossal bore.

The Terrible Nephew's gaze fell on the woman who was following Bertrice, and he frowned. "Miss Beauchamps," he said slowly. "What are *you* doing here? And with my aunt?"

Bertrice shook her cane once more. "*We* ask the questions, Robby Bobkins. Nobody cares about you."

Her nephew sighed with a heave of his shoulders and took a step toward her, lowering his voice furtively. "*Please*, Aunt Bertrice. I know your memory is...not as it once was, but I prefer to be addressed as 'Mr. Cappish.' It's my name. 'Robby Bobkins' is just a little infantilizing, don't you think?"

Bertrice frowned at him. "Robby Bobkins, do you actually *support* yourself with gainful employment?"

"Ack!" The Terrible Nephew took two terrible steps forward, clapping his despicable hands over her mouth. Bertrice didn't know everything he did with them, but she knew enough. She'd told him to never lay hands on her again after he'd knocked her out of her chair for calling the constable on him.

Not again. She was never going to tolerate being thrown about or silenced again, never, never, *never*—not by him, not by anyone else. She bit his fingers as hard as she could.

"Bleah!" The Terrible Nephew pulled away. He shook his hand and glared reproachfully at her. "Don't *say* such things, Aunt Bertrice," he whispered. "I'm a member of Glaser's. It's a respectable club. The members don't need to *work* for our upkeep—only for the betterment of society. It's one of our hallmarks. They'd toss me out if they believed I would be compelled to do such a thing."

"Well." She collected the taste of his vile flesh from between her teeth and spat on the ground. "*I'm* not the one infantilizing you, Robby Bobkins. I can't help it if you're an infant."

He sighed. "Do *not*. Call. Me. That. Please."

Bertrice pitched her voice to carry so that everyone nearby could hear. "Did I ask you what you wish to be called, Robby Bobkins?"

Here was the thing about being the wealthy aunt who her Terrible Nephew needed to please: He really could not be too rude to her in public. Even in private, his worst tendencies were somewhat restrained. She did not want to imagine what he did in his blind rages to women who would definitely *not* leave him forty-six thousand pounds.

The Terrible Nephew exhaled slowly and put a hand over his face, and when he removed it, he was sporting a crocodile's smile.

"Gentlemen," he called over his shoulder. "If you would afford me a little privacy to speak with my aunt? This won't take but a moment." He waited until the other two men moved back ten yards before turning back to Bertrice. "Aunt, if you prefer something more friendly, my intimate acquaintances call me 'Cappy.' I would like it if we were friends. We should mend our relationship." He perked up at this. "I think we would do well to apologize to each other."

Apologize? To *him*? First of all, there *was* no apology for what he'd done. Not for any of it. For another...

"Robby Bobkins," she said, enunciating the name and saying it as loudly as she could, "I am not here to mend our relationship. I am here to make your life a living hell. I have revoked the surety you fraudulently signed on my behalf with regards to the rooms you are letting. You will therefore agree to vacate your living quarters. Immediately."

Her Terrible Nephew's gaze flicked behind her to Miss Beauchamps. "Oh," he said idly, "that's not necessary. Miss Beauchamps won't have me tossed out on the streets."

Bertrice's gaze darted to Miss Beauchamps behind her. They hadn't talked nearly enough. But the woman had struck her as quiet—sturdy and capable, yes, but proper.

It had been a mistake not to make sure they were in full agreement. Miss Beauchamps might be *too* proper. A man with ill intent could easily break a proper woman. The way the Terrible Nephew spoke, it sounded as if he'd reached an agreement with Miss Beauchamps before, and he thought he could make her back down again.

They *should* have talked more, the two of them. The hairs on Bertrice's neck stood on end.

For a second, Miss Beauchamps looked at the pavement, and a disagreeable smile passed over her Terrible Nephew's face.

Then Miss Beauchamps looked up. Her spine straightened. Her jaw squared, and she looked as if she needed only a sword of fire to make her an angel intent on justice.

Up until that moment, Bertrice hadn't realized. It had been so long

—too long, really. Since Ellie had passed away a few years back and she'd fallen into a dark malaise.

But looking at Miss Beauchamps with her chin rising an inch and the last light of the sun reflecting on her eyes, Bertrice remembered all of a sudden what it was to want.

She'd spent all her life learning to stand up for herself. She'd learned to tell her husband no, and to mean it. She'd told the Terrible Nephew to go to hell some years ago, the day he'd broken her heart for the final time, when she'd had to admit to herself that he wouldn't change and nothing would bring back the child she'd loved. She'd been the one to stand up for Ellie when she discovered her accountant was swindling her. Bertrice was *good* at standing up. She was used to it.

She hadn't realized she wanted someone to stand up beside her until Miss Beauchamps did so. And maybe all the other woman wanted was the sixty-something pounds she'd been promised, but in that moment, when she decided to step forward, she seemed glorious in the most electrifying way.

"It seems," Miss Beauchamps said, with a quiet determination, "that you don't know Miss Beauchamps as well as you should."

~

When Violetta had signed that perfidious contract with Mrs. Martin, she had imagined standing in the background with her arms folded, nodding sagely, and collecting her money that same day.

She had imagined that Mrs. Martin would command Mr. Cappish's respect in a way that Violetta herself never had. So when he laughed off his aunt's statements and fixed his gaze on Violetta instead, her first response was to panic and drop her eyes, to hope that he'd look through her as if she weren't present, the way men always did.

Her second response was anger—anger that he'd always looked through her, anger that she'd spent her entire life being transparent.

She'd been a blur in the background, as uninteresting as a lime wash applied to the wall.

She was *tired* of not existing except as a tool to be brought out when needed. She'd spent all seven decades of her life saying *yes, sir, if you say, sir, I'll see to it, sir.*

But she wasn't an echo. She was a *person,* and if she was going to sign her full, legal name to a perfidious contract, she was going to fulfill its terms in their entirety.

Violetta's heart pounded. Her skin felt clammy, but she raised her head and looked at the spot just behind Mr. Cappish's head. "Won't she?" Her voice sounded braver than she felt. "*Won't* she have you tossed out on the streets?"

Mr. Cappish's eyes widened. He took a step toward her. He was tall, and at forty-nine, he was indeed young—young enough that he'd lost none of his height. The bulk of him was appallingly imposing, and he knew it. He knew how intimidating it was when he stood less than a hand's width from her. He towered over her and let his voice drop to a low growl.

"You may recall." He gestured behind him. "I'm a member of Glaser's, the renowned gentleman's club that stands as an edifice to all things manly. We are the ninth most renowned gentleman's club in London."

His performance should have sent a chill down her spine. Instead, the earnestness of his voice coupled with the reverence with which he spoke those words struck her as truly amusing.

She couldn't help herself. A snicker escaped Violetta's lips.

Mr. Cappish turned faintly pink. "That other list does *not* count. Imagine ranking Glaser's—*Glaser's,* which has been in continuous operation for seventy-two years—beneath those upstarts at Smith's. It's an *insult* to even think of us at number twelve in London. An absolute *insult.*" He looked at Violetta and gave her a firm nod, as if he had made a salient point.

Violetta almost backed down. She would have done; she *had* done, so many times before.

If she'd owned the rooming house. If she had still worked for Mr.

Toggert. If she were not so desperate, and this contract made of lies her only hope. Any number of ifs, and she might have been intimidated.

Instead, she decided to emulate Mrs. Martin—just a little.

"So?" she asked loudly. "Are you trying to make a point? Is it that the gentleman's clubs numbered one through eight wouldn't have you?"

"That's—" He sputtered. "That's not—dear God, of course I prefer the company at Glaser's! The gentlemen of Glaser's are renowned for their chivalry—"

"The chivalry of threatening two elderly women?" Mrs. Martin tsked next to him. "My, my, Robby Bobkins, what a *fine,* good specimen of manhood you've grown into, able to vanquish two aging ladies with no assistance but the four dozen men who you pay to call themselves your friends."

Violetta felt almost jealous just hearing that speech. It was so delightfully *cutting.* Why couldn't *she* think of insults like that?

"Careful." The Terrible Nephew raised a finger. "I wouldn't insult the men of Glaser's. We are powerful men, friends, dedicated to one another's mutual interest in all matters. Toss me out of your rooming house, and we will personally make your life miserable in ways that you cannot now imagine." He lowered his voice further, and leaned in to whisper in Violetta's ear. "I don't know what you've told my aunt, you old hag, but—"

"There is nothing wrong with my hearing," Mrs. Martin shouted. "How dare you threaten a lady older than you, you villain? For that, Robby Bobkins, you'll pay. I'll make sure of it."

Mr. Cappish just cast an indulgent look at his aunt. "You'll come around, Aunt Bertrice," he said. "I'm your only living flesh and blood. I'm your beloved sister's only son."

A look passed over Mrs. Martin's face—one that spoke of sadness and loss. She looked away.

Mr. Cappish straightened as if he knew he'd landed a hit.

"Her *only* son," he repeated, "and I know you promised her when she passed away that you would look after me."

Mrs. Martin swallowed, and Violetta felt her hopes of a swift resolution and a tidy addition to her self-funded pension slipping away. It wasn't as if she could enforce the contract she'd signed in Mrs. Martin's living room. What was she to do, go to a magistrate and demand reparations on account of the rooming house she demonstrably did not own?

"There's nothing that's gone wrong between us that we can't fix," Mr. Cappish said gently. "I'm sorry I treated your home with so little respect. See? Apologies are easy. Now, you say that you're sorry, too. My mother would want you to do it. For her, don't you think you can?"

Mrs. Martin exhaled slowly. "I miss her, too."

"I know, Aunt."

"I did promise her that I would do my best to stand in her shoes."

"There, there." Mr. Cappish smiled in satisfaction.

"So I will. Mabel Topham raised us, both of us," Mrs. Martin said. Her chin came up. "She was just a nanny, you might say, but she wasn't. We grew up alongside Sarah Topham." Her eyes lit, blue and fierce, ready to shoot fire. "She was like a sister to both of us. And Sarah's daughter, Lily. She was taking a course on shorthand while she was helping me along, and you—you utter useless cad—you came to my house and you didn't disrespect the damn *building,* you unthinking pile of fetid refuse. She wanted nothing to do with you, and you tried to rape her." Mrs. Martin stopped, her chin working. "I didn't want to see it. I avoided the possibility for years. I kept hoping I was wrong. But you showed your colors, and I'm glad my sister didn't live to see what you've become."

Violetta felt her stomach turn. God; she'd known that there was something wrong between the two of them. She hadn't known it was *this.*

"Aunt. Those words are so harsh. I've asked you again and again to see my side of it. I'm a *gentleman.* It wasn't rape; I would have paid her afterward. You've been sheltered; you don't know how these things work."

"I know exactly how they work," Mrs. Martin said. "I have money.

You have none. I will make your life a misery. I *promise* I will." She raised her voice even more loudly. "Gentlemen, toss this man out of your club. He'll get nothing from me. He'll never repay what he owes your coffers."

"Aunt Bertrice." The Terrible Nephew winced. "You don't *mean* that. I know you won't leave me with nothing. How will I survive?"

"Gainful employment is what most men in your shoes would consider."

Mr. Cappish made his voice a harsh whisper. "That's the second time you've mentioned it. I almost think you're serious, but you *can't possibly* be. Don't make such indelicate jokes around my friends. I know you're just teasing, but what will they think of me? It's one thing to work to fill your hours or to do good, but they must not hear you suggest that I *need* to perform actual labor in exchange for money. How crassly middle-class they would think me!"

"You hear that, gentlemen?" Mrs. Martin announced. "Robby Bobkins here needs to start earning wages for his labor."

"Aunt." He flushed and waved his hands, then turned back. "She's… quite old," he said to his friends who were looking at him from a distance with something like dawning horror. "We should respect her. Even if she's in her cups!"

"Go." She waved her hand in dismissal. "I see you need time to understand your changed circumstances. Go speak this over with your…friends. We'll talk in the morning."

Violetta watched Mr. Cappish retreat into the edifice of Glaser's. She sighed and turned to Mrs. Martin. "The morning? What will you do now? Had you planned to stay overnight?"

"Hmm." Mrs. Martin blinked, looking around at the darkening sky. "Well. I hadn't thought that far in advance. I'm here on doctor's orders, after all. I suppose that I must extend my trip." She frowned, considering. "I'll send for some of my things. See my solicitor, talk to my man-of-affairs, arrange for funds…"

"Where will you be staying?" Violetta racked her brains, trying to come up with a suitable place for a woman who lived in the sprawling expanse of a house that she'd visited out in the country. She'd never had need to think of London lodgings beyond the ones she managed. "Some hotel, perhaps? I suppose if I think, I would know where to inquire…"

"Perhaps." Mrs. Martin's nose scrunched. "Hotels. They're all likely to be far away, and they're so very large and impersonal. But what else am I to do?" She sighed.

Politeness made Violetta speak up. "Or, alternately…. My room isn't much, but…?"

Mrs. Martin brightened immediately, turning to Violetta with a smile. And what a smile it was. It lit her from within, making her seem like a bonfire in the cold air.

Do not, Violetta thought. *Do not invite this woman to stay with you. She is rich, and you have nothing. She's pretty, and you are plain. She's clever, and you're nothing but a boring woman with a head for figures.*

You're lying to her, and you don't need to like her any more.

Exactly the lecture she needed.

But Mrs. Martin's eyes were wide and she seemed almost vulnerable. "Oh," she said, as if Violetta's tiny room were a treat better than the fanciest London hotel. "Really?"

No, Violetta wanted to say. *Not really.* "It will be a little cramped," she said instead, "far less than you're used to. I don't have servants. We'll have to make our own dinner. I don't think you'll—"

Like it, she was going to say, but Mrs. Martin clapped her hands together. "I've never made my own dinner! If you wouldn't mind? I *did* want an adventure. And what could be better?"

CHAPTER THREE

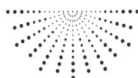

The place that Miss Beauchamps led Bertrice to was in a different building altogether, two streets down. The room was on the ground floor, thankfully; the hallway was darker and dingier than the rooming house she owned. Miss Beauchamps removed another, single, different key from her pocket to let herself into a single room.

It was smaller than Bertrice had supposed, and crammed with mismatched furniture—table, chair, rocking chair, and a bed covered with thick blankets.

"Not much," Miss Beauchamps said as they were hanging wraps on a hook, a faint flush that might have been embarrassment on her cheeks. "Most of the furnishings are left over from what the tenants abandoned over the years."

She ushered Bertrice to a rocking chair made plush with padded cushions and popped a kettle on the hearth.

The water had not yet begun to hiss, and Bertrice was already beginning to think she'd made a mistake. She'd imagined...well, *more*. A guest room, perhaps. Miss Beauchamps had said she didn't have servants, but Bertrice had expected at least a charwoman. From the state of the rooming house that Miss Beauchamps owned, she'd imagined she was rather more comfortable than this.

She hadn't wanted to be a bother, but... Hmm. She made a mental note of a question she needed to put to her solicitors, but since it couldn't be asked at this exact moment, she put it out of her mind.

"I know it's not much," Miss Beauchamps was saying, laying out the tea things, "and if you should want to leave after tea and find that hotel after all—"

"If you're trying to be polite and you want me out of your hair, do just say so," Bertrice interrupted. "These circumlocutions wherein one claims one thing and means another have never made much sense to me. Say what you mean! Indirectness is not my strong point."

"Is that so?" Miss Beauchamps murmured. "How nice to have my suspicions confirmed."

"I like it here," Bertrice told her. "It's cozy."

"No, it's—" Miss Beauchamps looked at her for a moment, before smiling brightly. "Never mind. For a second, I thought you were just being polite."

"And then you realized how ridiculous that sounded. Am I imposing on your kindness? Do you *want* me here?"

Miss Beauchamps looked up, pausing with a spoonful of tea on the way to the teapot. She did not meet Bertrice's eyes. Instead, she looked over her shoulder at some distant point; her eyes crossed slightly as she did.

"I'm used to doing whatever I wish," Bertrice said, "but I'm also used to people telling me to go to the devil if they don't want me about. By contrast, you're one of *those*."

"One of which?"

"One of those *nice* people. You do things you don't want to do all the time, don't you? You're *used* to it."

Miss Beauchamps's eyes widened, then narrowed.

"Go on," Bertrice said. "Spit it out, whatever you're thinking."

"The word for people like me isn't 'nice,'" Miss Beauchamps said. "It is 'not massively wealthy.' What you call 'doing things I don't want to' is what the rest of the world calls 'earning a living.' You lectured your nephew about it. You should recognize it."

"Oh." Bertrice blinked. "Oh. But I'm not employing you."

"We have a contract in which I have agreed to do a thing for you, and you have agreed to give me money for doing it, signed with herebys and everything."

So they did. Bertrice hadn't considered. It was less than a hundred pounds, scarcely anything compared to the chance to seek revenge on her nephew.

"I don't mind having you here," Miss Beauchamps said with a sigh. "I'm just embarrassed because my best is so far beneath your worst."

Bertrice sighed and stretched, rubbing her knee. "Don't be so sure. I've been very down recently. I'm actually fawningly grateful to you for rescuing me."

"Rescuing you from...?" The other woman frowned. "From your china and your tea and your servants? I would *love* to be burdened by your wealth. Do you know what I could *do* with it?"

"Have a perpetual stream of charlatans and liars attempt to remove it from you?"

Miss Beauchamps flushed and rearranged the teaspoons in front of her.

"I know," Bertrice said. "It's rude to complain about my enormous wealth. But I honestly forgot I was paying you. I've felt like there was nothing I could do about that weasel of a blood relation, and then you arrived. I'm grateful, that's all."

"Grateful." Miss Beauchamps stared at her spoons a little longer, before shaking her head and turning to the side. She took out a knife from a box and a half-loaf of bread from another. "Grateful," she repeated, cutting thick, perfect slices. She swept the crumbs into a napkin, and then found some cheese. "*Grateful.* Well, I suppose I'll let go of my petty jealousy then."

"I'll give you a fortune; you can see how you like it," Bertrice said.

Miss Beauchamps took this for a joke. "It's not just the money," she said. "I'm—how did you put it? I'm *nice*. At least, I do what people want. I don't make trouble. I've been doing it all my life, and I'm used to it." She seemed to catch herself, shaking her head and slicing cheese. "You say whatever you want, and I feel like I'm always scream-ing, deep inside where nobody can hear what I'm doing. It's become so bad that I'm afraid I might start doing it out loud."

Oh.

Miss Beauchamps set down the knife and squeezed her eyes together. "But enough about me. If you're going to stay here, I need to know something about you."

Yes, Bertrice thought, *I like women. Once I thought I liked men, too, but I had that burned out of me.*

"Your doctor. You said he suggested this." Miss Beauchamps gath-ered up the now-sliced bread and cheese and went to the stool near the fire. There was some contraption she had—a metal box of sorts, fire-blackened, with a wooden handle—which she manipulated with practiced ease, sliding the cheese inside. "Are you on the verge of dying? If you collapse, who should I fetch? What should I tell them?"

She sounded so matter-of-fact about the possibility of Bertrice keeling over that Bertrice wanted to laugh. Of *course* that comment about her doctor would sound dire to her. Technically, it would sound dire to everyone.

"It's nothing like that. He says I'll live decades longer. The problem is more that there's no joy in anything. Nothing tastes good. I scarcely want to get out of bed most days. He said that I should go on an adventure. He suggested taking the waters at Bath, but yelling at terrible men is far more restorative, don't you think?"

Miss Beauchamps stopped by the fire, tilting her head, as if consid-ering. After a moment she smiled. "Shockingly so!"

"What are you making?"

"Oh." Miss Beauchamps colored and looked away. "It's nothing much. Just a little toasted cheese with bread for dinner. I have some milk, still. And an apple, of course. An apple a day keeps the doctor away." She frowned. "Well, so does poverty, come to think of it. But that's a bit less healthful."

Mrs. Martin's cook served her bread toasted in thinly sliced points. She'd never watched the woman cut it. She hadn't eaten thick bread with slices of melted cheese since she was a child. She'd certainly never watched another woman swipe hair out of her eyes—dark eyes, deep eyes—and turn a little metal contraption above a coal fire.

"Don't they also say something about toasted cheese?" she asked.

Miss Beauchamps colored. "That those who eat toasted cheese at night will dream of Lucifer?"

"I had not heard of that one!" Bertrice leaned forward. "Is it true?"

"It always struck me as odd that the way to summon Lucifer was to eat poor man's food. The devil doesn't care about poor people any more than Parliament does."

"Oh." Bertrice looked at Miss Beauchamps, and then back at the cheese, then at the fire. Was Miss Beauchamps *poor*? She looked so… proper. But…there was the room. And there was the silent screaming. And there was that desperation over so tiny a sum as seventy-ish pounds.

Oh, dear. Bertrice wasn't much for niceness, but she did care about kindness, and the set of Miss Beauchamps's mouth suggested the other woman did not wish to speak of this any longer.

She changed the subject.

"Won't the cheese melt when you put it over the fire?"

"That's entirely the point."

A few minutes later, Bertrice could hear the cheese snapping inside the metal contraption. She could smell it cooking, salt and savory, and her mouth began to water. A few moments later, her stomach rumbled. It actually *rumbled,* as if she were a mere forty or so years old and hungry for a meal.

It had been so long since she had felt anything like hunger. She had been eating mostly because she was aware that putting food in one's mouth and swallowing it was a thing one was supposed to do if one expected to persist in a living state. She hadn't been hungry.

Her hunger felt like a miracle.

"It's not much," Miss Beauchamps said, maneuvering the cheese onto the bread. She put slices on two tin plates and passed one over to Bertrice. "But I hadn't expected company, and it's all I had."

The cheese was melted through and through. The bottom of the cheese had rested directly on the metal over the fire, and had been browned to a glorious crisp. She'd not been given a knife and fork, but Miss Beauchamps didn't seem to think one was necessary. She just picked up her bread and took one unceremonious bite. Melted cheese spilled over the edge, landing with a plop on her plate.

An adventure. Bertrice lifted her own bread and took a tentative nibble.

Oh. *Oh.*

Maybe it was the fact that the bread was thick enough to be toasted on the outside and still soft in the middle. Maybe it was the cheese. Maybe it was that hint of smoke that the fire had imparted.

Maybe it was that she was watching Miss Beauchamps roll the thick column of her neck, stretching it out.

It was good. It was all so good.

"This toasty cheese thing is so lovely!" she heard herself say.

Miss Beauchamps turned to stare at her.

"It is! I can't remember the last time I enjoyed a good toasty cheese thing."

Maybe it had been back with her sister and Sarah Topham, when they were children sneaking into the kitchen late at night, whispering together and giggling, trying not to wake their nanny.

Food was odd. It awoke memories she'd sworn she had forgotten. Memories of laughter, childhood, friendship…a time before she and her sister had married, when finding a man to tie herself to had been the only care she had in the world. God, it had all seemed so simple back then.

She took another bite. How strange it felt to have an appetite once more. Maybe it was the exertion of the day. Maybe it was the excitement. Maybe it was just the cheese toast.

Miss Beauchamps tentatively smiled at her, and Bertrice's feelings suddenly clicked into place. That light tickle of interest…she'd felt it since the moment she'd seen Miss Beauchamps in her home back in Surrey. The woman had seemed so proper, so prepared.

Bertrice had stood up for herself again and again, but saying *no* was a reaction, not an identity. Sometimes, it seemed she was nothing but a rejection of other people's demands. For all her certainty, she hadn't had solid moorings in ages. She'd drifted toward Miss Beauchamps—a woman who made perfect cheese toast and told Bertrice precisely what she needed—almost on instinct.

Bertrice had thought about hiring companionship, but she'd stopped letting herself hope for more. How *strange* it felt to have an appetite again. To suddenly find her mind engrossed, wanting details about how someone else's hair was pinned. To wonder about the pink of her lips, to want to know the feel of her hands. To wonder whether she'd ever wondered about another woman the way Bertrice did.

"I suppose it is good," Miss Beauchamps said. "I have it so often, I rarely think of it. If I had your money, I would..." But she trailed off and didn't finish.

"You would?"

"I can't choose," Miss Beauchamps said after a while. "There's too much. Sweets, I think."

A little silence fell. Another bite of that marvelous cheese toast; Bertrice chanced another look at the woman who sat across from her.

When Bertrice had been young and foolish, she'd thought beauty was as simple as clear, smooth skin, wide eyes, willowy silhouettes... the usual, really.

Decades of watching beauty had changed her. What was meant by "beauty" altered over the years—fashion demanded first plump, then slender. One year, brunettes were all the rage; the next, it was blonde hair. The noses that society raved over went from small to Grecian to snub.

Nobody would call Miss Beauchamps beautiful, she didn't think; even decades younger, had she been on the marriage mart, men known for sharp wits and sharper tongues would undoubtedly have amused crowds by mocking her.

Miss Beauchamps no doubt knew that. She probably knew in excruciating detail precisely what fun men might have at her expense.

Still, she drew the eye in a way that Bertrice could not explain, and did not want to attempt to understand. Her cheeks were round and ruddy, like a tea-kettle on the hearth. She sat stiff-backed, feet on the floor, but there was something about the way she looked at the wall that made Bertrice think she was seeing some country far beyond England.

She wanted to know what she was looking at. It wasn't just attraction. It was a pull within her, beckoning her closer.

"It must be nice," Miss Beauchamps said, "to not have to worry about money."

Bertrice worried about money; she worried a great deal about how she would leave it. But that wasn't what Miss Beauchamps meant.

"I suppose it is," she said slowly. "I rarely think of it."

Miss Beauchamps sighed and stood, slicing an apple before handing Bertrice two quarters. "Why did your doctor think you need a restorative treatment, then? If it's not too impolite to ask."

"Oh, I had fallen into a bit of a rut." She looked upward. "I didn't want to do anything. Nothing tasted good anymore. That sort of thing."

"Was there a reason?"

There was always a reason. Bertrice sat and breathed through the pain of hers for a moment before answering. "Well. Mrs. Lakeland passed away two years ago. Then Mrs. Nightwood. Then Mrs. Trouridge. There, just like that, in the space of nineteen months." Her voice did not tremble, not in the slightest. "My entire card group gone." Especially Ellie Nightwood, Ellie who had brought her through the worst of her marriage and saved her heart. "Everyone kept telling me to cheer up because I was lucky to still be alive and hale and hearty."

Miss Beauchamps made a sympathetic noise.

"I *am* lucky to be alive," Bertrice said, shaking off her shoulders as if she could shrug off that cloying sympathy. "I *am*. I don't want to be dead."

"Being alive doesn't spare you from grief. Rather the reverse."

She could feel a lump of emotion welling up in her, and Bertrice hated lumps of emotion. "It's hard to lose friends. And at this age…" No, there it was—stupid emotion again. She gritted her teeth and waited for it to pass.

"At this age," Miss Beauchamps finished for her, "everyone looks through you as if you're not even there."

"*Yes.*" Bertrice shut her eyes. "Precisely." That solid mass of emotion persisted, still damnably present. "So you know how it is."

Miss Beauchamps shrugged one shoulder. "I am what the papers call a surplus woman. There are so many of us—women who have never married, who make their own way in society—that we aren't even people any longer. We're just statistics to be presented. The most I can hope is that I'll be pointed to as a warning to young women, to secure their men before they turn into me. I wasn't alone most of the time. But my dearest friend went with her sister to Boston six years ago. Since then, I've been like this." She gestured around her. "Save for letters."

"Yes." Bertrice swallowed. "It's not the same for widows, but…it is. I had…" It was hard to talk about her friends still; her throat tightened with emotion. "My friends aren't here any longer, and now that they're gone I want to scream that I'm real, I'm still a person. I don't stop existing because I can no longer have children. There was no point in my life where I ceased having dreams for the future. There was no time when I stopped wanting friends and camaraderie and—"

She cut herself off.

Miss Beauchamps looked at her. "And?"

For one beat, Bertrice considered not saying a thing. But she'd learned long ago that there was no point in being circumspect. Her heart was wrapped in suffocating folds of cloth, each layer a regret made of things she'd never said. There was no point holding back. "Sexual attraction at my age is the worst," she admitted. "Everyone acts as if one should naturally outgrow all wants."

She still felt it beneath her skin—the desire to touch and be touched, to hold and be held. To be affirmed in the present. To be important to someone else. She'd once been thought beautiful—that had passed with her youth—but she still longed to be thought pretty. Just because she had grown old, just because she'd ceased to match the fresh-faced standard of loveliness, didn't mean that she'd lost her want.

People spoke of desire as if it were the province of the young. But here was Bertrice at seventy-three, still yearning.

"But you don't seem to like men," Miss Beauchamps offered slowly. "At all. Do you mean…?"

Again, Bertrice was past the point of dissembling. "If God intended women to only have relations with men, then why did He give women fingers and tongues?"

Miss Beauchamps tilted her head to look at her. She didn't often do it. Her eyes crossed just a little, giving the expression a hint of sweetness. Sweet, and for a second, Bertrice wanted to taste. She wanted to know more about the lines on her brow, the tips of her fingers. She wanted to lean in and—

Miss Beauchamps flushed and quickly dropped her gaze to her tea cup.

Just as well. Bertrice didn't need to do anything hasty. "Sometimes, I dream of finding a young thing of forty."

The tea cup slammed on the saucer. Bertrice looked up to see the other woman standing abruptly. She piled the empty dishes atop each other—loudly, angrily—and marched to a basin on the other side of the room.

Oh. *Oh.*

Bertrice watched as Miss Beauchamps violently wiped down the plates, then wiped the table where she'd cut the bread and cheese with a damp cloth. She went to the window, finally, opened it, and poured the gray water into the street below. A blast of cold air rushed in before she could close it once more.

"Miss Beauchamps," Bertrice started, "I didn't mean—"

"Never mind. It's nothing."

"That's just false. It is clearly *something.* When I said—"

"It's nothing," Miss Beauchamps repeated, securing the windows once again and setting the basin back in place. Belatedly, Bertrice realized that the woman had done all the labor that evening—the preparing, the toasting, the cleaning—and that there were no servants.

Oh. How rude. She hadn't thought. She hadn't helped. How... How utterly manlike of her. A flicker of shame went through her.

"It's nothing," Miss Beauchamps said a third time. "Just this—you want a forty-year old, and I'm standing right *here*. I told you how I felt, but even *you* don't see me as anything except surplus."

Oh. There it was, a second flicker of shame, this one deeper.

That's bad, Bertrice. Doubly bad, because it was true.

Miss Beauchamps just exhaled and shut her eyes. The anger in her pose tensed into stiff propriety once again. "Oh, dear." She turned away. "How very awkward of me. I shouldn't have—that is, I didn't mean to imply..." She trailed off. "Never mind it all. We should get ready for bed."

Bertrice hadn't really let herself think about bed. The single bed was large enough for two—maybe. Plenty of room if they didn't mind limbs touching. Scarcely enough, if they laid on their sides at the opposite edge of the mattress.

Miss Beauchamp's gowns seemed easier to undo than Bertrice's. It had been ages since she had undone her own gowns, and she didn't want to ask for help, especially now that she'd made such an ass of herself. She tried her best to undo the buttons up her back, but her arms didn't quite reach and her fingers cramped—

"Here," Miss Beauchamps said brusquely, and Bertrice shut her eyes at the dance of fingertips down her back. It was business-like, quick and impartial. *No, you don't understand,* she imagined herself saying. *I like you just fine.* It wouldn't make the situation less awkward.

"Thank you," she said, but Miss Beauchamps did not answer.

They washed in silence.

She needed to offer something like an apology. She knew it. When the pitcher ran low, she made sure to fill it from the bucket. She hashed through the muddle of her thoughts.

It wasn't until they'd gotten stiffly into bed—curling on opposite sides as far from each other as they could get, and yet so close that one wrong move, and they'd touch—that Bertrice spoke.

"What I meant." She swallowed. "I meant that I wanted someone who would be sure to outlive me. I don't want to suffer through another loss. The last one who left..." She couldn't find words. She could feel that dark malaise that had taken over her. She'd been adrift in grief. "It was too much. The one thing that having money allows is that I *could,* I suppose. Find a forty-year-old."

Miss Beauchamps did not respond, not for a long while. Her breath was even in the cold of the night—even, but not slow enough for sleep. Bertrice bit her lip. She was *not* a man, she wasn't. She wasn't going to demand forgiveness when she'd been the one in the wrong. She stared blankly into the dark.

"It still sounds to me as if you mean that someone like me hasn't anything to give you," Miss Beauchamps said.

It did, it did, but...

"And," Miss Beauchamps continued, "it sounds to me as if you're afraid you've nothing to offer but your money."

Bertrice breathed in that hurt. It was true—all too true. She knew how people talked of women like her—as if she were empty, all worth leached from her by the passing of time. Even her doctor, less terrible than most men, had thought of her as nothing but her funds.

She wasn't, though. She was real. She was still here, alive and dreaming.

"My dearest friend died two years ago." Bertrice hugged her arms to her chest. Friend wasn't a close enough word for what she had been. Lover wasn't a close enough word. What did you call the person who made your life worth living? What did you call her, when you weren't supposed to even have her at all? "I *am* lonely and I'm sad and I'm so, so scared. People tell me that I am supposed to mellow with age, but I care as fiercely as ever. And caring hurts. I'm frightened of caring."

Miss Beauchamps sighed.

"You're not surplus," Bertrice said. "No woman has ever needed a man to be enough."

"Tell the rest of the world." Miss Beauchamps turned in bed. "I don't dare stick my neck out, not once. If I had money, I'd…"

Once again, she paused. Once again, Bertrice asked. "What would you do?"

"I'd stop worrying," Miss Beauchamps breathed.

Maybe that was when Bertrice realized what she needed to do. Not much; just ease the burdens that made Miss Beauchamps's shoulders so tense. *Show* her that she wasn't surplus, because telling wasn't enough. Maybe confess the incoherent thoughts she'd had over dinner.

She could feel the other woman turning in the bed, and with it came the awareness that they were close physically, and not in any other way.

Start slow, Bertrice. You've hurt her, and you have questions to ask of your solicitor. Start slow.

She wasn't good at slow, but she tried. "Do you think you might show me how to use the…the cheese toasty thing? Tomorrow evening?"

A huff. "Yes," Miss Beauchamps muttered. "I suppose I could."

"I'm sorry I did so little to help with dinner tonight," Bertrice tried again.

"Your knee looked as if it pained you. I didn't mind. Truly."

The silence stretched longer. "By the way," Bertrice heard herself asking, "what do you suppose would be the most annoying way to wake up?"

One last huff. "Dear heavens. Do I want to know why you're asking me that? Or am I better off living in ignorance?"

Bertrice smiled in the dark. "Yes, I rather think you want to know why I'm asking. You'll like it. We're going to have fun."

❦

The sun had been two hours up. The streets were crowded. Violetta herself had never been the sort to lie abed letting daylight waste in any event; she would have personally called the hour closer to noon than morning. Nobody could have thought it *early*. Nobody rational, that was.

But then, they were talking about Mr. Robert Cappish. Rational had no place in the life of a man such as he. They stood just outside his door in the rooming house. They had waited until the last man other than Cappish had vacated the premises. Cappish was still in his rooms, no doubt sleeping the sleep of a man who had no idea what was in store for him.

"Here," Mrs. Martin whispered, as they got into position just outside his door. "You should have this."

A touch of her hand, skin against skin, and Violetta felt herself blush, remembering what she'd admitted last night. She had essentially implied that she found Mrs. Martin attractive, and *that* had been an embarrassment and a half. But Mrs. Martin was just giving her the stick, a firm wand of oak, as thick as her little finger, and twelve inches long.

"But—" Her protest was a whisper; why, she didn't know, when the entire point of this exercise was to be loud. "But I haven't the faintest idea how to—"

Mrs. Martin's eyes twinkled in her face. "That's the point. You don't need to *know*. Just do it."

It felt utterly ridiculous to turn to the small group that had gathered in the hall. Three men, two women. Violetta had met them years ago when they had gone caroling for charity. They had been the most successful charity carolers she had ever encountered, mostly because everyone they encountered emptied their pockets in a tremendous rush to hurry them on.

"On three," Mrs. Martin said. "One, two—"

Violetta knew nothing of conducting. She didn't know the music. She had no idea what she was doing. But there was no escaping the force of Mrs. Martin's personality. She raised the stick.

"Three!"

Down went Violetta's hand.

"Hallelujah," bellowed the chorus—off-key, out of synchrony, and extremely loud. *"Hallelujah."*

Beside her, Mrs. Martin begin laughing.

It was utterly ridiculous. Violetta had spent all her life trying to fit in, trying to be unobtrusive. And yet at the first sound of those notes, something inside her seemed to wake up—as if the out-of-tune song blew air over the embers of her anger.

Stupid Robert Cappish, stupid, *stupid* Robert Cappish. Stupid Mr. Toggert, stupid men everywhere who thought she was nothing, and stupid *her* for agreeing. For *letting* them think so.

She waved her arms wildly in what she hoped was the universal signal for *more noise, now, please.*

"HALLELUJAH, HALLELUJAH, *HALLELUJAH.*"

She would have bet anything that the chorus had no sense of music at all, but they responded to her gesticulations with wild enthusiasm, redoubling their volume.

"FOR THE LORD GOD OMNIPOTENT REIGNITH!"

A little doopsy-doo with her conducting stick—what on earth was the thing even called?—and they followed her cue, tilting even more off key.

Her face almost felt as if it would crack from the smile that grew.

Maybe Mr. Cappish was waking up. Maybe he was banging on the door. Maybe he was shouting for them to be quiet, but it wouldn't matter. They couldn't hear his protests. The cacophony was deafening; the man bellowing in the back had brought along cymbals, which he crashed together not at all in time to the music. It was the most glorious dissonance, and it went on and on.

"AND HE SHALL REIGN FOR EVER AND EVER."

Out of the corner of her eye, she saw the door behind her open; she turned quickly.

Mr. Cappish stood red-eyed and angry in front of them. He must have dressed hastily. The tails of his shirt were untucked; his jacket was twisted at the collar. His mouth moved. He was undoubtedly saying words. She couldn't hear a single one.

Violetta felt a wild surge of delight. He was talking to her, and she was drowning him out. For the first time in her life, *she* was drowning out someone *else*. She turned back to the choir and frantically waved her arms.

"KING OF KINGS!" they bellowed. "LORD OF LORDS!"

He stomped to stand in front of her, waving his arms, and—well—she supposed they *would* have to deliver their message eventually. Violetta sighed and let her arms drop.

The choir lapsed into silence raggedly, person by person.

"How dare you!" He glared at her. "Sleep is *important* to restore one's mind and health. To interrupt it in this manner is—it's really just entirely uncalled for, Miss Beauchamps. How *dare* you!"

"Robby Bobkins," said Mrs. Martin behind her, "if you have something to say, you should say it to my face."

It was interesting to watch his face turn white. First, the blood drained from his nose—impressive, considering how red it had been. Then from his lips. Then his forehead went pale, then his cheeks turned waxy. He turned around, looking almost green.

"Aunt…Aunt Bertrice." He plastered a fake smile on his face.

"Robby Bobkins, I *told* you I was going to make your life miserable. When have I ever not meant what I said?"

"Ah… But, Aunt Bertrice." He shut his eyes. "First things first. I must please, once again, ask you to not refer to me as…that name."

"Which name? Robby Bobkins?" Mrs. Martin spoke half as loud as the chorus had been singing—which was very loud indeed.

"Mr. Cappish, please. Or, as I said, you may call me 'Cappy.' I ask for only this small form of civility. I'm sure if we could just talk matters out, we could come to an understanding."

Mrs. Martin looked at him for a long moment, before nodding. "Yes, I think we can. Let us compromise. From here on out, I will call you 'Mr. Cappish, a despicable bag of diseased meat.'"

The Terrible Nephew blinked.

"Ladies and gentlemen of the choir, this is Mr. Cappish, a despicable bag of diseased meat." She looked at her nephew expectantly. "There, I've shown that I'm capable of compromise. Now will you promise not to rape women, or do you need an additional title?"

"I—Aunt Bertrice, that's—" He sputtered. "That's not any better than Robby Bobkins!"

"Men." Aunt Bertrice shook her head. "Never satisfied, no matter how hard you try to please 'em. Well, I tried. Miss Beauchamps, if you will do the honors?"

Violetta bit her lip, and then leaned into the choir, whispering her orders. They listened carefully.

"FOR BEHOLD," they began singing, "DARKNESS SHALL COVER THE EARTH."

Robby Bobkins groaned and retreated into his room.

Ten minutes later, he came out, freshly shaven and somewhat cleaned up. His ruffled collar betrayed his haste, however; he pushed past the throng at his doorstep, stumbling to the stairs and brushing lint off his coat as he went.

Violetta stopped her choir—when had she started thinking of them as *her* choir?—and let Mrs. Martin give instructions.

"We will be following him," she said. "Let's pick some good pieces?"

"I have an idea," Violetta heard herself say.

And so it was that they caught up with him three minutes later as he was strolling down the street, tipping his hat in a friendly fashion. He didn't see them coming behind him. He didn't even suspect it.

He had no idea what was about to happen, not even as Violetta raised her conducting-stick-thingy and waved it in the air.

"ROBBY BOBKINS!" the choir sang to the tune of the Hallelujah Chorus. "ROBBY BOBKINS! ROBBY BOBKINS, ROBBY BOBKINS, ROBBY BOBKINS!"

He broke into a run, and something stiff in Violetta's chest melted at that.

It was worth it. Whatever happened—whether Violetta got her money, or if she was exposed as a fraud and tossed in prison—it didn't matter. It was worth it to see him scamper off like a frightened rabbit. She and her ragged choir did their best to follow him—it didn't help the quality of the music any, but it could hardly hurt—all the way through "FRIEND OF FRIENDS!"

They followed until Mrs. Martin was lagging far behind. Violetta stopped two streets down, gestured the choir into silence, and waited for Mrs. Martin to catch up.

"He'll be angry about that," Mrs. Martin remarked. There was a small smile on her face.

"I know." Violetta tried to remember that she was in public. She straightened her shoulders and shoved that ridiculous desire to laugh deep inside her. "Isn't it glorious?"

CHAPTER FOUR

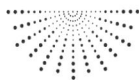

The sun was high and bright overhead. The chorus had been paid, and Bertrice had decided on the next entertainment for the day.

It was not quite two in the afternoon—the time when Bertrice usually found herself retreating to her room for a nap for want of something else to do. She'd spent months staring up at the canopy of her too-large bed, hoping for some surcease from her daily boredom.

Now, she sat in Hyde Park on a bench. They'd wandered here over several miles—mostly by hired cabs, stopping here and there to duck into shops. Bertrice's hips ached—a good ache, the sort of ache she'd not felt in years. Her knee…well, that was less of a good ache.

Lord, Bertrice sometimes forgot she wasn't forty any longer. She surreptitiously rubbed the joint. She'd need to find a cabriolet to take them straight back, no questions asked, *that* was for certain.

They'd sunk onto this bench, trees and grass and the distant glitter of silver waters all around them. She and Miss Beauchamps had procured jacket potatoes from an establishment at the edge of the park, cooked to perfection and slathered in butter and salt. They'd purchased bottles of soda water. They sat close to each other, wielding forks that Miss Beauchamps had produced from a pocket as if she were some sort of magician.

The first bite of potato was meltingly perfect. For so long, sustenance had felt like dust. She'd had no interest, no excitement. It had seemed a miracle last night to enjoy one meal; it seemed impossible that she could enjoy two. And yet here she was.

There was nothing she could point to that made this potato exceptionally good. Maybe it was the salt. Maybe it was the sun.

Maybe it was the way that Violetta Beauchamps sat next to her, ankles crossed demurely, potato in wax paper held in front of her.

She'd heard it said that hunger was the best sauce, but company was a seasoning that had been in short supply over the last years. Maybe that was it.

"I haven't had this much fun in ages," Miss Beauchamps said.

"Neither have I." She looked over at the other woman and felt an ache in her chest, the remnants of grief still lodged in her ribcage.

"All my life," Miss Beauchamps said, "I've done everything *right*. I was a demure little girl for my parents. I took care of them. I was introduced to men, and when nothing came of that, I…" She paused, her mouth temporarily thinning, then looked up with a sigh. "I… inherited the rooming house. And still I did precisely what I was supposed to do. I kept complete, fair records. I rented rooms to men of good families. I was polite and kind, even when my tenants were in arrears, even when they threatened me. I was always, always kind. I thought if I was, they'd have to be kind back. Eventually."

Bertrice sighed. "It was different for me. People *had* to be civil to me; I'm rich."

"Did they, though?"

She thought about the way her nephew talked to her—as if he always knew better, as if her eyes and her heart were suspect, as if she should be willing to substitute whatever facts suited him in place of what she knew to be true.

"It's a peculiar sort of civility. I must be humored. But they don't actually listen to me. Even if their words are polite."

Miss Beauchamps took another bite of potato. Her tongue flicked out to meet her fork, and for a second Bertrice felt as if her entire being was caught on that motion, so prosaic and yet so striking. Oh, to be a chunk of potato. Miss Beauchamps chewed and swallowed; it felt almost sinful to watch. She looked up to meet Bertrice's gaze, and, for a moment, paused, mouth open a fraction, before flushing and looking away.

"Tell me, Mrs. Martin. Do you often engage choruses to bebother men who have fallen from your graces?"

Mrs. Martin. It was polite, yes, but it felt so...so wrong. So *distancing.* Mrs. Martin was the label society applied to the wife of her husband, and that rat-fiend was long and thankfully dead.

"Bertrice," she said.

There was a pause. Miss Beauchamps frowned at her as if she did not know what she meant.

"My given name," she clarified. "It's Bertrice."

"I know? We signed a contract, did we not?"

"Well, use it," Bertrice told her. "Nobody has since my...dear friend passed away. It feels like it's getting rusty."

"And you expect me to polish it off for you?"

Bertrice felt herself flush. She hadn't meant to imply that she wanted the woman to act as if she were in service. But who did she talk to but servants at all any longer? "I didn't mean—that is, oh, *damn* it all—"

Miss Beauchamps's eyes flashed bright. "I was teasing. I can't call you Bertrice if I can't tease you, you know."

Oh. *Oh.* Miss Beauchamps bumped her shoulder, lightly, and Bertrice felt an irrepressible smile rise to her face. "Is that so?"

"It's so. I tease my friends, just a little." She looked over her shoulder, briefly. "I did before Lily went overseas, at least."

"Well." Bertrice looked over. *Teasing.* God, it hadn't been so long ago that she and her friends had all been alive. *They'd* teased her. They'd also sat with her during the worst of her marriage, finding excuses to get her out of London when he was in the city and reasons to bring her *into* London when he was rusticating. And she'd done her best by them, too.

Her friends had been an extension of her heart.

If Ellie had been here, she would have teased her, too—telling her to stop worrying, reminding her that she was alive.

Bright sunshine was spilling onto the crown of Bertrice's head. It felt like it was sinking into her being, lighting her to the tips of her toes. "That's...nice. That's very nice."

"My name is Violetta," said Miss Beauchamps. "And you haven't answered my question, you know. Do you often bebother men who fall from your good graces?"

Bertrice thought about the look on her Terrible Nephew's face. "Not often enough."

"It's awfully rude of us. I feel as if we shouldn't enjoy it."

"As rude as not paying rent for two years?"

Miss Beauchamps—no, Violetta—pursed her lips.

"They don't listen," Bertrice said. "And he doesn't listen to *you* differently than he doesn't listen to me—but he's still not listening. Following him around with a chorus has been the only thing that's received a response so far. Let's keep it up, shall we?"

The woman had—technically—signed a contract agreeing to do so, but nothing in the contract mentioned terrible carolers or farm animals or any of the other awful, vengeful ideas that Bertrice had been nursing in anger.

She held her breath as Violetta seemed to consider this.

"You know," Bertrice offered, "if you'd like, we could do it the easy way. Go to the constables; have him tossed out for failure to pay. But I tried purchasing his debts and having him tossed in debtor's prison. It didn't work."

That had been back in the days when rage was all Bertrice had. She had already felt empty and grief-stricken; rage had been welcome, as *some* sort of emotion rather than an absolute void of nothing. It had burned through her like a fire. She'd felt like she could have set the world ablaze. But she'd been contained in stone, doomed to burn and smolder impotently.

"What happened?"

"They found out I was his aunt and insisted it was a family matter, nothing for the courts." Bertrice sighed. She'd felt like cold ash for so long. No appetite. No longing. No hope, just the smothered embers of her resentment.

And yet here Violetta was, sitting beside her. Violetta's hand rested on her own knee; her knee was so close that if Bertrice leaned in even the slightest amount, their knuckles would bump.

"Ah," Violetta said softly. "Of course."

"I've screamed on the inside, too," Bertrice confessed. "I've screamed on the outside. I've screamed until I thought there was nothing left of me but my voice, and then I lost my voice. And still I kept screaming."

Violetta's eyes lifted to hers. It was just a glance—she seemed shy of the connection—but the dark glow in her eyes felt like a touch. Smoldering ember to ember, voice to voice, scream to scream. Then her head dipped down once more. "I never screamed aloud, and yet I lost my voice from disuse."

Bertrice let her hand drift to her right, a knuckle's width, enough to brush against the other woman ever so slightly. Ember to ember, spark to spark. She could feel it building inside her—as if the act of hearing and listening, repeated over and over, could make a furnace of her.

"It is up to the two of us, then," Violetta said. "Two is more than one."

One was impossible. One was contained. Alone, Mrs. Martin had felt cribbed in, made of complaints and unable to move. Two was a more dangerous number.

And then Violetta clinched it. She looked over at Mrs. Martin, and she asked the most wonderful question. "Well, then. What will we do to him next?"

≈

"Good Lord." The lodger stopped at the head of the rooming house stairwell, frowning at the procession that Violetta and Bertrice were heading. "What on earth are you intending to do with these animals?"

Drat. Violetta turned to him and put on her most placating face. They had made it up to the first floor, to within feet of Mr. Cappish's door, before being stopped, and she hardly wanted to give an explanation.

You see, Mr. Lornville, she imagined herself saying, *we are attempting to bedevil a horrible man.*

They'd come up with the idea together. Bertrice had sent a message by courier to her man-of-affairs. What the fellow had to do with farm animals, Violetta didn't know, but in short order, some poor clerk had procured a procession of women with geese in cages. The geese girls were currently carting their goods to the top of the stairs, while the birds hissed unhappily through the wooden bars. A few feathers marked their passage up to the first floor.

But Mr. Lornville was frowning at them. He was in his fifties—a barrister, although he scarcely practiced law—and very sure of his own significance.

To be fair, one didn't need to be particularly haughty to object to geese in one's rooming house.

"We're taking them up these stairs," Bertrice said. "Quite obviously. Have you no sense?"

Mr. Lornville's eyes narrowed. "I live up here." He peered into the nearest cage, and was rewarded with the responding hiss of the devil bird inside. "What do you intend to do with these geese in this rooming house?"

"Release them," Bertrice snapped impatiently. "Don't worry; they won't be in your quarters."

"They're loud," the man countered, "and geese are filthy, violent animals. They don't belong in *any* sort of house, let alone a rooming house. On whose orders is this being done?"

Bertrice gestured nonchalantly. "Miss Beauchamps approved it."

Violetta swallowed around a lump of fear in her throat.

It had only been three days since she had been sacked, and Mr. Toggert had obviously not informed the tenants of her displacement. But for a few scant hours, Violetta had been so immersed in their plans that she had forgotten the truth. She was not the owner of the rooming house. Mr. Lornville knew that, and he could expose her lies right now.

Mr. Lornville made an unhappy noise. "You can't do this, Miss Beauchamps. I don't know which tenant asked for such a ridiculous thing, but *I* don't approve, and I also live here. I would like to file a formal complaint."

"Oh," Violetta said through her fear. "Well."

What would Bertrice do? She wouldn't stand in place, rooted in fear. Bertrice, indeed, had not let so much as an eyelash flicker out of place during this entire exchange. Her arms were folded aggressively, cane dangling from one hand as if to suggest she could beat the man with it as easily as use it to assist her ascent of the staircase.

What would Bertrice say? She would—ah. There. Violetta drew herself up straight and made what she hoped was a gracious movement with her right hand. "Your formal complaint has been noted."

"Noted?" Mr. Lornville frowned. "Just noted? Have you not considered my request beyond that one second? I say, Miss Beauchamps."

"It's been noted," Violetta repeated. "The geese are allowed." Then, from some well of unknown creativity, she added, "We have agreed to conduct an experiment on living with fowl in London. Food practices which relegate the production of eggs and meat to far-flung farms may result in contamination during transport. We have therefore—"

Luckily, Mr. Lornville interrupted her before she had to provide any further explanation for this ridiculous flight of fancy. "I say. I don't wish to live on a farm. It can't be hygienic."

"The geese *are* trained," Bertrice lied next to her.

"Lots of people live on farms," Violetta added. "Many of them don't die, I've heard." Technically, they all probably died at some point. She amended her answer. "At least not out of turn." She hoped that was the case. She'd never been anywhere near a farm in her life.

"This is simply unacceptable. Listen to the noise! *Smell* them! If I have to, I will take this complaint—"

"To the authorities?" Violetta interrupted, before the man could go and ruin everything by mentioning Mr. Toggert, the man who had sacked her. She had a brief vision in her mind of how he would take this. Mr. Toggert, and his calm complacency. Mr. Toggert, and the look in his eye as he'd told her she had let profits fallen. Mr. Toggert, waving off the comment that he'd been the one at fault, waving off her proof, her entire life. It had been a pretense to avoid paying her pension—and he'd lied to her and held her to blame when she was the one who'd warned him in the first place.

Damn Mr. Toggert. Damn him to hell.

Better yet, damn him to unprofitability.

"Of course," she heard herself saying before she could think through the consequences, "I will release you from your lease. Due to changed circumstances and the like."

Bertrice looked at her in surprise.

Violetta had no authority to do anything of the sort. This was not the sort of lie she should tell—she knew it, the moment it came off her lips. But if Mr. Toggert lost all his tenants because he hadn't taken the necessary steps to replace her…whose fault was that, really?

Yours, actually, some portion of her mind that insisted on the truth whispered. *It's your fault.*

"I will give you two pounds," Bertrice said, "if you'll sign papers agreeing to quit the premises within three days."

Mr. Lornville blinked. So did Violetta.

"Well, he does have a valid lease," Bertrice pointed out, "and I do believe the experiments would be easier, if we had fewer people here. If you wish not to be part of it—by all means, we would be delighted to help you leave."

"Well." Mr. Lornville tilted his head. "Perhaps… I'll have to move all my things, you know."

"Four pounds," Mrs. Martin said with a shrug, and Violetta

refused to let herself feel anything more than a hint of jealousy at being able to throw around such a monstrous sum without blinking an eye.

"Five?"

"Only because these experiments are very important," Bertrice said solemnly.

Mr. Lornville smiled brilliantly and extended a hand. "That's very good of you. Very good indeed."

Bertrice did not shake his hand. Instead, she wrote out a draft on her bank, and had him sign a paper, before sending him on his way. The geese hissed angrily at him as he passed.

"Well?" Bertrice turned to Violetta. "What are you waiting for?"

Violetta took out the master key, which she had failed to return to Mr. Toggert, and unlocked the door to Mr. Cappish's room. He'd not emerged at all during the entire conversation—but it was nine in the morning, and a handful of geese and a bit of discussion were hardly enough to wake a man who required a deafening chorus to rouse him from slumber at that hour.

They gestured silently for the geese girls to enter; she could hear the *snick* as the cages opened. The women dashed back into the hall in a rush.

That was it. They'd loosed nine geese in the Terrible Nephew's room.

Violetta shut the door behind them. She locked it, for good measure.

"One," Bertrice counted. "Two. Three. Fo—"

"What in the blazing devil's hell is going on!" they heard Mr. Cappish shout from inside the room.

Bertrice dissolved into laughter.

And oh, Violetta should be scared. She was officially doing things that she had no business doing. She was now violating the law in new and interesting ways, and she should be too scared to do anything except cower.

But laughter was contagious, too, and she found herself cackling aloud as Mr. Cappish swore up a storm.

When they'd laughed so hard her sides ached, she turned to Bertrice.

"What would you like to do today?" she asked.

It was almost like being on holiday—a holiday where she lived in her own rooms and tormented men for fun and profit.

"Maybe see the Houses of Parliament?" Bertrice commented. "I never have before."

"Are you sure? They're full of men, you know."

"I know," Bertrice said glumly. "What's worse, they burned down decades ago, and I wasn't even there to see it. But we can have fun imagining what it was like, can't we?"

CHAPTER FIVE

Violetta managed to hold in her emotions for another handful of days.

Honestly, she hadn't realized she was holding anything. Or maybe she'd been holding on to so much for so long that hiding her pain felt normal.

In the end, a tree outside Westminster Abbey set her off.

The sun was out, and a few days of damp cold had given way to a bout of unseasonable sunshine. Perfect, Bertrice had said, for a little tour of London sights.

Violetta had agreed because Bertrice was something like an avalanche—there was no point trying to stop her. Besides, Violetta had discovered that there was a great deal of joy to be had when those rocks fell on other people.

It gave Violetta a tiny taste of what it might have been like, if her life had taken an upward turn instead of sliding down. If she'd had money. If her income had been just a twitch higher. If her parents had retained anything to pass on to her.

Bertrice had sent a note off to some man-of-affairs somewhere, and they'd been given a tour of the Abbey. After, a servant had blankets and a picnic lunch waiting for them. The man had stood under a tree—an old, gnarled oak with spreading branches—just to hold them a prime spot. The tree had dropped most of its leaves for the winter, and sunshine flickered through the branches.

It had *definitely* been the tree that had set Violetta off.

Certainly not Bertrice setting her hand on one rippling root, looking up through the branches at the blue sky overhead. She'd said absolutely nothing of import. Just this: "What a marvelous, beautiful tree this is!"

It *was* a marvelous tree, shaped by time and gardeners into twisted, labyrinthine splendor.

And yet that one remark stole the air from Violetta's lungs. She'd felt as if she were punched in the gut, as if all those years of grasping and holding everything in place were suddenly too much.

"Why?" Violetta had heard herself ask, her tone just a touch querulous.

Bertrice turned to her. "You don't agree?"

Violetta didn't know what to think. She hardly knew what she felt. "I just want to know *why* you think it."

"Well." Bertrice looked at the tree, frowning. "There's the bark, to start. Don't you think bark on old trees is picturesque? It's got—oh, I don't know the proper terms. But it's split. It's got ravines, you know. Proper texture. None of that smooth, boring stuff that young trees boast."

Something dark and sharp took form in Violetta's breast. "Go on." It came out on a hiss.

Bertrice looked bewildered. "Well...then...the shape. Look at that branch there, the way it dips and then rises. Or there, where those two branches have been rubbing together. Or *there*—there's a story about the left half of this tree, don't you think? I can almost imagine the gale that stripped away all but the heaviest branches, and they're only now growing back, a thicket of little twigs on a giant oak like this."

Violetta looked at the branches overhead, her teeth gritted, trying not to let her eyes water. Trying not to feel, just as she'd spent decades not letting herself respond to every last insult that she had been supposed to take as her due.

"All nature is like that, really," Bertrice had continued. "A boring straight stream is nothing compared to a rivulet that has carved its path deep into the forest, rock worn away, banks covered in moss. The human eye is drawn to difference."

The tight knot of hurt that Violetta had been nursing all her life flared. It flared into anger and self-pity and dismay. Then—like a wildfire set on a dry meadow—it raced past those simpler emotions directly into confounding rage.

"No doubt," she snapped. "Trees and streams and valleys and beaches alike. All of them grow more beautiful with age. Even men in their own way receive more respect. But it's not *all* of nature. It's all of nature except human women."

Bertrice turned to her, eyes wide.

"It's not me," Violetta snapped. "Nobody praises the texture of my skin, now that I'm no longer smooth as a sapling. Over the years, I've grown rounder and more lumpy, but when it's a human being with cares and feelings instead of a tree, *I'm* considered *disgusting.*"

"Violetta," Bertrice murmured. She tentatively reached out a hand. "*I* don't consider you disgusting."

"Even though I'm not a sprightly young thing of forty? How good of you. Even if it were true, you're one out of—how many people are there on this planet? Millions? Ha." She plucked morosely at the blanket beneath her. "But it's not just age. I've *never* been beautiful. My eyes cross, no matter how hard I try. My hands are so ugly that store clerks wince when I count change. Why is it that everyone can find a bloody *tree* more beautiful than a human woman who shares the same properties?"

She was raising her voice. A woman—much younger—gave her a disapproving glare and a sniff.

Violetta had never used the word *bloody* in her life. She hadn't even realized it was in her vocabulary.

She shut her eyes and felt her anger mingle with shame. She reached out, trying to catch hold of her unruly emotions. "I apologize for shouting. It's not *your* fault. It's been like this forever, and every time I think I'm at the bottom of humanity's care, I descend one rung further and discover how wrong I was. There's always another rung."

"There shouldn't be a bottom." Bertrice's hand was still stretched out, not quite reaching Violetta. Her fingers twitched forward, then stopped abruptly. "There shouldn't be a ladder."

Maybe she pulled back just now because she thought Violetta untouchably ugly. Maybe it was because they weren't the touching sort of friends. Whatever the reason, that hurt too.

Violetta felt little stinging beads of moisture form at the corner of her eyes, and let out a noise of frustration. Anger, and now this? Crying was for fools.

"Violetta."

She sniffed, refusing to look.

"You're right. It's not fair."

She shook her head. "My mother always told me it was what was inside that really counted, but I realized quickly it was a lie. They never say such things to pretty women."

"They don't," Bertrice whispered.

And Bertrice would know. Age had been kinder to her. Her locks were white and easy to pin in place, unlike Violetta's unruly mass of salt-and-pepper. Her hair had always been thick and curly; age had made her gray hairs coarser and downright untamable. Bertrice's features were pleasant and symmetric; she was slim enough that she had little to sag. She had wealth and beauty and the ability to command, and what did Violetta have?

Lies and a bank account that would deplete itself before she did everyone the favor of passing away.

She swiped away the moisture on her cheeks.

Bertrice's fingers once again twitched, then moved to lie still on her knee. "It's lies," she said. "They lie to us all. And sometimes we're idiots and we believe them, even if we know better."

"Yes."

"They lie to us, but we needn't lie to each other." She looked over to Violetta, looking *at* her, not through her. Her gaze touched her hands, then traveled up her arms. She took in every part that Violetta had ever been told was ugly.

"Don't you think?" Bertrice asked.

Yes, Violetta almost said. It nearly came out as a plea. And then she remembered the rooming house—the one she didn't own. She remembered the contract and the lie. She'd waited years and years, hoping someone would see the inner beauty her mother had told her was all that mattered. Sixty-nine years she'd waited. Sixty-nine years, until she'd given up. Because destiny was cruel, it had delivered that someone the very instant that she had capitulated.

Violetta closed her eyes.

Her fingers twitched of their own accord, moving toward the point where Bertrice's hand rested on her knee. So close she could almost feel the contact.

"I want it," she confessed to the tree and Bertrice. "I want honesty more than anything. But I don't believe it's possible anymore."

"You know what I see when I look at this oak?"

Violetta shook her head.

"Centuries have passed, and it's still here."

It survived. That was it—that was all Violetta could hope for, all she could ever have hoped for. She couldn't grow straight, not any longer.

She could survive.

"Well." Bertrice sat back, pulling her hand away. "We'll work on it, won't we?"

～

They did not work on it, not immediately. Bertrice had not imagined that it would be possible to make up for decades of pain in one afternoon, but she could feel the distance between the two of them like a yawning chasm as they packed up their picnic and beckoned the servant, who had been watching at a distance, to come take their things away. Clouds came and covered the sun; a fog crept in, and London returned to its typical winter gloom. Bertrice hired a cabriolet, which returned them to Violetta's room.

Still Violetta ignored her for the next hour, studiously reading a fading political circular, dated seven years prior. Bertrice couldn't forget the tree, the outburst. She'd been wrong. It wasn't the first time, and she didn't know how to fix it.

After an hour of near silence, Bertrice excused herself, claiming she had business with her solicitor. And she did—there was always something or other that her blasted solicitors needed answering or signing or complaining about. That, though, wasn't the reason she had left.

She returned with bread and cheese and tea and milk three hours later.

Violetta looked up and smiled—a pale thing, lips pressed together and vaguely turned up—and nodded politely once, before returning her attention to the same four-page political tract she had been perusing hours before.

WORKERS, read the front page. *ORGANIZE, ORGANIZE, ORGANIZE!!!*

Bertrice raised an eyebrow. "You're involved in radical workers organizations?"

Violetta primly turned the page. "I am educating myself."

"Good for you." Bertrice watched her a moment longer. Even proper and prissy, pretending she'd not lost her temper earlier, there was an almost magnetic quality to Violetta. As if the roiling tempest she'd let loose had been caged—for now, and for now only.

Bertrice wanted to see it loosed.

But there would be time for that. In the moment, she wanted to make dinner. She laid out the loaf and the cheese, found the knife and a wooden board, and proceeded to chop things up.

Or at least, she *tried* to proceed.

It wasn't easy, mainly because Bertrice had never held a knife before.

Oh, she'd held paring scissors and butter knives and steak knives.

She'd even held a little blade, one used to trim finger nails, for the space of five minutes.

But a knife? A *real* knife, with a serrated blade longer than her hand?

There had been servants for that. There had always been servants up until this exact moment.

She'd been so proud of herself, purchasing cheese and bread all on her own. Now she held the loaf in front of her, lifted the blade high—

"No," Violetta interrupted behind her, "*please* not like that. You must think of where your hand will be once the knife passes through the loaf. If you stab straight through that, the palm of your hand will be right *there*. Never use your flesh to stop a blade."

Bertrice wrinkled her nose. "I'm not an idiot. I would stop before then."

"Most of the time, I'm certain you would," Violetta said in a tone that suggested she was certain of no such thing. "But it's better not to have to rely on your skill. All it takes is one little mistake, and there you are, bleeding all over the bread."

"Hmmmph," Bertrice said, because it was becoming apparent she had no skill.

Violetta came to stand behind her, and ever so gently, she tapped Bertrice's knuckles. It wasn't sensual, but still, Bertrice sucked a breath in. "Here. Set the bread down. One hand to hold it in place. The other…"

Bertrice jabbed with the knife.

The knife lodged hilt-deep.

Violetta's hand stilled on hers. "Yes," she said after a long, drawn-out pause. "That's…definitely one way to start. Now that you've killed the bread, it's certain not to move about any longer."

Bertrice braced the loaf and managed to wrench the knife from where she'd buried it in the doughy deeps.

"So…like this?" She tried a motion as if she were slicing off a pat of butter.

"Maybe…" Violetta sighed. "More like cutting steak, less like cutting an apple? Slice. Don't push."

Bertrice tried again. Crumbs scattered like blood in an abattoir.

"Keep your hand steady, press straight down. Well. I suppose… that does serve much the same purpose. And it doesn't matter if it's jagged, once it's inside us?"

Violetta had made such smooth, pretty slices. Bertrice's bread fell apart in ugly, ragged, crumb-strewn chunks.

"Slice," Violetta said, and set her hands over Bertrice's. Her fingers were cool to the touch. But how could Bertrice possibly concentrate? Touches were rare in her life, except under the most impersonal of circumstances. Her maids had dressed and changed her with detached indifference; her doctor had methodically listened to her lungs and her heart; occasionally, a servant had brushed against her unwittingly in the hall.

Nobody had taken her hands with such gentleness since Ellie Nightwood had passed away.

"Like this," Violetta demonstrated. "See? The motion is all across; let the blade do the cutting, not your arm."

Even with instruction, the movement was unfamiliar. She felt as strange and clumsy as she had taking up needlework forty years ago, before the feel of thin metal at her fingertips became commonplace.

"You must think me a complete oaf," she said, after Violetta had guided her in chiseling off slices of cheese that looked as if they'd been hewn from rock by an inexpert stonecutter, and left her to bludgeon apples into shards.

Violetta glanced at her from her place at the fire, where she was turning the cheese toaster. Her lips pressed together; she looked into the sparking coals, as if seeing something that had long since disappeared.

"My mother didn't know how to cut, either."

Bertrice looked up from arranging her irregular wedges of fruit on two plates.

The other woman was still staring into the fire.

"She escaped the Terrors in France. She watched her own father die on the guillotine, disguised in servants' clothing at the edge of the crowd. She and my father fled in disguise. They came here. They had only the jewels sewn into her gown to sustain them. They were just important enough for the Revolution to target, but not quite interesting enough to gain entry to the top levels of English society." Violetta spoke evenly.

"I'm sorry." Bertrice had always been bad at showing compassion, but that seemed like a thing one should say at such times.

Violetta shrugged one shoulder. "I was born here. I never knew any differently. The money from the jewels ran short when I was almost an adult. There were no funds, not for maids nor cooks. My parents had no skills with which to earn a wage. My mother put a good face on it, of course." Another shrug. "It was easier for me to learn all these little things myself in order to make a penny stretch. And then it was easier for me to care for my parents than to try and educate them." A third shrug. "I ought to have married, but nobody wanted me, and the thought of men having their way with me made me feel nauseated in any event."

"Your mother must have been very fragile."

Violetta nodded her head. Still…

"No," she contradicted herself. "Maybe she wasn't. But strength is relative to situation, and she was pushed into a place where all her strengths—her confidence, her ability to order a household—became weaknesses."

Bertrice shut her eyes. "I married because my mother told me I would starve otherwise. She was not wrong. My father was the sixth son of an earl, and I was his second daughter. I would have no dowry. So I married the richest man I could find. It was the usual bargain—I served as his entry into polite-ish society; he provided for me as best as such a person could. But once we were married, he had his place in society secured and I still had need of his money, every day." She exhaled. "It was not an equal relationship. All the strengths that a woman needs to land a good match are unequal to the task of surviving that match when it goes sour. Sometimes I hate my mother for not letting me starve."

It was the first time Bertrice had spoken that aloud.

Violetta did not rear back in horror. Instead she shook her own head. "Sometimes I hate my mother, too. She didn't know how to do anything she had to do, and she didn't want to learn. Once the money ran out, she placed the burden of survival on me. She could have shown me how to hope, but instead, the legacy she left me was fear."

"Fear of violence." It was as close as Bertrice could come to talking about those dark years, locked deep in her heart.

"Fear of not having enough," Violetta whispered.

"Fear of not *being* enough, of sitting silent while others suffer in the exact same way."

For a long while, they didn't say anything.

Fear at seventy years of age was different than fear at seventeen. At seventeen, Bertrice had been walking down the so-called correct path, trying not to stray with all her might. Her fears had not been her own; they had been gifts from her elders. *They won't think you're proper if you do that. You might never find a match. Do you want to live in a garret alone for the rest of your life?*

Here was Violetta, living out the worst nightmare that Bertrice's seventeen-year-old self had harbored.

"If I hadn't married," Bertrice said, "I might have been you. I think of you, cozy in this room where nobody can touch you. I fear I could become jealous."

Violetta shook her head violently. "Do you think so? Do you think that just because nobody wanted me, nobody would touch me?" She didn't say anything more, but her eyes squeezed shut.

And no. Of course not. Bertrice knew men. They were opportunists, and what could be a greater opportunity than a woman nobody cared about?

Violetta went on. "You don't need to worry one ounce about what you will do when you're eighty and maybe ninety, with nobody to care for you. I think *all* the time about what I would do with your wealth. We met because I begged for a portion of it. Do you ever think about what we're doing now?"

"You refer to the geese?"

"And the chorus. And your Terrible Nephew."

Bertrice had tried not to think at all. She was having an adventure. She was trying to *enjoy.*

"Men inherit property," Violetta said. "Not fear. He expects *us* to be afraid. Don't you wonder what he might do to inspire that emotion in us?"

Bertrice exhaled. When she'd left on this adventure, she hadn't thought about what it would mean aside from a chance to do precisely what she wanted. She had tried to avoid thinking about the consequences. But even if she put it out of her mind, it stayed in her body, bringing heaviness to her limbs.

"I do," she said. "I do wonder. And..." Despite her bravery, there was always a tense expectation in her gut, one that counseled her to hide. She'd learned to push through it, but the worry never left. "And I *am* afraid. I just don't want to be."

"Neither do I."

Bertrice looked over. Women inherited fear, yes, but it was because women were expected to care. They were expected to look out for children and grand-nieces and servants, to fear for them if anything went awry.

Somehow, in the last few days, Bertrice had started to care about Violetta. To care was to be afraid.

"You know," Violetta said, pulling the toasted cheese from the fire, "I have no idea what I will do if he decides to attack me. He could hurt me, and I don't heal as swiftly as I used to." Her hands were trembling. "There's nobody to look after me."

Bertrice thought of Violetta's hands on hers, guiding her while she cut. She thought of the flush that had taken over Violetta's face as she'd led the choir. She thought of her friends who had passed away, Ellie Nightwood especially, and the empty cavern of her life. Ellie would have scolded her, if she had been here.

But when she tried to bring Ellie's face to mind to deliver that scolding, the image wouldn't hold.

Scold you for what? she imagined Ellie saying instead. *For mourning? For taking time? For missing me? I would never.*

Bertrice had been trying not to care for so long, but she cared so much. Of *course* she'd felt nothing. Of course she'd tasted nothing. She'd been too busy holding her own grief at bay to feel life as it went past. She'd made noises about seeking out a forty-year old to distance herself from the woman in front of her.

Here was life, gently reminding her that she could care again. That her grief was allowed, but so was her joy.

"Don't be silly," Bertrice said. "I'll look after you. I promise." She was surprised to realize that she meant it.

Violetta turned to look at her. She often looked as if she were seeing some point just beyond Violetta, and at first she did that. But then her gaze shifted to contemplate Bertrice directly, and Bertrice remembered what she had said earlier. *My eyes cross, no matter how hard I try.*

Bertrice met her gaze, reached out, and took her hand. "I promise," she said more fervently.

And for one bare moment, Violetta lit, blossoming at her touch, her eyes burning into Bertrice's with a radiant intensity. Then she sank back, pulling her hands away.

"Thank you," she said. Her voice seemed sad and small. "Thank you. But we have a contract, signed with herebys and everything." Her jaw squared. "And we have work to do. I don't need your promise." Her fingers clenched at her side, as if remembering that touch. "Let's take care of your Terrible Nephew. I'll take the money that's owed, and I'll…"

She didn't say what she would do, not for a long time.

"You'll…?" Bertrice prompted.

"I'll do what I've always done," Violetta whispered. "I'll survive."

CHAPTER SIX

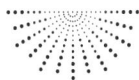

Two weeks later

Violetta stood at the top of the staircase in the rooming house she definitely did not own, about to execute what was both the brightest and the stupidest idea that she had ever had in her life.

She was going to hell. The only question was which path she would take on her road to the inferno.

She was certainly going to pay for her misdeeds. The last weeks had been torture. Torture for the Terrible Nephew; in the days past, they'd pelted him with eggs and dusted him with flour. They'd left putrid cheeses outside his room, and coaxed goats upstairs, convincing them to eat his undergarments.

They'd also been torture for Violetta. She'd pulled back from Bertrice as much as she could, limiting their physical contact to the brush of a hand. Sometimes she could not help herself, and their eyes met in a blaze of radiation that took her breath away. In those moments, she felt like her want was leaking from her, incapable of containment. She wanted to be loved. She wanted to be desired. She wanted someone who saw who she was.

But every time she allowed herself to let her guard down, she remembered the truth. She *didn't* want someone who saw her as she was, not at all. She was a liar. She couldn't want to be seen.

And so every time, she yanked her hand away or cut her gaze to a corner of the room, and gathered her wanting back inside her.

Violetta didn't know if her destruction would come in the form of Mr. Toggert, who—despite his foolishly lengthy absence—would soon discover that she was altering the leases of his tenants.

Perhaps it would be Mr. Cappish who brought the authorities on their heads. In the past few days, on the strength of Violetta's nonexistent authority, Bertrice had convinced every tenant except the Terrible Nephew to escape the hellish landscape that had once been a peaceful rooming house.

Maybe it would be Bertrice herself. She'd promised to look after Violetta, but that wouldn't last, not once she knew the truth.

It was just as the vicar had promised when she was young. One little lie sent out roots and branches, burgeoning in madcap fashion until her whole life was blossoming with falsehoods. She was probably going to hell. She was certainly going to prison.

And, well. It seemed a very far-off thing. She could panic about it later. Imprisonment was a form of planning for her dotage, wasn't it?

"Up here," she called to the plasterer she had engaged yesterday. "The work is up here."

Beside her, Bertrice snickered.

Oh, her current plan would not buy food. It would not keep her from any of the punishments that awaited. It would not give her anything except a private, desperate joy, but when shelter and food faltered in the years to come, it would be a joy she could hold on to.

Years ago, Violetta had been tasked with combining two rooms into one more luxurious set of rooms. It was from that experience that this idea had sprung.

Now she had only to execute it.

The plasterer came to stand beside her, frowning.

"You want me to plaster over this door?"

The carpenter was already at work. He had removed the door from its place and had fitted in a frame to cover the gaping hole. He was now nailing boards to cover the frame he'd built to block Mr. Cappish's entry.

"Yes, that's precisely the work you were hired for," Violetta said. "Plaster over the door. Make it look as if there's no entry at all into the room."

The plasterer frowned. "But there's still a room, there? That seems wrong."

"Um…" Violetta tried to come up with a good explanation.

But Bertrice never let anything stop her, and Violetta adored that. She opened her purse and shook the contents, heavy coins rattling in place. "What *seems* wrong is that I'm paying you five shillings for two hours of work. One of those shillings is for your work; the other four shillings are for not asking questions."

"But—"

"The more questions you ask, the fewer shillings I pay."

"I do not think you understand. My worry is—"

"What in the devil's name are the two of you doing?"

The angry delight in Violetta's heart froze in place. She felt her breath catch in her lungs.

They'd been so focused on the plasterer that they'd entirely missed Mr. Cappish coming up the stairs. He rarely returned this early in the afternoon, but here he was, frowning at them.

Violetta swallowed.

Bertrice did not shrink back, though. "What does it look like?" she demanded. "We are plastering over the door to this room. Keep on, keep on."

"*This* room," Mr. Cappish sputtered. "You mean the door to *my* room."

"I mean the room that you have *no right to enter,* as you've not paid for the lodging in two years!"

Mr. Cappish took four steps forward to tower over his aunt. "You mean the debts that *you* have not paid, despite your moral, familial, and ethical obligations to me, your only living relation!"

Bertrice's fists clenched. "I do not owe you anything. Not *one* thing."

For one long moment, the two glared at each other.

Bertrice would hate the observation, but in that moment, Violetta could see a family resemblance in their eyebrows, thick and angry, their cheekbones, touched with pink. There was a similarity in the way they both straightened their spines and threw back their shoulders.

The Terrible Nephew reached out and set one hand on Bertrice's shoulder. His fingers clenched; Violetta's heart leapt inside her, while her thoughts scattered. She couldn't just stand about and watch. She had to—

Bertrice brought her cane around and smacked her nephew in the knee, causing him to buckle, curse, and grab the wall to stay upright. "Get out of here."

Mr. Cappish stood, leaning against the wall and rubbing his leg. He was no longer glaring. Now he was looking off into the distance, his eyes narrowed as if focused on some unseen goal. "This has gone on long enough. I have been patient—very patient. But you've had your fun, and this is entirely out of hand. I am the patriarch of this family, aunt, and I intend to exercise my rights. End this now, or…"

"Or what? Are you threatening me? Because I haven't started yet. I haven't *begun* to start. Must I advertise what you are in every paper in London? I will do so." She raised her cane again.

Mr. Cappish straightened and skipped out of the reach of his aunt's cane. "I have been decent to you." He spoke in stilted, polite tones. "In light of your advanced age, I have given you every kindness. But you are placing an utter *nobody* over your own nephew. It's not right." He cast a glance at Violetta on the word *nobody,* and a little chill ran down her spine. "I won't hear of it any longer. If you keep on, I will stop you."

"I should like to see you try."

"I shan't even have to exert myself." His lip curled up, and he turned to the two laborers standing at the door. The carpenter had frozen in place, hammer in hand. "Stop this work at once. This is my lawful abode; I do not give permission."

"She's in charge of the rooming house!" Bertrice said, pointing at Violetta, and Violetta felt her stomach turn, waiting for the inevitable. "And *I'm* the one with the money. *He's* not capable of anything except manning about mannishly, and that's about as useful as a tea kettle made of ice!"

"If you board up my lawful residence," Mr. Cappish said to the carpenter, "I will inform my friends at Glaser's, and we shall make sure neither of you ever work again. Now, who do you want to anger —these two aging nothings or a select group of men who control the workings of London?"

"I knew there was something off about this," the plasterer said, shaking his head. He packed up his tools. "I simply *knew* it." He was off, down the stairs, three seconds later.

The carpenter looked at his hammer, then at the frame, then at the hammer once more. "I'm sorry," he at least had the grace to say, before gathering his materials and absconding.

Mr. Cappish watched them go, a gratified smile on his face. "You see how it is, Aunt? They will *always* listen to me. I'm your only living relative. They can *sense* that, you know. You think you're so smart with your carpenters and choruses, but everyone else knows the truth. I'm right, and they'll always know it."

He was right. Oh, not in the sense that his actions had any real connection with "truth" or "right." But he was right in the most basic sense—in a way that Violetta had learned over and over in her life. Money and skill and ingenuity and diligence and creativity never won. Not when wielded by women; not when there was a confident man proclaiming otherwise.

But Bertrice did not seem to notice. "Every threat you issue," she said, "will result in further retaliation from me. I have gone along nicely my entire life. I am done."

"You?" He scoffed. "Gone along? *Nicely?*"

"Nice-ish," she amended.

He took a step forward. "Listen to me, and listen well. I will have you declared incompetent unless you write a cheque upon your bank for ten thousand pounds. Right now."

"If you need money, obtain employment."

His jaw squared. "*That* again. I told you, I'm a gentleman. I shouldn't need to labor."

Bertrice just smiled. "Let's see who issues the threats here after all. I suspect your fine club will toss you out on your ear if they knew the truth—that you have no money, no prospects, and a mountain of debts."

Mr. Cappish flushed betrayingly red for one moment, before stepping forward and pushing a finger into Bertrice's chest. "I have prospects. Immediate prospects. I have simply chosen not to pursue them out of the goodness of my heart. You're not invulnerable. Neither of you are."

Violetta was vulnerable—so vulnerable. She'd spent the last weeks playacting, pretending that she could be as brave as Bertrice. But she never had been. Mr. Toggert was going to find out. She was going to prison—or worse. Was this a felony? Would they put her to death? When the possibility had been hypothetical, she had faced it with equanimity. But now, now that the constables might be coming…

Bertrice smacked the floor in front of her Terrible Nephew with her cane. "Get out of here," she said. "Go on. Do your worst. You can't touch us."

"You've made your last mistake," Mr. Cappish said. "I will put you away forever. Both of you. Just wait."

Violetta felt her vision darken at the edges. She was dimly aware of Bertrice waving her cane once more. She could scarcely hear Mr. Cappish's footsteps sounding on the stairs, dim and distant compared to the ominous thump of her heart.

"Violetta?" The words came from a long distance. "Violetta? Are you unwell?"

She couldn't speak for a moment. She could scarcely breathe. For a second, she could think only of a crowd chanting for her blood—of the incredible parallelism of being killed in public, just as her grandfather had been—

"Violetta." Someone took hold of her hands. The touch of fingers was warm against the clammy coolness of her palms. "Violetta, dear. It's going to be all right. I promise. Breathe. Breathe."

She did her best, struggling to inhale before realizing that she needed to let out the air she had been holding first. Air. Air was good. Air was excellent.

"Violetta, dear. Listen. I won't let anything happen to you. I promise."

"I can't," Violetta finally managed. "You don't know—it's—I have *nothing*, Bertrice, and I'm going to lose it all."

"No, you won't."

It wasn't a promise that Bertrice could remotely keep. She *had* to know that. Violetta had tried. She'd tried to make herself safe. She'd tried to make herself strong.

And what had it done? It had led her here—to this moment. She'd lied to Bertrice. She'd *lied,* and now Bertrice didn't even know how far she had been led astray. Everything was going to go up in flames, and it was her fault. If only Violetta hadn't involved Bertrice. If only she'd been smart enough, clever enough, to think of a solution besides fraud. If only—

"You won't lose anything," Bertrice repeated. "I promise you, you won't. It will all be well."

It wasn't a promise that could be kept, and yet that mindless reassurance calmed Violetta anyway. Her heart seemed to return to its normal rhythm; her vision cleared.

She pulled her hand from Bertrice's, straightened her spine, and stared at the unfinished wooden framework. "What do we do?"

Bertrice looked determined. "Now? Now we go on the offensive."

Violetta blinked. "I thought we were being offensive already."

A tiny smile played over Bertrice's face. "Oh, no," she said. "We've barely even started."

CHAPTER SEVEN

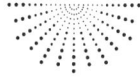

I t took almost twenty-four hours for Bertrice to escalate her tactics. She'd had to visit her solicitors—an *entire* office full of men who believed it was their occupation to comment on all of Bertrice's plans with such frivolities as, "you can't be serious" and "you cannot really intend to *do* that" and other similarly depressing inanities.

What was the point of giving people *money* if they kept asking you *why?*

Eventually, though, her money prevailed.

"Are you sure about this?" Violetta asked, as they approached the park the day after her nephew had accosted her when she had been rightfully trying to board up his room.

Bertrice was *not* sure. All the more reason not to admit it. "I'm sure as sunrises," she snapped.

"Oh, dear." Violetta glanced over at her. "That's bad."

"Do you believe in sunrises?"

"It's London," the other woman said with a lift of her shoulder. "It's winter. Nobody can see the sunrise through the fog of a London particular."

"Well, then." Bertrice refused to harbor feelings of uncertainty simply because it was logical to do so. "Pick a different analogy. What *are* you sure of? Death, they say, and taxes, but I can't see that either would make a productive comparison. What do *you* think you can count on?"

"Angry men getting their way," Violetta said dryly.

Damn. Bertrice felt her certainty slip.

"Pick something else," she said. "*This* evening, we're dealing with women."

And they were.

Normally, Bertrice preferred not to interfere with working girls—they had enough worries as it was—but when it came to relieving them of her Terrible Nephew's company, she felt as if she were doing them a favor.

It had taken a few questions and a few coins to discover his habits. Another handful of coins had guaranteed that a baker across the way would send a shopgirl to alert her when the Terrible Nephew emerged.

This late winter afternoon was near-dark, with a rolling greenish-black fog blanketing the park. Spindly, half-leafed trees seemed to come from nowhere, leaping out of the mist like phantasms.

She could hear the Terrible Nephew before she could see him—the grating, whiny tone of his voice seemed muffled at first, compared to the higher, clearer responses of his companion.

He was arguing. She couldn't make out what he was saying at first; his words didn't resolve into sentences until he was close enough to appear in the fog like a dark, shadowed, thing. He was standing too close to a cloaked woman who was trying not to look at him.

"Mr. Cappish. I have told you and told you again. The answer is no." The girl stood stiff-backed, her face tilted a quarter-turn away. She really *was* a girl; she could not have been older than twenty-four.

God curse Terrible Nephews the world over. Bertrice wasn't having it.

But the Terrible Nephew was not ashamed. "Molly," he was saying, "you're only saying *no* because you don't understand economics. What I'm offering is the same as saving—one puts money in the bank; it gathers interest, and your patience is repaid in a few years' time with a good return on your investment."

As they drew closer, Bertrice could see the girl's face. She was pretty, round-cheeked, and flushed red with something between fear and anger.

Molly narrowed her eyes. "Fucking you is like putting funds in a bank," she repeated dubiously.

"Exactly like that." He reached for her hand; she stepped away.

"Banks have money." Another suspicious look. "You don't. Get off already, won't you?"

He sighed. "In a few days' time, I shall have the means to be generous. Very generous. I will remember those who were kind to me. As I said, it's a simple matter of economics. Now, are you good at economics or are you poor at them?"

He set one hand on his hip and cocked one eyebrow as if this devastatingly terrible argument had proved some point. And maybe it had—just not the one he'd intended. Molly stared at him for a moment, as if she had no idea how to answer an argument that not only defied logic, but reason, sense, and propriety at the same time. Then she responded the only way possible: She burst into laughter.

"That," she said, wiping away tears of mirth, "is the stupidest thing anyone has *ever* said to my face. Are you sentient, man, or is your head made of bricks?"

"Well, actually," the Terrible Nephew said, drawing himself up, "it's funny you should mention bricks, because there's a well-known economic fallacy about construction material that I learned of in my Oxford days. Do you wish to be economically fallacious, Molly? I shall be kind and explain the whole to you. Suppose a man has a brick—"

So engrossed was he in his Oxfordian story of economic fallacy, that he did not notice Bertrice and Violetta approaching through the fog. Molly didn't look as if she needed saving, but honestly, it was kindness to interrupt.

"I will pay double your normal rates," Bertrice said, waving her hands from the five feet that still separated them, "if you will *not* engage in intercourse with him."

The Terrible Nephew turned to look at her. He let out a great sigh.

Molly, beside him, took the opportunity to put a few feet of distance between them. "You don't have to pay me, love. I've already said I'm not doing it."

"Aunt Bertrice," groaned the Terrible Nephew, raising a hand to touch his forehead. "You never learn, do you?"

Oh, they'd tried to teach her. Years and years and years, they'd tried to teach her. It gave her pride that she hadn't learned.

"He's my nephew," she explained to Molly.

Molly frowned. "Have you some religious objection regarding his immortal soul?"

"I'm fairly certain that whatever soul he was assigned decamped years ago. There won't be an angel in heaven willing to allow him entry once they get to the bit about how he claimed that fucking him is like putting funds in the bank. *If* they get there. He's done worse before. You *do* know him to some degree, yes?"

The corners of Molly's lips twitched. "I fucked him once before." A shrug. "He's fast, at least, but it's boring. I'm certainly not about to do it for free."

The Terrible Nephew gawped at this, then straightened. "I have explained and *explained.* It is like putting money in a *bank,* it is, and it's really, truly not my fault that women like you haven't the head to manage your own finances!"

Molly let out a louder guffaw. "Oh, is *that* what it is?"

"Robby Bobkins." Bertrice turned to him. "You have not been able to manage your finances since you were *thirteen.* You spent your inheritance from your mother in *five years.* You've been living on gifts from friends and credit you cannot repay for three. Why are you lecturing women about your inability to pay them?"

"How many times must I say it? Do *not* call me Robby Bobkins. My name is Cappish—Mr. Cappish. I once extended the offer to you to refer to me as my dear friends do, but—"

Bertrice leaned close to Molly. "Oh yes," she said. "He *did* tell me. His intimates call him 'Clappy.'"

Molly laughed harder. "I'll have to spread *that* one about. Lord."

"Here." Bertrice reached into her purse and took out a heavy coin. "That's for not fucking him. Please spread the word—not fucking Clappy here is like putting money in the bank, and I am the bank."

"It's *Cappy,* not *Clappy.* Aunt, perhaps you do not know, but when one says 'clap' in this particular context... It doesn't have positive connotations. It really doesn't. You might want to rethink what you are saying."

"What, in the context of banking?" Bertrice let her eyes widen innocently. "I hadn't realized. What could possibly be negative? Who *doesn't* want to clap when one visits banks?"

"Him," Violetta said behind her.

"Ah, right. He can't manage his funds."

"I don't know what you must think of me." Molly was staring bemusedly at the coin in her hands. "I didn't do anything. I can make my own way."

"Yes, well." Bertrice shrugged. "We women have to make up for the men in this world, don't you think? What has Clappy here ever done?"

Violetta flinched, and Bertrice could not help but recall their earlier conversation. What could be more certain than angry men getting their way? For a moment, she faltered. Just for a moment. Then she remembered. Oh, yes. Bertrice didn't *care* if it was impossible to prevail. She didn't care if foul men with good breeding almost never paid the price for their misdeeds. There had been too many foul men in her life—in everyone's life. She couldn't make all of them pay, but she had a chance to make *this* one do so.

"Aunt Bertrice," the Terrible Nephew said. "You have gone entirely too far. I warned you earlier that you had crossed the line. I must tell you that since last I saw you, I have visited a solicitor. As your nearest next of kin, I have no choice but to have you declared mentally incompetent. I have already filed the paperwork."

This was met with silence.

"Robby Bobkins," Molly finally said, dropping the coin in her pocket. "Your own aunt. How could you?"

He shook his head. "It's only a matter of time, now. Have your fun, Aunt Bertrice. Enjoy it while it lasts. Everything you do and have done—the flour, the geese, the plasterers—it all only proves my point. You are not capable. I don't need to wait for you to die; I'll be given charge of your funds as soon as the courts can see to it."

Bertrice refused to look at him. She stared instead at Molly, who looked back at her with something like pity.

"Have a nice day." Out of the corner of her eye, she saw the Terrible Nephew touch the brim of his hat and walk off.

She refused to watch him go.

It wasn't a surprise that he'd chosen this course of action. He'd always acted as if *her* money was really *his*. He signed fraudulent sureties in her name. He assured his fellow club-members that her fortune was coming to him. He even told women on the street that her money was like a bank. He was waiting for her to give in or die, and now that he realized that she had no intention of doing either anytime soon, he'd decided to make her wish she was dead.

"It was coming to this." Bertrice had known it deep in the pit of her soul, in the fears and nerves she hadn't wanted to acknowledge from the start. "It has *always* been coming to this."

~

Violetta had no idea why they needed chocolates, but Bertrice insisted, and she was not about to complain about being dragged to a chocolatier. She would not object to being made to inhale the seductive, luscious dark scent. She watched as Bertrice pointed to confection after confection on the chocolatier's counter, and when it seemed that the chocolates were overwhelming in number—an entire generous box of them—Bertrice turned to her.

"Which ones do *you* think we should add?" she asked.

Violetta had not had chocolate since she was a child. As a girl, these dazzling creations of sugar and gleaming brown cacao hadn't even existed. She remembered chocolate as something for drinking, and then only on special occasions.

For most of her life, it had seemed pointless to want chocolate. She could want and want and want, but she couldn't get it. Instead, she let herself yearn for prosaic things. She wanted a home, one she might stay in for the rest of her days, one that would be warm enough with gloves and a thick, wool blanket in the winter. She wanted the small joys: feeling sun on her face, or—luxury of luxuries—chicken soup on a cold day with doughy dumplings.

She could dare to want these things because they were within her reach. She did not know how to want glossy brown squares dotted with roasted nuts.

"That one," she said, jabbing her finger at the glass case at random. "And?"

And?

She jabbed again, careless, and the shop girl followed her commands, until that generous box became a ridiculous pack that would have bought chicken-and-dumpling soup enough to last half the winter.

Bertrice just nodded from the side.

The shop girl layered light paper over the top and tied the wooden box with a bright blue ribbon.

"A gift," Bertrice had said, tucking it under her arm. Maybe that was her plan to defeat her nephew—to find whomever would evaluate her mental competence and bribe them with sweets.

It wasn't the worst plan. Violetta wished people had tried to bribe her with chocolates at some point earlier in her life. She had thought herself moral and upstanding, when in reality, nobody had ever tried to corrupt her with anything she really wanted.

Instead, she swallowed her desire for a taste of sweetness. Easy enough; the knot of worry that Violetta had been holding in her stomach refused to untangle. Ignoring it had not yet made it better. It sat like a solid lump of brass, whispering the words that the Terrible Nephew had said.

It's been enough. It's been enough.

She had never been enough. Not to look at; not to bribe. The journey back to Violetta's room was accomplished in silence.

Violetta had spent all her life packed into that dull, sepia periphery of society. Living a careful life, one that was appropriate to her station. Now she'd shoved herself out onto center stage—carelessly, without any possibility of hiding behind the curtains. She had known perhaps from the first moment in Bertrice's parlor that it was all going to go horribly wrong. Now, her heartbeat seemed to encourage that final, inevitable doom with every thump.

But Bertrice did not seem to be bothered by the eventual outcome. She ascended the stairs to the building entrance the way she always did—slowly, one step at a time, but surely. *She* didn't seem to have the weight of the world burdening her shoulders; she carried only the weight of the chocolates she had purchased.

"Are you not worried?" Violetta asked, when they finally stood in her small room.

"Worried?" Bertrice wrinkled her nose as if this were the last thing she could possibly have considered. "Why the devil would I be worried?"

"Your nephew."

The nose twitched again. "We don't call him that."

"Your Terrible Nephew," Violetta amended. "You know, the truly awful absolutely no-good one who has filed papers to have you declared mentally incompetent? *That* nephew."

Bertrice blinked. "Him? Good lord, Violetta. I don't care what happens to him. Do you honestly believe I am supposed to be worried on his behalf?"

"Worried *about* him. Not worried *for* him."

"Oh." Bertrice looked as if the possibility had just occurred to her. "You think I should be worried about him? Oh, that's sweet. It really is. But dear, he's so *lazy*. What is there to worry about?"

"You have finally pushed him into action. Aren't you afraid?"

Bertrice removed her cloak and tossed it on a chair; Violetta hung it up for her, and when she toed off her shoes, aligned them as well. Bertrice sank onto the edge of the bed, still clutching the box containing the chocolates, with a sad little sigh. "No," she said, rolling her shoulders as she sat in place. "No, I'm not afraid of him."

"Not even a little?"

"The opposite of fear," Bertrice said, "is a plan, and I have a plan. So no, I am not afraid."

The definition of fear was someone *else* having a plan and Violetta having no say in it, even if that person was Bertrice. Maybe—if the last few weeks were any indication—*especially* if that person was Bertrice. "What's your plan?"

Bertrice set the box to the side. But instead of removing the ribbon, she reached into a pocket of her skirt and took out a piece of paper. She unfolded it from its square shape and handed this to Violetta.

Contract, it read, *for the sale of one (1) rooming house, located at...*

"To start, I'm going to buy your rooming house," Bertrice announced.

Violetta's vision blurred, then fractured. She inhaled and looked up, unable to read any further. Unable, even, to speak. Violetta *had* no rooming house; she had only her own too-threadbare lie. She'd not said a word, not as they went from bare acquaintances to friends to... to whatever this was. *Thump,* went her heart. This was how it ended. *Thump.*

"I can't." The words fell from her lips.

"You can't what?" Bertrice removed the box of chocolates and played with the ends of the ribbon holding the lid in place. "You can't sell it? I'm willing to pay two thousand pounds—more than its fair market value."

Violetta shook her head and pushed the document away. "Bertrice. It's not—" All their friendliness, all their camaraderie—it was all hollow if she did this.

But it was already hollow. And...two thousand pounds.

Oh, the things she could let herself want if only she had two thousand pounds! A little cottage in a village near the sea with an almost temperate climate. A garden; someone to see after her when she grew too old to do more than sit in her rocking chair and watch people pass.

The funds to give pennies to beggars, and pounds to girls on their wedding days...

She didn't even have to come up with a *different* lie; she just had to keep repeating the one she had already uttered.

"It's not *what?*" Bertrice asked, looking at her with that look that was not at all accusation.

"It's too much," Violetta seized on. "Too much—it's not worth that, you must *know* it's not worth it—"

"But aren't *you* worth it?" Bertrice's eyes speared her. "You've been of such immense value to me, Violetta. The world felt flat before you. I had *nothing* when you arrived, and now I feel…" She shrugged. "Well, I don't need to go further. I *feel* again, and I didn't before. Can't I repay you for that?"

"Don't." Violetta felt something like grief rise up in her. "Don't, please don't. I *can't.* I can't take this."

"You can't have someone see everything you've done and think well of you?"

Violetta choked, trying to swallow her sobs.

"You can't accept a reward for your hard work?"

She had waited and waited for someone to see her inner beauty. To value her for who she was. And when she'd given up and found Bertrice, she'd thought it was just her rotten luck to have finally missed her chance.

But now it felt like more than a missed chance. It felt like a tragedy.

"I can't sell you the building!" She almost screamed the words. "I'm not capable of doing so, because I do not *own* it. I have lied to you for weeks, and if the true owner ever realizes what we've done to his tenants, we shall both go to prison!"

Bertrice listened to this calmly. She didn't widen her eyes. She didn't gasp. She didn't scream for help. Instead, she gave a tug to the blue ribbon circling the box of chocolates. It came undone and slid to the floor. She opened the box, and the heady odor of chocolate filled the room.

"Here," she said, holding it out. "Have one."

"Did you *hear* what I just said?"

"That was a little dramatic." Bertrice shrugged. "We aren't going to prison, I don't think."

A possibility rose to Violetta's mind. "Oh—of course. You believed I owned the building. Likely, they'll let you off for that. I think." *She* would still be imprisoned, but that was almost inevitable. "I promise, I'll testify to that effect."

"Pooh," was Bertrice's response. "I knew you didn't own the building."

"I beg your pardon?"

Bertrice frowned into the box, and selected a dark brown oval. "I knew it," she said, "from the first day, because the maths didn't work out. You wouldn't be living *here,* without servants, instead of in the rooming house. You wouldn't be dressing like *that,* if you had that kind of property. You didn't have enough keys or enough money for this to make sense. I inquired of my solicitors. There's a register of who owns what and so forth. They found it out on the second day."

Oh. Violetta hadn't considered the possibility. She could scarcely fathom it now. Her mind felt blank.

"I asked my solicitors to look into it; they brought me the whole story. You labored for Mr. Toggert for almost fifty years and he sacked you to avoid paying you a pension. Typical story. Of course a man was at fault."

Violetta's head was spinning. She couldn't grapple with any of these revelations. There was one thing she could cling to. "You really shouldn't blame men for everything."

"No, just the ninety-eight percent of society's ills they're responsible for."

"That's—listen, Bertrice, that hardly seems fair. Men can't be responsible for *everything.*"

"Now we're just quibbling over what a fair percentage should be." Bertrice shrugged.

Violetta tried again. "Bertrice, I *lied* to you. Recklessly. Wantonly."

"So? You have some point here, I assume."

Violetta had thought that it was enough to say that she lied. She gestured, almost angrily. "How can you act like it's nothing? It wasn't *nice.*"

"Of course it wasn't." Bertrice looked even more baffled than Violetta felt. "We established that you were not nice on our first evening together. The word for people like you isn't *nice*. It's 'not massively wealthy.' I may be a cantankerous pain in the arse, but when someone explains a thing to me, I do try to listen."

The possibility that Violetta had been forgiven before she even had a chance to beg for it left her shaken. She fumbled for words. "Why didn't you say anything, if you knew all that?"

Bertrice shrugged once again and put the chocolate in her mouth. "I'm not stupid," she mumbled through a mouthful of candy, "and you had a good idea. No point embarrassing you when you'd already been treated so poorly. I purchased the building from Mr. Toggert myself, once I realized what we were about. Everything we did was perfectly legal."

"You were trying to buy the building from me, yet you'd already bought it? Bertrice, I don't understand."

One swallow, and Bertrice sighed. She suddenly looked more tired. "I was *trying* to give you money. In case..." Her hands twitched. She looked away. "In case my nephew succeeded in taking everything away. That way I would know you were safe and well. But here you are, being absolutely stubborn about it. Bah. I *told* you I had a plan, but *no*, you had to argue about it."

Everything fell into place so easily. The chocolates. Bertrice's plan. Violetta's own mistakes.

Bertrice wasn't confident; she was *scared*. And unlike Violetta, she hadn't conjured lies from the depths of her fear in an attempt to defraud someone else. No; she'd thought of Violetta first.

"Bertrice..."

"Oh, hmph." Bertrice tossed her head. "Don't take that sweet tone with me; what use is it? Have some damned chocolates."

"I thought you said they were a gift."

"They are. In part, they are a gift to myself, which is why I have eaten three of them. But they are also in part a gift to you, which is why I said 'have some damned chocolates.' It's a way of indicating that *you* are the person I am giving them to."

Here she was, being bribed with chocolate for the first time in her life, and Violetta couldn't even accept the terms.

"Why? Why me?"

"I see you, Violetta." Bertrice met her eyes, and Violetta could not look away. "You are brave and strong. You learned to stay silent because nobody listened, but you spoke as soon as you knew you could. You are like an oak—beautiful, every part of you. Your hands." She took them. "Your eyes." She looked into them. "You, Violetta. You."

These seemed like words about some other person—someone stronger, someone braver. Someone who had been more truthful.

"Bertrice. I...I can't?" Her voice ticked up, though, and Bertrice seized on her uncertainty.

"It's easy. Open your mouth and put a chocolate in."

The road to hell was surely paved with cacao. Violetta could not have said why she hesitated, but somehow, selecting one felt like the first step into something more honest and more frightening than the pretense she'd been engaged in. If she pretended to be worthy of the chocolate...

It was one piece of chocolate. Violetta was already going to hell. Could there really be any harm in allowing herself to be plied with sweets on the way there? No. No harm at all; just chocolate.

She examined the pieces carefully before selecting one—a candied slice of orange, vibrant as the sunrise, half-dipped in dark, shiny brown.

She took a delicate bite. The taste burst across her palate, citrus and sweet balanced with heady bitterness.

"So tell me," Bertrice murmured. "What is it you can't do? You can't let me help you? You can't assist me anymore in my quest with my Terrible Nephew? I don't think that's what you're saying."

It was too much. Violetta shut her eyes, but that made the sweetness on her tongue seem all the more intense.

"I think what you're saying is that you don't understand how anyone can care about you. And it's sheer cruelty that this world has made you believe that. I've cared about you from the moment you stepped forward and stood by my side."

Violetta opened her eyes to see Bertrice sitting next to her, her eyes round and soft, watching her with the most curious expression on her face. She didn't deserve it. She truly didn't deserve it, and yet—

The road to hell was paved with chocolate, and Violetta had already chosen her path. She leaned in and touched her lips to Bertrice's. She shouldn't. She *knew* she shouldn't. And yet Bertrice kissed back, leaning in with a soft sigh. The kiss was soft and brittle all at once—soft against her lips, soft in intentions, soft as if this were the start of a long journey. It was brittle because Violetta knew it was the end. Where could they go from here?

Bertrice had fought for Violetta, had pushed her to this moment. She'd known about her lies, and when threatened with the loss of both money and freedom, had tried to make her safe.

What had Violetta ever done to prove herself worthy of such care? She shut her eyes, but she couldn't shut off her questions. She couldn't shut off the feel of Bertrice. Bertrice's kiss whispered against Violetta's lips with a gentle certainty. How could she kiss like that, as if the world didn't matter? How could Bertrice take Violetta's wrist, promising safety and stability, when Bertrice was still at risk?

And—ah—that was it. Everything slotted into place. Their hands intertwined, palm to palm, fingers winding about each other, clasping each other tightly even as Violetta knew they'd never been at greater risk of separation.

Bertrice was offering Violetta what she could not have herself.

This kiss—this sweet touch of lips and limbs—it whispered of all the things that Violetta had never allowed herself to dream about. Dreams of companionship were like dreams of chocolate—impractical, when she had to worry about more prosaic things like bread and coal.

Yet here she was. Bertrice's hand slid up her inner wrist, to her elbow, pausing at every inch. At the scar on her forearm, left in an accident with a jagged nail; at the wrinkles of her elbow; at the loose folds that the decades had made of her upper arm. Violetta felt as if her skin was paper—too easy to rip—and yet she also felt as if she were illuminated from within.

Every part of herself that she was supposed to hate—every fold of skin, every discolored freckle—Bertrice touched and set alight. Violetta had never felt so seen.

And yet this kiss was a lie. *You will be safe,* Bertrice promised. *You will be loved. You will be beautiful.*

Bertrice's fingers landed lightly on her hair, petting the gray curls, acknowledging them.

Violetta had taken so much from Bertrice. She had lied to her. She took this, too, this offered affection. She drank it in as if she were dying of thirst, and only these falsehoods could quench it.

The road to hell was paved with chocolate and kisses, and Violetta gave into her damnation. She gave back her own truth to Bertrice's kind lies, letting her know with her own fingers, her lips, and her tongue. *You,* she thought, taking Bertrice's head into her hands. *You, with your Hallelujah chorus singing madly in a world that prefers silence, you offering comfort to everyone who needs it and stealing it from those who don't—you, you will be safe.*

No woman has ever before prevailed against an angry man, but you will. You will. She sent back all the love and beauty she saw in the other woman.

You, her fingers whispered, running down Bertrice's neck. *You, you, you. You are beautiful.*

She could feel the strength in the other woman, the muscle and sinew that had survived all these decades. Years of experience and hardship sang to her. Here, in Bertrice's flesh, she could hear all the things that they as women could not bear to say to each other, but must carry with them anyway—all the wounds that had healed into hard scars, carried by the sex so often referred to as soft.

Another kiss, and another. Bertrice's hands slid around Violetta's waist, holding her close. Another kiss, until Violetta could think of nothing but the kisses. The kisses gave way to little gasps—ones that said that whatever other lies Bertrice told with her flesh, in this moment, Violetta was beautiful to her. Nothing before had made Violetta feel so...grateful. So cared for. So seen.

It had been one thing to accept lies. Truth was too much.

Violetta tried to pull away. "I...I don't..."

Bertrice halted, her hands pulling from Violetta. Her eyes were unfocused for a second, before she looked into Violetta's face. "You don't want this?"

Violetta was near tears. "I don't *deserve* it."

"Violetta." Bertrice reached out and touched her cheek, and Violetta could not stop herself; she leaned into her palm. "Sweetheart. You deserve it. You deserve it all."

"I *don't.* You can't make a thing like that true just by saying words. When matters became difficult for me, I folded up my principles and I —I simply—"

"You simply went on," Bertrice said. "You refused to give up. You refused to doubt your own worth *then.* Don't do it now."

"But—"

"But don't take my word for it. Take your own. Deep down, you *know* you've done good things. So stop this nonsense right *now* and name one."

That direct tone caught Violetta up short. "I—well."

"*One* good thing, and don't tell me there haven't been anything."

"Well. I survived." It was all she had.

"Pah. So do cockroaches. So do eels. There's more."

"Before...before I was let go." Violetta swallowed. "I was good at what I did. I listened to people and helped make their homes comfortable."

"Yes, that's more like it. Keep going."

"I try to be compassionate when I can, and stern when necessary."

"Go on."

"I keep excellent records." Her voice sounded shaky. "I make cheese toast extraordinarily well." She paused, searching. "I...am good at identifying things I am good at?"

"No." Bertrice smiled. "You're remarkably bad at that. Do you not recall my needing to browbeat you on this very issue a mere minute ago?"

"Bertrice." Violetta leaned in and let her forehead rest against the other woman's. "You know that you're worthy, too? That you deserve comfort and safety?"

Bertrice gave out a little choked sigh.

And after that, it was easy to go on. It was easy to undo the buttons of each others' gowns, to kiss down bared shoulders, to lift up chemises—Bertrice's was edged in lace; Violetta's hem was bare—to show skin that was dusted with age spots and veined like the finest marble.

It was amazing how years of mere existence had taught Violetta to hate herself, as if simply existing in the impossible sea of society's expectation put hateful scales over her eyes and made her believe that her own body was unworthy of love.

Loving Bertrice—kissing knuckles that were swollen with age, running her hands up breasts that time had given a graceful sway—made those scales fall away.

Every act of gravity and time made beauty in nature—except when it happened to human women. Not any longer. Ravines carved in her forehead by time made a striking landscape. Grey hair between her legs made a gentle forest. Bertrice came to her, touching, exploring, telling her with every brush of her fingers that she *deserved* to be touched, *deserved* to be explored.

Bertrice's fingers pressed against Violetta's sex. She felt as if she'd been parched for so long that there could be nothing but dryness. But arousal came, and with it, moisture. Bertrice rubbed her thumb lightly against the lips of Violetta's sex, and then, when Violetta gasped and parted her legs, slipped her hand between them. Their kisses grew more frantic; Violetta's own hand went between Bertrice's legs, finding her wet, feeling her open for her. Each gasp felt precious. Each noise of encouragement made her feel as if she belonged, as if she were cared for, as if she were—

She came, arching her back, and Bertrice followed her down that path. Violetta was almost in tears as they leaned into each other. Bertrice felt warm and smelled sweet, and *oh,* it was such joy to feel this, and such sorrow to know it could be taken from her.

After they'd held each other a while, Violetta poured a basin of water; they cleaned each other. She couldn't think of tomorrow. She couldn't think of how to proceed.

"There," Bertrice said. "Don't you see? You deserve too much. You deserve everything."

"I..." Still she couldn't say it. She shut her eyes, unwilling to go along.

"I have always wanted to know what you would *really* do if you had my money. Come now; take a little of it."

If she took the money now, she would survive. But what about Bertrice?

"I'm going to give you two thousand pounds," Bertrice said. "There's a contract and everything. And...no matter what happens..." She trailed off. "I'll know. At least I'll know."

Violetta inhaled. "Why the chocolate?"

Bertrice just smiled at her. "I wanted chocolate. I could *guarantee* chocolate."

And I couldn't guarantee any of the other things I wanted, Violetta understood.

What *would* Violetta do if the Terrible Nephew won and the worst happened? If she had money, she could do anything. Buy a cottage. Purchase steamship tickets anywhere in the world.

The prospects for her old age were shifting from "certain imprisonment" to "cottage on the French coast."

She could have her safety, no matter what happened to Bertrice.

Bertrice was watching her. Violetta felt like a tree, rooted in a riverbank. She wanted to survive. It was a deep hunger; she felt her roots growing deeper still. She had always wanted to survive; now she felt that hunger growing. She didn't just want to survive; she wanted to survive with chocolates and joy and companionship.

"You have already given me too much."

"I haven't," Bertrice replied. "You gave me toasted cheese."

Violetta knew she didn't just mean toasted cheese. She meant everything they'd shared together—the joy of taking charge, even for a few moments. The pleasure of having a common enemy in the Terrible Nephew, and knowing that they were allies. The walks in the park and the moments when they'd been able to just be friends. More than friends.

Violetta didn't just want to *survive*. Instead of falsehoods about owning a rooming house, she wanted to promise certainty. She wanted to promise Bertrice that she could have security and companionship, that she would never be hurt or taken away to prison. She wanted to be able to deliver the things she most yearned for to this woman. But she didn't want to lie to her again.

"What are we going to do?" she asked instead.

Instead of sighing pensively or shrugging, Bertrice laid back in bed, a small, satisfied smile on her face.

"I bought the building," Bertrice said. "I will do exactly as I wish, and never mind what the Terrible Nephew says. Maybe he will stop me someday, but he hasn't succeeded yet, and I refuse to cede victory on the basis of his paltry threats. My lawyers will have something to say about those, I imagine."

There Bertrice was—sounding certain again, with her vulnerability hidden away. *I want this to be true,* Violetta thought. *I need this to be true.*

But that wasn't what she actually needed. What she needed was to do what she should have done from the start—open her eyes, look around her, and fight for what she deserved.

Violetta leaned forward and kissed the other woman's forehead. "Bertrice," she said, "if you buy a building you already own for two thousand pounds, you'll never prove you're mentally competent."

Bertrice shut her eyes. "Just let me be certain you're well, no matter what happens. That's all I ask for."

Violetta could weep. That was as close to *I love you* as she'd ever heard from a person who wasn't her parents.

"I have taken care of myself thus far," Violetta said. "I will take your chocolates. I will take as many boxes of chocolates as you can lawfully give me." She reached up and set the palm of her hand against Bertrice's cheek. "But I won't accept my freedom at the cost of yours."

It turned out that she could say *I love you,* too.

CHAPTER EIGHT

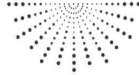

V ioletta woke the next morning.

The curtains were open an inch and dazzling sunlight spilled onto the wooden floors. It wasn't the first light of the morning, no, not by that angle. It wasn't even the second light of morning. It was maybe as late as nine, and Violetta could not remember sleeping so soundly since…

Well, maybe that one day twelve years ago, when she'd allowed herself to indulge in a long day at the fair and had been sore all the morrow. She stretched surreptitiously—there, sure enough, unfamiliar parts of her body protested. One didn't notice how many muscles one had in the body until one *used* them. And how deliciously she had used them.

The events of last night felt like a dream, gauzy and insubstantial. Bertrice, offering her a ridiculous sum. Wanting to hold and protect her, and not knowing how.

Violetta had never won what she wanted. Not safety, not security. After all these years, she had started to tell herself that she didn't really *deserve* them. The idea that she might was new, so new that she could almost smell it in the air—bitter and comforting at the same time, like a candied orange slice dipped in chocolate.

A small smile touched her lips and she shifted in bed again, stretching each muscle, bit by careful bit, her shoulders first, then her arching spine, then her toes, extended to their length, then her arms, stretching, stretching—

Her fingers found empty sheets. They closed almost spasmodically and she turned, her eyes wide.

No Bertrice.

Violetta's room was small—a bed, a table, and a wardrobe were all crammed higgledy-piggledy together, anywhere that there was space against the wall. There was nowhere to hide. If Bertrice was not in sight, she was not here. She'd left, and all last night's promises, spoken and unspoken, were dust.

Violetta should have known. She should have—her fears rose up once more, and then, as she glanced around the room, came to a halt.

There—on the table. There was a note.

Violetta shut her eyes.

Of course there was a note. Bertrice had no doubt…gone out to… fetch bread?

The half-loaf from last night sat on the table, wrapped in cloth, giving the lie to that possibility.

There was no point getting upset before she knew what she was getting upset about.

Violetta stood. The air was cold, her rough nightgown too thin after the warmth of the blankets. The rough floor froze her feet, and the hairs on her arms prickled.

She picked up the note.

Violetta,

I have to attend to some pressing business. Your presence is requested in the park in front of Glaser's at three in the afternoon.

Hereby signed,

Bertrice Martin

P.S. Bring the toasty cheese making thing, would you?

Not one word of affection. Violetta shook her head. Not one mention of what had transpired between them last night. Of course she wouldn't commit such doings to paper. Still.

Hereby signed. That was how they'd finished off the first contract. Violetta could almost hear Bertrice in her memory. "'Hereby' makes it more legalistic," she'd said. Legalistic. After last night…

Doubt was an old friend; it often came to keep Violetta company when she was lonely. Of *course* Bertrice had left. Of course she'd changed her mind, and of course all those words last night about beauty and safety and whatnot were meaningless. It had been sixty-nine years, and still Violetta had not learned—not truly, not as she should. She sat here, stupidly making excuses that she knew were lies, telling herself there was a reason.

But Bertrice had been as desperate last night as Violetta had been. She knew what she'd been threatened with. She cared—she truly cared—and what had happened last night *meant* something so long as Violetta held that meaning in her heart.

Violetta stood up.

Maybe she *didn't* deserve happiness.

But she didn't have *nothing*. She never had. She had her wits, her stubbornness, and fifty-seven pounds in the bank. Maybe *she* didn't deserve to be protected—maybe she'd forfeited the right when she told that lie—but by God she would fight anyone who said the same of Bertrice.

She needed what Bertrice would have had in her stead. She needed a plan. She was going to fight, and she was going to win.

"I promise," she said to the empty room where Bertrice was not standing, "that I will take care of you."

∼

The gentleman's club a few minutes before three in the afternoon was the site of much disturbance. Violetta had been sore that morning and spending the last four hours walking around would not help her on the morrow. But strangely—in the moment—she had never felt better.

She'd expected that Bertrice had arranged a confrontation at

Glaser's. She'd arrived assuming there would be one. But the scene she found was beyond comprehension.

First, there was a fire engine—a dark, hulking metal thing of pistons and cylinders, with a smoke-box rising from it. Dark hoses were coiled neatly nearby. Then there were the firemen—why were there firemen? Why were they digging ditches in the nearby park? Why weren't they wearing the Metropolitan Fire Brigade uniform?

That last was easy to answer. The brigade had only been formed a scant handful of years before, and it should not have surprised Violetta that private companies still existed. Their existence in *general* was not unusual; their presence *here* was a mystery. There was no fire. There wasn't even any smoke.

There was, however, a distinctive scent—a chemical, paraffin oil sort of smell.

And there was Bertrice. She stood in the center of this ruckus, surveying the goings-on like a general. Her hair was done up in complicated white braids. She walked about, nodding at the ditches, sniffing the air.

Violetta clutched the sack she had brought—containing her cheese toaster and the warrant that she had spent the remnants of her money and the last few hours obtaining—and took a tentative few steps forward into the madness.

"Bertrice," she said when she was close enough to be heard over the din, "what is going on?"

"Oh!" Bertrice turned, saw her, and brightened. "Violetta! How good that you are finally here. Now we can begin."

"Begin? Begin what?"

"You should move back," Bertrice gave her a brilliant smile. "Smoke inhalation is bad for the lungs. Take care of yourself!"

"Smoke inhalation?" Violetta allowed Bertrice to draw her back to the iron railing by the Thames. "What smoke? There's no smoke."

"Oh, don't worry about that. There will be, once I set fire to everything."

"*What?* You can't be serious!" But as soon as Violetta said those words, she wondered why she bothered. Of course Bertrice was serious. Why not fire? "What will burning anything accomplish?"

Bertrice just patted the railing. "Promise you'll stay here," she said. The other woman drew a small pack of matches from her pocket; Violetta was too gobsmacked in the moment to stop her.

Bertrice couldn't mean to burn down just the rooming house, could she? It was next to the gentleman's club—*right* next to it. It was impossible to incinerate one without scorching the other. Besides, both buildings were made of stone. Stone didn't burn.

Did it?

But there was a little pile of what had once been furniture near the door of the rooming house, now chopped into kindling. She could make out legs, bits of drawers...

Bertrice lit her match, dropped it on the pile, and...*whoosh.*

The entire mess burst into flame, catching almost immediately.

Bertrice whooped and retreated as swiftly as she could with her cane, cackling. "Here it goes!" She made her way to Violetta's side, grinning madly.

Violetta's jaw dropped. "Dear God, Bertrice. What are you doing?"

"Well, I can't *win* against the Terrible Nephew, but I can still make certain that he'll lose. I can't *wait* to see the look on his face. I said I would get him out, and by God, I will. It's *my* building; I can burn it if I want to."

Violetta glanced over at her. The fire was growing; the door caught first, before the flames spread with a *whomp* that she could feel deep in her spine.

"It's stone," she protested. "Stone can't burn. Can it?"

Bertrice's mouth twitched. "The exterior is stone. The interior? There's wood girders, holding up each floor. The stairs are wood. The furniture is wood. The carpet is extremely flammable, when it comes down to it. I don't suppose the stone will catch, but the rest of it?" A shrug. "We'll see how well it does."

As if to highlight this, flames leapt from an upstairs window. Then —oh, dear God—fire burst from a window in the gentleman's club.

"Bertrice." Violetta took hold of her hand. "It's spreading! You didn't buy the gentleman's club!"

"On the contrary. Giving money to a gaggle of men turned my gorge," Bertrice replied. "But it turned out *they* didn't own this building either. And their finances were terribly out of order. I purchased the building and had my solicitor negotiate with them to end the lease." The corner of her mouth ticked up. "Among other things."

Another window pane burst, this time on an upper level, and bright orange flame streamed from it.

The fire had taken over the two buildings so swiftly it could hardly be believed. In the few minutes since the blaze had started, a crowd had gathered, oohing and awing at the flames. Violetta could feel the heat, pulsing against her in massive wafts.

"Bertrice, you can't just...burn down buildings!"

"Oh, that's why the firemen are here—to make sure it doesn't spread. They've so much less work now that there's a public act. They were happy to help. According to that fellow there, the park is a bit of a natural firebreak, and we're here on the Thames, with water present. It's quite safe."

Violetta gave her a disbelieving look.

"Safe-ish."

Indeed, the firemen were presently hosing down a bush twenty yards from the house, soaking it in water so that the fire stayed contained.

Violetta tried again. "Don't you think it's burned enough? You might ask the firemen to put it out, now."

"Ah, well." Bertrice shrugged. "That's the danger of a fire started with oil. Apparently, one can't just douse it with water and expect it to go out? There's some details there. I'm not truly sure I understand. But I will leave *that* to the experts."

"Bertrice."

"Give me this," Bertrice said. "If the Terrible Nephew is to take over everything, allow me this memory—of watching everything important to him burn."

"This won't convince a magistrate that you're mentally

competent."

"Hmph. Only because they are men. If more judges were women, they would understand that it is a miracle we have not razed this city to the ground. I am as much in my right mind now as I have ever been."

They watched until the fire turned orange and ruddy, until the gray stone streaked black, and the black turned to gray ash. They watched until the window frames turned to cinder and fell to pieces. The heat slowly dissipated, and the noise of the conflagration dissipated from a full roar to a mere whisper against their faces.

Then Bertrice took Violetta's hand. "Come." She guided her forward.

Violetta balked, planting her feet. "What are we doing?"

Bertrice just grinned. "If I am going to set Glaser's afire, then we are going to make cheesy-toast over the smoldering remains. It's time."

What were Violetta's options? Refuse? There was no point; it had burned. There was no unburning, not now.

Why *not* make cheesy toast?

Violetta went. She and Bertrice found a smoking door, and set up the toaster over the blackened remnants of the once imposing entry to Glaser's. It didn't take long for the cheese to be good and toasted, and they swapped bites, feeding each other cheese that tasted of smoke.

"I can't say it's not worth it," Bertrice told her.

It was there, as they stood over the smoking embers, that he found them.

"Aunt Bertrice!" Mr. Cappish sounded utterly aghast. "What on earth are you doing?"

Bertrice cocked her head and considered her nephew. "You're not very observant, are you? I'm making cheesy toast over the remains of London's ninth most prominent gentleman's club."

"Aunt! That was my club. And the building next door—I *live* there. All my possessions are—" He made a disgruntled noise. "You can't just burn things down because you're a little angry about my personal choices!"

A *little* angry about his personal choices? Violetta considered hitting him with her cheese toaster.

Bertrice just shrugged. "Nobody was inside."

"It's someone else's property. Those buildings are not yours!"

"False. I bought them."

He frowned, struggling, before spitting out: "You can't just *burn* things! My club has a lease! People lived in that rooming house!"

"I bought everyone's leases! I negotiated with your stupid club to throw you out as a member and move away! They left this morning and they don't want you any longer."

This, more than anything, seemed to distress him. He put his hands to his temples almost despairingly. "You did what? *They* did what? What is *wrong* with you?"

"What is going on here?" interrupted yet another man, and Violetta looked up to see a constable arriving.

The Terrible Nephew pointed. "She did it! This crazy bat. She set *fire* to my gentleman's club. Just—ask her. Ask anyone!"

Bertrice narrowed her eyes. "There is some misunderstanding. I *own* these buildings. I have the deeds, I assure you." She tossed her head, as if she hadn't a care in the world.

The constable stared at her in disbelief. He looked around the park, at the fire engine and the gathered crowds, before looking back at her. "What has ownership got to do with anything? It's illegal to set fire to buildings even if you own them."

"Oh?" Bertrice straightened and bit her lip. "Is that so? I had…no idea." A frown passed over her face. "Oh dear. I will never hear the end of this. I did not consult my solicitors on that particular point; I assumed they would attempt to dissuade me. They often do."

The constable once again stared at her. His gaze fluttered down, then up, and he grimaced.

Violetta could not blame him for his discomfort. Bertrice spoke with the certainty of the wealthy and the accent of the upper class. Her gown was silk and lace; she positively dripped with an air that said she could not be touched. And elderly, wealthy women were rather hard to take into custody, even if they were admitted arsonists.

Alas; she was *clearly* an admitted arsonist.

"Well," Bertrice sighed, "I don't suppose it will matter. But I was burning down my Terrible Nephew's gentleman's club and rooming house because he threatened to have me declared mentally incompetent. You have to admit my reason was just. Or you would, if you weren't a m—"

Mr. Cappish took a step forward. "Sir. I should explain. I am her so-called 'Terrible Nephew.'" He chuckled, and tilted his head—a little gesture that seemed to shout *Listen to me; I am a man.* "And my aunt here has had the oddest notions in her head. You have to admit—setting fire to a building? It doesn't *sound* very mentally competent."

"No…" The constable trailed off.

Mr. Cappish smiled. He stepped next to his aunt and let a hand fall easily on her shoulder.

Bertrice twitched, pulling away, but he reached out and pulled her closer. "This is a family matter," he said in slick tones. "Release her to me, and I'll take care of it. If you would be willing to testify as to what you observed here today before a magistrate, we will put her away where she can't hurt anyone again. *Won't* we, aunt?"

"You—you—" Bertrice sputtered, but she was never at a loss for words. "Put me in his custody, and he will surely kill me. He *will*. You can't do it."

The constable hesitated. It wasn't much, but it was a moment, and Violetta only needed a moment. She gathered all her courage, all the promises she wanted to keep, and she stepped forward.

"Sir," she said. "I can make this simple for you."

The constable looked at her. Violetta *knew* what she looked like—an old, dumpy woman, grayish hair frizzled with age. Her eyes crossed in front of her. Her gown *wasn't* silk; nobody would ever take her seriously.

That was what they had wanted her to think all of her life.

"*You* can make this simple." The constable gave his mustache a suspicious rub. "How can anyone make *this* simple?"

"Like this." Violetta took a deep breath, and removed the receipts she had spent the morning collecting from her bag, along with the order from the court. "You cannot release Mrs. Martin into this man's custody, because he will not be able to take her. He has owed a great many businesses in the area for years. In order to facilitate collection, I have purchased one hundred and seventy pounds of his credit." His creditors had been delighted to get anything at all; she'd received a discount on his notes. "This morning, I visited a magistrate and obtained a warrant for the arrest of Mr. Robert Cappish. He is to be conducted to the Queen's Prison as a debtor."

Bertrice had told her that she'd already tried it—but that they'd dismissed her efforts, because she was a relation of the Terrible Nephew. Ha. Violetta was no relation, and she'd take great pleasure in holding him to account.

"What!" shrieked Mr. Cappish. "You can't do that! I'm a gentleman!"

"As the holder of one hundred and seventy pounds of his debt," Violetta said, "I assure you I *can* do this. Maybe a friend will take pity on you and arrange for your release?"

"But—but—*she's* my only relation!" Mr. Cappish said, pointing at Bertrice. "And you *can't* put me in jail. I'm a gentleman! *She* burned down a building!"

"Well." The constable bit his lip. "She *did* own it, after all. And I can't ignore a warrant—it's signed by a magistrate." He considered. "This is difficult. I believe I must put you *both* in jail. How's that?"

"You can't imprison me! I have to be at her mental competency hearing tomorrow," Mr. Cappish protested. "If I am not there, they'll dismiss it for want of prosecution!"

"Oh, no," Violetta said softly, shaking her head. "How sad. What an *unfortunate* side effect that would be."

Bertrice was watching Violetta, a soft smile on her face. It was silly, but Violetta found herself grinning back. She shouldn't feel so proud of herself. Bertrice was going to jail. And yet…

"Violetta, dearest," Bertrice said, brushing her hand against Violetta's elbow before the constable could conduct her away. "Could you contact my solicitors? I'd be most obliged to have your help with this small matter."

CHAPTER NINE

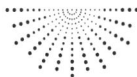

The courtroom the next morning was nothing like Bertrice had expected from reading Dickens novels. There were no shady looking figures lurking at the edges, wrapped in dark cloaks, nor was it a chamber of dark musty corners and unknown smells. It was just a room with benches, sunlight filtering in from back windows. There was no audience save for Violetta, dressed in her best gown, sitting demurely in the back. Bertrice's own gown was some blue lace-and-silk thing that made her look like a demure little doll. ("That *is* the look you are trying to achieve," her solicitor had advised.)

She felt like a child. *Sit straight. Smile sweetly. Don't blaspheme. Don't burn buildings, not even if it is the most effective method of evicting your Terrible Nephew.* Bah. Boring.

She'd already paid an enormous fine to the Metropolitan Fire Brigade that morning to win free of the jail. It felt like insult heaped upon injury to have to bat her lashes and look appropriately wounded for the magistrate.

"If you had consulted me," her solicitor was muttering, "we could have avoided all of this without burning any buildings at all." He sat beside her now, that rotten no-good spoilsport.

The magistrate wore a white wig, but no spectacles. The only point that seemed to match a typical Dickensian description was the man who must be some sort of assistant. He probably had a proper name to match his status, something like "clerk" or "mid-overlord" or whatever these folk called themselves. He would likely bellow if he heard himself called an "assistant."

He looked to be about twelve years old to Bertrice's untrained eye. Then again, she was pretty sure that everyone below the age of thirty looked like an actual baby to her, so that didn't mean anything.

"In re Mrs. Martin," the magistrate read. "Mr. Robert Cappish, prosecuting."

A silence reigned in the courtroom, disturbed only slightly by the noise Bertrice choked back in her throat. *He prefers Clappy,* she wanted to say, *or Robby Bobkins...*

Her rotten no-good spoilsport of a solicitor was almost certainly right on one point: Insulting her imprisoned nephew in court was a bad way to make her case for mental competence.

"Well?" The magistrate said. "Present the case."

The lawyers for the other side—and how Robby Bobkins had managed to pay a solicitor, let alone the slack-jawed besuited fellow who passed for a barrister on the other side, Bertrice would never know—shuffled papers before one of them stood. Likely he'd been chosen for the extreme slackness of his jaw, the slackest of slack-jaws among them.

"Your Honor," this man said. "We...know what Mr. Cappish's case is, but we are unable to prosecute it at the moment, as our primary witness, Mr. Robert Cappish himself, is indisposed."

The magistrate frowned. "He's ill?"

"Ah..." The man winced. "He's...in...a state which does not allow his presence here."

Heavens. Bertrice stared at the man. He must have trained for *years* to be able to stretch the truth to such bounds.

"What state is that?"

"The state of imprisonment," Bertrice heard herself interject. At her side, her own lawyer flicked what was supposed to be a quelling glance at her. Out of the corner of her eye, she saw Violetta behind her, ducking her head and hiding her smile. She should be proud; what an enormously lovely thing she had done.

Alas. Bertrice would have to allow herself to be quelled. It wasn't as if she *knew* how court proceedings were supposed to go on. If she took Dickens as her guide, they'd go on and on for six generations, and she hadn't the patience for that. Two generations was enough.

"Ah." The lawyer for the other side flushed. "Well. As to that... Yes. That would be the state in question. We would like to move for a continuance, if Your Honor would be so inclined, until such time as my client has an opportunity to...ah...attend?"

The magistrate sighed and looked upward. "Your client has requested custody of his elderly aunt, on the grounds that she is not mentally competent and requires guidance from a sober, staid gentleman such as himself. For what is he imprisoned?"

"Ah. A delicate matter."

"For nonpayment of debts," said Mrs. Martin's barrister. "The woman who holds his notes is in attendance, I believe, should you need to ask any questions of her."

The magistrate nodded and steepled his fingers. He turned to Mrs. Martin. "Mrs. Martin, do you believe yourself to be of sound mind?"

"Yes," she said. "I am old, and I am possessed of decided opinions, but I do think they're reasonably sound."

He nodded. "And—forgive me for being uncouth, but I must inquire—you are very wealthy, are you not? I notice you have employed Botts and Forthwell in your defense."

"My husband left me with a fortune of close to fifty thousand pounds."

"And your nephew...?"

"Has been cut off, since he will not treat the women in my household with respect."

"I see." The magistrate nodded again. "I could dismiss this case for want of prosecution, you know. Is that what you want?"

"Ye—"

"No," the barrister sitting on the other side of her solicitor said, picking up on some clue in the air that she had missed. "It is *not* what we want. Mrs. Martin believes that her nephew has had an adequate opportunity to make his case. It was outlined in the briefs he submitted, and it's nobody's fault but his own that he's not here to establish further particulars. We've submitted as evidence the proof that Mr. Cappish has already entered a false security on behalf of his aunt. I think Your Honor understands the precise contours of his veracity."

"Yes." The magistrate turned to Mr. Cappish's lawyers. "Your response?"

"Your Honor, this woman is deranged. The word we had of her goings-on yesterday involved arson and cheese toast. She cannot be trusted."

"Well," the magistrate said dryly, "I wasn't worried at all when you said 'arson,' but cheese toast, now, that's another story. How dare she be possessed of a fortune and burn her cheese toast."

Behind her, Bertrice heard Violetta make a small sound, not quite laughter, and she had to hold back her own chortle.

"I—Well, they're *connected,* you see, and it's not—"

"If all you have is hyperbolic stories about burning cheese," the magistrate said, "I believe we're done here. Tell your client that he's to pay his debts himself and to stop relying upon his aunt. Case dismissed with prejudice."

"With prejudice?" Bertrice leaned over and whispered in her attorney's ears. "That doesn't sound good. What does that mean?"

"It's not good," her lawyer replied, in low tones, "for Mr. Cappish."

She glared at him.

And—of course he did—he relented. "For your Terrible Nephew. It means he can't bring the case again."

"Oh." Bertrice said. "Oh."

She sat in place, hands clenching, almost unable to understand what it meant. She had won—not just a battle, but an outright war.

She'd won, and she hadn't been alone.

～

After she took her leave of her attorneys, there was nothing to do but wander about London in a daze, Violetta at her side. They found a path along the Thames and walked. A cold breeze blew in over the water.

"This isn't over," Bertrice said. They weren't touching; it was too cold to remove gloves, and holding hands through two layers of wool felt odd.

"No?" Violetta glanced over at her. "I thought that was what 'dismissed with prejudice' meant. That it was over."

She sighed. "One of his horrible friends will give him money, perhaps. Just because the club voted him out doesn't mean that someone won't take pity on him."

"Perhaps."

"Or perhaps Parliament will finally pass one of those debtor's reforms that it keeps promising to consider and he'll have to stop moldering in a cell."

"To be fair," Violetta said delicately, "I personally think that debtor's prison is uncommonly cruel. I wish they *would* pass those reforms."

"Me too." Bertrice sighed. "I hate having political principles. And once he's out, he'll start scheming again. If it's not him, it will be some other person. It never truly ends. There are always men."

Violetta glanced at her. "To be fair," she said once again, "that judge who summed up the entire affair in about three seconds of glancing at the evidence was a man. They're not *all* bad."

Perhaps. Perhaps they were not all bad. Bertrice considered the possibility. Her consideration lasted two seconds. "That's like saying that not *all* rats are invasive pests," she replied. "I can't tell if the ones who *aren't* attempting to enter my home and eat my food stores respect my private property or if they simply haven't had the opportunity. I don't wish to inquire as to the difference."

Violetta just shook her head and smiled. "Well, take it as you will.

But there's hope. Men may make up the police, the courts, the lawmakers. They may be husbands and brothers and nephews and uncles. Their voice may always be louder than ours."

"That's your version of 'there's hope'?"

"Yes, because despite all of that, we've discovered that we can be happy." For some reason, Violetta blushed. "If we're lucky, we may have decades of happiness left, still. Maybe men are all bad—I won't grant you that, but *maybe* they are. But if they are *all* terrible, then they are also so incompetent at ruining women like you and me that there is always hope. They can't take our joy away, and they've tried."

Bertrice bit her lip.

"They've had seventy-three years to defeat you," Violetta said, turning to her. Her eyes were wide and dark, and she was almost certainly the dearest thing that Bertrice had seen in years. "What do you think it means that they've yet to accomplish it?"

She looked upward. "It's only because I had *you* that I won this time."

"And it's only because I had *you* that I believed I could make a difference."

Their path along the Thames intersected the remains of the rooming house and the gentleman's club. The burned buildings looked dismal. Stone streaked black with smoke, dark gaping holes where there had once been wood window frames—it would take a while to restore them.

The park was a little disturbed—the firemen had, in fact, dug up a bit of it to be certain the fire didn't spread—and the girls in the park were clustered together, talking.

Bertrice frowned. There was something wrong with that, there was. It took a moment for the answer to arrive, and as it did, she grimaced. "You know, Violetta, I have made mistakes."

Violetta looked at her. "You, admitting it?"

"I have *all* this money," Bertrice said mournfully, "and I utterly *wasted* it burning down the ninth most influential gentleman's club in all of London."

"Good heavens." Violetta looked at her. "I can't actually believe you're admitting it. I do have to agree, it was…fun while it lasted, but arson is probably—"

"There are *eight more of them* out there," Bertrice interrupted, "bastard strongholds of masculine stupidity that they are, and I went for number nine. What idiocy! What ineffectiveness!"

Violetta threw her head back and laughed. "I should have known. Please, consider that one arson per week may stretch my meager limitations."

But Bertrice hadn't taken her eyes off the girls congregating in the park. Molly, hadn't that been her name? And others. The gentleman's club had burned down, and men were the police, the magistrates, the lawyers, and the lawmakers.

"No," Bertrice said. "Why burn them down, when there are so many better ways to set fire?" She started off across the way. The park, on closer inspection, was far the worse for the wear. The grass near the fire was singed black; slightly farther away, it was merely scorched at the tips. The women looked up as she approached.

No point beating around the bush. "Here now," Bertrice said. "You —Molly, yes? Have we altered your income?"

Molly stared at her, and then looked around the park, empty of men, and sighed. "It will all work out, I'm sure. We'll just have to make some adjustments."

Bertrice pressed her lips together, considering. "Would you want to learn a respectable trade, if someone offered you the money to do so?"

Molly shrugged. "I *know* a respectable trade, but what with the new machines, lace-making hardly pays the coal bill in winter."

"Huh." Bertrice should not have been surprised that the newspapers were all wrong when it came to ladies of the night—or of the late afternoon, as these women might have been called. Newspapers were generally written by men; why *would* they understand women? "And what if I offered to hire you?"

Molly's eyes narrowed suspiciously. "To do what? I don't want any charity, and I'm rather tired of making lace."

"Look," Bertrice said, "here's how it is. I have a great deal of money, and I'm trying to get rid of it before my nephew inherits it. I've tried to give it to parishes and the like, but they've not used the money in a manner I approve of. What would *you* do if you had thirty thousand pounds to do good with?"

Molly choked. "To do *what* sort of good with?"

"Why are you asking?" said one of the girls near her. "Who would say no? I'll take it, if she doesn't want it."

"I don't know," Bertrice said. "I don't *know* what to do with it. But here I am, with too much money and too few real relations to leave it to, and here you are, with a temporary lapse in gainful employment. If I gave you access to thirty thousand pounds and said that I wanted you to make this world a better place for women—any women—what would you do?"

Molly frowned. "I would have to consider. It would be a huge responsibility. I don't know what you wanted to hear—likely not that—so—"

"Exactly that," Bertrice said. "You're hired. I shall pay you…three hundred pounds a year to get rid of my money? Is that sufficient?"

"Oh my God." Molly shook her head. "This is a dream. Or you're lying. I don't *want* charity."

"It isn't charity. You are going to make it so that when my Terrible Nephew gets out of debtor's prison, which he undoubtedly will in truly terrible fashion, there's almost nothing he can inherit. It will make my life immeasurably better, believe me. Now, do you accept?"

"I'm not an *idiot*," Molly said. "I only stopped making lace because I can do arithmetic, and this is by far a better offer."

"Then," Bertrice said, holding out her hand, "we have a deal. I'll have my solicitors draw up the whole thing."

～

The way back to Violetta's apartment seemed different. Next to Violetta, Bertrice was smiling and humming something—Violetta rather thought it was an off-key version of the

Hallelujah Chorus. But despite those outward markers of happiness, there was…something to her stride. Maybe it was the way she gripped her cane. Maybe it was the fact that she'd just agreed to give away a huge portion of her fortune.

Maybe…

"Now that that's out of the way," Bertrice said briskly, in an almost business-like manner, "I suppose we should visit my solicitors and get you a cheque. I feel the need to pay you back for what you did today, at a handsome return. Two thousand—no, five thousand pounds. Have you decided what you want to do?"

Violetta turned to her. "Bertrice."

Bertrice just gave her a weak smile. "There are so many options, you know. You could get a cottage on the coast. Or purchase the building where you live." Her smile brightened. "Buy the building where Mr. Toggert lives, and add a flock of geese to his life."

"*Bertrice*," Violetta said, with a little more emphasis.

Bertrice seemed not to notice. "Or, I don't know. You could do anything you like."

"I don't know if I can do *anything* I like," Violetta said. "Am I allowed to stay with you?"

There was a long pause. Bertrice flushed pink, two little spots on her cheeks, and exhaled slowly. "Well. I wouldn't have wanted to assume that you'd…want that sort of thing."

Violetta had to hide a grin. "There's a vast difference between assuming and trying to send me off to a cottage on the coast. And I don't think you have to *assume* that I want that sort of thing, since I very much enjoyed myself every minute I was with you. Especially what happened two nights ago; I hadn't thought I was terribly shy about letting that be known."

"No," Bertrice said. For some reason this made the tips of her ears turn red. "I suppose not. But…you do understand, after you get that cheque, and after we figure out the commitment I've made to the women in the park… I'm not going to be all that wealthy. I did just set fire to some of my property."

It was obvious that Bertrice seemed to think that this might be a problem. The way she looked at Violetta—through her eyelashes, holding back just a little, as if waiting for rejection—was adorable.

"Oh, no," Violetta said. "I have spent my entire life chasing the wealthiest people possible, and alas, I have been stymied at this final moment."

"I'll just have thirteen or fourteen thousand pounds," Bertrice confessed.

"Shame," Violetta said, "I suppose you'll only be allowed to buy thirteen thousand pounds worth of love from me. That's a real tragedy."

This had the intended effect. Bertrice turned to her. Her hands fluttered on the word *love;* she bit her lip, considering. "How much is thirteen thousand pounds worth of love?"

"It's sold by the weight."

"How much does love weigh?"

"Nothing," Violetta said, "which is very inconvenient for the seller who intends to make a business purveying it to the general public. Damn my poor business sense. If only we had someone at hand to explain how bricks worked."

"You're…teasing me," Bertrice said.

"And doing a fine job of it," Violetta told her. "Listen to you, you goose. I'm not sure which is worse—your belief that thirteen thousand pounds is a mere nothing, when it is in fact a ridiculous fortune, or your belief that your wealth is why I have come to care about you. I love you because you never let your fears stop you. I love you because your heart is soft—at least, to people who aren't men—and kind. I love you because when I was at my most desperate, you gave me choices instead of tossing me out. I love you because you're beautiful, and because you make me feel beautiful. I don't know why you think your money would factor in."

A slow smile spread over Bertrice's face. "Well. If that's the way it is, let's go home and have some more of those cheesy toast things."

Violetta sighed. "Bertrice."

"Violetta."

"Bertrice, you know that's not how it's done. I put my heart out into this cold weather, and you just demand cheese toast? You can do better."

"Oh, well." Bertrice sniffed and adjusted her collar. "I love you, but I've been terribly obvious about it. *Now* can we have cheese toast?"

EPILOGUE

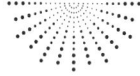

A home in Boston, one and a half years later

Violetta came back from the market with a loaf of bread and a bouquet of bright yellow crocuses, fresh from the spring market, to find Bertrice poring over a letter.

"Bertrice?"

Bertrice looked up. "Vi, darling. Aren't those lovely?"

"Yes—are you crying, Bertrice?"

"No. Why would I do a thing like that?"

"I see little tracks of moisture on your cheeks."

Bertrice straightened, swiping at her face. "Nonsense. I've just had news. You know how we were worried because the Terrible Nephew was to be released from Debtor's Prison?"

"Oh, no." Violetta stepped forward, coming to sit by Bertrice. "Never say he's out. But he hasn't found us, has he?"

"No," Bertrice said. "But he went to my former bank and gave them a forged cheque, which he claimed was on my account."

"Oh, *no.*"

Bertrice's smile curled upwards. "Oh, yes. And they fetched a constable on the spot. Right back into prison. How glorious."

"What an oaf."

"Ten years, my solicitor writes. Hard labor. What utterly lovely news."

"Isn't it, though?" Violetta smiled, and felt one last, lone worry dissipate. "Let's eat in the sunshine, shall we? It's such a beautiful day."

They packed up sandwiches together, before heading across the street to a park. Boston was lovely; Violetta had found her old friend, Lily, and they had restarted their friendship. Now they both had friends to spare.

The park, when they arrived, was pretty—trees with pale, spring-green leaves dancing in the sunshine. They laid a blanket on a bench and sat, enjoying the warmth.

"So," Violetta said, after they'd finished their sandwiches, "why *were* you crying?"

Bertrice sighed. "It's going to sound stupidly sentimental."

"Oh no, not sentiment."

"I was just thinking how glad I was that you came my way. That's all." Bertrice spoke gruffly.

Violetta found herself smiling. She reached out and took the other woman's hands. "That's all?" Her heart soared. "I think you mean, that's all I could possibly have wanted."

"Nonsense." Bertrice gripped her hands back and smiled. "You should want everything. Let me manage dinner tonight. I know just the thing."

PART I
BACK MATTER

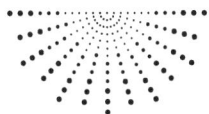

AUTHOR'S NOTE FOR TALK SWEETLY TO ME

THE IDEA FOR THIS BOOK came from two places. The first was a course in quantum mechanics that I took way back in 2001, one taught by Dr. Jerzy Cioslowski. Dr. Cioslowski was the sort of person who told a million extraneous stories as he taught. One of his stories was of Hartree, one of the early giants of quantum mechanical computations. His main advantage, Cioslowski said, was that his father was a computer: He would calculate all his sums for him, leaving Hartree free to do most of the work.

Once, he told us, the computer was a person. In fact, computers were often women. He said this—leaving half the (female) class sputtering, and then went on blithely.

There isn't much known about the history of female computers. They came into prominence in World War II, when female computers served in the Manhattan project, and helped crack the German's Enigma code. But they existed before that. Very little is said about the computer, either male or female, so I've had to interpolate.

The other source of inspiration for this was a real woman. Her name is Shakuntala Devi, and she was known as the human computer for her ability to calculate complex cube roots in her head in a matter of seconds. Her roots were modest—her father was a circus performer

—but not only was she a mathematical genius, she also wrote cookbooks, nonfiction on homosexuality, nonfiction on learning mathematics, and novels (many of these are available as ebooks today). She even ran for office.

In terms of the work Rose was doing, I ended up deleting a lot of astronomy and mathematics from this book as written. (I'm sure you're shocked to hear that.) One of the things I deleted was a reason why she'd be using the law of gravitation to calculate the Great Comet's trajectory. This was actually a huge open problem in astronomy at the time: everyone knew that comets didn't purely obey the laws of gravitation in their trajectory around the sun, and nobody could figure out *why* they didn't. It was a source of some serious disagreement. People came up with all kinds of theories as to the source of the discrepancy. The real answer—asymmetric outgassing of cometary materials as the comet approached the sun, and a few relativistic effects—was not known for many years yet. Rose's goal in her calculations would be to try to fit the theory of gravitation with the other known theories to see which of those theories best approximated reality.

Yes, there was once a lengthy explanation of this in the book. Yes, I deleted it.

As for Patricia's husband, the brief account that Rose gives is also accurate. Africanus Horton, the first black doctor in England, was sponsored by the editor of the *African Times*. Thereafter, several others were sponsored regularly, many of whom married women in England (some white). While we don't have statistics of this by race, by 1882, Britain had probably trained at least as many black doctors as there were dukes. There were also a number of middle-class black families like the one Rose comes from—shopkeepers, lawyers, and the like. I don't pretend there were many of them as a proportion of the population as a whole, but especially in the areas of the country that were near the major ports—Liverpool, London, Manchester and the like—there were known concentrations of people of color. I'm indebted to the book *Black Victorians, Black Victoriana* for their work in peering into the historical record on this point.

Finally, a brief note on the transit of Venus. Just about everything Rose says about the transit of Venus is true. I made one alteration to reality for the purposes of the story. In reality, the snow on December 6th started before the transit did, and so the transit was not visible at all in London. I moved the storm back a few hours, and gave Rose that first glimpse of the phenomenon. I hope you'll forgive that tiny alteration.

AUTHOR'S NOTE FOR HER
EVERY WISH

I had the initial idea for this book a long time ago—in 2011, when I was doing research for *The Duchess War*. I ran into a bit of something in the Leicester archives advertising a charity loan for young residents of the parish looking to start a new trade or business. I remember reading the language very carefully and thinking to myself, huh. They don't say you have to be a man to apply.

I thought I knew precisely what to do with that. Except the problem was finding an appropriate hero. I tried someone who was in the competition against Daisy, but unfortunately, didn't like that dynamic. I tried one of the judges. I tried someone who was tasked with persuading her to withdraw. None of those things worked for me for a number of reasons.

And then, when I was writing, *Once Upon a Marquess*, a random minor character appeared on the screen and I called him Crash. I don't know why. It's not exactly a name one would normally use. But as soon as I wrote the name—Crash—I figured out that his real name was Nigel, and everything sort of followed from there.

The word "bicycle" was in use back in 1866, although rarely; I've chosen to use the word "velocipede" almost exclusively because the velocipedes of 1866 were dissimilar from today's bicycles in a number of ways. For one, there was no bicycle chain in most production models. There were definitely no shocks. And bicycle helmets are an incredibly recent invention. Nonetheless, the bicycle was an amazing invention, and it became all the rage late in the 1860s. Crash would have been perfectly positioned to take over the craze.

Britain was an empire, and for a very long time, one of the chief products that empire sought after was labor. It was involved in the African slave trade for a very long time, until slavery was outlawed in Britain itself in 1772, followed by the abolition of the trade in slaves in 1807, and finally by slavery in British colonies in 1833. This did not end the thirst for cheap labor. In lieu of African slaves, Britain would impress sailors (both domestically and internationally). It was one of the global players engaged in what was colloquially known as the "pig trade"—which involved Chinese laborers who were indentured servants, where some of them entered their period of servitude more involuntarily than others. And of course, Britain ruled over numerous colonies where cheap, abundant, exploitable labor was used—India being one of them.

These workers were often impressed into doing grunt work for the merchant marines. As you can imagine, worker safety was not highly valued, and workers who were injured on the job back in those days had little by way of regulatory protection. The global empire of Britain is littered with stories of sailors from around the world being marooned in various ports. If they weren't able to work to the rigorous standards of an oceangoing vessel, they might find themselves far from home with no way to return.

Britain didn't obtain racial data in its census for quite some time, and so reconstructing questions like how many people of color were in Britain in the latter half of the nineteenth century is difficult. But how many is not relevant to the question of their general existence: They were absolutely there, and it's probably reasonable to assume that those who ended up in London for one reason or another tended to band together.

When I was doing research for *Talk Sweetly to Me*, I read an essay about how a photographer in the 1920s who was taking pictures of working-class people discovered a tiny neighborhood in Bristol near where the slave ships had docked over a century before. In this area, nearly everyone was some shade of brown, the result of people who had been stranded generations ago and had intermarried with each other and the local population and various sailors of every ethnicity who had wandered by.

When I wrote Crash and his aunt and their group of friends, I was imagining that sort of Bristol neighborhood in London. Given the number of people from around the world who ended up stranded in London, such a place would have to exist.

When Crash says that much of England would refer to his aunt and his friends as whores, this is not meant to be descriptive as many people would understand that term. One of the main problems that authorities had in the 1860s is that it was difficult to corral the spread of STDs because it was hard to tell who was involved in sex work and who wasn't. This is in part because upper-class English gentlemen were jerks who thought they could have sex with anyone poor, and in part because prostitution just didn't work the way they thought it did. There were some people who only earned a living in prostitution, but a huge number of people who might be classified as sex workers back then had a regular job, and then maybe a man or three on the side. Many authorities basically assumed that anyone working jobs that earned little enough money had to be involved in prostitution on the side.

Finally, a note on two items mentioned in the book. The velocipede really did start to become popular at the end of the 1860s, and it has basically never stopped since, despite significant advancements in transportation technology. Crash would have gotten his foot in the door right at the start. Crash is also (basically) right when he says that you're more stable on a bicycle the faster you go. For the same reason, tops wobble less when you spin them faster. It's a physical phenomenon known as precession. I didn't want to go into too much detail, because obviously the faster you go, the more you can hurt yourself.

Second, there is such a thing as a carbolic smoke ball, and that (like other random things that show up in my book) is a joke between me and ten thousand law students who will all say, "ARGH, CARBOLIC SMOKE BALLS!" There's a famous case from 1892 involving an advertisement for a carbolic smoke ball.

The basic idea behind a carbolic smoke ball was that the ball contained carbolic acid, which interacted with the air and filtered it. The makers of the ball claimed it would filter out, say, influenza germs. Like about 95% of the purveyors of Victorian-era medical equipment, they were totally wrong. The actual Carbolic Smoke Ball Company featured in the 1892 advertisement didn't exist in 1866, but upon research, I did find references to early inventions that were basically carbolic smoke balls that were period. So I hope you enjoy it.

Printed in Great Britain
by Amazon